SECRET

OF THE

DRAGON

Tor Books by Margaret Weis and Tracy Hickman

Bones of the Dragon
Secret of the Dragon

SECRET
OF THE
DRAGON

MARGARET WEIS

AND

TRACY HICKMAN

TOR®

A TOM DOHERTY ASSOCIATES BOOK

NEW YORK

SECRET OF THE DRAGON

A Tor Book
Published by Tom Doherty Associates, LLC
175 Fifth Avenue
New York, NY 10010

www.tor-forge.com

Tor® is a registered trademark of Tom Doherty Associates, LLC.

ISBN 978-0-7653-1974-6 (hardcover)
ISBN 978-0-7653-2692-8 (first international trade paperback edition)

First Edition: March 2010

Printed in the United States of America

0 9 8 7 6 5 4 3 2 1

To Brian Thomsen,
with much affection

Kingdom Chart of the Khrakis

OCEAN ESTARTHIA

OCEAN AYLITHIA

Island Hesvia

Hesvolm Sea

Nurn Straights

Dragonholm

Karais

Kilenholm Mountain

The Congersluie

The Steppe Oans

Urda'an

Eastern Expanse

The Forged Kingdoms of Thur

The Oran Empire of Light

The Dansbo Westreach

Fae Tribes (Uncharted)

The Stormlords

Sea of Tears

DRAGONSHIPS

Miles 100 300 500 700 900

30000 ft	-0 ft
27000 ft	-3000 ft
24000 ft	-6000 ft
21000 ft	-9000 ft
18000 ft	-12000 ft
15000 ft	-15000 ft
12000 ft	-18000 ft
9000 ft	-21000 ft
3000 ft	-24000 ft
	-27000 ft
	-30000 ft

PROLOGUE

"I am Farinn the Talgogroth, the Voice of Gogroth, God of the World Tree. Attend me! For now I will tell the tale of Skylan Ivorson, Chief of Chiefs of the Vindrasi, the greatest of the Chiefs." He paused and then said, with a sigh, "The greatest and the last."

The pause was for dramatic effect. The sigh was genuine. Farinn the Talgogroth was an old, old man, the oldest in the Vindrasi nation. Being a Talgogroth, he knew the history of the Vindrasi, and he maintained proudly that he was the oldest Torgun who had ever lived, reckoning that he had seen eighty-five years. He was the only living Vindrasi who had actually known and sailed with the fabled Skylan Ivorson on his epic voyage in the dragonship that was now almost as legendary as its master, the *Venjekar*.

There was some bustle in the hall, as the women poured mugs of ale, then sat down on the long bench beside their men. Children ceased romping and ran to sit on the floor in front of the Talgogroth so as not to miss a word, for the old man's voice—once a vibrant tenor—now tended to be thin and cracked. The Vindrasi had heard this story many times before, but it was one of their favorites and they never tired of listening. Every child there, boy and girl, dreamed of growing up to be a hero like Skylan or Garn or Aylaen or Bjorn or Erdmun or the others whose names rang through the hall.

All now dead. All except the one who had been the youngest on that voyage. The old man regarded the children with wistful sorrow.

The tale he told could be likened to a tapestry in which bright colored threads were stitched close together to form a stirring and beautiful picture of brave men and women doing battle with fearsome enemies. Viewed from the front, the tapestry appeared flawless. Every stitch was perfectly sewn, each thread blending together in harmony with every other thread to form a wondrous picture.

Seen from the back, the picture was not as pretty. The embroidery that was smooth and beautiful and glowing on the front looked broken and fragmented when viewed from the other side. Threads were knotted, snarled, or tangled. Some of the threads had snapped and had to be tied to other threads. If the strand had frayed, the thread was pulled out and tossed away and another, stronger thread used in its place.

Farinn the Talgogroth told the tale as seen from the front. He knew quite well that if the people saw it from the back, no one would ever want to listen to it. All men need heroes and they need their heroes to be perfect; never mind that it is the knots in the threads on the back of the tapestry that make the work strong and enduring.

The Talgogroth's grandson, who was now in his forties and would be Talgogroth when his grandfather died (Farinn had outlived both his sons), brought the old man a mug of ale. Farinn took a drink, to ease the dryness in his throat, and began to speak.

"Hear now the tale of Skylan Ivorson, son of Norgaard Ivorson, Chief of the Torgun during the time of what would become known as the Last War, the War of the Gods.

"Skylan Ivorson had seen eighteen winters when the first spark of the raging fire that would eventually consume the world was struck. Ogres, sailing in their ships with the triangle sails, crossed the sea and landed on Torgun shores. The ogres did not come to fight, as you would expect. They came to parley and Norgaard Ivorson, as Chief, had no choice but to make them welcome as his honored guests.

"The ogres brought dire news. They told the Torgun that the gods of the Vindrasi had been defeated in a great battle in heaven. They said the gods of the Vindrasi were now dead. To prove what he said was true, the Torgun godlord came to the feast wearing the sacred Vektan Torque, the spiritbone of one of the Vektia Dragons. The torque had been given to the Vindrasi by the dragon goddess, Vindrash, and was valuable beyond all measure. Horg Thekkson, Chief of Chiefs of the Vindrasi, of the Heudjun clan, had given the torque to the ogres."

The children interrupted, hissing and booing at this point. Horg was the villain of the tale, at least at the beginning.

Tangled threads, thought Farinn as he waited for the clamor to die down. So many tangled threads.

"Horg claimed he gave the torque to the ogres to prevent them from attacking the Heudjun, an act of cowardice and dishonor that would bring down on him the wrath of Torval."

The children clapped at this juncture and leaned forward eagerly. They all knew what was coming.

"The Torgun lit a beacon fire, asking their neighbors, the Heudjun, for help to defeat the ogres in battle. The Heudjun did not come. Skylan was war chief of his people, for his father, Norgaard, was crippled by wounds of honor, taken in battle. Skylan led his warriors against the ogres. The Bone Priestess, who was then Treia Adalbrand, summoned the Dragon Kahg, and the Torgun defeated their foe, though they were outnumbered a hundred to one."

Farinn smiled to himself. That was not quite true, but it made for a good story.

"Alas, though it seemed the Torgun won, in truth they lost, for the treacherous ogres used foul shamanistic magic to steal the sacred Vektan Torque. The ogres sailed away with the Torque and there was nothing the Torgun could do to stop them.

"The Torgun turned their wrath upon their cousins, the Heudjun, who had failed to come to their aid in a time of desperate need. Norgaard, Chief of the Torgun, determined to challenge Horg Thekkson in the Vutmana, a battle sanctioned by the gods in which one chief may challenge another to determine who has the strongest claim to be Chief of Chiefs.

"Norgaard was a cripple and could not fight, and the law states that a Chief may choose a champion to fight in his stead. Norgaard chose Skylan, his son, to do battle. The Torgun warriors sailed across the Gymir Fjord to confront the Heudjun. Draya, Kai Priestess, revealed to the Heudjun that Horg had given the Vektan Torque to the ogres; the Torque had not been stolen as he had basely claimed. She called upon Torval, god of the Vindrasi, to judge Horg.

"Horg Thekkson and Skylan Ivorson fought the Vutmana—"

"Sing the story of the battle!" cried a little boy.

"Another time," said Farinn gently.

Long ago, he had composed a lay that told the tale of the epic battle. His song detailed every heroic sword thrust and parry. But Farinn disliked singing the lay and avoided it when possible. He had known when he was composing it that the story he told was a lie. He had kept silent out of respect, and now he was the only one who knew the truth. He would carry the secret of what had truly happened during that battle to his grave.

Farinn went on with the tale. "Skylan Ivorson was victorious. As winner, he had the right to choose if he would make his father Chief of Chiefs or if he would decide to be Chief himself. Skylan had taken an oath to Torval that he would make his father Chief. Skylan broke that oath and claimed the chiefdom for himself."

The children were silent, wide-eyed. Oath-breaking was very terrible and they all knew Skylan would be punished.

"Some say that Torval cursed Skylan for his oath-breaking," Farinn continued, "and the tragedy that befell him afterward was due to Torval's curse. Others say it was a traitor god who caused all the trouble. Skylan always said it was he himself who brought about his own downfall, for he was an arrogant youth and would listen to no man's advice."

Parents frowned at their children, warning them to take heed. The children brushed this lesson aside in anticipation of the rest of the story.

Farinn paused a moment, then said softly, "The wise say it was Skylan's wyrd."

The hall was hushed. The men and women silently nodded their heads.

The wyrd is spun by the Norn, three sisters of the god Gogroth, who came at Torval's summons to plant the World Tree. His three sisters sit beneath the tree, one twisting the wyrd on her distaff, one spinning the wyrd on her wheel, one weaving the wyrds of gods and men on her loom. When the thread that ties a babe to the mother is cut, the thread of that child's wyrd begins. Every person has his own wyrd, as does every god. The wyrds of men and gods together form the tapestry that is life.

A single thread is fragile. The tapestry itself is strong.

Farinn went on to relate the various adventures and misadventures that befell Skylan Ivorson, Chief of Chiefs.* The tale was a long one and when the old man's voice began to give out and the children were unable to stifle their yawns, he brought the tale for this night to an end.

"The Bone Priestess, Treia Adalbrand, sister to Aylaen, the woman Skylan loved, accused Skylan of having cheated in the Vutmana, claiming he had treacherously murdered Horg Thekkson and thus robbed Torval of his choice.

"Skylan had by this time come to believe that his misfortunes were due to the curse of the god, Torval. Plagued by guilt, Skylan confessed to the crime of having murdered Horg Thekkson—ironically, the one crime among many of which Skylan was truly innocent.

"The Torgun turned on Skylan. They made him a prisoner and threw him into the hold. Justice done, the Torgun warriors prepared the funeral biers for their dead warriors. As the smoke rose, carrying the ashes and the souls of the dead to heaven, the Torgun were ambushed by soldiers of Oran, Empire of Light. The Torgun were captured and made prisoners on their own ship.

"And that is where the tale ends for tonight," said Farinn.

Even though they were dropping from sleep, the children wailed in protest. Farinn smiled and took a long pull from his mug.

Benches scraped along the floor as people rose. Fathers lifted their sleepy children in their arms and carried them out of the hall. Mothers walked alongside, draping blankets over the smallest children to fend off the night's chill. The young unmarried men stayed behind in the hall to finish off the cask of ale and tell their own tales of valor. The young women, demurely accompanying their parents, glanced over their shoulders to make sure that the young men were watching.

Farinn rose stiffly from the stool on which he'd been seated. His grandson tried to take his arm, but Farinn irately shook off the assistance.

"I might be old and I might be slow, but I can still walk on my own two feet," he said testily.

Farinn made his way to his longhouse. He did not go to bed. He

---

*For those who have not been fortunate enough to hear the Talgogroth recite it, the tale of Skylan Ivorson begins in the book *Bones of the Dragon,* Volume One, Dragonships.

did not require much sleep these days. He fixed himself a honey posset to sooth his throat and, sitting before the fire, he thought back to that time when young Skylan Ivorson, once Chief of Chiefs, had been made a slave. Farinn would resume the telling of the tale tomorrow night. He always liked this part.

This was where Skylan's story took an unexpected turn.

The Vindrasi believe that every person has his own wyrd, as does every god. The wyrds of men and gods are intertwined, often to the detriment of man, for the gods are all-seeing, whereas man is blind. But sometimes the gods discover that foresight is a curse, not a blessing. For though a god may believe he is sure of the future of creation, no god can ever be truly confident that what he sees will come to pass, for no god can dictate the actions of men.

For men are free to choose. And thus men may unwittingly unravel the plans of the gods. . . .

Skylan Ivorson, Chief of Chiefs of the Vindrasi nation, sat in the sand and watched half-naked men with hammers crawl over the side of his ship. He was reminded of flies swarming over a carcass.

The damage the *Venjekar* had suffered when the ship ran aground on a sandbar was greater than Acronis, the Legate of Oran, had first thought. After capturing the ship, the Legate had ordered his men to make some cursory repairs to the hull and then sail with the tide. The *Venjekar* had taken on so much water so rapidly that Tribune Zahakis, chosen by the Legate to captain the ship, had barely made it back to shore.

Skylan had felt a grim sort of satisfaction in the failure. It was as if the *Venjekar* knew she had been taken captive and had chosen to sink to the bottom of the sea rather than submit to her captors. Skylan prayed to Torval that the foul Southlanders would not be able to repair the *Venjekar*. Let them take away his sword, haul him off in chains; he would find some comfort in the fact that his ship had steadfastly defied her foes.

The *Venjekar* had not been given the choice. The Legate carried carpenters on board his ship, a war galley which the soldiers called a "trireme" because it had three banks of oars. Acronis sent the carpenters to make repairs. Zahakis ordered the Torgun prisoners to be removed from the ship. They now sat in the sand, their hands and feet shackled, bound to each other by chains, and watched over the soldiers of the Legate in their glistening segmented armor and leather skirts.

The Torgun warriors, bereft of their armor, were now only seven in number. Almost thirty had set sail on the *Venjekar* when Skylan had begun this god-cursed voyage. Some had died fighting the giants on the Dragon Isles. Some had been wounded in the battle against the Southlanders. They had survived their wounds only to die later with the others, victims of a strange sickness, the likes of which the Torgun had never known before.

The sickness came on suddenly, beginning with fever and chills, stomach cramps and bloody diarrhea, and ending in death for many. Others, like Aylaen and Treia, Erdmun and the youngster, Farinn, had caught the sickness, but recovered. Skylan had not been affected by it at all, possibly because he had remained isolated from the others, a prisoner in the hold. The sickness had not struck Wulfe either, possibly because the boy had run away. Terrified of the strange soldiers, Wulfe had stayed away from the camp for days. He was gone so long Skylan had thought the boy had run off for good this time. But then Wulfe had returned, showing up unexpectedly, saying he was hungry.

Skylan had feared the soldiers of Oran would try to shackle Wulfe. The boy had a marked aversion to iron, swearing he could not touch it or it would hurt him. Wulfe could not even bear to smell it.

The Southlanders did not shackle Wulfe. They had no manacles that would fit over the boy's scrawny wrists, and no one considered the eleven-year-old boy a danger. They didn't particularly care if he ran away again, and so the soldiers left him alone. If Raegar had been on shore, he could have told them that Wulfe was extremely dangerous. He would have urged the soldiers to bind him hand and foot and lock him in the hold. Raegar was not there, however. Skylan had not seen his traitor cousin for days. Wulfe crouched by Skylan's side, keeping his distance, for fear he might accidentally touch one of the iron shackles.

The prisoners were not chained up to keep them from running away, but rather to discourage the "savages" from attacking their guards. The Torgun warriors had already tried twice to fight their captors, not with any hope of escape, for they had no weapons, but simply with the intent of killing as many as they could before they themselves were killed.

The Torgun blamed Skylan for everything—the storm that had blown them off course, the disastrous encounter with giants, their enslavement. They even blamed him for the sickness. The Torgun could not blame Skylan more than he blamed himself. Nor could they hate Skylan more than he hated himself.

Skylan had often dreamt that his soul went to Torval's Hall of Heroes. As he stood among the valiant warriors who had died with swords in their hands, his hands and feet were bound by chains. Torval and the other heroic warriors had roared with laughter, driving him from the Hall. He would constantly awake from that terrible dream in a cold sweat.

Skylan now watched the carpenters. He had to admit, grudgingly, that they knew their business. He turned to Wulfe, who was digging holes in the sand.

"I asked you a question. Where has Raeger been keeping himself?" Skylan said. "I would think he would be hanging around like he did at first, gloating and jeering at us."

Wulfe shrugged. "He is probably somewhere rutting with Treia."

Skylan stared at the boy, incredulous. "Treia? And Raegar? Treia may be a venemous snake, but she is Vindrasi. She is loyal to her people and to her gods. Raegar betrayed her as he betrayed the rest of us. She would scratch out his eyes if he came near her."

"I saw them," said Wulfe. "In the temple. Rutting."

"What do you mean, you saw them in the temple? What temple? Where?" Skylan demanded.

"The temple here," said Wulfe. "The temple with the big statue of a dragon inside it."

Skylan frowned. "This isn't another of your stories, is it? Like claiming you can talk to satyrs and dryads."

"I *do* talk to satyrs and dryads," said Wulfe. "And I *did* see Raegar and Treia."

Skylan was dubious. He believed the boy lied, but his lies had the value of being entertaining. "Tell me what they said. And keep your voice down."

An armed guard, looking hot and bored, paced about the sandy shoreline.

Wulfe leaned a little nearer, keeping a wary eye on the iron clamped around Skylan's wrists and ankles, as though he expected it to leap up and bite him.

"You remember when the dragon goddess came to you?" Wulfe asked. "Right before you fought the giants?"

Skylan remembered that encounter only too well. He gave a brief nod; his lips tightened. "I remember. Go on."

Wulfe continued. "The dragon goddess scared me and I ran away. I found Garn, but he was holding a sword and there were more men with him holding swords, and that scared me more than the dragon, and I ran away from them, too. That's when I saw Treia. She was tearing her hair and wringing her hands and talking crazy to herself, all about how Raegar was dead and no man would ever love her."

Skylan nodded. Wulfe's story fit with what Garn had told him, about how the distraught Treia, grieving over the supposedly drowned Raegar, had gone off by herself. No one knew where. The Torgun had been going to search for her, but then the giants had attacked them and they were fighting for their lives.

"I didn't know where you were or how to get back to camp," Wulfe said. "I thought Treia would know the way so I followed her. But she didn't go back to camp. She went into the temple with the dragon. And there was Raegar, alive, lying on the floor. His clothes were all wet."

"Of course they were," said Skylan. "He didn't fall off the ship. He jumped overboard and swam ashore."

"Maybe." Wulfe shrugged. "Raegar told Treia a god had punished him. Treia was so glad to see him she began to rut with him then and there. Afterward she asked why he was being punished. He said it was because he was keeping your secret. And then he told her your secret, about how you and Draya murdered someone named Horg. Did you murder someone named Horg?"

Skylan sighed and was silent for long moments, gazing out over the clear, waveless sea. At length, he shook his head.

"But someone named Horg was murdered?" Wulfe asked.

"Yes," said Skylan.

"But you didn't murder him?"

"No. I fought cleanly. As Torval is my witness!" Skylan said vehemently. "I did what I believed to be right. Why is it," he asked in frustration, "that every time I think I am doing right, it turns out to be wrong?"

"Maybe you should do something wrong and then it will turn out right," Wulfe suggested.

Skylan smiled bleakly. "Maybe I should. Garn knew. Garn always knew what was right. He tried to tell me and I wouldn't listen. And now Garn is dead and I am a slave and my people are slaves."

"All because of Treia." Wulfe growled, sounding so much like a dog that the soldier whistled and looked around in search of an animal.

"I can't blame her," said Skylan. "She trusted Raegar. We all did."

Wulfe snorted. "She likes rutting with him."

"How do you know Raegar was lying? Maybe it *was* a miracle. Maybe Vindrash did save him."

Wulfe snorted. "Vindrash wears boots then. The floor was dusty and I saw the footprints. I saw Raegar's footprints. His feet were bare and wet. I saw two pairs of prints of men who had been wearing boots and they were dry. They stood and talked to Raegar. The dry boots left and Raegar stayed."

Skylan frowned. "If that's true, Raegar knew Treia would go to the temple. She is our Bone Priestess. She would go there first to pray. Raegar was waiting for her!"

"I tried to warn you about her," said Wulfe. He gave Skylan's arm a sympathetic pat, though he was still careful to keep his distance from the iron manacles. "I hate her. And I hate Raegar. He hit me!"

"Why? What did you do?"

Wulfe muttered something.

"What?" Skylan nudged him. "Speak up."

"He caught me spying on them," said Wulfe sullenly. "And he hit me. Someday I'll kill him."

"Get in line," said Skylan.

He was silent, then he asked the question he'd been afraid to ask. "How is Aylean? I heard she had the sickness, but that she survived. I also heard that she tried to fight the soldiers. They didn't hurt her, did they?"

"I don't know. She's in the Big Ship out there."

Wulfe pointed to the trireme, which floated at anchor some distance away, near the sandbar on which the *Venjekar* had disastrously run aground. Compared to the sleek, graceful, dragon-prowed *Venjekar,* the trireme with its large hull and oars and beaked snout looked like some sort of gigantic seagoing turtle.

"Don't worry," said Wulfe. "They won't hurt Aylean or Treia. Raegar told the soldiers both women were Bone Priestesses and his god wanted them safe."

"I wonder why his god wants Bone Priestesses," Skylan muttered. He shifted in the sand, trying to find a more comfortable position, causing the chains to clank. The guard cast him a sharp glance.

"You two—shut up! No talking!" the soldier shouted.

Skylan glared at him and started to say something else. The soldier walked toward them. Wulfe jumped to his feet and scrambled off.

The soldier paid no attention to the boy. He kicked Skylan in the ribs. "What were you two talking about?"

"Go diddle yourself," said Skylan.

The soldier started to kick Skylan again. Skylan had been spoiling for a fight and this seemed as good a time as any. He jumped to his feet and swung the chain that hung from the shackles at the soldier's head. The heavy leg irons hampered Skylan's movement; his swing was slow and clumsy. The soldier ducked, then drew his sword and struck Skylan on the side of his head with the flat of his blade.

Skylan fell sprawling in the sand. He could taste blood in his mouth. His ears rang.

"Better hope you didn't kill him," said another soldier. "The Legate will be furious if you did. He expects this one to fight in the Para Dix."

"Bah! I didn't hurt him. These savages are like mules. You have to hit them to get their attention."

The soldier started to kick Skylan again. Skylan twisted around, grabbed hold of the man's foot, and yanked him off balance. The soldier landed on his butt in the sand.

His comrades chortled and jeered. The soldier, his face red with fury and embarassment, scrambled to his feet. He would have probably killed Skylan if the Tribune had not come up at that moment.

"Harm him, Manetas, and the Legate will have his price out of your pay," said the Tribune. "You men, chain him more securely."

The Tribune's name was Zahakis. Skylan had taken particular notice of him. The man was tall for a Southlander; his body was all muscle. His nose was misshapen. He was dark-skinned, darker than most of the swarthy Southlanders. An old scar sliced across his face from cheek to chin. He was, perhaps, in his early thirties. He was a man of few words, quick decision.

The main reason Skylan found Zahakis interesting was that there was no love lost between the Tribune and Raegar. Skylan had observed the animosity between the two the first time he saw them together.

Raegar had given the soldiers orders regarding the *Venjekar*. The soldiers had listened to Raegar, their faces expressionless. After Raegar had gone, the men had looked to Zahakis.

"Carry on with what you were doing," was his order.

The soldiers, grinning, had obeyed Zahakis.

Skylan was not certain what use he would make of this animosity between them, other than he was glad to find someone else—even an enemy—who despised Raegar as much as he did.

Zahakis was watching in silence as the soldiers wrenched Skylan's arms behind his back and bound him by the wrists, then thrust a wooden pole through the bend in his elbows, between his arms and his back, forcing his arms into an awkward and painful position.

This done, Zahakis said, "We have new orders. Some of you, come with me."

The soldiers walked off after their commander.

Skylan sat hunched over, spitting blood and sand. He glanced at the other Torgun. The grim and dour Sigurd, friend of his father's and now nominal Chief of the Torgun. Bjorn, prone to gossip and laughter, his best friend next to Garn. Erdmun, Bjorn's younger brother, gloomy, never happier than when he was expecting trouble. Grimuir, friend and ally of Sigurd's, he had never liked Skylan. Farinn, the youngest, quiet and withdrawn, mostly kept to himself. Aki the Dark; he had only recently come to the Torgun from another clan and Skylan did not know much about him. The warriors looked at Skylan, and then they looked away.

Skylan sighed. He didn't know what he'd hoped for. Not love or friendship. But maybe admiration? Nothing. They despised him. They didn't care if he lived or died. Perhaps they were wishing him dead. All he had to show for his trouble was a bloody gash on his head, throbbing pain in his ribs, and despair in his heart.

Skylan shifted his gaze to the charred and blackened spot on the sand that had been Garn's funeral pyre. Tears filled Skylan's eyes. He was ashamed of them and, fearing his men would see him weep, he lowered his head, letting his long, blond, lank hair fall forward to hide his face.

The tears mingled with the blood that dribbled into his blond stubbly beard. Skylan tasted salt and iron in his mouth. He would have prayed to Torval, but Skylan feared that Torval, like the Torgun, would look at him and then look away.

The sisters, Treia and Aylaen, had been captured in the ambush. Treia had been presiding over the funeral pyres of the Vindrasi dead and had been horror-stricken at the sight of the black-haired, brown-skinned soldiers in their strange-looking armor. Treia was nearsighted and in her bleary vision, the soldiers in their shining armor were gleaming retribution emerging from the smoke of death, coming to drag her off to the Nethervarld, where the God of the Talley, Freilis, would cast her to her daemons.

The soldiers had grasped Treia roughly by the arms, bound her hands behind her, and threw her into a tent they had erected with disciplined swiftness on the shore. Feeling their rough hands on her and smelling the stink of sweat and leather and listening to the crude talk, Treia had realized these men were flesh-and-blood and that she was their captive.

She had known fear, then, cold and sickening in the pit of her stomach, fear over what men did to captive women. She sat in the tent, trembling with terror, but all the men had done was drag Aylaen to the tent and toss her inside.

"The savage bitch bit me!" one had muttered, exhibiting a bloody bite mark on his forearm.

"You'll soon be foaming at the mouth," his comrade had predicted jokingly.

"It's not funny," his friend had grumbled.

Aylaen had a bruised face and swollen knuckles and a sprained wrist, but considering that she had fought her captors with the fury of a catamount, she was probably fortunate the soldiers hadn't beaten her senseless.

Treia had done what she could to treat her sister's injuries, which wasn't much, for they wouldn't let her back on the ship to fetch her healing salves and potions. And so, Aylaen and many of the other Torgun had contracted the terrible sickness.

The Legate's soldiers had said it was an illness common among city dwellers, known as the "bloody flux." The Legate had sent a man they termed a "physician" to help and, finding that Treia was a healer, this man had permitted her to treat her suffering people.

Having never before seen such an illness, Treia had not been able to do much for her patients except bathe their fevered bodies and close their eyes when they died. Those few, like Aylaen, who had survived had done it on their own. Others, like Treia and Skylan, had not been affected at all.

Once Treia had presided over the funerals of her dead, the bodies had been burned, along with all their clothing and anything they had touched.

Free of the grip of the sickness, Aylaen recovered rapidly, a fact she seemed to resent. She had watched the dead being consumed by flames with a look of envy. After that, she had gone into the tent and thrown herself down onto her blanket and stared into the darkness, tears flowing unchecked down her cheeks.

Treia had at last grown exasperated. "Garn is dead," she had told her sister. "You must accept that and go on. You will make yourself ill again if you don't."

Aylaen had been so lost in her grief she had not even seemed to hear her.

This morning, Treia sat in the sand outside her tent, watching the soldiers shackle the Torgun prisoners together and dump them onto the sand while the carpenters made repairs to the ship. Out to sea, the strange-looking war galley rocked gently at anchor near the sandbar on which the *Venjekar* had run aground.

Treia was not shackled or bound in any way. No one considered her a threat, nor were they concerned that she might escape. The soldiers sometimes stared at her and sometimes they seemed to talk about her, laughing in a way that made her cheeks burn, but none had molested her or Aylaen. She might have worried about that if she had not been in such inner turmoil, wondering what had become of Raegar, wondering why he had abandoned her, wondering if he was dead.

She saw Skylan get into a fight with the soldiers and her mouth curled in a contemptuous smile to see him knocked to the ground. He had not even been sick, the others had told her. He should have died! He was the one responsible for their suffering. Some god must love him, Treia thought resentfully.

She sat watching the soldiers and their commander, Zahakis, walking across the sand and felt a flutter of alarm. They were coming toward her tent. Treia hoped that they were going off into the underbrush to hunt, as they had done in the past.

But their heads in their helms with the flaps that covered their cheeks were turned toward her, as were their steps. Treia crawled back into the tent and shook Aylaen by the shoulder.

"What is it?" Aylaen said, rolling over with a groan. "Why did you wake me?"

"The soldiers are coming for us," said Treia, her voice tight.

Aylaen sat up. Her face was pale and thin from her illness. Her red hair, which she had cut short as a dedication to the goddess, had grown back in a cluster of curls that straggled over her forehead and down her neck. Her green eyes were sunken and smudged by dark circles. She was only seventeen, but illness and sorrow had aged her. Treia, in her late twenties, seemed the younger by comparison. Aylaen's eyes had been clouded and dull before this. When Treia mentioned the soldiers, she was pleased to see a spark of fire in the green depths.

"I will die before I let those sons of whores touch me," Aylaen said, clasping Treia's hand tightly. "You and I—we'll fight them."

Aylaen tried to stand. Her weak legs would not support her and she ended up falling on her hands and knees. Treia had to help her sister out of the tent. "If you would not lie in your bed all day, you would be stronger," Treia scolded.

Aylaen stood blinking in the sunlight that hurt her eyes, holding on to her sister's arm to help her walk. The women stared, white-faced, at the approaching soldiers and their commander, who seemed to know what they feared.

Zahakis came to a stop in front of them and said in formal and dispassionate tones, speaking slowly so that they would understand, "I have orders to remove both of you to the galley. You will not be harmed, I give you my word as a Tribune of the Third Legion. Be so good as to accompany my men in a peaceful manner and you will not be bound."

"Go to hell," said Aylaen.

"Sister, you can hardly walk," Treia said in a low voice. Aloud she said, "Why are you taking us to your ship?"

"Because those are my orders, Madame," said Zahakis.

Treia bit her lip. If Raegar was alive, he might be on the galley. "We will come with you," she said, and she pinched Aylaen when her sister started to argue. "For once in your life, don't cause trouble!"

Aylaen would have probably fought her captors if she had been strong enough to resist. As it was, she was already feeling faint and dizzy in the hot sun. Rather than appear weak, she suffered the soldier to grasp her by the arm and lead her across the beach and into the water.

Treia followed, accompanied by another soldier. At the sight of their womenfolk being taken away, the Torgun warriors raised a shout and jumped to their feet.

Zahakis ordered his men to keep going. "I'll go deal with them."

The water from the shoreline to the sandbar was only about hip-deep. The soldiers waded into the sea, hauling the women with them. Treia floundered through the waves, her movements hampered by the skirts of her long linen smock. She had taken off the woolen apron dress she usually wore over it. The summer days were hot, too hot to wear the overdress or her priestess robes.

The water splashed over her, soaking the linen chemise that clung revealingly to her body. One of the soldiers glanced at her and made a comment to another.

His friend gave a grunt. "I would not let Raegar hear you say that. He gave orders to treat these women with respect."

"So he can enjoy them all for himself," the soldier said with a leer.

"Raegar says this woman and her savage bitch of a sister are Bone Priestesses or something."

"A boney priestess is nearer the mark," returned the other soldier, and both men laughed.

Treia stared at them in astonishment. She had difficulty understanding the language of the men, for though many of the words of their language were the same as hers, the Southlanders spoke rapidly, the words seeming to slide off their lips as if coated with oil. Yet she had heard the name, Raegar, clearly. They had spoken of him as though they knew him. Something about giving orders regarding her and Aylaen. But how was that possible? These men were Southlanders. Raegar, though he had lived for many years in the Southland, which he called by their name, Oran, was Vindrasi.

Treia's shock and bewilderment increased immeasurably when she was taken on board the Southlander's galley. The soldier escorted her up a ramp. The moment she set foot on the deck, she heard her name.

"Treia! Thank Aelon you are safe!"

The voice was Raegar's. The eyes were Raegar's, but she did not recognize any part of the rest of him. He had shaved off his blond hair and beard, leaving his scalp and the lower part of his face white with a suntanned strip across his nose and eyes. He sported the tattoo of a serpent on his skull. He wore the same segmented armor as the soldiers, with the addition of a red capelet, adorned with serpents stitched in golden thread around the hem.

This strange Raegar strode toward her, his hands extended. He spoke to her as though nothing was wrong, as though the world had not changed.

"I am so glad to see you. I feared you would catch the flux. And Aylaen. I heard she was ill, but that she recovered, thank Aelon! I prayed for her."

Treia recoiled from him as she would have recoiled from a daemon.

"What does this mean?" she cried, upset and confused. "What has happened to you? Don't touch me!"

Raegar raised his hands and backed away from her.

"I am sorry, Treia," he said coolly. "I thought you understood."

"Understood what?" she asked, bewildered.

"Who I am."

Raegar ordered the soldiers to take her below.

"This is a war galley. We do not have facilities for women," Raegar explained. "I have made arrangements for you and your sister to berth in the storage room. It has a lock on the door."

The soldiers took her away. She stumbled down a ladder, tripping over her wet skirts, that led to a narrow corridor. They took her to a large, dark room filled with two-handled jars that, she would later learn, held oil and water and wine, and sacks containing corn, grain, beans, smoked and salted meats, and fish. Someone, probably Raegar, had made a bed of sacking. The soldiers gave her food and water and then left.

The smell of the fish made her gag, but she drank some of the water. She had been offered dry clothes, but had refused. She crouched on the blanket, shivering in her wet chemise. She was like a person stunned by a blow.

The soldiers then brought in Aylaen and shut the door behind her. Aylaen peered about in the darkness, waiting for her eyes to adjust from the bright sunshine. Seeing Treia, she hurried to her.

"Did you see Raegar? That whoreson! He betrayed us! He's one of *them*!"

Treia didn't answer.

"Treia, did you hear me?"

Treia made no response.

Aylaen regarded her sister in silence, then she said quietly, "I'm sorry, Treia. I know you loved him."

Treia sat staring into the darkness that smelled of fish until weariness overcame her and she slept.

Treia woke suddenly, wondering if she had heard the sound of footsteps or only dreamed them. She glanced over at her sister. Aylaen was asleep. Treia heard a key rattle in the lock to the door, and she rose stiffly to her feet. The door opened. Sunlight, flooding into the darkened storage room, blinded her. Squinting, she saw a large man wearing long robes.

"Who are you?" she asked tensely. "What do you want?"

"Treia, it's me, Raegar—" he began, but before he could get another word out she had flung herself at him, striking him with her fists. He caught hold of her arms.

"Hush, Treia. I'm not going to hurt you. I love you," Raegar said, and he kept saying it until she relaxed and broke into wrenching sobs.

"There, there." Raegar soothed her like a child, stroking her hair and rocking her gently. "There, there. You're safe now, my love."

When she had grown quiet and quit trembling, he said softly, "I need to talk to you." He glanced at Aylaen, who was still asleep. "We must speak in private. Will you come with me? You must be quiet. If you make a fuss, you will bring the soldiers down on us. Promise?"

Treia nodded. Hearing his voice, feeling his touch, warmed by his embrace, she was with her lover once more. The strange Raegar was gone. Well, almost gone. She still found it hard to look at him; he was so different. She could get used to him, but it would take time.

He led her from the storage room and closed and locked the door behind them. They went to another room nearby; a small cabin. The only furnishings were a desk, two chairs, and a crude bed.

"This is the Legate's cabin," said Raegar, shutting the door and locking it from the inside. "Don't worry. Acronis won't disturb us. He has gone ashore to inspect the repairs on the *Venjekar*, which are taking longer than he first supposed. We will be alone."

He began to kiss her passionately. Treia resisted him at first, but her body truly yearned for him and she returned his passion with passion of her own. She took off her damp clothes. He flung off his robes and they made love on the crude bed, carefully, for the cot creaked beneath their weight. Raegar cautioned her to silence when she moaned by putting his hand over her mouth.

Sated with pleasure, his body covered in sweat, he rolled off her and stood up and began to dress himself. She gazed up at him, reluctant to move.

"I brought you some dry clothes," he said. "I don't have a chiton, which is the proper dress for a woman of Oran, so you will have to wear one of my long tunics."

The robe was plain, without adornment, and of fine wool, smooth to the touch. Treia put it on. The tunic was far too big, but she didn't mind.

"It smells of you," she said, and she twined her arms around his neck.

"Sit down," he said, gently withdrawing from her embrace. "I have to tell you what is going on and we don't have much time—"

"Before you lock me up again!" said Treia angrily. She sat down on one of the odd-looking chairs and looked up at him, trying to see past the bald head, the snake tattoo, and his now unfamiliar face.

"You lied to me!" She glanced over at the bed. "Was our lovemaking also a lie?"

"I swear, Treia, the last thing I wanted to do was hurt you," said Raegar. "I longed to tell you the truth, that I was a warrior-priest of Aelon. I did tell you some of the truth when we were together in the temple. I had hoped you would understand—"

"I understand that you are a traitor!" Treia cried, rising to her feet. "You betrayed your own people. You betrayed me!"

"Hush! Keep your voice down." Raegar caught her by the wrists. "I did what I did for your own good, my love. I'm trying to save you, Treia."

"By making me a slave?"

"Not you, my love. You will not be a slave. Neither will your sister. I swear. If you will trust me and listen to me, you and Aylaen will be loved and honored. As for the others," Raegar continued, his voice hardening, "Skylan and your stepfather, Sigurd, and the rest, do you care what happens to them?"

Treia said nothing. He took hold of her hands, kissed them, and clasped them in his.

"They have no respect for you, my love," said Raegar. "I have often heard them make jokes about dried-up old virgins. . . ."

Treia stiffened. She had often heard the laughing and sniggering behind her back. She was twenty-eight years old and unmarried in a society where most girls were married by the age of sixteen. After several failed attempts to arrange a marriage for her, her stepfather, Sigurd, had told her he had taken her off the market.

If she had been ugly, she might have understood why no man wanted her. But she wasn't ugly. Her brown hair was thick and luxuriant. She was slender with a good figure. Her eyes were large and dark; though due to their weakness, she had developed a squint. Treia couldn't understand it. Ugly women got husbands all the time, and she could not.

"You are right," she said harshly. "I don't care."

He kissed her and she pressed against him. He held her close and whispered softly, his breath brushing her cheek, "There is one thing you must do for me."

"Anything, my love."

"When the *Venjekar* is repaired, you will use the spiritbone to summon the Dragon Kahg and order him to sail the ship to Oran."

Treia pulled away from him and shook her head.

Raegar eyed her with displeasure. His voice was cool. "What's wrong, Treia? You are not going to refuse to do this for me, are you?"

"I want to please you," Treia said confusedly. "It's just . . . What if . . . for some reason . . . I can't summon the dragon? . . ."

"Then I would be very *dis*pleased with you, my love," Raegar said, his voice growing colder still.

"I want to!" Treia said fervently. "But you know the Dragon Kahg is obstinate and sometimes he won't come. . . ."

"He came when you summoned him to fight the giants. The Legate watched from the ship. He saw the dragon battling the giants. Acronis was most impressed."

Treia shivered. She had not summoned the dragon. She had not even been there. She had been with him in the temple. She opened her mouth to say this, but her courage failed her.

"You will summon the dragon," Raegar told her.

Treia gave him a smile that she hoped didn't look as false as it felt. She tried desperately to think of some lie, some way to put him off. A thought came to her. Before she could tell him, she was startled to hear the blaring of a trumpet.

"The Legate has returned," Raegar said. "I must take you back."

Treia grabbed her wet chemise from where she had dropped it on the floor, and he took her back to the storage room.

"I am sorry I have to leave you locked up in here," said Raegar. "When you summon the dragon for me, perhaps I will be able to prevail upon the Legate to release you."

"I would do anything for you, Raegar," she said. "You know that. But I am afraid for you; the Dragon Kahg will view you as a traitor. He might take out his fury on you."

Raegar smiled. "The dragon has no power to harm me. I don't have time to explain now. I will come back to you this evening."

He shoved her into the storage room and shut the door.

"My love! Raegar!" Treia pleaded. She heard him drop the bar that locked the door, heard him turn the key in the lock, heard him walk away.

She closed her eyes and leaned her forehead against the door. She had no choice. Somehow she had to find a way to do what he wanted. She could not lose him. She turned and fell over an amphora she had not been able to see due to her poor eyesight.

She caught herself and waited until her eyes grew accustomed to the dim light that filtered through the chinks in planking of the ship's hull. When she could see well enough, she groped her way through the storage room to where Aylaen lay, fast asleep.

"Aylaen, wake up!" Treia said urgently. "Aylaen. I have to talk to you. It's important."

"What? I'm awake." Aylaen sat up, staring about in confusion. "What is this place? I don't—"

Her voice died. Her eyes darkened. "I remember. Raegar! We're prisoners—"

"Listen to me, Aylaen," said Treia sharply. "This is about Raegar. I need the spiritbone. You must give it to me. Now."

Aylaen looked puzzled. "But I don't have the spiritbone, Treia. It fell into the sea when the Dragon Kahg was wounded. You know that. You helped me search for it."

"I don't believe you," said Treia flatly. "I think you are lying to me. You have the spiritbone. You've had it all this time, hidden away. You want to keep it for yourself."

"Treia, you're wrong. I swear to you—"

Treia slapped her across the face. "Give it to me!"

Aylaen put her hand to her stinging cheek. Tears flooded her eyes, and she turned away from Treia and lay back down.

Treia fell on her, grasping her, holding her close. "I am sorry, Aylaen! So sorry! Please forgive me. I am frightened of what might happen to us. You know what men do to captive women! Give me the spiritbone, and I will summon the Dragon Kahg to come save us!"

Aylaen rolled over and looked up sadly at her sister. "I wish for your sake and mine and for the sake of our friends that I had the spiritbone, Treia. But it is lost. You must believe me. I'm not even sure the Dragon Kahg is still alive. He was badly injured. He may have gone away to die. . . ."

"Don't say that!" Treia said fiercely. "He is alive. The dragon is alive!"

"You believe me, don't you?" Aylaen said wearily.

"I suppose I have to," Treia said churlishly.

"I think I'd like to go back to sleep now, Treia. I'm not feeling well." Aylaen lay back down with a sigh.

Treia walked away and tripped over a sack of something and hurt her toes. Behind her, she heard the sounds of Aylaen shifting her body about on the hard floor, trying in vain to find comfort.

Treia sat down on a pile of sacking and calculated how long she had to wait until Raegar returned.

Raegar came to her that night, as he had promised. Treia stood by the door. She'd been standing there since the last rays of the sun vanished and left the storage room in pitch darkness. He lifted the bar, opened the door, and drew her out into the corridor, which was as dark as the hold. He had not brought a light; he spoke in a whisper.

"You've had time to think, Treia. Will you summon the dragon for me?"

Treia braced herself for his displeasure.

"I can't. Hear me out, my love," she said, feeling his body grow rigid with anger. "I don't have the spiritbone. Aylaen has it and she is keeping it from me!"

"Aylaen," Raegar repeated, startled. "Why would she have the spiritbone?"

"I gave it to her before the battle. I thought you were dead! I didn't care what happened anymore. Aylaen was the one who summoned the dragon to fight the giants. She claims the spiritbone is lost, but I know she is lying."

"Why would she keep it from you?"

"Out of spite. Jealousy. Because I have you and she has no one now that her lover, Garn, is dead."

"I will speak to her, persuade her—" Raegar said. He looked as though he might enjoy the persuasion, and Treia felt a twinge of jealousy. She had sometimes seen Raegar's gaze stray from her to her more attractive younger sister.

"Aylaen is stubborn. But there is a way."

"Yes, what is that?" Raegar looked dubious.

"We must trick her," said Treia.

A ylaen slept because being asleep was better than being awake. She felt no pain in her sleep. Garn was alive in her sleep. She was back home in her sleep. Waking was a horrible dream. Sleep was blissful peace.

Until the gods intruded.

Aylaen was walking with Garn on the beach, basking in the warmth of the sun of a late spring day. Suddenly, without warning, the wind changed, shifting from a warm spring breeze scented with sage and flowers, to a fierce, bone-chilling blast. The gray waves crashed onto the shore.

The wind brought with it snow, a few flakes at first, and then a howling blizzard. The snow was so thick it blotted out the foaming sea. Aylaen was dressed for summer in a linen smock. The fierce, cold wind pierced the thin fabric. She was wet through and shivering. She reached for Garn, but he was gone. She could not find him in the heavy snowfall. She called to him. The wind flung her cry back into her face.

Aylaen had to seek shelter or she would perish in the storm. The sea was before her. The village of Luda lay behind her, and she turned her footsteps that direction, slipping in the snow that was already starting to whiten the ground. The wind pummeled her. Ice pellets stung her skin. Her hair was caked with white. The cold made her fingers ache and burn. Her toes were numb. She could not feel her feet and so stumbled and fell.

She staggered on through the raging storm, but could not find the village. She should have reached it by now and she knew, in despair, she must have gone the wrong way. She was so cold and so tired. She longed to drop to the ground and not get back up, to let the snow cover her like a soft wool blanket. She would go to sleep and never wake. She was just about to sink down onto the frozen ground when she saw lights ahead of her.

She recognized the Chief's Hall, ablaze inside and out with flaring torches. Voices came from within. There were no sounds of revelry, though. No laughing or singing. Not a wedding, then, or there would have been raucous merriment. Perhaps a funeral, honoring the dead. No matter. For her, there was warmth, light, life. She fought her way through the snow toward the hall. With every step, the bitter wind seemed intent on pushing her back.

Finally, she reached the door and it opened to her touch. Light flooded out of the hall, dazzling her. Warmth embraced her. Aylaen hurried inside the hall and the door slammed behind her, shutting out the cold, keeping out the night.

A man sat in the Chief's place at the head of a long table. The man was old with long gray hair that fell over his shoulders. He was accoutered as though for battle, wearing plate armor and chain mail. His helm was adorned with dragon wings. His shield, painted blue and gold, stood against the wall behind him. His hand rested on the hilt of an enormous two-handed great sword.

The man had a beaked nose and a far-seeing gaze, a strong jaw and jutting chin. His eyes were blue and piercing. He was a mighty warrior. His breastplate and helm were dented. His sword was red with blood. His expression was grim and dour. He glared at her in anger.

Aylaen did not know what she had done to deserve his wrath, but she felt guilty and she looked from him to the other people in the room.

A woman stood beside the man, her hand on his shoulder. The woman wore armor that sparkled in the light. Her armor had been wonderfully designed to resemble the scales of a dragon. Her helm was adorned with dragon wings. Her face was familiar. . . .

"Draya!" Aylaen exclaimed, astonished.

Draya had been Kai Priestess of the Vindrasi. Aylaen had seen the woman only once, after the Vutmana, when Draya and Skylan had been wed. Treia had claimed that Draya and Skylan had conspired to murder Draya's first husband, Horg, during the Vutmana. Which meant that Draya must be abhorred by the gods, especially Torval, for she had taken away his judgment.

"Yet you are here, Draya," said Aylaen, startled and confused. "You have an honored place among the gods."

"Look more closely, Daughter," said Draya.

Aylaen looked into Draya's eyes and saw not years, but eons. She saw the stars and the sun and the moon wheeling in the heavens. She saw the endless cycle of the tides. She saw the passing of the seasons.

"Vindrash!" Aylaen breathed, awed.

"My beloved servant, Draya, sacrificed herself that I might find refuge in her body. Thus, in this disguise, I hide from my enemies."

"I don't understand, Blessed Vindrash." Aylaen blushed in confusion. "Was Draya a murderer?"

"Draya repented of her crime and she was forgiven. Her soul resides with Freilis. She is at peace."

"And Skylan? Was he involved?"

"Skylan made mistakes. Whether or not we forgive him remains to be seen," said Vindrash.

"I will never forgive him," said Aylaen harshly.

Vindrash smiled gently. "In time you might forgive him. In time you might forgive yourself. But we did not bring you here to discuss that. Look around."

Aylaen did as she was told. The other men and women seated at the table were grim and downcast and barely glanced at her, except one, who raised a mug of mulled wine in a jovial, mocking salute.

Two chairs at the table were empty. A place had been set for someone, as though the guest was expected to arrive any moment. The other chair was wreathed with flowers. A mug lay on its side, the wine spilled.

Aylaen shivered. Her gown was sodden, her hair wet with melted snow. Her teeth chattered.

She knew where she was. She was in the presence of the gods of the Vindrasi. Since she was a little girl, the gods had peopled her imagination, coming to comfort her when her father died, giving her courage when her stepfather beat her, befriending her when she was lonely.

"Torval," said Aylaen, naming the God of War. "Vindrash," she said, naming the dragon goddess. She looked around the table at the other gods, named them all.

Skoval, son of Torval and Vindrash, the God of Night. He was a secretive, bitter, dark-avised god, who ruled over dreams. Skoval's love for Aylis, the Goddess of the Sun, had turned to hatred when she spurned him, and now he spent eternity chasing her. Skoval smiled at Aylaen, not with his lips, but with his eyes, as though the two shared a secret. Skoval had rebelled against his parents and been banished to darkness. Aylaen had always disliked him, but now she understood him. She felt he understood her.

Aylis of the Sun. Her fiery gaze was fixed on the two empty chairs, one of which belonged to her daughter, Desiria, who had been killed in battle with the Gods of Raj. The other empty chair belonged to another god. Aylaen wondered who was missing.

Hevis was here. God of Fire and Power, deceit and treachery, he was the son of Volindril, Goddess of Spring and Rebirth, and the Five Vektia dragons. His flames could either warm man or burn flesh from bone. Hevis was thin and dark, with sleek hair. He looked very much like Skoval, for the two were brothers. Hevis's fire lit Skoval's darkness. Neither one was to be trusted.

Akaria, daughter of Aylis, was goddess of the sea, and she was beautiful as calm water at sunset and lethal as the undertow that sucked men to their deaths. Beside her was Svanses, Goddess of the Wind and Winter's Cold, daughter of Sund and Volindril, wild and unpredictable. Whenever Akaria and Svanses did battle, waves rose and ships sank, rivers flooded and men drowned.

The two were rivals and generally despised each other, but now they sat side by side. Svanses was also the goddess of revenge. Akaria, furious over her twin sister's death, had allied herself with her foe.

Volindril, Goddess of Spring, had once been beautiful, with golden hair and green eyes, but now she was faded, pale and sad and frightened, cloaked in sorrow, grieving.

The god who raised his mug to Aylaen was Joabis, God of the Feast, pleasure, wine, and practical jokes. Joabis had been invited to join Torval when the god took over the world, for Torval was fond of feasting and merriment. Joabis was fat and jolly and no one took him seriously. Everyone thought him harmless, though those who had imbibed too much ale in the night often cursed him in the morning.

Two gods, brother and sister to Torval, sat at the end of the table. Gogroth, who was god of the World Tree, and Freilis, Goddess of the Talley, ruler of the Nethervarld, the realm of the dead. Gogroth had planted the World Tree at Torval's command. The tree's branches extended into heaven. The tree's roots reached deep in the Nethervarld. Torval's vast hall was made from the wood of the World Tree. The Norns, the three sisters, sat beneath the World Tree, spinning the wyrds of men.

Freilis, clad in dark armor and carrying the Sword of Retribution, ruled over the dead. She stalked the battlefield, taking the Talley, sending the souls of the heroic dead warriors to join Torval in his hall, there to feast with their womenfolk throughout eternity and, if need arose, join Torval in heavenly battle. Freilis took to her realm the souls of children, men and women who had died of illness or old age, and the souls of those who died dishonored. The latter were chained to rocks, to be tormented by her daemons that embodied their crimes.

Then Aylaen knew who was missing: Sund, the God of Stone, foresight, and history, thought and contemplation. A friend of Torval, Sund had been invited to help govern creation because of his ability to see through the tangled wyrds into the myriad futures of gods and men. If Sund was gone, the gods were blind.

As blind as man.

"Where is he?" Aylaen asked in sudden fearfulness.

"Sund will be here," said Torval firmly.

Vindrash said nothing to contradict him, but her eyes flickered. Her face was pale.

Aylaen sensed her fear, and her own soul shrank in terror.

"Why did you take Garn from me?" she cried out. "Why did you send winter's cold to ruin my springtime?"

"We did not," said Vindrash.

Aylaen heard the wind howling outside the Hall like some awful beast, smelling fresh blood, trying to batter its way inside. She felt again the bite of cold, and she looked at those seated around the table, and there was the goddess of the wind and the goddess of the snow and the god of night. All wore armor that was battered and dented. All carried swords. All except the god of the feast, who chuckled drunkenly and quaffed his wine.

Aylaen stared at the gods in horrified realization.

"Why are you here? Outside the storm rages and the dark night reigns. What is happening?"

"Simple," said Joabis, pouring himself another drink. "We are getting our godly asses kicked."

Torval swore at the god in anger. "At least some of us fought our foes—"

"And two of you are dead," said Joabis snidely.

"Sund is not dead!" Torval roared, louder than the wind. "He will be here."

Taking off his helm, Torval flung it on the floor. His iron gray hair fell about his face. He looked very old and very tired. "Sund will be here."

Vindrash came to her husband and rested her head upon his shoulder. He grasped her hand and held it fast, pressing it against his wrinkled cheek. The other gods looked down at the table or into their mugs, anywhere except at Torval. All except Joabis, who poured wine into a mug.

She recoiled from him in disgust, and he smiled and drank the wine himself.

"If you ask me, my dear," Joabis said in a confidential whisper, his breath stinking of wine, "the old man's biggest fear is that Sund is *not* dead."

From outside the Hall came the sounds of blaring trumpets and drums beating and the clash of steel. Torval shoved himself wearily to his feet. The other gods drew their weapons, lifted their shields.

Vindrash flung open the door. The fierce wind blew the snow inside. The goddess turned to Aylaen and pointed out into the night.

"You must leave now," said Vindrash.

Aylaen shrank from the darkness and the cold and the sounds of battle. "I want to stay here, where it is safe."

"Nowhere is safe," said Vindrash.

The wind buffeted Aylaen. She shivered. "But I have no cloak. I did not know winter was coming!"

"Yet winter always comes," said Vindrash. "If you were not prepared, that is not our fault."

"It *is* your fault!" Aylaen cried angrily, forgetting herself. "I loved Garn and you took him from me!"

"Thus the bard sings, 'The thread is twisted and spun upon the wheel. Then I snip it and he dies.' What is the song about?" Vindrash asked her.

"Death," said Aylaen bitterly.

"Birth," said Vindrash. "Creation. Remember that."

Aylaen stared at her. She stared around at the other gods. They stared back, impassive, unmoved.

"I don't understand."

Vindrash dragged Aylaen to the door. "You do not belong here. You must leave."

Aylaen clung to her. "When I was little, you came to me and held me and gave me comfort. Why won't you do that now?"

"Because I have no comfort to give," said Vindrash. "What I do have to give you is that song. Remember it, if you remember nothing else."

Vindrash seized hold of Aylaen and flung her out into the snow and the night.

Aylaen awoke, shivering with the cold. She felt a qualm of terror, thinking she had fallen into a snowbank and was going to freeze to death, only to find that she had done nothing more than kick off her blanket.

Still shivering, she wondered how long she had been asleep. The sun still shone, gleaming through the chinks in the planks of the ship's hull. By the way the shadows fell, it must be late afternoon.

Treia was seated, straight-backed, on a box near the door, her arms crossed over her chest, her feet flat on the floor.

Aylaen did not want to talk to her. Moving stealthily, she took hold of a corner of the blanket and slowly drew it up over her. She shifted position, as quietly as she could, but apparently not quietly enough.

Treia said sharply, "Aylaen! Are you awake?"

Aylaen kept silent.

"I know you are," said Treia sharply.

Aylaen sighed and rolled over. "I had the most horrible dream."

Treia snorted. "You and your dreams."

Aylaen wrapped the blanket around her shoulders. "Or maybe it wasn't a dream. It seemed very real. Vindrash came to me. The goddess spoke to me—"

"The goddess is always speaking to you!" said Treia angrily. "Why not me? I am the Bone Priestess. I spent my life on my knees, praying for the goddess to talk to me! Never once! But she speaks to you, and what did you ever do? Pretend to want to become a priestess so you could be with your lover!"

Hurt and astonished by her sister's sudden rage, Aylaen had no idea what to say. Fortunately she was saved from responding by the sound of the key in the lock.

"Raegar?" Treia called eagerly, and she forgot Aylaen and sprang to the door.

Raegar did not enter. He remained in the doorway. The two whispered together for a moment, then Treia left with him, shutting the door behind her.

Aylaen sat staring into the darkness, thinking of the dream, hearing her sister's words and the sad strains of a song.

"The thread is twisted and spun upon the wheel . . ."

BOOK ONE

Upon his return to the ship, Tribune Zahakis reported to the Legate that the *Venjekar* had been repaired and could once more take to the open seas. The makeshift rudder was crude, but would serve the purpose.

"The problem, my lord, is that we do not have men to sail her," said Zahakis. "My soldiers know nothing of sailing and would be far more likely to send the ship to the bottom of the ocean than they would be to row it safely to Sinaria. Not to mention the fact that it will take every single man I have to guard the prisoners. I never saw such a barbarous lot. They are savage as wild beasts. I am beginning to think the stories I have heard about these Vindrasi are true."

"What stories are those?" Acronis asked, interested.

"They live only to fight. Their bloodthirsty warrior god will not take them into the afterlife unless they die in battle. One of the barbarians attacked his guard out of sheer cussedness, using his chains as a weapon." Zahakis chuckled and shook his head. "And you want to train them for the Para Dix!"

"Which man was that?" asked Acronis.

"His name is Skylan Ivorson. He used to be their chief, apparently, but he broke some law and is now an outcast and disgraced. None of the others will have anything to do with him."

Acronis and Zahakis stood on the deck of the trireme. Across the bay, the *Venjekar* floated in the shallow water. Zahakis had ordered his men to haul her into the waves in order to test the rudder and make certain it worked. The experiment had been successful. The soldiers had reloaded the stores they had removed from the *Venjekar* and dragged the prisoners back on board.

Zahakis had been going to shut the men up in the hold, but Raegar had announced that he had been ordered to bring the two women back to the ship, and he was going to house them in the hold. Zahakis left the Vindrasi warriors, chained together, sitting on the deck, with four archers standing with arrows nocked and ten marines guarding them. After the altercation with the barbarian Ivorson, Zahakis would have liked to use the full complement of twenty marines attached to the *Light of the Sea* to guard these dangerous men, but his soldiers had to eat and sleep sometime.

"Speaking of the Para Dix," said Acronis. "I know you are not a fan of the game—"

"It makes war a game and that demeans the true soldier. People come to believe battle is nothing more than grand and glorious sport."

"Would you have the contestants fight to draw blood, Zahakis? That would get very costly. I would soon run out of champions."

"Not such a bad thing, my lord," Zahakis said.

"Well, well, we will not quarrel. I suppose in some respects you are right. I would not participate in these contests myself, but Chloe takes such pleasure in the contests."

Zahakis smiled. "I think your daughter knows more about the game than either of us, my lord."

"She does indeed," said Acronis proudly, adding, "Point out this Ivorson to me when we go on board."

Zahakis promised he would, and the two returned to their original discussion. "I don't suppose you can spare sailors from this ship to handle the barbarians?"

"Not a chance."

Zahakis shook his head. "Then as I see it, Legate, we have no choice but to tow the ship to Sinaria. Either that or leave it here until we can return with enough men to sail it back."

The two stood gazing out at the *Venjekar,* rocking gently at anchor.

"She is a lovely thing," said Acronis, admiring the sleek, clean lines and dragonhead prow. "Say what you like about these barbarians, they can build ships. Picture her, Zahakis, on my estate. Fresh paint for the dragon. His eyes gleaming red. His scales bright blue and green. Chloe will be enchanted. We *must* take it back with us."

Acronis leaned on the rail, keeping the *Venjekar* always in his sights. "According to Raegar, we do not need to worry about manning the ship. He plans to summon a real, live dragon. The same dragon we saw fighting the giants. If you remember, we wondered where it had come from and where it went."

"These *are* known as the Dragon Isles, my lord," said Zahakis dryly.

"According to Raegar, the name comes from the Temple of the Dragon Goddess, which is located here. Dragons don't live here. They don't live in this world at all, apparently."

"So what does the dragon have to do with sailing the ship, my lord?" Zahakis asked, dubious.

"From what Raegar tells me, the dragons have made a pact with the Vindrasi. A dragon such as the one that belongs to this ship consigns his spirit to a ship in the form of a spiritbone and carries the dragonship over the seas. In turn, the Vindrasi give all the jewels they capture in their raids to the dragons. Don't ask me what the dragons do with jewels, Commander," Acronis said. "I asked Raegar and succeeded only in insulting Aelon, though I am not quite sure how."

Zahakis was skeptical. "Dragons have wings. At least, the one we saw had wings. Why don't they simply fly wherever they want to go?"

"For the same reason we ride horses, Zahakis—to spare our feet. Dragons are large beasts, and though they are strong, they grow tired when they are in flight and must often stop to rest. The ship, powered by the dragon's spirit, carries the dragon's bone with it. The dragon can spring to life if he is needed and remain in spirit form when he is not."

Zahakis wrinkled his brow. "And you believe this faery tale, my lord?"

"Oh, I must, Commander," said Acronis with mock solemnity. "Aelon commands me."

Zahakis grinned. He was about to make some comment when he saw Raegar emerge from down below and come up on deck. Zahakis gave a meaningful cough. Acronis glanced over his shoulder and lowered his voice.

"Still," said Acronis in thoughtful tones, "you and I both saw the dragon fighting the giants. And I have read accounts written by people who have survived Vindrasi raids. Many relate how dragons fought alongside the warriors. Some claim that the ship itself changed into a dragon. Others claim that the dragon materialized out of thin air."

Acronis leaned his arms on the railing and gazed with admiration at the dragonship. "I would like to see for myself, Zahakis."

"You're not serious, Legate."

"I assure you I am," said Acronis. "I am a man of science, Tribune. We saw a dragon fighting the giants. If the dragon will come when this woman whistles or prays or whatever she does, then I must take advantage of this opportunity."

"And if she orders the dragon to kill us all?" Zahakis asked wryly.

Acronis glanced at his friend with a slight smile. "Are *you* now a believer in faery tales, Zahakis?"

"You pay me to be prepared for all eventualities, Legate," said Zahakis.

"So I do, Tribune. Raegar claims this woman is in love with him and that she will do whatever he tells her. We have nothing to fear." Acronis clapped Zahakis on the shoulder. "It will be exciting, Tribune. A break in the dull routine."

"If you say so, sir," Zahakis said.

"We will make the attempt tomorrow morning. Take whatever precautions you feel are necessary. And don't forget to show me which of the savages is Ivorson."

Acronis paced the deck, his gaze always on the *Venjekar*.

"If I see a dragon and live to tell about it," Acronis said to himself, "what a wonderful story I will have to take home to Chloe."

Skylan watched the sun set from the deck of the *Venjekar*. Aylis, the Sun Goddess, slid out of a cloud bank, where she had been hiding most of the day. Hot and molten, she began to melt into the water. In the last minutes, before she sank, she seemed to glare at him, point at him with a red, accusing finger that lanced across the sea.

"What are you doing, sitting there like a lump?" the goddess seemed to ask him. "Are you giving up? We need you to fight for us. . . ."

"What are *you* doing?" Skylan was tempted to ask her back, for even as the goddess chided him, she sank into the sea and the water closed over her.

As if in answer, Skoval, God of Night, began to skulk about among the tree trunks and slide slowly out of the distant mountains, stealing up on the world stealthily, as though afraid someone might notice. The commander of the Southlanders, Zahakis, returned, bringing with him ten soldiers and dismissing those who had been guarding the Vindrasi all day, sending them ashore to get some sleep. He ordered the archers back to the galley, telling them to eat and rest, for they would be needed in the morning.

Skylan wondered why. What was going to happen in the morning that required archers? Was there going to be a battle? Had they sighted an enemy? Two other Vindrasi dragonships had set out for ogre lands along with the *Venjekar*. Skylan had lost contact with his two ships during the storm. He hoped that they were now sailing to his rescue.

Skylan's head told him this was improbable, that the other two ships had likely sunk or were lost at sea in battle, but his heart wanted to believe. He imagined the ships attacking the *Light of the Sea,* warriors hurling spears and firing arrows to kill as many men as possible before they boarded the galley and finished off the rest.

He himself would kill Raegar. Skylan, chained up on the deck of the *Venjekar,* wasn't certain how that would come about, but this was *his* dream and he gave himself his sword, Blood Dancer, which Raegar had taken from him. He put himself on board the galley where he single-handedly fought and killed Raegar, then rescued Aylaen, who would be so thankful that she would fling her arms around him and tell him she loved him. He would carry her back in triumph to the *Venjekar,* where he would be welcomed as a hero and men would once more call him Chief of Chiefs.

Skylan was jolted suddenly back to bleak reality. Aylaen and her sister, Treia, came walking up the gangplank of the *Venjekar.* The two were escorted by Raegar.

Treia cast a look of sullen defiance at the warriors, especially her stepfather, Sigurd, who shouted out, "You foul bitch! What are you doing here in the company of that traitor? You are no daughter of mine. You and your whore of a sister."

"We are *not* your daughters!" Aylaen said scathingly, her green eyes flaring in the fading light. "A blessing for which we thank Torval daily!"

Aylaen put her arm protectively around Treia, and the two walked across the deck to the ship's hold. Raegar pulled open the hatch and the two women descended down into the small cabin below. Aylaen paused before she went down to cast a sweeping glance around the deck. Her gaze found and fixed on Skylan.

He took this for a hopeful sign, but he was mistaken. Her narrowed, glittering eyes told him as clearly as words how much she hated him. When she was certain he understood her, when his gaze dropped beneath her withering fire, she made her way down the ladder.

Raegar remained on deck. Bjorn, Grimuir, and some of the other Torgun warriors took this opportunity to jeer at Raegar, calling him traitor and coward, saying his mother had rutted with a snake (a reference to the serpent tattoo on his head), hoping to goad him into a fight.

Skylan kept silent. He could have told them they were wasting their breath. Raegar grinned at the insults. He did not care what these people called him or what they thought of him.

But he does care what his men think of him, Skylan realized, watching as Raegar cast surreptitious glances at the soldiers guarding the Vindrasi, making certain they noticed how little attention he paid to the insults being hurled at him.

The faces of the soldiers were frozen, expressionless as long as Raegar had his eye on them. When he went down into the hold with Zahakis to make certain that all was secure with the women, the soldiers exchanged glances and one made a remark that caused the others to glower and nod. Skylan could not hear what was said, but he understood.

No man likes a traitor, even if he's on your side, Skylan reflected. For you can never be sure he *is* on your side.

When Raegar returned to the deck, the Torgun greeted him with more insults.

Raegar now seemed annoyed.

"Tomorrow morning you will witness the power of Aelon," he announced. His gaze swept over the Torgun and went to the soldiers, and he added sternly, "All of you."

Raegar leaped over the side and splashed through the shallow water to where the galley, *Light of the Sea,* rode at anchor. Once he had gone, the soldiers looked at each other. Some snickered, others grinned and shook their heads. The Torgun fell glumly silent.

Skylan tried to go back to his daydream, but it had turned to ashes. The dream was stupid, a waste of time. His wrists and ankles were rubbed raw and bloody from his efforts to try to free himself from the manacles, efforts that had utterly failed.

His sword, along with the rest of their weapons, was stored in a locked chest in the hold of the *Venjekar*. Skylan took some comfort in the fact that the weapons were still on board the ship, though, he reflected gloomily, they might as well be on the other side of the world for all the good they could do him.

Hope flickered again briefly when he considered that Aylaen and Treia were both down in the hold with the weapons. He wondered whose side Treia was on. He knew she was in love with Raegar, or rather she *had* been. But how could she love a traitor? Treia was a Vindrasi; she would be loyal to her people. Then Skylan thought of what Wulfe had told him and he wasn't certain about her. Aylaen, on the other hand, was loyal. She would have no love for Raegar. But she did love her sister.

As he was thinking about this, he realized he wasn't alone. Sigurd had also been thinking about his stepdaughters, and started to rail against them.

"The two spent the night on that galley doing the gods know what. No man will marry either of them now. Not that any man would have married Treia before. Dried-up old sour apple like her."

The other Torgun frowned and shifted uncomfortably, their chains clanking. Sigurd was in his forties, the eldest among them. He was valiant and courageous, a skilled warrior, but he was also a dour man, a hard man who had married his dead brother's wife to make certain the land stayed in the family, not because he had any great affection for her. He openly kept a mistress and had fathered sons by her. None of the warriors particularly liked Treia and they might have all agreed in secret with what he said, but she was their Bone Priestess and she deserved their respect.

Sigurd continued, complaining about Aylaen. "I would have made a good marriage for her. I was in negotiations with a wealthy landholder from Vindraholm who was willing to pay me two times the customary bride-price because his son was so besotted with her. Then she spoiled everything by cutting off her hair and cavorting around as a man and—"

"She dedicated herself to the goddess," said Skylan.

Sigurd glanced at Skylan and said to the other warriors, "I thought I heard a noise. Like the yapping of a dog. Did anyone else hear it?"

"I heard only the prattling of a coward," said Skylan. "Only a coward would insult a woman, especially a woman who saved the coward's miserable life."

Sigurd scrambled to his feet and, hampered by the manacles around his ankles, made an awkward lunge for Skylan, who rose up to meet him. Two soldiers went over to break up the fight. They halted when some of their comrades shouted to them to let the barbarians slug it out.

"My money on the young one," said several.

An angry shout ended the match. Zahakis came up out of the hold, yelling to his men, who hurriedly drew their swords and intervened. They seized Sigurd's chain and dragged him down onto the deck, then clouted him over the head. Another hit Skylan for good measure.

Sigurd picked himself up off the deck. His face was bruised and bloody. He glared at Skylan, who wiped blood from a split lip and spit out a tooth.

"We were only going to let the barbarians fight it out, sir," said one of the soldiers. "It gives us something to do besides being forced to sit here and smell their stench."

"Who started the fight anyway?" Zahakis asked.

"The older man, the one with the scar across his nose and the gray in his beard. I don't know what the fight was about, sir, I wasn't paying attention. But he went for the young one."

"The young hothead again. The Legate was asking about him," said Zahakis. He turned to look at Skylan. "Acronis is considering him for the Para Dix. He has the physique of a fighter. Look at those thighs. Good biceps and chest musculature."

"Clean him up and the ladies will love him," one of the soldiers said.

"He'll have to be trained," said Zahakis. "I hear the barbarians' idea of battle is to form two lines and start bashing each other over the head."

The soldiers laughed. Skylan blazed with anger. He was tempted to challenge the soldiers then and there, never mind that he was chained, outnumbered, and weaponless. He lifted his hand to touch the amulet of Torval he wore around his neck, commending his soul to his god. Then he paused; an idea came to him.

The plan was desperate and Skylan wasn't sure he liked it, for it required subtlety and Garn was always telling him that he was about as subtle as a shield wall made up of ogres.

Skylan started to rub his aching jaw. Seeing the soldiers watching, he lowered his hand. He glanced at his fellow Torgun.

"For good or ill, I am still Chief of Chiefs until the judgment of the Vutmana," Skylan said to himself. "I am the one who is responsible for my people. I am the one who has to fix my mistake."

He turned his plan over in his head.

The night deepened. The soldiers lit a lantern and gathered at one end of the ship to play some sort of game involving pebbles thrown out of a box onto the deck. The game seemed childish to Skylan. There was no strategy involved. One man threw the pebbles and the others placed bets in advance on how many he would toss. The game was simply an excuse to gamble. Small wonder the soldiers were bored.

Skylan lay on the deck trying to sleep, which proved impossible. Whenever he dozed off, his chains would clank and wake him. He was just about to slip into slumber, clanking chains or not, when he felt a touch on his arm.

Wulfe, sopping wet, squatted down beside him. The boy had been gone all day. Skylan would have once worried about him, but he had learned that Wulfe could take care of himself.

Skylan grunted and rolled over. "Where have you been?"

"Talking to the oceanaids," said Wulfe. He cast a wary glance at the soldiers. Seeing they were involved in their game and had apparently not noticed that he had climbed over the ship's side, he settled himself comfortably on the deck.

Skylan yawned and closed his eyes. "So what did your dryads have to say?"

"Oceanaids," Wulfe corrected. "Oceanaids are different from dryads. Dryads live in trees and oceanaids live in the ocean."

Skylan was glad for the darkness; Wulfe couldn't see his smile.

"What did these oceanaids have to say?" he asked drowsily.

"Your gods are still alive. They're holed up in their Hall, under siege. The Gods of Raj and the Gods of the New Dawn think that your gods have been defeated and now they are going to fight each other."

"Good for them," said Skylan.

"The oceanaids told me that a fleet of ships has set sail from the ogre lands. The ogres are going to attack the lands of the Gods of the New Dawn. The oceanaids were going to sink the ships, but then they decided it would be more fun to watch you Uglies kill each other. When that happens, they say all the gods will go away and we faery folk will take back the world."

Wulfe curled up beside Skylan, pressing his back to his friend's back to keep warm.

"If that happens, I won't kill you," Wulfe told him sleepily. "I'll let you stay with me. I'll use my magic to protect you."

"Why don't you use your magic to free me from these chains?" asked Skylan.

"Do you want me to?" Wulfe asked, rousing. "I could do it. I was going to, but I was afraid you'd be mad."

Wulfe had once told Skylan that his mother was a faery princess and that his father had been a wolf. An outrageous lie, but an amusing one.

"Sure. Use your magic," said Skylan. "Turn my chains into flowers."

"I can't work magic on iron," said Wulfe. "But don't worry. I'll think of something."

He fell asleep and Skylan must have, too, for he dreamed of Torval in his Hall with the other gods, all of them wearing armor and carrying swords, ready for the last battle. The souls of the dead heroes were with them. Skylan looked for Garn, for Garn had died a hero's death and he should be among them.

Skylan spent all night searching for his friend among the honored dead and couldn't find him.

The hold of the *Venjekar* was dismal and dark and cluttered, but it was better than the storage room of the galley, if for no other reason than that it didn't smell of fish. Aylaen lay down on a blanket, saying she was tired, but Treia was restless and insisted on talking to her about the spiritbone.

"I don't know why you're treating me so badly," said Treia.

Aylaen sighed. "If I had the bone, don't you think I would use it? I would summon the Dragon Kahg and tell him to carry me to Garn . . ."

Treia regarded her uncertainly, then said slowly, "So you really do not have the spiritbone?"

"I've told you time and again, Treia, the bone was lost at sea," Aylaen said wearily.

"But then . . . what I am supposed to do?" Treia asked, dismayed. "Raegar expects me to summon the dragon tomorrow morning."

Aylaen was so startled, she sat up. "Why would Raegar expect you to summon the dragon? If you did summon Kahg, the first thing he would do would be to kill Raegar."

"The dragon won't kill anyone."

"How do you know?"

"Raegar says Aelon has been victorious in battle against our gods. He holds Vindrash hostage—"

"That's not true," said Aylaen sharply. She was about to say she had seen Vindrash in her dream, but she feared Treia would scoff. "Even if it is, it doesn't matter. The spiritbone was lost—"

"I've been thinking," said Treia. "When a wounded dragon heals, he returns the spiritbone to the priestess. The Dragon Kahg may have hidden his bone somewhere on board the ship. We have to look for it."

"If the dragon wanted you to have it, why would he hide it from you?" Aylaen asked, perplexed.

Treia glared at her. "I'm trying very hard to be patient, Aylaen, but you make it difficult. The dragon would not hide his bone from *me*. He would hide it from our enemies."

Aylaen had to admit this made sense, more sense than anything else Treia had said. There was something more to this desperate need for the spiritbone, something Aylaen did not understand. But she loved Treia and she wanted to please her and, above all, she wanted her to leave her alone. And so she helped Treia search.

The sisters lifted the lids off barrels and fished about inside. They shook out blankets and empty sacking. They opened the lids of all the sea chests except one, which was locked, much to Treia's ire. The chest was heavy and gave off a metallic clanking when Treia kicked at it in frustration.

"Raegar ordered his soldiers to lock our weapons in here," said Aylaen.

They had taken away her sword, a gift from Vindrash. She had found the sword in the Hall of the Gods back in Luda. The sword had been an offering to the dragon goddess from some long-ago warrior. It had been stashed away with other gifts and forgotten.

Aylaen had been proud of it. The blade was old, but Skylan had assured her the workmanship was very fine, the steel good quality. Skylan and Garn had taught her to use a sword, back when they were children playing shield-wall.

Tears filled Aylaen's eyes at the memory. She hurriedly wiped them away. If Treia saw her crying again, she would be annoyed.

"The Dragon Kahg wouldn't hide the spiritbone in a locked chest," Aylaen pointed out.

"Here is my sea chest!" Treia exclaimed, astonished, from where she was groping about in a shadowy corner behind the ladder.

"Well, what of it?" asked Aylaen.

Treia dragged the chest out from beneath the stairs. "I searched for it after the storm, but could not find it. I assumed it had been washed overboard. I searched in exactly that place. It wasn't here. I'm positive."

"It's hard to see down here," said Aylaen. "Everything was so confused then. You probably just overlooked it."

"No, it was not here."

There was no mistaking the chest, which had been a parting gift from the Kai Priestess, Draya. It was the only sea chest with a rune, the symbol of Vindrash, carved on the lid.

Treia lifted the lid and gave a glad cry. "Here are my clothes, clean and dry."

Reaching in, she drew out a dress for herself and another she handed to Aylaen. "You can stop pretending to serve the Goddess. You no longer need to dress like a man."

Aylaen shook her head.

"You might as well," Treia urged, thrusting the dress into Aylaen's arms. "We both know why you made that vow to be a man-woman. You didn't really intend to become a Bone Priestess. You wanted only to be with Garn."

Aylaen smoothed the fabric of the apron-dress. Though her clothes were wet and grimy, she wanted to wear what she had on: a man's wool tunic and leather trousers and boots. She wanted to stay as she was, where she was in time. She did not want time to move, unless time moved backward. Change of any sort seemed a betrayal of her love for Garn.

Aylaen folded the dress. She was about to place it back inside the chest when something fell out of the folds and landed on the deck with a thud.

"What is that?" Treia asked, blinking, unable to see in the dim light.

The knife was small, the kind used by fishermen to cut fouled lines and gut fish. Aylaen picked it up, touched it gingerly. The blade was sharp. She slipped the knife into the top of her boot.

"Only a brooch that fell off the dress," she said. "There's nothing else in here."

"Are you certain?" Treia said suspiciously. She came up behind Aylaen and tried to see over her shoulder.

Aylaen was annoyed and about to tell her sister she could look for herself, when she gave a little gasp. The spiritbone lay at the bottom of the chest.

"Sister, I found it!"

Aylaen lifted the spiritbone and sat back on her heels, gazing at it in wonder. "How is this possible? The bone fell into the ocean. How did it come to be here?"

"You 'found' it!" Treia said with a tight-lipped smile. She snatched the spiritbone out of Aylaen's hand. "I thought you might 'find' it if we looked long enough."

Treia held the bone close to her weak eyes to study it, as though she feared it might be fake. "I will take it for safekeeping."

"You can have it," said Aylaen. "The gods know I don't want it."

She thought back to the battle with the giants. If she had stayed on the beach to fight with Garn and Skylan, not gone running out into the sea to retrieve the spiritbone, Garn might still be alive. Aylaen hated the very sight of it.

"I am glad you understand, Sister," said Treia.

Aylaen didn't, not in the least, but she was thankful that she could stop searching. She could feel the cool blade of the knife in her boot.

"Are you hungry?" Treia asked. "I will ask for food."

She climbed the ladder that led up out of the hold and began to beat on the hatch, shouting that Raegar had promised them food and water. Footsteps sounded on the deck above.

Aylaen drew the knife from her boot.

"If Garn will not come back to me," said Aylaen softly, running her finger over the blade's sharp edge, "I will go to him."

6

The next morning, Zahakis ordered his soldiers to haul the *Venjekar* across the shallow water of the bay to within hailing distance of the *Light of the Sea*. The Legate was on the deck, flanked by four archers and ten soldiers, as well as the ship's crew, who stood ready to raise the sails and set out to sea should flight become necessary. Acronis ordered the rowers stationed at their oars, which were belowdecks, not only to be ready to row the galley out of danger, but for their own protection. Most of the men, not wanting to miss the spectacle of a dragon, crowded close to the oarports in order to get a good view.

Raegar stood on the deck of the *Venjekar* before the dragonhead prow. He wore a suit of ceremonial armor and a surplice embroidered with serpents eating their own tails, the vestments of the warrior-priesthood of the New Dawn.

The sun shone brilliantly this morning. Raegar, looking at the fiery orb, saw Aelon's glory, for Aelon ruled the sun, as he ruled all above and below. Skylan, looking at the sun, saw the goddess Aylis glaring at him and the other Torgun warriors in fierce anger, intent on making them sweat.

The prisoners had been herded together at the back of the ship, as far from the prow as possible, with ten soldiers and Zahakis to keep close watch over them. Skylan sat on a sea chest, his feet and hands chained, and wondered what was going on. Erdmun claimed he had overheard one of the soldiers say that Raegar was going to summon the Dragon Kahg and order him to sail the ship. Skylan scoffed at this, as did the other warriors.

"Not even Raegar's that stupid," said Sigurd. "The Dragon Kahg would have his balls for breakfast."

The others laughed and added their own crude remarks.

"Unless our gods are dead," said a quiet voice. "Maybe his god rules everything now, even the dragons."

The young man who had spoken was named Farinn. He had not been long among the Torgun, having only recently moved to Luda to live with relatives following the death of his parents, who had been killed when their longhouse caught fire. He was fifteen and this was his first voyage, the battle with the giants his first battle. He had accorded himself well; at least Skylan assumed he had. He couldn't remember that Farinn had even been there, though he must have been. The battle with the giants had been chaotic and confusing and Skylan could recall it only in horrific flashes. Farinn was so quiet people tended to forget he was around. Even now, when he spoke, men looked surprised. And troubled.

Skylan did not know Farinn well. Looking at the other Torgun, Skylan realized he did not know any of these men well, though he had lived with most of them from childhood up.

He could not have said, offhand, what Sigurd liked to eat for supper. Skylan might have been able to put names to Grimuir's children, at least the boys, for he sometimes played war games with them, but he would have been hard-pressed to say whether Grimuir had three sons or four.

Sklyan knew his comrades only as warriors. He knew where to place each man in the shield wall, knew how well each handled sword and spear and axe. He had relied on Garn for the rest. Garn who seemed to know everything about everyone, not because he loved gossip, like Bjorn, but because he had genuinely cared about his friends.

"How can I care about these men when I might have to send them to their deaths?" Skylan had once asked Garn.

"That's just an excuse," Garn had told him with a laugh to take the sting from his words. "The welfare of one person absorbs you completely. And that person is Skylan Ivorson."

Skylan remembered Garn's laughter and his heart ached. He stared out at the waves lapping against the ship's hull and listened to the talk that, not surprisingly, excluded him. No one asked his opinion or what he thought. They kept their backs to him.

"Our gods are not dead," Bjorn said firmly.

"Then where are they? Not around here, that's for certain," Erdmun returned. "I heard Treia was going to summon the dragon. She *is* a Bone Priestess. If anyone would know whether or not our gods are dead, it would be her."

The others looked uneasy at this. Skylan stirred and considered speaking out, denying Erdmun's claim that the gods were dead, but he knew no one would listen to him. Skylan focused his attention on Raegar. It was hard to stomach the sight of the traitor pacing proudly back and forth beneath the dragonhead prow, casting a critical eye over the *Venjekar* as though he was her master.

The others continued talking. The soldiers generally broke up conversations among the prisoners, for fear they might be plotting to escape. Skylan was surprised they were allowing it until he noted Zahakis, their commander, lounging nearby, listening intently. He was finding this discussion about dead gods and dragons very interesting, apparently. Skylan was about to order his men to keep silent, until he remembered that they would refuse to obey.

"The spiritbone is lost," said Bjorn. "It fell into the sea when the Dragon Kahg was wounded and left to return to his own realm. I should know. I helped search for it."

"The spiritbone always comes back to the Bone Priestess. She must have found it. Raegar wouldn't risk making a fool of himself otherwise," Grimuir argued.

"He isn't just risking making a fool of himself," said Sigurd. "He knows that the Dragon Kahg could send that monster of a ship to the bottom of the sea with a twitch of his tail. Raegar knows something. Or thinks he knows something."

"He knows our gods are dead," said Erdmun stubbornly.

The sea chest beneath Skylan began to shake, and he kicked it to make it stop. Wulfe had woken before dawn and had started to leave the ship, as usual, to keep out of the way of the iron-wielding, iron-wearing soldiers. Skylan had stopped him, telling him that if the ship sailed, he would be marooned on the island by himself.

Wulfe had said that if Raegar caught him, he'd be dead here by himself and Skylan had told the boy to hide in the sea chest. Wulfe was slightly built and could bend his lithe and skinny body as if he were made of willow branches, and he had no trouble fitting into the chest. But he'd been there a long time and he was probably finding his hiding place cramped, hot, and uncomfortable.

"Be quiet," Skylan told the boy in a low voice. "Something's about to happen."

Raegar ordered one of the soldiers to give the signal. The man blew a blast on the trumpet. Once he had everyone's attention, Raegar began to speak in a booming voice designed to carry over the water to the galley, loudly expouding upon the glories of Aelon and how they would witness those glories by seeing that even a dragon known to serve the Vindrasi gods would bow to Aelon.

He spoke with conviction. Skylan, glancing around, saw that his men were grim-faced and downcast, as men look when they have no choice but to concede a bitter truth.

What did Raegar hope to accomplish? Skylan wondered. Raegar must be confident that this god of his could exert control over the dragon, otherwise he would not risk summoning Kahg, who could reduce the *Light of the Sea* to the *Blazing Heap of Ashes*. Skylan felt a nagging doubt. Farinn was right. The gods did appear to have abandoned their people. He did not believe the gods were dead, but it could be that Torval and Vindrash were not strong enough to intervene. What if this god, Aelon, was able to compel the Dragon Kahg to obey?

"Then that will be a sign," Skylan said softly.

Raegar continued with his exhortation. The soldiers were well-disciplined and stood unmoving beneath the merciless sun. They all wore their best armor, the helms with the cheek flaps, the leather skirts, and they must be broiling. Their faces and bare arms glistened with sweat. Skylan more than once cast a longing glance at the cool seawater, rolling beneath the keel of the *Venjekar*.

Skylan wondered if the soldiers were wishing they could jump into the water or wishing they could throw in Raegar. There was no telling how long the warrior-priest would have gone on praising Aelon. He was interrupted, cut off mid-sentence by the Legate.

"I trust Aelon will forgive me for rushing him," Acronis called out from the deck of the war galley, "but we are all slowly roasting to death. Get on with it."

Raegar frowned, deeply offended. "One of you men fetch the Bone Priestess," he said with what dignity he could muster.

Skylan looked intently at Raegar, searching for any sign that he was at all doubtful or nervous. To the contrary, Raegar appeared smugly confident.

Skylan sighed, and hearing a growling noise coming from the sea chest, he kicked it again.

Down in the hold, Treia was dressed in her ceremonial robes, which she wore over the apron dress, wearing that over the linen smock. She was sweating profusely in the close, confined area of the hold. Aylaen remained in bed.

She could hear Raegar's loud voice coming from above deck, going on and on about his god. The droning put her to sleep. She was awakened by the sound of someone coming down the ladder.

"Priestess," said the soldier curtly, pointing at Treia and gesturing to the deck above. "You are summoned. Make haste."

Treia looked at Aylaen, who made no move to rise.

"Aren't you coming with me?" Treia asked, startled.

"Why?" asked Aylaen. "You have the spiritbone."

Treia cast a glance at the soldier. "Tell Warrior-Priest Raegar I will attend him shortly."

She waited until the soldier had gone back up the stairs, then she hurried over to Aylaen and knelt beside her. "We should both pray to Vindrash to summon the dragon. Just to be safe."

Aylaen thought of the dream, of Vindrash casting her out into the cold. She shook her head.

"The goddess isn't interested in hearing from me."

"Treia!" Raegar shouted angrily from the deck. "I sent for you! What is this delay?"

"You have to come, Aylaen!" said Treia insistently. "Please!"

Aylaen sat up, her arms on her knees.

"I don't see why. . . ."

"Because sometimes the Dragon Kahg doesn't come when I summon him," Treia said, her face strained and tense and glistening with sweat.

"The dragon will come, Treia. You are the Bone Priestess."

Treia's lips tightened. She was holding the spiritbone in her hand, and suddenly she thrust it in Aylaen's face.

"The Dragon Kahg gave the spiritbone to you. *You* are the one who found it. That means he wants you to have it."

"But I don't want it," Aylaen said, shocked. She stared at her sister in dismay. "I don't want anything to do with this!"

"Then our people are doomed," said Treia coldly. "And you have doomed them."

Slowly, reluctantly, Aylaen took the spiritbone from Treia's hand.

On the war galley, Acronis walked the deck, trying to find the most advantageous position from which to see what was happening on board the *Venjekar*. He could hear Raegar summoning the women. There appeared to be some sort of problem, for there was a momentary delay, but then they appeared, one wearing what looked to be ceremonial robes and the other dressed like a man. According to Raegar, this female had taken some sort of vow to her barbaric gods to become a "man-woman."

Acronis found this practice curious, and he had made a note of it. He had been disappointed to find that Raegar could not provide him with more details.

"I have not lived among them for years," said Raegar dismissively. "Thank Aelon I've managed to forget all their savage ways."

Poor Raegar. An ambitious man, he could capture all the dragons in the world and he would never gain what he sought—acceptance in Sinarian society. He would always be an outsider. Acronis had once tried, kindly, to explain to him the facts of the matter. Raegar had flown into a rage, yelling and cursing—merely confirming what everyone knew. He was, beneath his fine clothes, an uncivilized barbarian.

The two women stood close together. They were sisters, though Acronis found that difficult to credit, for they did not look much alike. The one who dressed as a man had green eyes and a crop of red curls. The other had long blondish hair and dark eyes. The red-haired woman was a beauty or would have been if she had combed her rampant curls and washed her face. Her older sister might have been attractive, but for the fact that she squinted and walked with the slight stoop one often saw with those who had poor eyesight.

The ritual to summon the dragon was apparently about to start, for the older sister had hold of an object that must be the vaunted spiritbone. She lifted the bone in front of her and began speaking to the wooden head of the dragon.

Acronis was too far away to see the bone or hear what the priestess was saying and he regretted that he was not present on the *Venjekar* to observe and take notes. He had considerd it, but had at last agreed reluctantly with Zahakis that the Legate's place was on his own galley, ready to order his men to take action should the dragon attack.

Raegar had promised he could control the beast—or rather, Aelon could control it. Acronis was dubious and, frankly, at this stage, after sweltering in the sun listening to Raeger drone on and on, Acronis was rooting for the dragon.

The Vindrasi prisoners were silent, watching their Bone Priestess. The blond, young hothead named Skylan sat by himself.

"He is undoubtedly praying to his savage gods that his dragon will kill us all," Acronis remarked to his scribe, who was by his side. "I don't suppose I can blame him."

The priestess quit speaking. Holding the spiritbone, she placed her hands into a bucket of water, scooped up seawater, and held it and the spiritbone in her cupped palms.

The Torgun warriors rose eagerly to their feet, ignoring the soldiers who angrily ordered them to sit down. Raeger glared at all of them and demanded silence.

The water in the priestess's hands dripped onto the deck. Nothing happened.

Acronis glanced at his archers, who must be growing weary of keeping their arrows nocked. He did not give them the order to stand down. Not yet. Even at this distance, he could see Raegar's face darken in anger and concern.

Raegar said something to the priestess, who said something to her sister, the man-woman, and thrust the spiritbone at her. The Torgun warriors began to yell, urging her on. The man-woman shook her head. Her sister spoke to her at length, and, finally, the man-woman gave way. She took the spiritbone from her sister, dipped her hands into the water, and then, before Raegar could stop her, she flung the spiritbone into the sea.

Acronis was startled. Was this part of the ritual? He didn't think it was, for Raegar was choking with fury and yelling for someone who could swim to jump into the shallow water after it.

Ripples from where the spiritbone landed were still spreading. Then, the seawater began to swirl.

Acronis leaned over the rail to get a closer view. The swirling motion grew stronger, causing the war galley to rock at anchor and sending waves splashing into the hull of the *Venjekar*. The sea began to rise, kicking up foam. Sea spray rose into the air, whirling like a water spout turned upside down.

Acronis watched, transfixed, as the rising surge of water took shape, forming around the single bone that had been thrown into the sea. Bone sprang from bone, muscle wrapped around bone, heart beat beneath bone, skin and scales flowed over bone, wings jutted out from bone. A magnificent head lifted on a great, curved neck. Red eyes flared.

Acronis caught his breath.

The dragon spread his wings and rose from the water that cascaded off the glistening body in sheets and rained down on the lifted faces of those who stared up at him, awestruck and terrified.

Acronis saw movement—one of the archers, raising his bow.

"No!" Acronis cried, and he jostled the man's arm.

The dragon circled the two ships slowly. He was the green of the sea when a storm is coming. He was the blue of the sea when the water is calm and children play in the waves. He was the gray of the sea in the winter when the waves break against the rocks along the shore. His crest was white as sea foam.

Acronis gazed upward as the water poured off the dragon's body, spattering cool on his face. Across the water, the Torgun prisoners shouted at the dragon, calling him by name, urging him to attack.

The dragon turned flaring red eyes upon Acronis, who stood transfixed by the awful beauty of the creature. The sunlight shone through the membrane of the wings. The dragon was so close Acronis could see the branching blood vessels, red amid the green. The Dragon Kahg began a stooping dive.

Raegar called out the name of Aelon and demanded that the dragon obey him and surrender. His words bounced off the dragon, who paid no heed. The crew on board the galley shrieked in terror and fell over each other trying to seek shelter belowdecks. The soldiers drew their weapons. The archers raised their bows.

Acronis might be dead in the next few moments, and all he could think of as he stared at the marvelous beast was that death was a small price to pay for having been privileged to see such magnificence.

Raegar shouted again, calling for Aelon.

"Kahg!" The Torgun shouted the dragon's name in warning and pointed. "Behind you!"

The dragon snaked his head around. Three winged serpents, creatures of Aelon, skimmed over the top of the ocean, speeding toward the dragon like a flight of arrows, slicing through the tops of the waves.

The Dragon Kahg reversed his dive, clawing at the air to gain altitude, wings beating. He sucked in his breath, his rib cage expanding, and spewed forth a great gout of white foaming water.

The water struck the lead serpent with the force of a tidal wave. The serpent twisted, flipped, and flailed, and sank into the water with a bubbling hiss. The other two serpents sped toward the dragon, separating, outflanking him, attacking from the left and the right.

Kahg could not evade them, and they struck him before he had time to draw another breath.

The serpents attempted to wrap their bodies around the dragon, trying to squeeze the breath from his lungs and crush his bones. The Dragon Kahg slashed at the serpents with his clawed feet and tore at them with his fangs, ripping out chunks of scaly flesh that he spit into the sea.

Blood rained down on Acronis. One of the serpents, bleeding from a ragged tear that had nearly split its body in two, sank beneath the waves. The other struck at the dragon's hindquarters with its tail. The Dragon Kahg caught hold of the serpent in his claws. The serpent writhed and coiled and struck repeatedly at the dragon's head and wings.

Some fool archer let loose an arrow, aiming for the dragon. Kahg, battling for his life against the serpent, never saw it. The arrow fell harmlessly into the sea.

The wind strengthened, whipping up the waves so that the *Venjekar* and the *Light of the Sea* rocked violently. Dark clouds boiled up from the horizon. Thunder rolled and lightning flared. The blasting wind seized the dragon and the serpent and carried them, still battling, up into the clouds. The dragon and the serpent, tangled together, were swallowed up by clouds and vanished from sight.

The Torgun fell silent. Raegar stood on the deck of the *Venjekar*, glaring at the heavens. Men on board the galley were dazed, dumbstruck.

Acronis was the first to speak, and his voice shook with rage.

"I want the man who fired that arrow whipped!"

On board the *Venjekar*, the Torgun gazed into the thunder-clouds, praying desperately that the Dragon Kahg would fly back to destroy their enemies. Time passed. The thunder ceased. The clouds drifted off, casting dark shadows on the sparkling water. The dragon did not return.

"This proves our gods are dead," said Erdmun glumly.

"The Dragon Kahg killed two of his foes," said Skylan. "The dragon and our gods are alive and fighting. If you want further proof," he added with grim satisfaction, "look at Raegar."

Raegar's face was purple, his neck red, cords bulging, blood vessels throbbing. He had just seen the creatures of his invincible god go down in defeat. He was so furious that he lost control and raised his hand to strike Treia, blaming her for his failure. Aylaen stepped between Raegar and her sister.

"Touch her," said Aylaen, "and you will die."

Her voice was soft with menace and, though she had no weapon to carry out her threat, Raegar lowered his hand. The Torgun were shouting and yanking on their chains. Zahakis decided this had gone far enough and he stepped in to try to regain control.

"One of you men, take the women below," he ordered sharply, then turned to confront Raegar.

"What the hell are you doing? Your kinsmen are trouble enough without watching you mistreating their women. Keep it up and they will rip their chains out of the bulkheads to get at you!"

Raegar glowered, hands clenching and unclenching. He began to try to say something, but Zahakis coolly cut short the man's raging.

"We have bigger worries. How do you propose we sail the ship now that the dragon is gone?"

"I will order the prisoners to sail it," said Raegar. The flush was slowly fading from his face, leaving it an ugly mottled color, red with whitish-yellow spots.

"I'm sure they'll be eager to obey you," said Zahakis dryly.

Raegar gave an unpleasant smile. "Leave it to me, Tribune. I know these brutes."

"Because you're one of them," muttered a soldier standing near Skylan.

Raegar walked over to face his former friends and kinsmen, who told him what they'd like to do to him. Raegar looked smug and Skylan tensed.

Whatever the whoreson is planning, he is confident of the outcome.

"You will sail this ship," Raegar said loudly, "or I will order Tribune Zahakis and his men to whip you until the flesh falls from your bones and you bleed to death. You will go to Torval in chains, bloody from the lash, the mark of the slave upon you. Is that how you want to die?"

Skylan held rigidly still. The Torgun fell silent. No man moved. No man spoke.

To die a slave was to die dishonored. Torval would spurn them, turn them from his Hall. They would be forced to spend the afterlife alone, separated from their loved ones, who would refuse to acknowledge them out of shame.

Skylan rose slowly to his feet. "Release me. I will sail the ship."

"Coward!" Sigurd sneered, spitting the word from the side of his mouth.

The others by their baleful expressions agreed with him.

"I will not die in chains," Skylan said. "And I swear to Torval I will not die without first taking my revenge on the man who betrayed us."

Bjorn and Aki muttered agreement and it seemed they might join him, for both stood up. Sigurd barked a sharp command. Erdmun whispered something and Bjorn, casting a glance at Sigurd, sat back down. No one else raised his head.

The Torgun could not always rely upon the dragon to sail their ship, for the dragon was often away on his own business. In that instance, the Torgun would raise the sail or row the ships themselves; each warrior sitting on his sea chest, plying an oar.

Skylan reached down to his sea chest and yanked it open. Wulfe stared up at him. Skylan gave a nod and the boy, relieved, scrambled out. The soldiers all laughed and even the stern Zahakis smiled. Raegar glared, not amused.

"What is he doing here? That boy is the spawn of daemons!" Raegar said, seething. "Throw him over the side."

"The boy is just a boy," said Skylan. "If you want me to sail the ship, I will need his help."

Zahakis looked across the sea at Acronis. The galley's crew was raising the sails. The galley had two—one in the center and one in the front. The sails billowed, catching the wind, and the galley began to glide through the water. The Legate stood on the deck, watching the proceedings on board *Venjekar*. He could not hear what was going on, but he could undoubtedly guess. Acronis, seeing Zahakis's glance, nodded his head. The Legate was impatient to return home.

"Strike off this man's chains," said Zahakis. "Do not remove the leg irons. I don't want him tempted to take a swim. As for the boy, he does look dangerous, I admit, but I think twelve armed soldiers can handle him."

His men grinned. Raegar muttered something and stalked off.

He must be questioning his god about now, Skylan thought. Either that or asking Aelon to send down his holy fire to consume everyone on board, starting with Zahakis.

They took the manacles off Skylan's wrists and freed him from the chains. With Wulfe's help, Skylan raised the *Venjekar*'s single sail, then he pointed to the stern to the single oar-like rudder.

"I must use that to steer the ship."

"I will come with you," said Zahakis. He placed his hand on the hilt of his short sword. "In case you decide to run the ship into a reef, I will take Raegar's advice regarding the boy and throw him overboard."

Skylan grasped hold of the tiller. He felt it bite and steered the ship so that the wind caught the sail. The galley was well ahead of them. The *Venjekar* followed in her wake; the lighter, swifter ship soon gained upon the massive galley.

"You are a wise young man," said Zahakis, taking his place along-side Skylan. "Sometimes it takes more courage to live than to die."

"I'm alive for one reason," said Skylan coolly. "So I may have the pleasure of killing you. *After* I gut Raegar."

Zahakis smiled briefly and shook his head. Leaning on the rail, he gazed out over the sea.

"I am thankful that dragon of yours didn't rip our heads off," he said, and he added as he walked off, "but wherever the beast does its fighting, I hope it wins."

The *Venjekar* and the *Light of the Sea* put into shore that night to take on fresh water and send out hunting parties. Finding game had proved a failure on the Dragon Isles. The men could see the tracks, but traps and snares caught nothing and hunting parties returned empty-handed.

Raegar took advantage of the opportunity to transfer from the *Venjekar* to the *Light of the Sea*. He did not take Treia with him. He still blamed her for his failure to command the dragon.

After the ship made landfall, Treia and Aylaen were permitted to leave the hold. Treia watched in bleak unhappiness as Raegar walked up the gangplank onto the *Light of the Sea*. He did not spare a glance for her.

"He asked me if the Dragon Kahg was dead. He thinks I should know," Treia told her sister.

"Do you?" asked Aylaen.

"No," said Treia bitterly. "Do you?"

Aylaen shook her head.

Their captors escorted them to a freshwater stream to perform their ablutions. The women had no privacy; the soldiers kept close watch on them. Aylaen laved her face and neck with the cold water and then sat on the bank of the stream, shivering in the waning light.

Treia rinsed her long hair and wrung it out. She scrubbed her face and washed her body as thoroughly as she could, given the fact that she could not take off her clothes.

She is trying to make herself pretty for Raegar. Aylaen did not know whether to weep for her sister or slap her.

Once their bath was finished, the two returned to camp. Treia gripped Aylaen's arm and, keeping an eye on their guards, whispered, "If the spiritbone comes back to you as it did the last time, you must tell me!"

Aylaen turned to her, eyed her coldly. "I swear to you, Treia, that if the spiritbone came back to me I would crush it to powder beneath my heel."

She broke loose from her sister's grasp and walked off. Treia hesitated a moment, then hurried after her.

"You don't mean that," said Treia. "Raegar says—"

"Raegar!" Aylaen repeated angrily. "Raegar is a traitor to our people. He is a traitor to you, Treia! Can't you see that? How can you still love him?"

"Raegar has the good of our people at heart—"

"His god wants to destroy our gods, Treia! Why is that good?"

"Our gods brought their doom upon themselves," said Treia. "They were careless of their creation."

Back in camp, a bright fire burned. A hunting party must have been successful. They smelled roasting meat.

Aylaen's stomach turned. "I'm going back aboard ship."

"You have to eat," said Treia.

"I'm not hungry."

"You'll make yourself sick. . . ."

"Good!"

"Sister, I know you are angry with me, but think about this." Treia paused, then said abruptly, "How can you believe in gods who let Garn die?"

The sky was gray. The sea was gray. A light rain began to fall. Drops splattered on the burning logs and hissed and sizzled. Aylaen lifted her face to the rain, let it run down her cheeks. She tried to weep for Garn, but the tears would not come. She had no more tears left.

The sky wept for her.

Skylan and the others did not receive a share of the roasted meat. They were forced to sit and smell the tantalizing aroma that made their stomachs growl and their mouths water. They were given a noxious paste of ground fish known as *garum,* bread, fresh water, and the fruit of Oran known as olives. Skylan ate the strange food, even choked down the fish paste, determined to keep up his strength.

After the meal, those soldiers not on duty guarding the slaves held a wrestling match. They drew a crude circle in the sand. Two of the men stripped naked and, stepping into the circle and sweating and heaving, each tried to force his opponent to step out of the circle or pin the opponent so that he could not move and was forced to give up.

Punching was not permitted. The men had to rely on strength and quickness and agility. Zahakis acted as the judge. When a man broke one of the rules, Zahakis separated them and forced them to start over. Acronis was an honored guest, and he clapped and called out when one of the wrestlers did particularly well. The Legate made wagers with his soldiers and crew, laughing good-naturedly and paying up when he lost, waving away his winnings when he won.

The Torgun warriors at first tried to pretend they weren't interested. But wrestling matches were extremely popular among the Vindrasi. Men and women both took part (though they did not fight naked, which the Torgun found shocking). Eventually the warriors gave up the pretense and began to watch.

Aki, a renowned wrestler himself, was so impressed that when one of the wrestlers flipped the other over on his back with a skilled maneuver, he gave a shout of approval. The other warriors glared at him, and Aki flushed and grinned and shrugged.

When the matches ended, the losers paid up or promised they were good for it, and everyone made ready for sleep. The fires were allowed to burn out. The soldiers wrapped themselves in blankets. The sentries paced the beach in the fitful rain. The prisoners lay down in the wet sand and tried to sleep. Zahakis had ordered the Vindrasi to be chained together, side by side. Skylan had managed to see to it that he was chained to Sigurd.

Skylan kept an eye on the sentry, waited until he was some distance away, then said softly, "Sigurd, I need to talk to you."

"Go talk to yourself, piss-shit coward," Sigurd muttered, rolling over, turning his backside to him.

Skylan managed to control his anger, though the bile burned holes in his stomach.

"I have a plan for us to escape," said Skylan.

Sigurd was silent a moment, then he started to turn.

"Don't move!" Skylan cautioned. "Just listen."

"Well?" Sigurd said churlishly.

"These Southlanders enjoy a good fight. Let's give them one."

Sigurd shifted position slightly, managing to peer at Skylan over his shoulder. "I'm listening."

"We will wait until we have been out to sea for several days, when the soldiers are good and bored, then you and I will get into a fight. The soldiers will break it up. I'll tell Zahakis—"

"Hush!" Sigurd warned.

Boots crunched in the sand. The sentry was making his rounds. Skylan closed his eyes, feigning sleep.

When the sentry had passed, Skylan said softly, "I will tell Zahakis that you have challenged me for the right to be chief of the warriors and that we must fight to see which of us it will be."

Sigurd grunted. "A Vutmana?"

"Of sorts," said Skylan.

"Go on," said Sigurd. "I'm starting to like this."

"I will say that tradition demands that you and I fight with sword and shield. We will start our battle, and when the soldiers relax their guard, we will stop fighting each other and turn on them."

Sigurd snorted in disgust. "Even a blind cat can still smell the rat. The Southlanders are stupid, but not that stupid."

"Like I said, I have a plan."

"We all know your plans have worked out so well so far," said Sigurd, sneering.

"Are you with me or not?" Skylan asked.

"On one condition."

"What is that?" Skylan asked warily.

"We fight the Vutmana for real. Whoever draws first blood is chief."

Skylan hesitated. Once he would have agreed immediately, certain that Torval would not let him lose. But Skylan was not so sure of Torval's favor these days. He had broken an oath to the god. He had lied, invoking Torval's name. True, he had fought a heavenly battle against serpents at Torval's side, though he had to admit that might have been a dream.

Skylan put his hand to the fresh weal on his chest obtained when the tail of the serpent had lashed him, knocked him out of the heavens, and sent him tumbling back to earth. If it was a dream, it had left its mark. He had faith in Torval, whether Torval had faith in him or not.

"I agree," he said. "In Torval's name."

"So what is this plan?" Sigurd asked.

"We start by convincing the Southlanders we want to kill each other," said Skylan.

Sigurd grunted and grinned. "I think I can do that."

Wulfe had not gone ashore with the rest, but had remained on board the *Venjekar*. The soldiers frightened him. They stank of iron. He waited until all of them were quiet except for their snoring, and then he softly and silently crept off the ship.

He was bored. He tended to sleep a lot during the daylight hours, dozing in the sun. He liked being up at night, when he could do what he wanted with no Ugly to yell at him. He thought he might go talk to Aylaen, who had returned to the ship, try to cheer her up. He had come to like Aylaen. But Treia was down there with her and Wulfe hated Treia.

She and Raegar had caught him practicing his magic, bringing flocks of seagulls to save Skylan and the others from the giants. Treia had termed him "fae," hissing the word. Raegar had done worse, calling him "daemon spawn." Wulfe was not even sure what a daemon spawn was. If it meant he had frequent battles with the daemons who lived inside him, who often urged him to do terrible things, then Raegar was right. Wulfe wanted to do terrible things to Raegar and to Treia, but Owl Mother had warned him that the daemons were evil and he must not give way to them.

"They seek to harm you, to get you into trouble," Owl Mother had told him. "That is because they are miserable and they want you to be miserable, too."

Wulfe was miserable now and he hadn't even given in to the daemons. He was miserable because Skylan and his friends were miserable. Wulfe tried to be hopeful. He had his magic. If only he could figure out a way to use it to help.

Wulfe pattered down the gangplank, grateful for the rain that blotted out the light of moon and stars and hid him from the sentries. He waited until no one was looking, then he scampered onto the beach, ran across the sand until he reached the treeline, and vanished into the shadows.

He tried to strike up a conversation with the dryads, who lived in the trees, but they were sleepy and told him to go away. The animals that prowled by night were intent upon their own business and wished him well and scurried past. Wulfe walked in the woods.

He always hoped, on these walks, that some night he would venture into a coppice and there he would find his mother, beautiful as a moon glade, her hair bound with stars, dancing with the other faeries. He imagined her catching sight of him, laughing with joy and holding out her hands to him, calling him to come join her. He would dance with her and she would take him back to the faery kingdom and they would be happy together always.

"Still, then I would have to leave Skylan," Wulfe said to himself. A hard choice. He could never decide, from one night to the next, which he would choose.

Fortunately, this night, Wulfe was not called upon to make the choice. He saw no faeries. On a drizzly, dark night like this, they were probably snug and cozy in their underground dwellings, sipping honey wine from clover cups and listening to beautiful songs about how wonderful their world had been before the gods of the Uglies had come and ruined it.

Leaving the woods, Wulfe returned to the beach. He had traveled a good distance away from the ships and the soldiers with their horrible smell of iron. He took off his clothes and left them on the beach and ran into the water. The oceanaids—beautiful denizens of the sea, guardians of the sea and all who lived within it—were awake and they came to play with him.

The Uglies could not see the oceanaids, for their skin was translucent, taking on the color of the water in which they lived. The oceanaids brought dolphins for Wulfe to ride and kept him company until the sky began to grow light. He bid them goodbye. He had to sneak back on board ship before anyone saw him.

He shook off the water like a dog and, shivering a little in the cool air, he put on his clothes—a pair of wool trousers and a wool tunic. He had been given stockings and boots, but he never wore them and had no idea where they had got to.

He ran down the beach, keeping watch on the sentries, planning to time his dash up the gangplank the moment no one was looking. Wulfe was drawing near the *Venjekar*. So were the sentries, but, fortunately, they stopped to talk. Wulfe started heading for the ship, then something white, sloshing about in the waves, caught his eye.

He thought it was a fish, caught in a tide pool, and he went to free it. Drawing nearer, he saw that it wasn't a fish. He wasn't certain what it was—a large shell, maybe. He was curious now and he squatted down to pick it up. When he knew what it was, his hand froze in midair.

It was a spiritbone. The spiritbone of the Dragon Kahg.

Wulfe felt eyes staring at him, the dragon's eyes. He trembled, afraid to look up at the dragonhead prow, knowing he would see the dragon's eyes, red and baleful. The Dragon Kahg did not approve of him, or so Wulfe believed, for the dragon always seemed to be glaring at him.

"Don't worry!" Wulfe said to the dragon, risking a glance at the head that towered above him. "I won't touch it!"

He stood up and heard one of the men yell, "Hey, someone's out there!"

"Put your sword up. It's only the kid," said his comrade.

"What the devil is he doing traipsing about in the middle of the night?"

"Up to no good, I'll wager. Hey, you, kid—" The soldier shouted and began running toward him.

He would see the spiritbone in the water. He was bound to see it. Wulfe snatched up the spiritbone and shoved it hastily in his trousers as the soldier came splashing through the water. The man made a grab for Wulfe.

Terrified, the boy dropped down to all fours and ran off, dashing over the sand on his hands and feet. The soldier was so startled by this odd spectacle that he stood and stared.

"Would you look at that? Kid runs like a goddam dog!"

The soldiers laughed and, seeing that he went back on board the ship, they walked off, continuing their conversation.

Wulfe crouched among coils of rope in the stern, far from the eyes of the dragon, and wondered what to do. He should go down to the hold, take the spiritbone to Aylaen. He would have if she'd been alone, but Treia was there and Wulfe knew that she would be horrid and nasty. She would probably accuse him of stealing the spiritbone. She would turn him over to Raegar, who wanted him dead.

Wulfe pulled the spiritbone out of his trousers. The spiritbone reeked of magic, dragon magic. He didn't want it and he was tempted to throw it back into the water, but he was afraid the dragon would be mad at him. Wulfe longed to talk to Skylan, to ask him what to do. That meant leaving the safety of the ship and venturing onto the beach, where Skylan was sleeping. The soldiers would catch him.

Wulfe made up his mind. He rose from his hiding place and crept across the deck. When Wulfe had first come to Luda with Skylan, after his disastrous adventure with the druids, the boy had lived aboard the *Venjekar*. He spent much of his time wandering around the village of the Torgun and he often found objects imbued with faery magic; objects the Uglies had either discarded or misplaced or, sad to say, that he stole.

Among these magical objects were a child's tooth, a wooden thimble (which he'd picked up by wrapping a bit of cloth over it), a charred finger bone from the site of Garn's funeral byre, and locks of hair belonging to Skylan, Aylaen, and Treia. Wulfe had planned to sneak off with some of Raegar's hair, but Raegar had foiled him by shaving his head.

Wulfe had discovered a loose plank on the bulkhead directly beneath the dragon's head. He had worked diligently to pry it from the nails that held it in place. He made a cubbyhole in the bulkhead, lined it with some of the cloth used to make sails to keep it dry, and then deposited his treasures inside. Now he removed the plank, taking care to avoid looking at the dragon, and thrust the spiritbone inside. Wulfe closed up the compartment and, putting his hand on the plank, whispered a little rhyme.

> *"Keep safe from thieving hands.*
> *Keep safe from spying eyes.*
> *Let them meet a swift demise."*

He wasn't certain what a "demise" was. His mother had taught him the magical rhyme and she had not bothered to explain. Probably she didn't know either. His little song sung, he yawned and walked across the deck to where he had made himself a bed. Turning about the blanket three times, he curled up and went to sleep.

The next morning, Sigurd tried to strangle Skylan.

Skylan was barely awake. He was stumbling groggily to his feet when Sigurd jumped him from behind, flinging the chain that connected the manacles on his wrists around Skylan's neck and jerking him backward. The two crashed to the ground, kicking and flailing.

The soldiers immediately broke it up, dragging the two apart. Skylan's neck was bruised and bloody, and Sigurd was limping from where Skylan had kicked him in the shins in an attempt to make him loosen his hold. Neither was seriously injured. Both of them glared at each other from the grasp of their captors.

"You two again," said Zahakis, regarding them grimly. "I swear by Aelon's arse, I'm tempted to slit your throats and leave your bodies here to rot! You're more trouble than you're worth. Take them on board," he ordered his men. "And no food, only water for the rest of the day!"

Skylan sullenly took his place at the tiller. Sigurd made a muttered remark as he limped past him. Skylan clenched his fists and started to rise. Zahakis shoved him back down.

"Why is there bad blood between you two?" Zahakis asked as the *Venjekar* set out to sea, following in the wake of the war galley.

"He challenges my right to be chief," said Skylan, casting a dark glance at Sigurd, who continued to glower at him from where he sat chained to the bulkhead.

"You a chief?" Zahakis said, amused. "You are just a boy!"

"I have seen eighteen winters," Skylan said. He started to say, "Our god made me chief." But he knew that was open to question. He touched the silver sword he wore around his neck, asking Torval's forgiveness and his blessing and said instead, "I fought a battle against the old chief and I won."

"So what right does Graybeard over there have to challenge you?"

Skylan swallowed. He didn't like admitting the truth, but Zahakis might ask for confirmation from Raegar. Skylan had to make this convincing.

"Sigurd thinks I cheated in the ritual contest. He believes that I murdered Horg, the old chief. Poisoned him."

Zahakis raised his eyebrows. "Did you?"

"No," said Skylan.

"So did you kill him in combat or was this Horg poisoned?"

Skylan stared moodily out to sea and did not answer. Even now, he did not like to think about that time. He had been so proud of himself, so cocksure that he had broken his oath to his father, to his god. Only to find out that it was all a lie.

"You people really are savages," Zahakis said. He leaned against the rail, making himself comfortable. They had a long journey ahead of them and nothing to do. "Tell me about this ritual combat."

Skylan related the history of the Vutmana, describing the battle in detail, how the priestess measured out the ceremonial cloth on which the warriors stood, how each warrior was given three shields and one sword, how each had to stand still and take the blows from his opponent until first blood was drawn.

"That means our god, Torval, has made his decision and the priestess declares the winner," Skylan said.

"So you had to stand there and let this Horg try to kill you? You couldn't fight back or defend yourself?" Zahakis shook his head. "That takes guts. I would like to see this Vutmana."

"You can," said Skylan. "Let Sigurd and me fight. This night when we make landfall. Let me prove to my warriors that Torval chose me!"

He spoke with an anger and intensity that was not feigned. Skylan wanted this fight and he knew, from the bruises on his neck, that Sigurd wanted it as well.

"If you keep on getting into trouble, I will kill both of you before the voyage ends," Zahakis remarked. "You might as well entertain us. I will speak to the Legate. You are his property, after all."

When Zahakis walked off, Skylan looked across the deck at Sigurd and gave a slight nod. Sigurd rubbed his chin and nodded back.

They made landfall that night. The next day, according to Zahakis, they would head out to sea and not see land again for weeks. The Legate was not happy with the amount of meat they had salted down for the long sea voyage and he again sent out hunting parties to acquire more. Zahakis took advantage of the opportunity to speak to Acronis about Sigurd and Skylan, proposing that the barbarians be permitted to settle their differences.

Acronis listened with interest as Zahakis described the strange way in which the barbarians conducted their ritual combat.

"You are right, my friend," said Acronis. "One man forced to do nothing except defend himself while the other tries to slaughter him requires extraordinary courage. It does sound entertaining."

"Too bad it's just a ruse young Skylan is using to try to escape," said Zahakis, grinning.

"Do we really appear to be that stupid, Zahakis?" Acronis asked, half in jest and half serious. "Do they honestly think we would give them shields and swords and that we would then be shocked when they left off fighting each other and turned on us?"

"The two men do appear intent on killing each other. We could let them fight when we are in open water, far from land. It would help alleviate the boredom. We'll see how the voyage goes."

"An excellent idea!" said Acronis.

He glanced over to where Skylan sat on the ground, eating fish paste with his fingers and every so often casting a glance in their direction.

"He knows we're talking about him," said Acronis. "So the young man is a chief. I look forward to seeing how he handles himself in a fight."

He added, as an afterthought, "I suppose we must consult Raegar in this? He is our priest, after all, and concerned with our spiritual well-being."

"I already did," said Zahakis. "Raegar is opposed, of course. He says that the ritual contest will only encourage the Vindrasi in their barbaric beliefs. He wants them to turn their thoughts to Aelon."

Acronis sighed. "I don't mind confessing to you, Zahakis, that I find Aelon to be a very tiresome god. He pokes his nose into our affairs, keeps his eye on us at all times, demands that we do this, do that . . ."

"Rather like my wife, sir," said Zahakis.

Skylan was forced to tell Sigurd that there would be no Vutmana, at least not tonight. Sigurd grumbled that Skylan must have said something or done something to spoil their plans. Skylan said Sigurd was an ass and once again the soldiers had to step in to break up the fight.

The next day dawned fine. The wind continued blowing strong and the *Light of the Sea* and the *Venjekar* sailed out into the Sea of Tears. They had now entered waters unknown to the Torgun. Accustomed to sailing within sight of land, navigating by landmarks, the Vindrasi had no idea where they were. They knew by the position of the sun that they were heading south, but that was all.

The concept of sailing at night was unknown to them. Sailing in the dark was dangerous within sight of land. A ship could founder on rocks or run aground. There were no such dangers in the middle of the ocean. The main danger there was in losing their way. Without landmarks, Skylan had no idea where they were.

Raegar had tried to show Skylan how to read a map, to use it to tell where he was and determine where he was going and how to get there. The maps had proven useless to Skylan. Neither he nor any of the other Vindrasi could read or write.

He had come to see how maps could be of value, however. The thought had come to him that once they escaped, he would have to sail the *Venjekar* home through these strange waters. He began to think that the ability to unlock the mystery of these baffling lines and squiggles might be worthwhile.

Zahakis had a map on which he noted the progress of the *Venjekar*. When Skylan expressed an interest in learning about such means of navigation, Zahakis pointed out to Skylan where they were, where they were headed, where they had been. He showed

Skylan his own homeland, tracing the route they had followed with his finger.

"What is the route you took to reach my homeland?" Skylan asked.

Zahakis glanced at Skylan sharply. Skylan kept his gaze fixed on the map, feigning interest, though to him it was nothing but scrawls and pictures.

"We sailed east from Oran and then north."

The wind is blowing us south to Oran, Skylan considered. If we take back our ship, we would not have the wind. We will have to row and our numbers are few. We would have to sail close to land, make landfall every night. The voyage will be a long one, but we could manage.

"Raegar told me that men could find their way across the open sea using some sort of tools that take measurements of the stars or something like that," said Skylan. "I didn't believe him," he added hastily, not wanting Zahakis to think him gullible.

"On the contrary, this time Raegar was telling you the truth," said Zahakis. "I don't understand the workings of such scientific instruments myself. They make little sense to me. The Legate is adept at their use. He takes readings daily and marks down our position on his charts."

Skylan thought this over. He had lots of time to think, sitting at the tiller, and he came to the sobering realization that his world, a world he had once proudly thought he ruled, was not a world at all. It was only a small piece of a much larger world, a measly morsel of bread torn from an enormous loaf.

He listened to Zahakis describe the city of Sinaria, capital of the land of Oran. Zahakis told of its wonders, the vast numbers of people who lived there (more people in one city than in all of Vindraholm). Zahakis told him more about the Legate, a man who was so wealthy he had commissioned the construction of not one, but two triremes. He paid for the men to sail his ships and the soldiers who defended them.

"The Legate was a territorial governor for many years. He and his legion defended the northeastern provinces of Oran from the raids of your people and the ogres and Cyclops. Ostensibly the legion was under the command of the Emperor, but being so far away from the capital, the Legate was forced to take control of the legion himself, and, gradually, the men came to look upon him as their commander.

"This was fine while we were far from Sinaria, but then the Emperor, under the influence of the Priest-General, became nervous that the Legate was gaining too much power. He ordered the Legate to return home, where he could keep an eye on him."

Skylan understood. Horg had feared the Torgun's rising influence, one reason he had sold them out to the ogres. Men were men, it seemed, whether they had swarthy brown skin or fair skin or hairy skin (like the ogres).

As he steered the *Venjekar* through the vast ocean, with only sea below and sky above, Skylan saw his wyrd unwinding before him, running straight and true across the sun-spangled water toward the blue haze of a far horizon. He wanted to sail like this forever, leaving everything behind: guilt, murder, lies, regrets, sorrow.

Sail on with the wind in his face . . . and stinging saltwater in his wounds. His skin, rubbed raw by the manacles, burned from the seawater that splashed up onto the deck.

Skylan winced and grimaced and came back to bitter reality with a thud. He wasn't leaving anything behind. His wyrd bound him to the past, a chain that could never be broken.

All he could do now was to try to set right what had gone so disastrously wrong.

Aylaen watched the sunlight creep through small chinks in the wood planking of the hold, dappling parts of the deck, leaving much of the hold in shadow.

Most of the time, the two women were alone. Zahakis would check on them once a day, always treating them with courtesy and asking if they needed anything. He had given Treia and Aylaen permission to come up on deck to take the air, but only Treia took advantage of the offer. Aylaen didn't like the way the soldiers stared at her.

Sometimes Wulfe came down to visit. The boy was given free run of the ship. He still didn't like Treia, but he was bored and being around her was slightly better than being around the soldiers. Aylaen listened to his stories of being raised by his father, the wolf, and his mother, the daughter of the faery queen, and she marveled that he could come up with such amazing lies. But the boy's visits were an irritant to Treia. She complained to Aylaen and finally Aylaen told Wulfe it would be better if he didn't come.

After that, the two women wrapped themselves in the shadows and hugged the darkness close.

Aylaen watched the sunlight creep across the floor, marking the passing of time. Treia sat curled up in a far corner, her arms around her bent legs, her chin resting on her knees, her gaze fixed and staring.

She had spent the last two days turning the hold and everything in it upside down, searching for the spiritbone of the Dragon Kahg. Treia hoped that if she found the bone, Raegar would no longer be angry with her. She had constantly scolded and nagged Aylaen into helping her.

But the spiritbone, it seemed, was gone for good this time. Treia had finally given up looking. She gave up doing anything except staring into the shadows.

Seeing her sister absorbed in her own misery, Aylaen stealthily removed the knife from her boot.

She had not found the time yet to use it. Treia was always watching her. True, there were the nights when Treia was asleep and Aylaen, who spent most days sleeping, lay awake, tossing and turning. But it seemed to Aylaen that every time she reached for the knife, Treia would moan in her sleep or cry out or shift restlessly. Aylaen, terrified her sister would catch her, would roll over and lay still.

Now she held the knife in her hand, watching a sliver of sunlight play upon the blade. She turned the knife; the light flashed and faded, flashed and faded.

"What do you think you are doing?"

Treia's voice seemed to explode around Aylaen like a lightning strike. Her heart lurched, her hand shook. She dropped the knife and made a reflexive grab for it and sliced open the palm of her hand.

"Look what you made me do!" Aylaen cried accusingly.

Treia snatched the knife away and flung it across the deck. She turned Aylaen's palm to the light to look at the cut.

"This is deep. It will leave a scar," said Treia, her voice trembling. "You are a fool! A stupid little fool!"

She was truly upset. Aylaen regarded her sister in wonder. She had never thought Treia cared much about her.

"Put pressure on it, like this," Treia ordered. "I'll fetch the salve and some bandages."

Aylaen pressed her left hand over the cut. Blood welled up around her fingers. Tears welled up in her eyes. She felt like a fool, sniveling over a cut on her hand when she had been about to drive the knife into her belly.

Treia came hurrying back, stopping to pick up the knife on the way. She cleaned the wound and rubbed in the salve and then bound Aylaen's hand tightly with a strip of linen.

"What were you going to do? Kill yourself?" Treia asked.

"I want to be with Garn," Aylaen said, keeping her head lowered, not looking at her sister.

Treia snorted. "If you believe in such things, Garn has gone to the Hall of Heroes. Do you think he would welcome you there? He would turn his back on you in shame. Torval would pick you up by the scruff of your neck and throw you down to Freilis, who would give you to her daemons for their sport."

"What about the old songs that tell about wives who were so stricken with grief that they threw themselves into the fire of their husband's funeral boats? According to the songs, Torval honored their sacrifice."

"And who wrote such songs?" Treia asked scornfully. "Men wrote them. They would have us think we could not live without them."

"I *can't* live without him," Aylaen said.

"That is because you are weak," said Treia.

"When you thought Raegar was dead, how did you feel?"

"I didn't try to kill myself," said Treia.

She wrapped the bandage so tightly that Aylaen gave a little gasp. "You need to loosen it. I can't feel my fingers."

Treia finished the wrapping and sliced off the end of the cloth with the knife. Blotches of blood began to seep through the bandage. The wound ached and throbbed.

Aylaen sighed. "Garn *would* be ashamed of me, wouldn't he, Treia? He would turn his back on me."

"He would," said Treia.

"Thank you for helping me." Aylaen swallowed, then said, "Will you give me the knife back?"

Treia cast her a suspicious glance.

"I'm not going to kill myself," Aylaen said hurriedly. "To be honest, I don't think I could have gone through with it anyway. But we are the only two women on a ship filled with men and it's a long voyage and we should have some way to defend ourselves. . . ."

Treia silently handed over the knife. Aylaen tucked it into her boot, then, impulsively, she put her arms around her sister and hugged her close.

"I love you, Treia! I'm so glad to know you love me!"

Treia stiffened in Aylaen's grasp. She gave her sister an awkward pat on her shoulder.

"I'll change the bandage and put more salve on the wound to-night. If that man, Zahakis, asks what happened, make up some story. Don't say anything about having a knife."

"I'll tell them I fell down the ladder," said Aylaen. Treia had been so kind, Aylaen wanted to do something to please her. "Would you like to look for the spiritbone again?"

Treia gave a tight and bitter smile. "Useless. A waste of time."

"You think the Dragon Kahg is gone for good?"

"I think the dragon is dead," said Treia.

The *Venjekar* and the *Light of the Sea* had been at sea seven days, making good time, for they did not have to use the rowers. Zahakis told Skylan that in this part of the ocean, the wind blew steadily from the north, driving the ships in a southerly direction. Skylan was starting to think glumly that Zahakis had either forgotten about the ritual combat or he had figured out that it was all a ploy. Sigurd was angry and accused Skylan of being a coward, of trying to weasel out of the contest.

Then one night, trouble broke out on the *Venjekar*. For once, it was not started by the prisoners. The soldiers were playing their usual gambling game with the stones, when one accused the other of cheating. Men took sides. Fists flew. The next day there were split knuckles, swollen lips, and black eyes. Zahakis was livid with fury.

That morning, he scribbled something on a scroll of papyrus, wrapped it in a sack, and weighted it with a rock. Bringing the *Venjekar* within hailing distance of the *Light of the Sea*, Zahakis flung the weighted sack into the air. It landed on the deck of the galley. Acronis's scribe retrieved it and took it to the Legate. An answer came back.

Zahakis told Skylan that if the weather was fine, they would hold the Vutmana tomorrow.

All Skylan could see as far as he looked was the vast emptiness of the ocean. "Are we that close to land?" he asked.

"We are not close to land at all," said Zahakis.

"Then how can we fight the Vutmana?"

"On board this ship."

Skylan didn't know what to say. He had never considered this possibility.

"But . . . we can't fight on board a ship," he said, floundering. "It's not . . . proper. The gods wouldn't like it."

"Then I guess you won't fight at all," said Zahakis, shrugging.

Skylan sat at the tiller. All his careful planning, gone overboard.

"Very well," he said glumly. "We will fight the Vutmana on board the ship."

"You should be honored," Zahakis said, grinning, as though he could see inside Skylan's head, know what he was thinking. "The Legate himself will be coming over to see you fight as well as your kinsman Raegar."

"That whoreson is no kin of mine," Skylan said.

Zahakis chuckled. "I can't say I would claim him either. He's coming on board this afternoon to make preparations for the Vut—whatever you call it."

"Set me free," Skylan said, "and I will welcome him."

Zahakis laughed, but he did not take him up on the offer.

Skylan sighed. So much for his plans. He had assumed that the fight would be held on land. When the war galley made landfall, the Legate sent the rowers and soldiers ashore. They made up hunting parties, hauled water, and did other chores. They lit fires, cooked hot food, made themselves comfortable for the night. Skylan had figured that once he and Sigurd had their weapons, they would first kill Zahakis. The loss of a commander always threw even the best-trained forces into confusion. Skylan would set his fellow warriors free. They would take control of the *Venjekar* and sail away. By the time the Legate had managed to collect two hundred crew members and order them back on board and set them to work, the *Venjekar* would be well on her way home.

That had been the plan. A good plan, Skylan thought as he sadly bid it farewell. He spent the rest of the day thinking and revising.

For his new plan to succeed, Skylan needed the key that unlocked the prisoners' manacles. Zahakis carried the key with him always—wearing it on his thumb like a ring. Skylan pondered long and hard on how he might acquire it. Aylaen and Treia could not be of help, for Zahakis had ordered them to remain in the hold. Skylan and his friends were chained hand and foot. That left Wulfe.

The boy had the run of the ship. The soldiers were starting to like him, had made a sort of pet of him. He would run about the deck on all fours and they would roar with laughter and give him food. They tried to give him coins, but he was terrified of the money, which was made of metal. The soldiers found that even more hilarious.

Wulfe could get close to Zahakis. The boy could move silently and stealthily as a stalking cat. The only problem was the boy's fear of anything made of iron.

That afternoon, when Zahakis went down into the hold to check on the women, Skylan motioned for Wulfe. The boy crouched eagerly beside Skylan.

"Did you talk to your oceanaids today?" Skylan asked.

"Of course," said Wulfe.

"They didn't happen to mention how close we are to land, did they?" Skylan said.

"I can ask. Do you want me to?"

"Sure, go ahead."

Wulfe dashed off and was soon hanging over the rail, yelling at the waves. The soldiers watched him and chuckled. Skylan felt more than a little foolish as he waited to hear what Wulfe and his fae friends had to say.

"Two days," Wulfe announced on his return. "So long as the wind doesn't shift direction. And they don't think it will."

Two days. They could sail to land in two days. Skylan didn't know whether he believed Wulfe or he simply wanted to believe. Either way, he decided, it didn't matter. This was the only opportunity for escape they were likely to have. They would have to take it and trust to the gods.

He told Wulfe what he wanted him to do.

Wulfe shook his head violently and started to make a dash for it.

"Come back here," Skylan said sharply.

Wulfe came back, dragging his feet.

"You want to get away from these soldiers, don't you?" Skylan said softly, keeping an eye out for Zahakis.

Wulfe nodded slowly, still suspicious.

"You want to see Raegar dead, don't you?"

Wulfe nodded again, this time emphatically.

"Then you have to get that key for me," said Skylan. "You're the only one who can do it."

"But it's made of iron. It will burn me," said Wulfe plaintively.

Skylan might not have believed this, but he had seen Wulfe's fingers the one time he'd forced the boy to clean his sword. His fingers looked like Wulfe had put his hand on a red-hot kettle.

Wulfe's brow puckered. "Why do you need this key anyway?"

"Because it unlocks the manacles," said Skylan. "You've seen a key work."

Wulfe shook his head. "The druids never used locks or keys."

After he thought about it, Skylan was not surprised. From what he had seen of their village, the druids had nothing of value to lock up.

Skylan pointed to the leg irons. "See the metal box that looks like a barrel? You put the key in there. The key touches a spring. The spring releases and the manacles pop open. I'll need to keep the key for a long time, so Zahakis can't wonder where it has gone or start looking for it."

Wulfe grinned. "You want me to steal an iron key that I can't touch off the Ugly's thumb so he doesn't notice it's missing."

Skylan gave a frustrated sigh. The boy was right. It seemed impossible.

"Wulfe," he asked abruptly, "can you talk to Aylaen or Treia?"

"I won't talk to Treia. Ever," said Wulfe emphatically.

"Well, then, can you talk to Aylaen? Have you talked to her?"

"Yes," said Wulfe. "I've been telling her stories about my mother and father. They cheer her up. Why?"

Skylan glanced around to make certain no one was near, then he said softly, "I was just wondering if she said anything about finding the spiritbone."

Wulfe gave a nervous start and peered warily at Skylan from beneath shaggy bangs. "It was lost. It fell in the sea."

"I know it fell in the sea," Skylan said impatiently. "But that doesn't mean it's lost. The spiritbone will come back to the person the dragon chooses to keep it safe."

Wulfe stared at him. "It does? It comes to the person the dragon chooses?"

"Yes," said Skylan. "Why? What's the matter?"

"Nothing," Wulfe said. He cast a sidelong glance at the dragon-head prow.

"I'll think about the key," he said, and jumped up and ran off.

Skylan had been going to ask Wulfe to tell Aylaen about the plan, to see if she could help. Now that he thought about it, he was glad he didn't. Aylaen would tell Treia and Treia would be certain to warn Raegar.

Skylan looked up at the carved head of the dragon, asking for a sign, a glimmer of light in the wooden eyes that would fill him with hope. But the dragon's eyes were blank, gave away nothing.

He saw Wulfe leaning over the rail, waving his hand to the waves and talking again with the sea spray.

"He won't touch iron because it burns him. He believes his grandmother is the Queen of the Faeries, and he talks with spirits who live in the ocean."

Skylan sighed and muttered, "But he's all I've got."

Wulfe sat cross-legged on the deck, watching Zahakis. Wulfe had seen the key before, but he hadn't known what it was or what it did. He had just thought it a piece of ugly jewelry. Wulfe considered various ways of acquiring it. There were magical spells he could cast on the man that would cause Zahakis to drop the key. Wulfe could make the man's hand wither so that the key would slide off. He could cause the key to go red-hot and burn him and he would have to take it off.

But that wouldn't work, Wulfe realized, because then the key would be so hot Skylan couldn't touch it.

The true drawback to all these ideas was that they smacked of magic. Owl Mother had warned Wulfe that if he used his magic, he should disguise it as a natural phenomenon. Otherwise he would be putting himself in danger.

Remembering the moment he summoned the seagulls and how Raegar had struck him across the face and knocked him unconscious, he really, really wanted to see Raegar dead. Wulfe knew he had to give the problem of stealing the key his full attention.

———

Raegar came aboard late in the afternoon. Skylan had wondered if he was going to swim, but the war galley hoisted out a plank meant for boarding enemy ships, and when the *Venjekar* sailed near, they lowered the plank onto the deck. The sea was calm. Raegar crossed without incident and was greeted formally by Zahakis and loudly and obscenely by the Torgun. Raegar made a point of asking about Treia and Aylaen and was assured they were well. He said he needed to speak to them and he went down into the hold.

Skylan had not seen Aylaen all the time they had been at sea. Treia came up sometimes for air, but Aylaen remained below. Skylan knew she was grieving for Garn. He, too, was still grieving the loss of his friend, and he wished he could comfort her and find comfort in talking about their friend. It seemed to Skylan that he and Aylaen were the only two who mourned Garn's loss. Bjorn and Erdmun had both been Garn's friends. They were sorry he was dead, but his passing had not left an empty feeling in their chests as it did for Skylan. Sometimes it seemed as painful to Skylan as if he had been pierced by a spear.

More painful, he reflected, for a wound will heal and be forgotten, but the pain of loss and the anguish of knowing that Garn's death was my fault will be with me for the rest of my life.

Then Wulfe came sidling up to him and Skylan had to quit thinking about the dead and turn his thoughts to the living.

"Don't go to sleep tonight," Wulfe said softly.

And before Skylan could ask Wulfe what he was going to do, the boy ran off.

Zahakis sometimes steered the ship himself at night to allow Skylan to rest. Zahakis would chain Skylan to the bulkhead near his fellow Torgun, who greeted him with sullen looks or paid no attention to him at all.

That night, as Skylan lay down beside Sigurd, he whispered, "Stay awake. Tell the others."

Sigurd's dark eyes flashed. He nodded and, rolling over, whispered to Bjorn, "Stay awake. Pass the word."

Night fell as the god, Skoval, took over rulership of the world.

The full moon rose. The tops of the waves were gilded with molten silver. Raegar emerged from the hold. His face was dark. He was upset about something.

Two soldiers were on duty guarding the prisoners. Another was at the tiller and the others were playing the usual game of stone-guessing. Zahakis stood near the rail in the stern, gazing out at the moonlit ripples. Wulfe was nowhere in sight.

Raegar joined Zahakis at the rail.

"I still do not approve of this fight," Raegar announced.

"I am sorry you feel this way," said Zahakis in a tone that meant exactly the opposite. "Did you inform the Legate?"

"I did," said Raegar, frowning. "He knows that these two brutes are fighting for the favor of their heathen god. Indulging them in this barbaric ritual only encourages them to believe in gods who are dead."

"I take it the Legate was still not impressed with your argument," Zahakis said.

"He was not," said Raegar angrily. "Acronis said the soldiers were bored and that this would provide some amusement and break up the routine. I have spoken to the Bone Priestesses, however," he added stiffly. "Neither of them will take part."

"As I understand it, the priestess is important to the spectacle. Perhaps they will attend if I ask them nicely," said Zahakis with a half smile.

Raegar sucked in an irate breath, but Zahakis walked off, not waiting to hear what the priest had to say. Raegar muttered something, then stalked over to where the soldiers, who had been listening to this exchange with interest, hurriedly returned to their game.

"Gambling is illegal!" Raegar said. "Go to your beds."

The soldiers glanced at Zahakis, who gave a slight nod, and the men, grumbling, did as they were ordered.

The *Venjekar* glided over the silver waves.

Skylan was sleepy and he wished irritably that whatever Wulfe was going to do, he'd go ahead and do it. He was just thinking this and wondering what Wulfe had in mind, when Zahakis gave a yell and sprang back from the rail, shaking his left hand frantically.

His startled cry woke everyone. Soldiers fumbled for weapons. The Torgun sat up, staring at Zahakis, who appeared to be wrestling with something that glimmered white in the moonlight.

Bjorn suddenly began to laugh. "It's a jellyfish!"

The sea creature's poisonous tentacles wound tightly around the commander's hand. The soldiers hastened to his aid, though when they reached him, none of them had any idea what to do. No one wanted to grab the thing. Swearing and yelling in pain, Zahakis at last managed to shake the jellyfish loose. It landed on the deck with a soggy plop.

Zahakis wrung his hand and continued to swear. Skylan had been stung by jellyfish before, like hot needles being jabbed into the skin.

Zahakis's hand was starting to swell from the poison. He grabbed hold of the key ring and yanked it off and flung it to the deck. Then he doubled over, cradling his hand and groaning.

His soldiers gathered around him, all of them offering advice on what to do. One of the men kicked at something at his feet and Skylan saw Wulfe, crawling about on the deck. The soldiers swore at him and told him to get out of the way. Wulfe scuttled off, carrying something wrapped in a bit of cloth, which he dropped in Skylan's lap.

Skylan rolled over to hide his movements and unwrapped the cloth to find the key ring inside. He was about to slide the key stealthily to Sigurd with orders to unlock his leg irons, when a shadow blotted out the moonlight. Skylan glanced up to find Raegar looming over him. Skylan hurriedly slid the key onto his thumb and closed his fist over it.

But Raegar was not interested in Skylan. He was after other prey. Reaching down, Raegar seized Wulfe by the hair and yanked him to his feet.

"Here is the culprit!" Raegar cried. "He did this to you, Tribune!"

"Did what?" Zahakis asked irritably.

"He sent the jellyfish to attack you," Raegar said balefully.

The soldiers began to roar with laughter. Zahakis's mouth twitched.

"Let the kid go, Raegar—"

"Since when have you seen jellyfish fly?" Raegar demanded angrily. "The boy is evil, I tell you. He must die! Aelon commands it!"

Lifting Wulfe off his feet, Raegar flung him headlong into the sea.

The boy landed with a splash and a shriek and immediately sank. For a moment everyone stood staring stupidly at the waves, unable to believe what they'd seen. Then suddenly everyone was shouting and moving at once.

Skylan jumped to his feet, forgetting in his fear for Wulfe that his legs were chained. He tripped and crashed headlong to the deck. Several soldiers ran to the side, searching for the boy. Wulfe came bobbing back to the surface, his arms flailing. The soldiers yelled and pointed.

Wulfe sank again. Zahakis shouted for one of the men to dive in after the boy when, without warning, an immense wave reared up from a calm sea. The wave rose higher and higher, until it hung poised over the *Venjekar* like a hand ready to smack a fly, then crashed over the bow.

The *Venjekar* heeled. Men grabbed anything they could find to keep from being washed overboard. The deck canted. Skylan clung desperately to his chains and stared in astonishment to see Wulfe rush past him in a great gush of seawater. The boy fetched up against a sea chest and lay on the deck, coughing and spitting up water.

The sea calmed instantly, but it was a sullen calm that sent waves slapping against the sides of the hull. Zahakis knelt beside Wulfe, pounding him on the back and asking him if he was all right.

Skylan had thought he'd seen faces in the wave, faces of beautiful women, beautiful *enraged* women with sea-foam hair. He didn't have time to think whether he believed what he'd seen or not. The angry soldiers crowded around Zahakis, urging him to let them toss Raegar overboard. Skylan crawled over to Sigurd and handed him the key.

"Tell the others to unlock the manacles and then pretend they're still locked. Not you," he added, reaching down his hand to prevent Sigurd from unlocking his own manacles.

Sigurd looked at him, frowning.

"We're going to fight tomorrow," said Skylan. "How will it look if Zahakis comes to unlock our manacles and finds them already unlocked?"

Sigurd took a moment to think this over, then gave a nod and handed the key to Bjorn, whispering instructions. Bjorn swiftly unlocked his manacles and passed the key to Erdmun. The key traveled down the row of warriors. A few fumbled with it, trying to find the keyhole. The sound of the key scratching against the metal seemed loud enough to be heard back in Vindraholm, and Skylan winced, certain that the soldiers must hear it, too.

None of them were paying any attention, however. Zahakis had quieted their fury, and ordered them to wring out their clothes and spread their bedding to dry and assemble their gear, which was strewn all over the deck.

Zahakis, his face grim, walked over to confront Raegar. "You are lucky I don't do what the men want and throw you overboard."

Raegar began to sputter. "First the jellyfish, then the wave. This was all the boy's doing."

Zahakis walked off.

"Let him live and you will be sorry!" Raegar called after him.

Zahakis said something Skylan couldn't hear. Another wave slapped the ship. Raegar went to the hold, lifted the hatch, and stomped down the stairs. Zahakis came over to stand in front of Skylan, who tensed, acutely aware of the key making its way down the line. He saw, out of the corner of his eye, Grimuir palm the key and keep still.

Skylan grinned up at him.

"I've heard that urine causes the pain of the jellyfish sting to ease. I would be glad to piss on you, Tribune."

Zahakis shook his head and muttered something and continued on his way.

He has forgotten the key, but he will recall it soon enough, Skylan thought, and he looked down the line.

Grimuir was busily unlocking his fetters. He handed the key to the warrior next to him. Wulfe was waiting next to Aki, the last man in the line. When Aki had freed himself, he gave the key to Wulfe.

The boy jumped to his feet and ran off, dropping the key quietly on the deck, not far from where Zahakis had been standing when he flung it off. Sometime later, one of the soldiers stepped on it and took it back to Zahakis. Skylan breathed a sigh in relief. So far, so good.

The soldiers were wiping the saltwater off their swords and polishing their armor to make certain they didn't rust. Zahakis filled a helm with seawater and was soaking his hand. The Torgun pretended to sleep.

Wulfe lay down beside Skylan. "My blanket's wet," he grumbled.

"Stop complaining. You're lucky you're alive," said Skylan.

"Not lucky," said Wulfe. "The oceanaids saved me."

Skylan remembered the faces in the wave. He eyed Wulfe. "How did that jellyfish get on board?"

"It was funny, wasn't it?" Wulfe said. "Watching Zahakis jump up and down and shake his hand, trying to get it to let go."

"Wulfe—"

"I'm sleepy," he said, and he curled up in a ball and pressed his back to Skylan for warmth.

Sigurd dug his elbow into Skylan's ribs.

"Whoever draws first blood is chief. You agreed to that. You swore by Torval."

Skylan didn't answer.

10

The day of the Vutmana dawned bright and clear, cool and cloudless. Skylan took the sunshine for a good omen; Aylis was smiling on them. The sea was flat, no wind at all. The ships would have had to use rowers, but the Legate had declared today a holiday. The *Light of the Sea* and the *Venjekar* bobbed gently up and down on the smooth water. The sailors lowered the gangplank, and Acronis, accompanied by his bodyguards and a servant carrying a collapsible stool, crossed from the galley to the *Venjekar*. The crew of the *Light of the Sea,* including the rowers, gathered on the deck to watch the spectacle of the barbarians fighting each other.

"What happened to your hand?" asked Acronis, noting the red weals on the Tribune's fingers, palm, and wrist.

Zahakis described the night's events.

"How very odd," said Acronis. "Raegar flings the boy into the sea and the sea flings the boy back."

"So it would seem, my lord," said Zahakis.

Acronis glanced at the soldiers. "How did the men react?"

"Raegar tried to drown the boy, sir. The troops didn't like it."

"The same soldiers who would think nothing of butchering this boy if they came across him while sacking his city are upset when a priest tries to drown him," said Acronis. He shook his head.

"It is one thing to kill in the heat of battle, my lord, and another to watch a man throw a helpless child into the sea," said Zahakis, mildly reproving.

Acronis frowned. "Yes, well, I can't say I blame them." He drew in a deep breath of the sea air, glad to change the subject. "Are the barbarians prepared for the fight? Raegar does not approve of this, you know."

"Raegar's not having a good voyage, my lord," said Zahakis with a smile. "All is in readiness. The men have their orders."

"Very well," said Acronis. "Let whatever this is called begin."

Down in the hold, Raegar paced the small area, a difficult feat for a man of his height. He had to keep his head bowed and shoulders hunched. Aylaen would have ignored him, as usual, but she was curious to know what had happened last night. All the women knew was that there had been yelling and shouting and the ship had heeled violently, sending them both careening across the deck of the hold. Then the ship had righted itself and all had been quiet and the women had no idea what had happened.

Aylaen was angry at herself for being curious, for wanting to know what had happened. Garn was dead. She shouldn't be taking an interest in life. Yet she had to hide a smile when she heard Raegar claim that Wulfe had caused a jellyfish to leap on board the ship and attack Zahakis. Apparently she didn't hide it well, because Treia cast her a rebuking glance.

"The boy is a danger," Raegar continued. "I have tried to warn these fools, but they won't listen. Aelon commanded that I take action. I threw the boy in the sea—"

"You did what?" Aylaen cried in shock.

"Quite right," said Treia severely.

"Sister, how can you say that? Wulfe was just a boy and this man murdered him!"

"He is not dead," Raegar said. "His daemon friends saved him. A wave threw him back on board."

Aylaen opened her mouth to point out that this was ridiculous. Treia frowned at her, and Aylaen kept silent. Her sister was happy again. Raegar had forgiven Treia for the failure with the dragon and had once more deigned to honor her with his attentions. Aylaen might have been pleased about this for Treia's sake, but she had noticed that Raegar was starting to favor her with his attentions, as well. He had said nothing, but she didn't like the way he kept looking at her.

"So are Sigurd and Skylan going to go ahead with this supposed Vutmana?" Treia was asking. "Why would the Legate permit it?"

"The soldiers want amusement," Raegar stated sourly. "They need a Bone Priestess, however. I told the Legate that neither of you will have anything to do with it."

"I might," said Aylaen, just to be contrary and annoy Raegar.

Treia cast her a shocked glance. "You will do no such thing. I forbid it."

"You might get hurt," said Raegar in solicitous tones that made Aylaen's skin crawl.

"How could I possibly get hurt?" she asked tartly.

Treia and Raegar exchanged glances.

"It is all a plot by Skylan to escape."

"It is?" Aylaen stared at him.

"Of course!" said Raegar dismissively.

"But why would the Legate let them fight, then?"

"Acronis is not stupid. He has taken precautions."

"But don't you *want* to escape?" Aylaen asked Treia. "Don't you want to go back home?"

She saw Treia gazing up at Raegar with adoration and knew the answer.

A wave of homesickness swept over Aylaen. She longed for her mother, who had not wanted her to go on this voyage, who had wept and pleaded with her to remain. She longed to be back in the fields where she and Garn had worked, to sit in the grove where they made love in the afternoon. She dreaded the thought of being a slave, dreaded what horrors the future might hold. Her heart leaped at the idea that they might have a chance for freedom. She hated Skylan, but she never doubted his courage and resolve. She wondered suddenly if the strange events of last night were a part of Skylan's plan.

Aylaen glanced sidelong at Raegar, who was sitting beside Treia, airing his grievances to an appreciative audience. Seeing that he was, for the moment, not paying any attention to her, Aylaen slid the small knife out of her boot and swiftly thrust it into the leather belt she wore and arranged the folds.of the tunic she wore over it, making certain that it was well concealed.

"You have not found the spiritbone?" Raegar was asking her sister.

"No," said Treia, and she shrugged. "I doubt if we will ever find it. The Dragon Kahg has abandoned us."

Raegar nodded in satisfaction. "That means your gods have given up."

A soldier shouted down into the hold. "Warrior-Priest Raegar, you and the women are wanted on deck."

Raegar assisted Treia to climb the ladder. He turned to assist Aylaen, but she drew back from his touch. He gave her a smile and shrugged and followed Treia. Aylaen came last, feeling the cold steel of the knife in her belt.

Our gods won't give up, she thought. And neither will we.

Raegar stepped onto the deck. The Legate and Tribune Zahakis stood together in conversation in the place of honor near the dragonhead prow, watching while the soldiers erected an awning made of canvas on the deck, which would shade the Legate from the sun so that he could better enjoy the spectacle.

Acronis should have invited Raegar to join them. He was, after all, the Warrior-Priest assigned by the Priest-General to serve on the *Light of the Sea*. Acronis saw Raegar and he said something to Zahakis, who grinned. Raegar guessed that they were discussing him. He gave a bow. Acronis inclined his head and turned away.

Raegar was angered. As the representative of Aelon, Raegar was responsible for the souls of all those on board and that included the Legate and the Tribune. Raegar did his duty, preaching to the men about Aelon and how the God of Light cared for them and wanted them to live good and productive lives.

Raegar was sincere in his belief in his god. He was sincere in his belief that all men must be brought to Aelon for the salvation of their souls. Raegar truly believed he had the good of the Legate and the crew and even the good of his Vindrasi kinsmen at heart. True, he had betrayed his kin into slavery. But as the Priest-General often said, if Aelon sometimes casts a dark shadow, it is only because the light behind him shines so bright.

Life in Sinaria was not easy for a freed slave. Raegar had turned to Aelon out of desperation and Aelon had picked him up out of the dust and rewarded his hard work and dedication. Raegar strove to open the eyes of these people. What he did, he did for them. Yet, because he had blond hair and blue eyes, the brown-eyed, brownskinned Southlanders saw only a barbarian, a man who had once been a slave.

"What is the matter, my love?" Treia asked, seeing his face darken.

The soldiers were having some difficulty with the awning, giving them time to talk.

"Look at those two," Raegar said. "They should have listened to me. They will be sorry. I warned the Legate about my cousin.

"Aelon warned me that Skylan and the others were a danger to the faith," continued Raegar in a low voice.

"Aelon speaks to you?" Treia asked.

"Not in words," Raegar said, "but in feelings. When Skylan Ivorson first told me he was Chief of Chiefs of the Vindrasi, I felt in my heart and my soul that he had to die."

Treia raised her eyebrows. Her eyes widened.

"I have experienced such strong feelings before and the Priest-General says they come from Aelon and that I should act on them. I told the Legate he should kill Skylan and the others. Not Aylaen," Raegar added hurriedly, glancing around for her. She had gone off by herself, was standing at the rail, gazing out to sea. His voice softened. "I have hope your sister will become a convert to Aelon as you have."

Raegar had strong feelings for Aylaen, though these feelings did not come from Aelon. He had always thought her beautiful and desirable, but he knew she was in love with Garn and he could never hope to win her away. Garn was dead now and Raegar thought he might have a chance with her. He was careful not to mention his hopes and his plans. Not yet. Treia was jealous of him. He would have to ease her into his way of thinking.

"If Aelon is so powerful," Treia said, "why is he afraid of Skylan?"

He gave her a frowning glance and asked sternly, "Do you mock the god?"

"Of course not," said Treia hurriedly. She closed her hand over Raegar's in apology. "I meant only that Skylan is a mortal. He is your slave. Aelon is a god and all powerful. . . ."

"I do not question," said Raegar. "I only know what I felt. If you think I am wrong—" He started to pull his hand away.

"No, no!" Treia clutched him. She looked at her stepfather and the other men, chained hand and foot, and her lips tightened. She said abruptly, "I think you are right."

"I warned the Tribune about these men. He laughed at me. He

walks in darkness, Treia," Raegar said earnestly. "I seek only to try to bring him into Aelon's light. Yet he has no respect for me. Why is that?"

"You are an outsider. No matter that you have lived among these people for years, you are not one of them and you never will be. I know," Treia said bitterly. "They treat me the same way. Forget about trying to help them and concentrate on helping yourself."

Raegar thought about the insults, some veiled and others not. He thought about the fact that he—a high-ranking priest—was never invited to the homes of the nobles. When Raegar had wanted to marry again, he'd sought the hand of a well-born woman. She had laughed in his face.

Raegar brought Treia's hand to his lips. "You are a wise woman, my love."

Treia flushed in pleasure.

The soldiers finally completed the task of raising the awning. The Legate's servant had brought the collapsible stool and placed it in the shade. The Legate sat down; Zahakis took his place next to him.

The soldiers unlocked Skylan's leg irons and freed Sigurd from his leg irons and manacles. Accustomed to walking with the heavy weight on his ankles, Skylan took a step and almost fell over. Sigurd stood chafing his bruised wrists. Skylan searched the deck for Wulfe and was worried, at first, that he couldn't find him. Then he realized that he was probably hiding in the hold, away from the swords and the fighting.

Acronis indicated he was ready to begin. "I understand that the Bone Priestess will be the judge of this contest." He looked at Treia.

Raegar spoke up. "Bone Priestess Treia will have nothing to do with this heathen bloodletting."

Sigurd and Skylan exchanged grim glances.

"I'll kill that whoreson," said Skylan.

"Not if I get to him first," said Sigurd.

"Winner of the Vutmana gets to gut Raegar."

"Agreed," said Sigurd, and then he added gloomily, "If there *is* a Vutmana. What if Acronis won't allow it now?"

Aylaen turned from the rail. Her green eyes fixed on Skylan. "I will judge the Vutmana," she said. "This man does not deserve to be Chief of Chiefs."

Zahakis sent his soldiers down into the hold where they had stored the Vindrasi weapons with orders to bring two swords and six shields, three for each man.

The Torgun watched in a tense and brooding silence, broken only by Erdmun, who was nervously fiddling with the lock on his leg irons.

His brother, Bjorn, jabbed him in the ribs and whispered, "Stop that! You'll attract attention."

Erdmun whispered back fretfully, "I don't know what we're supposed to do!"

"Wait," said Bjorn. "You'll find out soon enough."

"All that means is that you don't know what we're supposed to do either," Erdmun grumbled.

His brother ignored him.

Skylan burned with impatience. Sigurd stood scratching his jaw. A soldier led Aylaen to the crude circle that had been painted on the deck. Raegar had flushed in anger when she had come forward and had started to try to stop her. Treia had said something to him and he had kept silent. Aylaen paid no attention. The expression on her face was grave and solemn.

"Do you think she knows? Guesses?" Sigurd muttered.

Skylan shook his head. He had no idea.

Aylaen's gaze went from one of the men to the other. "Do both of you agree to abide by the judgment of Torval?"

"I trust to Torval's judgment," said Sigurd.

"Do you, Skylan Ivorson?" Aylaen asked, and then added with a tremor in her voice, "You are the one who lied and cheated and committed murder. Do you trust to Torval to judge you?"

Skylan was startled by her brutal words. He opened his mouth to say that he did trust in Torval, but the words suddenly stuck in his throat. Torval had punished Skylan for his crimes, for what could be worse than being a slave? Still, Torval was known to be a vengeful god with a memory as long as time. Perhaps he had not yet finished with Skylan.

"I trust in Torval," Skylan said at last and he knew, in his heart, that he meant it. Whatever happened, he had faith in his god.

Aylaen's green eyes turned gray as the sea. "I pray that Torval will judge you as you deserve."

"If he does, I'll be chief," said Sigurd. "First blood, remember?"

Aylaen directed the two combatants to their places, facing each other on opposite sides of the circle.

Acronis explained the rules to his men, relating how each of the barbarians would be given a chance to strike his opponent, who was permitted only to deflect the blow with shield or weapon. He could not defend himself or fight back. Either man who was forced out of the circle was disgraced, dishonored.

Last-minute bets were exchanged. Current money was on Sigurd. Everyone except Raegar and Treia settled themselves to watch. The disapproving priest and priestess showed their disdain by walking off to stand at the stern, as far from the fight as they could get, and feigned disinterest by looking out at the water.

Skylan saw without seeming to see Bjorn and Grimuir and the others start surreptitiously to quietly free themselves from the manacles which they had unlocked the night before.

Skylan, as the one challenged, had the right to strike the first blow. He hefted one of the shields and grasped his weapon. The soldier had chosen weapons at random. Skylan had no idea what had happened to his sword, Blood Dancer, but had been hoping Torval would drop it into the soldier's hand. Either Torval didn't want Skylan to have his sword or the sword wasn't even there. He recognized the blade the soldier had chosen for him. Skylan had given the sword to Bjorn as a gift before they had sailed. He looked at Bjorn and raised the sword in salute. His friend gave him a half smile and a nod.

Sigurd planted his feet on the deck and lifted the shield, bracing himself for the blow. He and Skylan had agreed that they would fight a few rounds, wait until the soldiers were concentrating on the battle, and then attack their foes.

Skylan stood poised for his charge at Sigurd when he was halted by a gasp and a cry. He turned to see a soldier holding Aylaen, a long-bladed knife to her throat.

"She will not be harmed," Acronis called from where he sat at his ease on the stool beneath the canopy, "so long as you use those swords on each other and not turn them on me."

Sick with defeat, Skylan struck Sigurd's shield with a strength born of rage and frustration. Sigurd staggered beneath the blow and almost fell. His shield split in two. His arm tingled from wrist to elbow. He flung down the pieces of his shield. Skylan walked back to his place in the circle, as the rules required, waiting for his opponent to recover.

As he did so, he glanced at Bjorn, who scratched his beard and gave a jerk of his head. That was the signal; the men were all free of their shackles and ready to fight. For all the good that would do them now.

Sigurd picked up another shield. His expression was grim and dark. His fingers hovered near the hilt of his sword and suddenly he grinned—the wide, crazed grin that he wore when he was standing in the shield wall covered in his enemy's blood. Sigurd wasn't supposed to draw his weapon. By the rules of the Vutmana, he had to stand there and take the hit. Skylan knew the moment he saw Sigurd's mouth split in that rictus grin that Sigurd didn't give a damn about freeing himself or the others. He was out for Skylan's blood.

Skylan dropped his shield and advanced, sword in both hands. He struck Sigurd's shield and, watching his enemy's feet, saw Sigurd shift to bring up his sword. Skylan was hampered in his attack by the fact that he needed Sigurd alive. Skylan twisted, kicked, and, dropping to the deck on his hip, slid feetfirst into Sigurd, taking him out at the knees.

The astonished Sigurd pitched over Skylan's head and landed on top of Skylan. He lay there a moment, gasping. Skylan throttled him; he had to half choke him to get the blood-crazed man to listen and then he had to repeat his words twice.

"Our warriors are free! You stupid bastard, our warriors can fight!"

Sigurd grunted, then he clouted Skylan in the mouth, splitting open his lip.

"What about Aylaen?" Sigurd asked.

"I'll take care of her," said Skylan, and he flung Sigurd off and scrambled out from under him.

"This is against the rules," called Acronis, and he sent Zahakis to break up the fight and send each warrior back to his own side.

As Sigurd walked past Skylan, he grinned and pointed and said, "First blood."

Skylan could taste the blood from his cut lip in his mouth. Sigurd picked up his shield, and Skylan walked slowly back to his place.

Ordinarily the Torgun would have been yelling and cheering, but they were too tense, waiting for the order to attack. That was all wrong, and Skylan was surprised Zahakis didn't notice. The soldiers of Oran were making noise enough, each shouting for his man. Money switched hands. Acronis watched with interest. Pointing at Skylan, the Legate said something to his scribe.

Skylan, feigning a limp, took his time retrieving his sword. He looked about, taking note of everything and everyone and, as sometimes happens on a winter's day, when the sun makes the snow sparkle and the air is breathless and nothing moves and there is no sound, he saw everything in stark, clear detail.

Acronis, seated beneath the dragonhead prow, was wearing loose-fitting robes, comfortable in the heat. He was not armed. His body-guards, standing one on either side, wore armor and each carried sword and shield. The other soldiers were scattered about the ship, either leaning on the rail or squatting on the deck. Some wore armor, some did not. All wore their short-bladed swords.

Aylaen and her guard stood close to the circle marked off for the fight. Zahakis, in full armor and wearing his sword, was about two strides away from Aylaen. The Torgun were chained to the bulk-heads, near the stern.

A desperate plan formed in Skylan's mind. His only concern was how he was going to rescue Aylaen. He looked at her. Their eyes met. He knew that outthrust jaw, the quivering lips, the green fire in her eyes. Aylaen wasn't afraid. She was angry. She dropped her gaze.

Her hand stole to her belt. She made the motion of fingers closing over a hilt.

She was telling him she had a weapon. She could take care of herself.

Skylan picked up his sword. Sigurd held his shield, yelling and jeering at Skylan, urging him on. As Skylan took a step, he saw Aylaen's hand dart to her belt. A flash of metal, and the soldier holding Aylaen gave a horrible cry and dropped his knife to grab hold of himself. Blood poured from a wound in his groin. Moaning, he fell to the deck and lay rolling about in agony. Aylaen dragged the man's sword from its sheath.

Skylan ran for Zahakis and barreled headlong into the man, taking him down onto the deck before he could draw his sword. He could hear behind him the battle howls of the Torgun warriors as they threw off their chains and came thundering across the deck.

Skylan slugged Zahakis across the jaw twice, saw him go limp, and was on his feet, running toward Acronis with Sigurd on one side and Aylaen on the other.

"Capture the Legate!" Skylan yelled at Aylaen. "Take him alive! Don't kill him!"

Aylaen looked astonished, but she gave a brief nod. The Legate's bodyguards had their swords drawn and were standing in front of him. Skylan took one guard and Sigurd took the other. Sigurd was used to fighting with spears and axes. He was clumsy with a sword, and ended up using it like a battle-axe, chopping and bashing at his opponent's head and shoulders. The guard sliced open Sigurd's chest, but Sigurd never seemed to notice. His blood was up, the madness of Torval had seized him, and his foe withered under Sigurd's brutal assault.

The madness of Torval seemed to have claimed all the Torgun. Either that or the madness of freedom. Using the manacles and chains that had bound them as weapons, the Torgun knocked swords out of hands, struck men across the face, tangled their legs. When a soldier fell, one of the Torgun was on him, seizing his sword and turning to fight the next.

Skylan, trying to watch his foe and keep an eye on Aylaen, who was circling around Acronis from behind, made a mistake that was nearly his last. Thinking to end the fight quickly, he feinted and then drove home his blade, only to realize at the last moment that the soldier was waiting for him. A frantic sideways leap saved Skylan, but just barely. The blade scraped along his ribs.

Skylan drove his sword into the soldier's hairy armpit, left unprotected by the segmented armor, severing tendons and breaking bones. Skylan yanked his sword free and jumped over the soldier as he was falling.

"I have him!" Aylaen cried.

She stood behind Acronis, smiling in triumph, her sword at his throat.

Acronis did not appear unduly alarmed. He seemed detached, as though all of this was happening to someone else. His scribe was on his knees on the blood-covered deck, his hands in the air, shaking and pleading for his life.

Skylan looked around the ship and found, to his amazement, that they had won. Some of the soldiers had jumped overboard. Others were being tossed over the rail by the Torgun who first stripped them of their armor and weapons. Only one person was missing.

"Where's that bastard, Raegar?" Sigurd shouted.

The last Skylan had seen Raegar, he was standing by the stern. Skylan whipped around, but they were too late. Both men turned in time to see Raegar leap into the water. Treia was screaming. He was calling to her. Treia hesitated a moment, then climbed over the rail and dropped into the sea.

Aylaen cried out and dropped her sword to run to the rail. Leaning over, she called to her sister. Raegar had hold of Treia and was half swimming, half dragging her through the water. Treia couldn't swim and she was gulping and choking and clinging to him with a deathlike grip. She stared at Aylaen and then looked away. Aylaen fell silent and stood watching, stricken.

Sigurd now had hold of Acronis. Erdmun was binding the man's hands behind his back.

"What do we do with our friend the Tribune?" Bjorn asked grimly.

Zahakis had recovered consciousness and was on his feet. Bjorn and Grimuir had bound his arms behind him with rope.

"I say we slit his throat!" Aki said, and the other Torgun shouted in agreement.

Zahakis faced Skylan and smiled as best he could with a broken nose and a split lip and one side of his face bruised and bloodied.

"He lives," Skylan said shortly, raising his voice so that it could be heard throughout the *Venjekar* and across the water to the *Light of the Sea*. "He lives so that he may tell the world that the Torgun are valiant warriors who will never be slaves to any man!"

Sigurd didn't like it, but the other Torgun were pleased. The Vindrasi often set free foes who had survived a battle, knowing that their tales of the Vindrasi's ferocity and courage would spread fear throughout a region.

Skylan took charge of Zahakis. Placing his sword in the man's back, he gave him a shove toward the ship's rail. Once there, he cut the man's bindings.

"I owe you for saving the boy," Skylan said quietly.

Zahakis gave a rueful smile. "I underestimated you barbarians. What will you do with the Legate?"

"Use him as a hostage."

Zahakis nodded. "I will come after you, you know."

"I know," said Skylan. "And we will be ready."

He yelled for Bjorn to help him. The two picked up Zahakis and heaved him over the rail. He landed with a splash, floundered a bit as a wave swamped him, then began swimming with swift, strong strokes for the ship.

Aylaen gazed sadly across the water to where men were dragging Treia onto the trireme. The rest of the Torgun raised a cheer. They were free and they were on their way home.

The sail hung limp. The sun-baked air was breathless. The seas flat. Unless the dragon returned, the Torgun would have to man the oars, and there were only seven of them. If the dragon had been with them, Kahg could have sailed them to the World Tree and back. Skylan cast a pleading look at the carved head on the prow.

The wooden eyes stared impassively at nothing.

Skylan sighed and shook his head and took grim stock of their situation. Most of his men had suffered some sort of injury in the battle, though none severe. They had taken the Southlanders completely by surprise. Few of the soldiers had been able to draw their swords before the Torgun were on them. Fighting had been hand-to-hand, resulting in split lips and swelling eyes, bruised cheeks and bloody knuckles. He had a wound in his side, but it wasn't severe. Grimuir had a knife slash across his shoulder that would leave a fine scar to attract the women, so he said with a grin.

The Torgun were excited now. Their freedom had gone to their heads like strong wine. They were disappointed that the gods were not helping, but they did not fault them or complain. The gods of the Vindrasi were stern parents who went their own way, lived their own lives, and expected their mortals to do the same. If life knocked you down, you got back up, wiped off the blood, and charged back into the fray; you didn't run home sniveling.

The Torgun shoved the sea chests into place and began hauling out the oars. Sigurd roamed the deck, issuing orders, urging the men on. The Torgun knew what they were about, however, and no one needed Sigurd to tell them how to thrust the oars into the oar-locks or ready themselves for rowing.

When they were settled and the oars bit into the water and the ship lurched forward at a dismal crawl, they raised their voices in an ancient sea chant. Skylan couldn't bear the pain. He went down into the hold, muttering something about going to fetch their weapons.

The chest where their swords and battle-axes were stowed was open. He could see tiny slivers of sunlight shining on the blade of his sword, Blood Dancer. He did not pick it up. He stood in the darkness of the hold and he leaned his head against one of the beams and he closed his eyes in despair.

Was he the only one who understood that their predicament was hopeless? They had no dragon to lend his spirit to the ship, carry it over the sea. They were a long way from land with only a vague notion of their location in this vast ocean. Their numbers were far fewer than they needed to row the ship. They were weak from being chained to the deck for days and eating nothing but fish paste. And, not far off, Zahakis walked the deck of the war galley, with two hundred rowers, rested and well-fed.

Skylan sighed deeply. No good would come of cursing the darkness. He buckled on the sheepskin sheath that he'd had specially made for his sword, sheathed the fine weapon, and felt better. He went back up on deck to seek out Aylaen, who was standing at the rail, staring across the water at her sister. Skylan motioned her to walk with him, away from the others, over to the ship's prow. She went, but she made it clear by her stiff back and rigid posture that he was to keep his distance.

Skylan spoke in a low voice, so that the men did not over-hear. "Aylaen, does Treia have the spiritbone? Did she take it with her?"

"No, of course not!" said Aylaen, rounding on him angrily. "If she did, don't you think she would have asked the dragon to help us?"

Skylan looked across the sea at the war galley. He could see Raegar on deck, Treia standing beside him. Aylaen saw his gaze go to her sister on the enemy ship, and Aylaen's eyes flared.

"You think *she's* a traitor, too!"

"Aylaen . . ." Skylan began in mollifying tones.

"She doesn't have the spiritbone. I know she doesn't because we searched for it! Both of us!" She added in a choked voice, "You know as well as I do that if the Dragon Kahg wanted us to have the spiritbone, we would not need to search at all. Face it, Skylan. The dragon has abandoned us. The gods have abandoned us!"

She lowered her head, blinking her eyes rapidly.

"Aylaen—"

"And it's your fault!" she cried.

"I know it is," said Skylan, his voice somber. "But that thread has snapped and I can't tie it back together, no matter how much I want to. I need you to forget about blaming me. I need you to forget about your sister. She made her choice and it was hers to make. I need you to be a warrior, Aylaen. You will have to stand guard over the Legate. All the men will be needed at the oars." He handed a sword to her, wrapped in its sheath. "I found it in the hold."

Aylaen wiped her eyes and, taking hold of the sheath, drew out the shining steel blade with its worn ivory hilt, the sword that she had found in the temple of Vindrash. The goddess had given the sword to Aylaen, or so Aylaen believed. Her hand closed over the hilt. The sword was smaller than a man's, weighted to suit a woman.

She hefted the sword and gazed at Skylan, then shifted her gaze to Sigurd. She called out to him, "I will guard the Legate, Chief. You need all the men for rowing."

Sigurd waved his hand in approval. Aylaen thrust her sword into the sheath and buckled it around her waist. She turned on her heel, without a word, and walked across the deck to where Acronis sat on his collapsible stool, his arms bound behind him, his feet tied at the ankles.

He watched Aylaen walk toward him, regarded her with a bemused smile. "You won the day for them. Stabbing your captor like that took courage and a cool head. Are all the barbarian women trained in the art of warfare?"

Aylaen shook back her red curls. "I would like very much to jab my sword into someone's belly right now," she said, her voice grating. "If I were you, I would keep my mouth shut."

The Legate raised an eyebrow. Skylan was going to take his place at the tiller, but first he stopped to make certain their captive was securely bound.

"I take it you are using me as a hostage," said Acronis. "You will kill me if Zahakis attempts to recapture the ship."

"Something like that," Skylan answered.

"Your plan was brilliant and well-executed," the Legate said. "I would be interested to know how you managed to get hold of the key to the manacles from Zahakis."

Skylan could have said he was interested in knowing the same thing. That made him remember Wulfe and he realized he had not seen the boy since the fighting began.

"You did make one mistake," Acronis added.

"What was that?" Skylan asked.

"You should have killed Zahakis. He has been the commander of my forces for many years and he is very loyal. He will come after you."

"I am counting on that," said Skylan.

Acronis frowned, puzzled.

"Zahakis is *so* loyal," said Skylan coolly, "that when I bind you with chains and throw you into the sea, he will stop his pursuit to try to save you."

Skylan went back down into the hold, yelling for Wulfe. He found the boy hiding in an empty barrel.

All that day, the *Venjekar* crawled over the water. Skylan took his turn at the oars, sending Erdmun to man the tiller.

The gods were not only disinclined to help them, the gods seemed to be actively working against them. The sun goddess, Aylis, beat on them relentlessly. Svanses held her breath. Akaria caused her waters to roll sluggishly beneath the keel.

The men stripped bare to the waist, wearing only their trousers. Sweat rolled off their bodies and dripped from their hair and beards. Days of inactivity and poor food had weakened their muscles and drained their stamina. But every man, whenever he grew weary, looked at the chains that had once bound him and found new strength.

The *Light of the Sea* was far behind them, but not as far as they had hoped. Zahakis was an able commander and he had managed to drag his soldiers out of the sea and put an end to the crew's confusion and fear over the loss of the Legate. He ordered the rowers to the oars and the war galley was able to chase after the *Venjekar* after only a brief loss of time. Not only that, the galley was making better time than they were.

Every man on board the *Venjekar* could see that the trireme was slowly gaining on them.

"If only we had the dragon," the Torgun said.

Wulfe heard the men talk about the dragon. He heard their prayers to the dragon goddess, Vindrash, and he didn't know what to do. He had overheard Skylan talking to Aylaen about the spirit-bone. That was when he'd decided to run and hide in the empty water barrel.

He knew where the spiritbone was—it was secreted in his little cache in the bulkhead right under the dragon's nose. The spiritbone had come to him—Skylan had said so. The dragon wanted him to have it.

Well, maybe.

Wulfe wasn't exactly sure about that. Perhaps the dragon had wanted Aylaen or Treia to have it and Wulfe had just stumbled upon it by accident. In that case, he had taken what didn't belong to him and he was certain to get into trouble. Skylan might punish him by making him clean his sword again.

Still, Wulfe thought, Skylan and the others might be so glad to have the spiritbone and the dragon that they wouldn't be mad.

Wulfe spent the day dithering. He watched the men working and suffering at the oars, sweating in the bright sun. The war galley that looked like an ugly snapping turtle with a hundred legs crawled in-exorably toward them. Wulfe made up his mind.

Wulfe could not possibly walk across the deck with the eyes of everyone on him and retrieve the bone. Everyone on board the ship would know about his hiding place, and while he liked some of the Uglies, such as Skylan and Bjorn and Aylaen and maybe Farinn, there were others, such as Sigurd and Grimuir, Wulfe didn't like one bit. The only two Uglies he trusted were Skylan and Aylaen, and Wulfe's trust in them went only so far. Skylan had made the boy clean his sword and the iron had burned him.

Aylaen was Treia's sister and Wulfe hated Treia and Aylaen told Treia everything. Wulfe had eavesdropped on the sisters enough to know.

Wulfe decided to wait until darkness fell, when everyone would be asleep. The chase would come to a halt at night, for the rowers on both ships would have to rest.

The sun was still a blood-red stain on the horizon when Sigurd gave the order for the men to cease rowing. The order was hardly necessary. Only a few had kept grimly to the task. Progress was almost negligible. He woke those who had already fallen asleep where they sat, and they drew in the oars and stacked them in the center of the ship, ready for use in the morning. Skylan raised the sail in hope that a breeze might come up in the night. The sail hung limp and drooping; a banner for their spirits.

Skylan walked over to check on the Legate. Both Acronis and Aylaen had fallen asleep. Aylaen lay on the deck, her hand resting on her sword's hilt. The Legate slept on his stool, his chin on his chest. His position was uncomfortable, his hands were bloody from the tight ropes. He'd been given water to drink, but Sigurd was rationing the food and he'd had nothing to eat. Acronis had made no complaint, sat stoically upon his stool.

Skylan cast a last, weary glance at the *Light of the Sea* before the sun sank and the ship, swallowed up by darkness, would vanish from his sight. He saw, to his vast relief, that she was bringing in her oars, as well. He had been afraid that the zealous Zahakis would push his men, force them to row long into the night.

But then, why should he? Skylan asked himself bitterly. Unless the gods relent, Zahakis will easily overtake us, perhaps as early as tomorrow.

Skylan looked at his men, sleeping where they had fallen on the deck, too tired to make beds or even to eat. Their skin was sunburnt, their hands raw meat. The Torgun rarely had to row their ships. They could generally count on either the wind or the dragon to carry them over the seas.

Perhaps, this night, there would come a miracle.

Skylan touched the amulet and prayed to Torval more fervently and earnestly than he had ever prayed in his life.

"I don't care what you do to me, Torval," Skylan said. "Let your wrath fall on me with the full force of a hammer blow from your strong arm. Crush me and feed me to Freilis's daemons. Save my men. Save Aylaen."

He lay down on the deck, stared up at the stars, and he did not fall asleep so much as drop into an exhausted stupor.

Wulfe waited impatiently until he saw Skylan's head loll to one side, his eyes close, and his breathing grow regular. Even then, Wulfe waited a little more to make sure Skylan and the others were deeply sunk in sleep. When he was certain that he was the only person awake on the ship, Wulfe stole noiselessly on bare feet across the deck to the dragonhead prow.

Wulfe worked free the wooden "plug" and removed it. The spiritbone was still there, nestled inside, snug and safe. Glancing back at the slumbering men to make certain no one was watching, Wulfe reached his hand into the niche.

He had the feeling someone was watching him. Wulfe froze and looked around. The men were asleep. Aylaen was asleep and so was the Ugly who sat tied up on the stool. Wulfe slowly lifted his gaze. The dragon's head faced straight out to sea, but Wulfe was certain the dragon's eyes were glaring at him. The sight startled Wulfe so that his hand jerked back.

"I don't want the spiritbone." Wulfe sought to reassure the dragon. "I'm going to give it to Aylaen."

He reached again into the niche. He wanted nothing more now than to be rid of the spiritbone. Once it was gone, the dragon would leave him alone.

As if Svanses had been holding her breath until it hurt and now she was forced to let it go with a whoosh, the wind for which Skylan had been praying blasted across the sea and struck the *Venjekar*. Wulfe heard a splintering sound above his head. Looking up, he saw the fierce head of the Dragon Kahg swooping down.

Wulfe shrieked in terror and crouched, screaming, as the carved wooden head of the dragon toppled to the deck and landed with a crash on top of the oars, barely missing braining the boy. The freakish wind died away as if it had never been, leaving not a whisper behind.

Wulfe stared in terror at the wreckage. He saw again the head coming straight at him and, in his mind, he knew the dragon had tried to kill him because he'd been going to touch the spiritbone. Wulfe slammed the wooden plug back into the cache and made a dash for the hold.

Skylan was wrenched from a black sleep by a horrific noise. He was on his feet before he was awake, staring about dazedly in the lambent light of the stars and a thin, sullen moon. Sigurd and the others were all awake, stumbling about, demanding to know what was going on.

"What the—"

The words died on Skylan's lips. He stared in appalled disbelief, his insides twisting like worms in the mud, at disaster.

The head of the Dragon Kahg lay on top of a pile of broken oars. The head was intact. It had not been damaged in the fall.

The dragon's empty eyes stared into the empty heavens.

The next day, Zahakis captured the *Venjekar* without a fight.

The Torgun, stunned by despair, sat listlessly on the deck, paying no heed as the soldiers locked the iron manacles and reattached the chains. Zahakis freed the Legate and he returned to his war galley. Men stretched a heavy cable from the *Light of the Sea* to the *Venjekar* and took the broken ship in tow. Treia shouted across the water, trying to persuade Aylaen to come aboard the *Light of the Sea*. Raegar added his pleas, as well. Aylaen would not speak to either of them.

A favorable wind, sent by Aelon, filled the sails of the *Light of the Sea*. The war galley sailed south to Sinaria—a wealthy city, a fat city, a city that knew it was destined to be the capital of an empire that would someday rule the world. The *Venjekar* rolled and bobbed sluggishly in the galley's wake. The head of the dragon lay on the deck, seemed to glare at the Torgun accusingly.

Skylan stared at the broken prow, feeling the heavy weight of the manacles on his legs and thinking that the weight was heavier on his heart.

"Maybe the gods have abandoned us," he said to no one in particular.

To his surprise, it was Aylaen who answered.

"When you are in battle, you cannot hear your children wail," she said, speaking softly, more to herself than to him. "You hear only the clash of arms. So it is with our gods."

BOOK TWO

The *Light of the Sea* sailed slowly into the Trevalis Bay early in the morning. Though the sun had barely risen, the day was already hot. The Torgun hated the heat. In their homeland, the days were pleasantly warm in summertime, the nights were always cool. In this part of the world, the heat was constant. The only change night brought was that sometimes the wind died, leaving them sweltering and sweating and unable to sleep.

As the heat rose in shimmering waves off the still water, Skylan sat in chains on the deck of his captured ship and stared in dazed amazement at the sights of the city known as Sinaria that was yet in the distance. Zahakis had said that the population of Oran's capital city, Sinaria, was greater than the population of the entire Vindrasi nation.

Skylan had, of course, not believed him.

Now he stared at the rows upon rows upon rows of buildings made of stone and wood, stacked one atop the other, covering the sides of the hills, jutting from the tops of the hills, spreading into the valleys. Narrow streets, twisting like snakes, crawled up and down and slithered sideways among the buildings.

The port was crowded with vessels of all types, from small fishing boats to merchant ships loaded with amphorae and passengers lounging on deck beneath awnings. The moment the war galley was sighted, boats put out from the shore, their occupants offering to sell everything from wine to food to whores, who brazenly showed *their* wares and called out the names of the streets on which they could be found.

Warehouses lined the port. Wagons carried goods from the ships to the warehouses. When night fell, the wagons would roll into the city. The streets were so crowded and narrow that wagons were not permitted to enter the city until after dark. Behind the warehouses, guard towers constructed of wood rose at intervals from a high wooden fence that formed the port's fortifications. The hot wind blowing from the land carried with it the stench of the docks, mingled with smells of smoke, fish, rotting garbage, refuse, and filth.

"What are those buildings?" Skylan asked Zahakis, who had come on board the *Venjekar* along with a master seaman to undertake the tricky maneuvering of the broken ship in the crowded port.

"Homes, shops, businesses," Zahakis answered.

Skylan stared, incredulous. "They look like the outbuildings we use to keep our pigs from wandering off."

"Your pigs probably fare better than those who live in those hovels," said Zahakis. "Sometimes twenty people—the old, the young—are packed into a dwelling that consists of only a single room. They sleep there, eat there, cook there, rut there, die there." His tone was grim and Skylan, glancing at him, saw the man's face was dark.

"Which is the Legate's dwelling?"

Zahakis gave a brief, mirthless laugh. He pointed off into the distance. "You see the muddy river water that pours into the sea over there? That is the River Cydron. Sail up that river and eventually you will come to Acronis's grand estate. That is where you will be living."

"Not living. I will be a slave," said Skylan.

Zahakis shook his head. "You think yourself ill-used, young man, but when you walk the streets of Sinaria, you will realize you are fortunate to be a slave of the Legate and not one of the poor devils forced to live in the city's slums. At least the Legate will see to it that you do not starve, that you are not knifed in a fight over a rotten cabbage, that you do not have to teach your sons to steal or prostitute your daughters for food."

Zahakis stood gazing at the slums, his jaw working, his eyes shadowed with pain.

"You wonder why I am loyal to the Legate," Zahakis said suddenly. He nodded in the direction of the city. "Acronis saved me from that life. I was nine years old. I tried to rob him. He could have killed me on the spot. Other men would have done so and not given it a second thought. Acronis took me to his fine house. He fed me and clothed me. He located my family and sent them to one of his farms where there was work. When he returned to the provinces, I went with him. He saw to it that I learned to read and write. I joined his legion, when I was old enough, and, although I had his favor, he made me sweat my way through the ranks. That is why I am loyal to Acronis and why I will be loyal to him to my death."

Zahakis leaned on the rail. "No crops grow on those hills. Only misery."

"What about your ruler?" Skylan asked.

Zahakis gave a snorting laugh. "The Imperial guard dare not set foot on many of those streets. They are ruled by gangs whose leaders hold more sway over the populace than does our newly crowned Empress. The gangs could take over the city if they wanted. They don't. There's no profit in it."

"Why doesn't this god of yours, this Aelon, do something to help his people?" Skylan asked.

"Aelon is no god of mine," Zahakis said grimly. "Still, I have to give him credit. He did try to clean up the city. One night a fire swept through the tenements located on the north side of the river. The fire consumed block after block, moving so fast people had no time to flee. Thousands died, including Raegar's wife and children. Aelon's priests claim that the fire was sent by the god, a cleansing fire, to burn away the sins of the people."

"And you call us barbarians," Skylan muttered.

Zahakis gave a thin-lipped smile. "There will come a reckoning. Even now the pot simmers. Someday it will boil over." He remained silent a moment, then shook his head and continued pointing out the sights of his city. "You see those twin hills there. The building on the hill hiding behind those great stone walls is the Imperial palace. Our new Empress and her family live there in that complex. The very grandiose building on the hill opposite is the Shrine of Aelon. There used to be a temple of the old gods on the site, but Aelon's priests tore it down. The old temple was lovely: white marble, surrounded on all sides by a columned portico, simple and elegant. Aelon demanded something more splendid.

"The Shrine of Aelon is surmounted by a golden dome. The sunlight reflects off the dome with such brilliance that it seems to be another sun come down from the sky to grace our city. Even at night, the dome of the shrine continues to shine, its light brighter than the moon. People who live near it claim it is so bright they can't sleep."

Skylan listened in wonder. He had never heard words such as "slum" or "palace," "Imperial" or "Empress." He stared until his eyes ached at the Shrine of Aelon and its surrounding gardens and fountains and the other structures that dotted the hillside, white against the green of the clipped lawn. He could not comprehend such wealth, such magnificence. The Hall of Vindrash, which was the largest and most beautiful building Skylan had ever seen, could be dropped down whole into the Shrine of Aelon and go unnoticed.

Skylan could not comprehend such wretched poverty either.

We may not build such grand and imposing structures, but we do not let our children grow up in pigsties, he thought.

The *Light of the Sea* crept forward at a crawl, mainly to avoid running down the flotilla of boats that had swarmed out to greet her. Some of these now brought men of prominence, who came on board to speak to Acronis. Skylan thought they must be merchants or nobles, but Zahakis laughed and said that, no, they were fellow scientists, eager to hear about his voyage. He pointed to Raegar, who stood apart, frowning at them in haughty disapproval.

"The priests do not approve of thinking," said Zahakis wryly. "People who think begin to question. Aelon does not like questions."

"You speak of the old gods," Skylan said, eyeing Raegar balefully. "What were they like?"

"From what you have told me, our old gods were much like yours," said Zahakis. He shrugged. "Who knows? Perhaps our gods *were* your gods. Just called by different names."

Before Skylan could make a cutting remark, Zahakis was hailed by Acronis's scribe, shouting from the deck of the trireme.

The ship dropped anchor at last, some distance from the docks. Word of their arrival had spread, including word that they had brought back a dragonship filled with barbarians. Raegar had gone ashore, saying he had to report to the Priest-General.

While he was gone, Aylaen transferred to the war galley at Raegar's insistence. She argued against going, but not very hard, Skylan noted. He could not blame her. She had lived alone in the hold on board the *Venjekar* and undoubtedly missed her sister, unworthy as that sister was. Treia waited impatiently for Aylaen and, putting her arms around her, hustled her belowdecks.

Raegar was gone for almost the entire day, returning at night with word that the Empress had decreed that a parade would be held in the Legate's honor, the chief feature of which would be the fearsome dragonship he had captured. Unfortunately, the *Venjekar,* to the Legate's vast disappointment, did not look all that fearsome.

Carpenters from the *Light of the Sea* had worked diligently throughout much of the voyage to try to restore the dragonhead prow. For some reason that they could not explain, whenever they tried to mount the dragon's head on the stump of the prow, the head fell off.

The first time, the head of the Dragon Kahg splashed into the sea and had to be fished out. The attempt to retrieve it cost the Legate a day's sailing. The second time, the head toppled onto the deck, nearly killing the carpenter's son. The carpenter told Acronis he could not work properly while they were at sea. He would mount the dragon's head once the ship reached land.

The stubborn refusal of the Dragon Kahg to cooperate did much to lift the spirits of the captive Torgun. Skylan knew what his friend, Garn, would have said. That the prow was only a piece of wood carved to resemble a dragon, that it did not have a mind or a will of its own, that a log could not rebel.

Skylan honored Garn's memory, but he knew in this regard his friend was wrong. Perhaps somewhere the Dragon Kahg was being held captive. Perhaps the dragon was fighting back the only way he could. The wooden eyes of the dragon no longer seemed empty.

"Don't give up," the eyes seemed to say.

The ship behaved sluggishly and erratically, much to the frustration of Zahakis, who could not understand what difference the loss of the decorative prow could make to the sailing of the ship.

"This proves our dragon is not dead," Skylan told him.

"It proves the Legate hired bad carpenters," said Zahakis.

Despite this disappointment in the matter of the dragon's head, Acronis was pleased with the spectacle he was going to give the people. Raegar demanded the honor of carrying the head of the dragon, insisting that Aelon had prevented the head from being mounted on the ship. The Legate told Zahakis, with some amusement, that he did not see why Aelon had the right to ruin his parade, but if Raegar wanted to walk miles in the heat carrying the heavy head, who was he to argue?

Acronis would ride in his chariot with an honor guard of his soldiers, marching in formation. The men had spent the long days at sea polishing their armor and helms to a blinding sheen. With them marched the rowers, a reward for their hard and back-breaking labor. The *Venjekar,* mounted on wheels, would be hauled through the city by the Torgun warriors. The two captive barbarian women would be displayed with the ship.

Zahakis explained to the Torgun warriors what they were going to do. The men listened with disdain, their eyes staring out across the water, refusing to acknowledge the man's existence. That ploy didn't work for long.

When the Torgun heard they were to drag their beloved ship past gawking crowds, they were enraged.

"We will die first!" Sigurd cried.

Zahakis pointed to the *Light of the Sea.* The men turned to see Aylaen and Treia standing on the deck, an armed soldier beside them. So that was why they had taken Aylaen.

"We hold your women hostage," said Zahakis.

"Our women will die as well!" Sigurd said angrily.

"In that case," said Zahakis, his calm voice overriding the tumult, "I will have you chained to the hull of the ship and you will be whipped through the streets of Sinaria. Think about it."

He walked off, leaving the Torgun in an uproar, swearing that they would let their skin be flayed from their bones before they would give in. Skylan was as angry as the rest. The thought of being put on display, like a fat sow at the market, made his gorge rise.

They won't have to kill me, he spoke to himself. I will die of shame.

Zahakis, passing close by him, paused to say, out of the corner of his mouth, "I think you should know that Raegar is hoping your men will refuse. The guards who will be walking the streets with you will be warrior-priests, like himself. If you and the others do not obey, they have orders to beat you to death."

"Your Legate wants us alive," said Skylan, frowning, his anger burning. "I've heard the two of you talking. He wants us to fight for him in some game."

Zahakis stopped and, under pretext of adjusting the ties on his boots, said softly and quietly, "Acronis won't have anything to say about it. He will be riding at the end of the procession. You will be with the warrior-priests. For some reason, Aelon wants you dead."

Zahakis straightened. "If it were me, I wouldn't give the god the satisfaction."

"Why do you care what happens to us?" Skylan demanded.

"Damned if I know," Zahakis muttered. He glanced over his shoulder at Skylan and shrugged. "We have a saying here, young man, 'The enemy of my enemy is my friend.' "

He walked off, heading back to the *Light of the Sea* to continue his preparations for landing.

Skylan pondered the man's words. He didn't understand what was going on. The nature of the animosity between Acronis and this god, Aelon, was beyond Skylan. He didn't really give a rat's ass anyway. Let their serpents devour them all. What he did know was that he might be able to use this animosity between the Legate and Raegar to his benefit.

Provided they stayed alive.

Skylan listened to the men raving and raging and he gave an inward sigh. He, the wild, impetuous, never-look-before-you-leap Skylan Ivorson, was going to be the voice of calm reason. In Torval's Hall, Garn was laughing.

Skylan drew in a breath. He was about to make himself very unpopular.

"I say we do it," said Skylan. "We obey the Legate's orders."

"Bah!" Sigurd shrugged. "All know you are yellow as dog piss."

"We are Torgun," said Skylan sharply. "We are prisoners in the city of our foes. Do you want us to enter this city as slaves, hauled through the streets, driven by the whipmaster?"

Sigurd sneered and turned away, muttering to his buddy, Grimuir. Bjorn looked thoughtful, however; his brother uneasy. The rest at least decided to hear Skylan out.

"Would you enter this city as a slave or will you walk through the

ranks of our foes proud with your head held high and songs of defiance on your lips?" Skylan asked.

Sigurd scoffed at them. "Don't listen to this barking pup. Go lick
Zahakis's ass, Skylan, and leave us men alone."

"I want to hear him," said Farinn, quietly defiant.

"I am Chief," said Sigurd angrily.

"And this is a council meeting," returned Bjorn. "All have the
right to speak. Go on, Skylan."

"Look at us." Skylan lifted his manacled hands. "We stink like
pigs. Our beards are long. Our hair is filthy and matted. What do we
look like? What do we smell like?"

"Slaves," said Erdmun.

"We look and smell like slaves. I say we show these Southlanders
that although they have chained our feet, they can never chain our
souls."

The others nodded at this. Even Sigurd quit scowling.

"What is your plan?" Bjorn asked.

Skylan explained. The others listened and looked at Sigurd. "I
guess it might work," he said grudgingly.

"I like it better than being whipped to death," Erdmun said in a
low voice to his brother.

That night, when Zahakis came back on board, Skylan met him
on deck.

"We will do what you ask," Skylan said. "We will haul our ship
through the streets."

"You're a clever bastard," said Zahakis. "How did you get Graybeard to go along? Last I heard, he was all for dying just to spite us."

"I want something in return," said Skylan.

Zahakis snorted. "Slaves don't bargain."

Skylan shrugged. "Your Legate wants to impress the people. If
you grant our request, we will put on a show that the populace will
be talking about for months."

"What do you want?" Zahakis asked, a smile flitting over his lips.
"Your weapons? You tried that once and we fell for it. We're not
likely to do that again."

"We want to take a bath," said Skylan.

Zahakis looked startled. He started to laugh, then stopped, for he
saw that Skylan was in earnest. Zahakis eyed Skylan suspiciously.
"What are you up to, young man?"

"Do you want live slaves or dead ones?" Skylan countered.

"I will speak to the Legate," said Zahakis.

Skylan heard laughter and glanced back at his comrades. Sigurd was grinning at him. He said something in a low voice to Grimuir, who gave a snigger.

Skylan turned away. In death, valiant heroes meet in Torval's Hall, friends and enemies alike. A man who dies in combat will share a drink with the honorable foe who killed him.

I will drink with Zahakis in the afterlife, Skylan determined. I will slug Sigurd.

Zahakis crossed the gangplank to the *Light of the Sea*. The galley rode at anchor, waiting to sail into the harbor tomorrow in triumph.

Zahakis found the Legate in his small office, planning his triumphal entry. Acronis's eyes widened in disbelief.

"They want to *what*?"

"Bathe, my lord."

Acronis shook his head. "This is a strange request. They are plotting something."

"Of course they are, though I admit I do not know what, unless they plan to try to swim for freedom."

"Skylan may be clever, but he is not foolhardy, nor is he stupid. He must know that any attempt by his warriors to try to flee will be hopeless. We hold his womenfolk hostage and I've seen the way he looks at the red-haired beauty. He is hopelessly in love with her. He would never leave her behind. And if these barbarians did somehow manage to escape, where could they go? With their blond hair and blue eyes, they could not very well lose themselves in the crowd."

Acronis pondered long and hard. Zahakis waited, keeping his thoughts to himself.

At last Acronis shrugged and said, "I say we let them clean themselves up if that's what they want. Dress them in their armor and their winged helms. Put on a spectacle. Then, when they fight in the Para Dix, crowds will throng into the arena to see them. Besides," Acronis added in softer tones, "Chloe will love it."

Zahakis smiled to himself. Chloe was the real reason. If Chloe had asked for the stars, Acronis would have found some way to rip them from the heavens. He was planning this triumphal parade solely for her benefit. A man of science, a philosopher, Acronis disliked ostentatious display. He would have been happy to have gone quietly to his villa and shut himself up in his library. Chloe adored parades and nothing would please her more than sitting with the Empress and the other noble ladies of Sinaria, watching her father, crowned with laurel leaves, as he rode in triumph past the reviewing stand.

The Torgun stripped off their clothes. The soldiers unlocked the manacles and, freed of their chains, the warriors jumped into the sea. Zahakis had posted archers on deck, their arrows nocked and ready to fly.

Once in the water, the Torgun forgot for a moment they were captives. They began to roughhouse, pushing each other underwater, splashing and kicking. The boy, Wulfe, jumped in with them, chattering and laughing. Aylaen watched from the deck of the *Light of the Sea*. By the wistful expression on her face, she would have liked to have joined them. Her sister, Treia, found her there and, looking scandalized, for the men were naked, she dragged Aylaen away.

Back on board the *Venjekar,* Skylan and the other Torgun scrubbed their clothes and plaited their long hair and combed their beards. They would have liked to have shaved their beards, as warriors did in the summer months—the fighting season. Beards were grown for warmth in the winter. Skylan had asked Zahakis for a razor. The Tribune had laughed heartily at that and refused.

Skylan was astonished beyond measure when Zahakis told him that he and his warriors were going to be permitted to wear their armor and helms. The soldiers hauled the armor up from the hold where they had kept it in storage. Skylan's eyes blurred with tears as he rubbed a cloth lovingly over his chain mail. He should be wearing his armor proudly as he stood in the shield wall. He should not be wearing it as a slave, dragging his broken ship through the streets of his enemy. Skylan grit his teeth and let his anger burn away the pain. He touched the amulet to Torval.

"I hope you can take time from your battles to look down on us," he said to the god. "We will make you proud."

Wulfe put on the clothing given to him by the soldiers. They had started to think of the boy as lucky, for he could make dolphins come at his call, and dolphins were friends to those who sailed the seas. Boys in Sinaria wore sleeveless, short wool tunics, belted at the waist. Wulfe had grown some during the voyage, but, much to his despair, he was still not very tall. He wanted to be as tall as Skylan.

Wulfe had talked to his friends, the oceanaids, and he was worried. He sought out Skylan, found him polishing his helm. The helm being metal, Wulfe kept his distance.

"The oceanaids say that Uglies in this land hate the fae. They kill them. You won't let them kill me, will you?"

"I won't let them kill you," Skylan said, only half listening.

Wulfe gave a sigh of relief and crept a little closer. "The oceanaids told me that the ogre fleet is halfway across the sea. The ogres are coming here to fight the Southlanders."

Skylan grunted. He was concentrating on trying to remove a stubborn bit of rust and only after a moment did he realize what the boy had said. Skylan quit polishing, stared at him.

"Your oceanaids say that an ogre fleet is sailing here to Sinaria?"

Wulfe looked hurt. "I already told you that."

"They are coming here to make war?"

"I guess," said Wulfe. "Why else would the ogres come?"

Skylan spit on the metal and rubbed it with a cloth, all the while keeping an eye on Wulfe. He did remember Wulfe telling him something about ogres sailing to Sinaria. Something about Uglies killing one another.

Wulfe left Skylan staring at him and wandered away to lean over the rail, watching the oceanaids cavort among the waves. He watched his friends so he would not have to look at the dragon, whose head lay on the deck. Wulfe didn't like the way the eyes stared at him.

Wulfe had not breathed a word to Skylan or anyone about the spiritbone, which was, so far as he knew, still hidden in the niche in the hull, guarded by the magical spell he had cast on it. Wulfe had been terrified that the carpenters might discover the spiritbone when they were trying to reattach the dragonhead prow, but the magic worked, for they had not found it.

Skylan and the rest might think the dragon was dead, but not Wulfe. He alone could see the faint glint in the eyes; the eyes that were always watching him. Wulfe did not know what the dragon wanted from him. He wished he had never found the spiritbone.

The last time he had been ready to tell Skylan about the spiritbone, the Dragon Kahg had swooped down and tried to eat him.

Skylan thought the dragon's head had broken off.

Wulfe knew better.

BOOK TWO

Acronis entered the city in triumph. But it was the Torgun warriors who were the true victors—unusual for slaves.

The procession was led by Raegar, who had demanded the honor
of carrying the dragonhead prow. He pictured himself proudly
walking the streets with the decapitated dragon, symbolizing the
victory of Aelon over the gods of the barbarians. Raegar would be
impressive, imposing.

But when he lifted up the dragonhead prow and started walking
along the parade route, he was greeted by laughter. The sight of
Raegar carrying the dragon's head made it appear as if the dragon
were out taking a stroll. To make matters worse, the head seemed to
have taken on a life of its own. It lurched and bobbed and occasionally made unexpected lunges at the crowds, terrorizing small children and eliciting gleeful hoots from the adults.

The jokesters who think it their duty to provide entertainment no
matter what the occasion shouted out ribald remarks that increased
the audience's mirth. As Raegar walked down the street, he could
actually see merriment expanding out in ripples ahead of him, as the
crowds, hearing the commotion, leaned forward to see the fun.

Before he'd traversed more than a few city blocks, Raegar was
sweating, annoyed, and angry. If he had not been assured by Aelon
that the gods of the Vindrasi were crushed and shattered, on the
verge of utter annihilation, Raegar would have said the goddess
Vindrash and her dragon were making him look foolish.

Zahakis, who witnessed Raegar's ordeal, was thankful he was
wearing his helm; its hinged cheek pieces concealed his broad grin.

The sailors and oarsmen of the *Light of the Sea* walked in the parade, waving proudly to friends and family. Sure, living conditions on board ship were harsh, their jobs were backbreaking and often dangerous, but these men were not slaves. They were free men, citizens of Oran, and Acronis treated them as such. This was a proud moment in their difficult lives and they walked and waved, sometimes picking up their children along the way and carrying them on their shoulders.

The soldiers marched next, resplendent in their shining armor; faces stern, eyes forward, their standard bearers leading the way.

After them, the Vindrasi captives.

Men had mounted the *Venjekar* on wheels and attached long ropes to the ship so that the Torgun warriors could haul it through the streets. The ship was no great burden to the warriors, who were accustomed to hauling it out of the water and dragging it onto the shore.

The burden that nearly crushed them was in their hearts. The knowledge that they were slaves, conquered, vanquished. The humiliation of being forced to exhibit their defeat to gaping crowds of foreigners. The misery of being strangers in a strange land, far from their homes and loved ones. Their grief over the loss of comrades. The bitter realization that they were in this battle alone, that their gods were either unable or unwilling to help them. The unspoken fear that they could not escape their fate. The death of hope.

Aylaen had chosen to walk with the warriors. Acronis had first decreed that the women should stand on the deck of the *Venjekar*. Aylaen had told him defiantly that he might as well kill her now, for she would sooner die.

"You should have seen the fire in her eyes," Acronis would later tell Zahakis. "The set of her jaw, how she held herself. It was at that moment I conceived the idea of fighting her in the Para Dix. I will call her the Ogressa. The Barbarians and the Ogressa. Has a nice sound to it, doesn't it?"

Keeping this in mind, he told Aylaen she could walk with Skylan and the other Torgun males. Now she wondered if she had made a mistake. She stared in dismay at the narrow, twisting streets, the enormous buildings that seemed to enclose her like the walls of a tomb. She was appalled at the size of the city and at the sheer numbers of its people. But what she noticed most and what she would never forget was the smell.

Thousands of unwashed bodies pressed together in the blazing heat of a summer's day. Garbage rotting in the alleyways. Gutters overflowing with brown, stinking water. Smoke from forge fires and cook fires hung on the breathless air. The stench made her sick to her stomach. She felt bile rise in her throat and she feared she would vomit.

"How do they stand it?" Erdmun asked, gagging. The Torgun stood beside their ship, waiting for the orders to haul on the traces. "This is worse than a shit hole!"

Aylaen tried to block out the smell by pressing her nose and mouth into the sleeve of her tunic, but when the time came that they had to start hauling on the ropes, she had to breathe it in.

The people stared—particularly at her, as she stood among the ranks of the men—and jeered and hooted. Aylaen's face burned, her body shook, her legs trembled. She thought she would die of shame. She *wished* she could die. She saw that she was not alone. Skylan's face was pale and strained, his lips compressed and his jaw clenched.

But then he lifted his head and licked his lips and raised his voice in an old, old song.

> *"We sing our praise to Torval.*
> *We ring his name with our bright steel.*
> *The name of Torval sounds in the clash*
> *Of sword on shield*
> *Hammer on the stone walls of our enemies.*
> *Strong and mighty though they be*
> *We are stronger.*
> *Torval puts flame in our hearts*
> *And spear tips catch the god's fire."*

Skylan's voice grew louder and more confident as he sang. He gave a heave and the rope line tightened and the other Torgun joined him, tugging on the rope and lifting their voices in the song that was often sung by those standing in the shield wall to give them courage.

Aylaen had never sung this song, for it was a warrior's song, a man's song. Skylan was at the head of the line, standing alongside Sigurd. He looked back at the Torgun and his look embraced them, as his song embraced them, and they were one, all of them standing together, as in the shield wall, their foe despair.

The Torgun raised their voices in a defiant shout. Skylan led them in another verse. The *Venjekar* lurched forward. The Torgun broke into a run, startling the soldiers marching ahead of them. Sigurd started to grin, that crazed grin he wore only in battle. Bjorn ran beside Aylaen. He was yelling himself hoarse. She began singing—somewhat tentatively—and Bjorn smiled his approval. Grimuir, in front of her, looked back and nodded.

The Torgun refused to let hope die. They chose to bear their burden with jaws outthrust and heads high. They chose to sing to their god, Torval, though he might be bloodied and battle-scarred and besieged. They shouted his name as they ran defiantly through the streets, pulling their ship, keeping uncomfortably close on the heels of the soldiers, forcing them to set a swift pace or be run down.

The Torgun would pay for this moment. This sense of exultation could not last, for they were slaves and the gods alone knew what suffering and humiliation lay ahead of them. Aylaen did not think about the future. She concentrated on the present and the words of the war chant and she could no longer smell the horrible smells. She did not see the staring eyes or the gaping mouths or hear the taunts and jeers.

She had a sudden vision of Torval, striding through the heavens, pulling on rope lines that were tied to the world, dragging the world behind him. He was old and weary and his wounds were many. His armor was dented, his shield splintered. Yet he ran on, defiant.

"Your gods are dead," Raegar kept telling them.

Beaten down. Desperate. Dying, maybe. But not dead.

Aylaen lifted her woman's voice and joined in the song. Rich and mellow, her voice soared on the crests of the deeper voices of the men. She pulled on the ropes until her hands were blistered and bloody and sang herself hoarse in praise of Torval.

The crowds had turned out to jeer or gawk at the barbarian slaves. But their mocking laughter was drowned out by the singing. Many

Sinarians who had come to sneer and pity ended up admiring and applauding. The streets that day were full of slaves. They looked up from their onerous chores: cleaning the muck from the gutters, carrying slop jars, shuffling in long chained rows to work in the mines or the clay pits, hauling their masters about in curtained chairs, cooling their mistresses with fans. They saw the Torgun, this new crop of slaves proud and defiant, and for the first time some dared to find hope in their hearts.

The Torgun fought their own battle that day. They had no care for the battles of others. They would never know it, but they lit sparks in the hearts of many. They started tiny fires in the wet and filthy straw, and because no one was paying attention, no one noticed the thin, wispy, ominous puff of smoke.

The all-seeing Aelon saw, however. He saw much as he gazed into the future.

Last came Acronis riding in his chariot. He had created a public sensation; this parade of his would be the topic of discussion among the populace for days, perhaps months. His friends would be pleased for him, his enemies consumed with jealousy. But he thought little of all that. He rode through the streets, paying scant attention to the cheering throngs, impatient to reach the end. He wanted to see the smile on one face, to see the light in one pair of eyes.

The Torgun hauled their ship toward a vast arena. They had no idea what it was. It looked like a bowl sunk into the ground surrounded by benches. In the center was what appeared to be a large fire pit. The remnants of circles and lines that had been painted on the grass could still be seen; the rain had not yet washed them away from the last Para Dix game. Large boulders, some as tall as a man, were placed at various intervals around the field. A track for wagons and chariots and other vehicles circled the center playing field.

Acronis entered the Para Dix arena to the cheers of the audience. The Torgun pulled their ship into the arena and, at Zahakis's direction, came to a halt. Skylan tried to keep his face stern and impassive, hoping he did not show his feelings of bafflement and confusion. He had seen sights this day that he could not have imagined. A glance at his friends told him they felt much the same.

Acronis in his chariot rolled up to the royal stand. He bowed to his new Empress—a vapid woman wearing an elaborately coiffed red wig. Her eyes were painted with kohl, her lips with carnelian.

She rewarded weeks of danger and monotony, death and hardship, with a tepid smile and a vague nod and held up her pug dog so that he could get a better view.

In truth, though he bowed to the Empress, Acronis saw only one person—a slight girl of about fifteen years, small in stature, thin for her age, seated on cushions several rows removed from the Empress and her party. The girl's eyes were large and brown and shining with pride. Her smile was Acronis's sunrise. She was clapping so hard her hands must sting.

She pointed to the barbarian ship, the *Venjekar,* and mouthed the words, "For me?"

Gods in heaven, Acronis thought, his heart aching, how he loved her!

All around him, women tossed roses. Men cheered.

"Die now!" they cried, an ancient blessing, which meant that Acronis should die now, at the height of his glory, rather than go on living with the knowledge that he would never be as happy as he was on this day.

Acronis, being in extremely good health, went on living.

Acronis's estate was a sprawling complex consisting of the beautiful villa that had been in his family for many generations, barracks for the soldiers, outbuildings that included stables, bakery, smithy, and bath houses, all surrounded by a brick wall. The villa graced the top of the highest hill in this part of Oran. From the portico, Acronis could see his olive groves, his fields of grain, the green hills dotted with sheep and cattle, and the compound in which he would house his newly acquired slaves.

Beyond, the River Cydron wound about at the foot of the hill. He could trace the river's sparkling meanderings to the sea. Acronis loved the river. He liked to think that it represented the past, life as it had been lived in his youth—placid, slow, refined, and dignified.

The living area in the marble and granite villa was built around a central atrium—a paved courtyard open to the air. Adorned with marble fountains, bronze statues, ornamental trees, and fragrant flowers, the large and spacious atrium served as a reception area for guests.

The doors and windows of the central rooms could be opened to the atrium, receiving the benefit of the cooling breezes, perfumed by the flowers. The largest and prettiest of these rooms belonged to Chloe. The dining room and the room Acronis used as his office also looked out into the atrium. The only rooms in the villa that were not attached to the atrium were the bedrooms for the house-slaves, the lavatory, and the kitchen, which was located at the far end of the house, near the bakery.

The Palace of the Empress, the Shrine of Aelon with its garish light, and the city with its noise and stench and crowds were many miles distant, separated from his villa by the surrounding hills.

The weary captives saw the villa—its white walls stained pink with the setting sun—only from a distance. The villa was so different from their own longhouses that they had no idea it was a dwelling. Nor did they care. The Torgun were exhausted and disheartened when they straggled onto the spacious grounds, dragging their ship behind them. Their high spirits, their defiance, was gone. Their song had come to an end.

Muscles cramped. Their hands were raw, their hearts ached. When told that they had arrived at the compound they would henceforth call home, they were so tired most collapsed, never bothering to look at their surroundings.

Skylan looked and his brow furrowed. "This is odd," he muttered.

The compound looked like an old pen that had once been used to hold sheep. A stone wall, squarish in shape, enclosed a large grassy sward located at the bottom of a hill. A rusty iron gate had been set into the wall. Inside the compound, a few wedge-shaped tents made of goatskin were being set up by the soldiers. Skylan could see, in the distance, the waning sunlight drifting on the surface of a body of water, probably a river.

What was odd was that the wall came only to Skylan's thigh. He could easily hop over it. What sort of prison was this?

They hauled their ship into the compound. Acronis had been going to mount his trophy in front of the villa, but not until the dragon's head prow had been repaired. Until then, the *Venjekar* was also a prisoner.

The warriors sat on the ground like men stunned.

Wulfe appeared suddenly at Skylan's side and settled himself down on the grass. Skylan had been wondering all day what had become of the boy.

"Where have you been?" he asked.

"Hiding in the ship's hold," said Wulfe. Edging closer, he said, "I hate this place. When are we leaving?"

Skylan looked at the boy and looked away.

Aylis, the Sun Goddess, was giving up her fight and sinking into the west. Red streaks smeared the sky. The shadows lengthened. Many of the Torgun had already fallen asleep on the grass. Though he was exhausted, Skylan was uneasy and restless. He had a feeling worse was to come to them before the end of this day.

The Legate would not keep slaves in a compound from which they could easily escape without some means of controlling them. Skylan's feeling was confirmed when he saw four strange-looking wagons pulled by horses come rolling to a stop at the compound.

The wagons looked like small dwellings on wheels. Constructed of wood, the walls and arched roofs protected the occupants against inclement weather. Side panels could be opened or closed, permitting the occupants to see out or remain private. A door at the end allowed entry. Raegar, accompanied by six priests and two soldiers, emerged from the carriages and walked toward them. Zahakis and twenty soldiers, armed with spears and swords, guarded them.

"Trouble coming," Skylan warned his men.

Bjorn shook Erdmun awake. The rest were already on their feet. Wulfe started to run, but Skylan grabbed him.

"Too late. Raegar saw you. Go to Aylaen. She'll take care of you."

"I don't want to leave you," Wulfe said.

"There's going to be a fight," said Skylan, and Wulfe ran over to Aylaen and ducked behind her. She gave him an uncertain smile that wasn't much comfort.

Wary and suspicious, Skylan and the others watched Raegar approach. The two soldiers must have been warrior-priests, for they wore the same armor, marked with a serpent and sun, as did Raegar. The other six priests were dressed differently. They all had shaved heads, like Raegar's, and the serpent tattoo. But they wore long, belted gowns that flowed from their shoulders. Golden bracelets wound like snakes around their bare arms.

"Their men dress like women," said Sigurd with a snort.

"Their men *are* women," said Bjorn, incredulous.

A closer look proved Bjorn was right. Skylan could now see the more delicate feminine bone structure of the faces of the six priestesses. As the women drew closer, Skylan saw to his astonishment that the bracelets on their arms were not bracelets. Living serpents twined around the bare arms of the women. The serpents twisted and coiled and flicked their tongues.

"This is bad magic," said Wulfe. "Very bad magic."

Skylan didn't need the boy to tell him. He could feel the badness crawling around him, see it slithering toward him. He would have rather faced axe-wielding ogres.

He glanced at Zahakis, saw the man's face was grim and stern. Whatever was about to happen, Zahakis didn't like it.

Raegar came to a halt in front of the Torgun. He lifted his head and raised his arms to heaven. He was about to launch into a speech, when Aylaen called out, "Where is my sister?"

Raegar was annoyed at the interruption, but he managed a smile. "Treia is safe within the Temple enclave. You will see her shortly. I will take you there this night—"

"No, you won't," said Zahakis in flat tones. "The Legate wants her for the Para Dix. She is his slave. He was generous in giving you the other woman. Now get on with what you came here to do so that we can all go to our beds."

Raegar flashed Zahakis an irate glance. He seemed about to make some argument, then thought better of it. Drawing himself up, he addressed the Torgun.

"Aelon has tried to bring you people into his blessed light, but you have refused. Aelon does not blame you. The god realizes that you are stubborn and rebellious children whose parents have long spoiled you. Aelon knows that, like spoiled children, you truly yearn for discipline and authority."

"I truly yearn to kick you in the balls," said Sigurd, and Skylan and the others laughed loudly.

Raegar did not grow angry, which Skylan took as a bad sign. He kept his eyes on the female priestesses with the serpents.

"I have brought with me those we call Spirit Priestesses. Their task is, among others, to help guide those stumbling in darkness to Aelon's light. You men are stubborn. You stop your ears to my words. You refuse to heed my teachings. Therefore, the god will speak with you directly. You will be branded with the sign of Aelon."

The Torgun said nothing. They came together, shoulder-to-shoulder, silently forming a shield wall to face their foes. They had no weapons. They had no shields. They did not expect to survive this encounter, but Torval would smile upon them when he welcomed them to the Hero's Hall.

Aylaen started to join them. Wulfe gave a low cry and clutched at her hand, holding her back.

"Don't leave me," he begged. "Don't let him take me. He's going to kill me!"

"Hush, Wulfe, no, he's not," said Aylaen, but she stood apart from the others, holding on to Wulfe's hand.

Skylan thanked her with a smile. She pretended not to see him.

Raegar watched them and shrugged. "You make it all too easy."

Skylan tensed, expecting Raegar to order Zahakis and the soldiers of the Legate to attack. To his surprise, Raegar gestured to the six priestesses.

"Prepare these barbarians to receive Aelon's blessing."

"What about the boy and the woman?" a priestess asked.

"The boy comes with me," said Raegar harshly. He added, his voice softening, "The woman is under my care."

Raegar smiled at Aylaen, an ingratiating smile, his eyes glittering. Skylan's stomach roiled. His hand itched for a sword to cut that smirk off Raegar's face. Aylaen flushed deeply and, to avoid looking at Raegar, bent down to say something comforting to Wulfe, who crouched, quivering, at her side.

The six priestesses with the serpents coiled about their arms joined hands and began to chant, calling upon Aelon. Wulfe shrieked in terror. Aylaen tried to hold on to him, but he pulled free and started running. Raegar barked a command to his warrior-priests, who ran off in pursuit, armor rattling and clanking.

Skylan did not look to see what became of Wulfe. He could not take his eyes from the chanting women. The words to the prayer slithered into his head like the snakes they wore on their arms and twined about his brain, hissing. He tried to shut out the voices. He wanted to cover his ears, but his arms wouldn't work.

Skylan was tired, tired of fighting, tired of hoping, tired of hurting. Even drawing in his breath seemed to take more effort than he had to give. Much easier to let go.

Much easier . . .

Skylan was sitting on the grass. Night had fallen and he had no memory of how he had been there. Two of the snake-singing priestesses were kneeling in front of him. One had hold of his hands and was examining both of them by torchlight. Skylan watched with detachment. Why should he care? The hands were not his. They belonged to someone else.

Raegar stood over him. "This one is right-handed. Put the tattoo on his sword arm."

The priestesses nodded. One of them held a bowl of dark liquid, which she placed on the ground. She drew out a vial filled with tiny crystals that sparkled in the torchlight. Removing the stopper, she carefully measured out a small portion of glittering, multicolored crystals into the dark liquid.

"Pulverized gemstones," said the woman, noting Skylan staring. "Crystals of quartz, amethyst, and other semiprecious gems, all blessed by Aelon."

She gestured to her forehead where red rubies gleamed in the light.

"There is nothing to fear, young man," she said. "We have received Aelon's blessing ourselves. The god speaks to us as he will speak to you."

Skylan didn't like that. In his mind, he was struggling, fighting to escape. His mind could not connect with his body, which wasn't his body. It belonged to someone else. Someone who was sitting on the grass, watching the gems lose their luster in the dark liquid.

"Squid ink," said the woman, stirring the crystals into the ink. "The sacred mixture is ready."

The other priestess drew a slender knife made of silver from a pouch. The blade was decorated with serpents holding suns in their mouths. The handle was made of bone and was old and worn and yellow with age.

Skylan watched as the woman rested the knife's sharp point against the skin of his right forearm. He watched the knife pierce his flesh, watched the red blood well up from the wound. He watched the trail of blood follow the sharp blade of the knife down his arm to form a crude S-like shape that reminded him of the snakes the women wore on their arms. He watched. He knew he should do something to stop this, his brain raged at him to fight, but he was under the thrall of this strange lassitude.

The priestess dropped the bloody knife in the grass and began to spread apart the lips of the fresh wound. The other priestess poured the squid ink laced with the crystals into the fresh wound and then began to grind them deep into his flesh.

The pain was excruciating. Skylan cried out in wrenching agony and fought to get away. He didn't move. His body persisted in just sitting there, watching.

Her work with the crystals finished, the priestess wound a bandage tightly over the wound. Skylan watched the blood mingled with dark ink seep through the bandage.

"Do not take off the wrapping for several days," said the priestess with the crystals.

Rising to her feet, she moved on to young Farinn, who had been observing Skylan with a look of horror on his face. When the priestess lifted Farinn's arm, he flinched. He did nothing else. He sat on the ground and watched them put the tip of the knife against his flesh.

Skylan was outraged. The sight of them hurting Farinn pierced him worse than the blade of the knife. Skylan had grown to like the quiet young man, who sometimes sang to himself very softly when he thought no one heard him. In his mind, Skylan was leaping to his feet and attacking the priestess, twisting her wrist to make her drop the blade, breaking her arm if he had to. He sat and watched them slice open Farinn's arm, watched the blood flow, watched the young man shiver in pain, and, to his shame, he did nothing.

Skylan was suddenly reminded of the terrible time back in his homeland when the ogre shaman had cast a magic spell on him, freezing his limbs, preventing him from fighting.

"Bad magic," Wulfe had warned him.

Skylan shuddered and even that seemed to take an immense amount of effort.

When the priestesses finished their work, they emptied their bowls and packed up their silver knives and their squid ink and crystal vials.

"We will go back to the carriages and wait for you there," one said. "What do we do with the woman?"

They were talking about Aylaen, who had been watching the proceedings with a bewildered expression on her face.

"She stays here," said Zahakis. "To begin her training."

Raegar scowled. "I will speak to the Priest-General about this. He will not be pleased."

Zahakis shrugged. The priestesses who had been holding Aylaen released her. She hurried to join the warriors. The men sat on the ground, staring listlessly at nothing. Aylaen eyed them helplessly, not knowing what was wrong, uncertain what to do. The priestesses departed.

Raegar remained, waiting impatiently for the return of the warrior-priests he had sent off in pursuit of Wulfe.

"You and your soldiers can leave now," Raegar told Zahakis with a dismissive gesture. "Your swords are no longer needed. The Torgun are not a threat."

"I have orders from the Legate to escort you and your people off the premises," said Zahakis.

Raegar scowled and drew in a seething breath, but he made no argument. Skylan wondered what Raegar meant about them no longer being a threat. For himself, he planned to be a threat to Raegar so long as the traitor drew breath.

"You're never going to find the kid in the dark," Zahakis added caustically. "Call off the chase."

"I will not have that fiend running around loose," said Raegar. "You and your men can leave, go to your beds. As I told you, you are not needed."

Zahakis shook his head and remained where he was, keeping his soldiers on the alert.

Skylan's wound throbbed and burned and stung. The bandage was too tight. He decided to take it off and he was surprised and gratified to see his hand obey his brain's command. He was fumbling at the strip of the cloth, trying to find the end to start unwinding it, when he heard a shrill screeching.

The two warrior-priests had hold of Wulfe. The boy squirmed and twisted and kicked wildly. Looking very grim, the two men dragged the boy back to where Raegar was standing.

"What do we do with the little turd?" one asked.

"Take him to the Temple," said Raegar.

Wulfe cried out in terror and struggled frantically to escape.

Skylan rose to his feet. The strange and frightening lethargy appeared to be wearing off. "You're not taking him anywhere, Raegar. The boy stays with me."

He started to take a step toward the warrior-priests who had hold of Wulfe. Pain shot through Skylan's right arm. He gasped and stifled a groan.

Raegar continued to issue orders. "Take the boy to the enclave.

Lock him in the special prison cells where we keep his kind. I will attend to his purging tomorrow—"

Wulfe twisted about and sank his teeth into the priest's arm. The priest gave a cry and let go his hold. Wulfe squirmed out of the other guard's grip and ran to Skylan.

"Don't let him take me," Wulfe cried. "He's going to murder me!"

"Fetch him," said Raegar, glowering at the priests.

Skylan put his arm protectively around Wulfe. "He stays with me—"

The pain was like nothing Skylan had ever experienced, as if he'd thrust his arm into a kettle of bubbling, red-hot, molten iron. He doubled over, clutching his arm and moaning.

The other Torgun watched in uneasy silence, not sure what was happening.

"Thus does Aelon punish those who defy him," said Raegar. He gestured. "Take the boy."

Wulfe gave a howl. Skylan could do nothing to help him. He felt as though his arm were being burned off. Aylaen took hold of Wulfe and wrapped her arms around him.

"You can leave him with me, Raegar," she said. "I will be responsible for him."

Raegar hesitated, not quite certain how to handle this situation. He did not want to offend Aylaen, but he did want the boy.

"You do not understand, my dear," he said at last. "I am taking him to the Temple because he puts all of us in danger. I am doing this for your own good. He is a child of the fae. He is a danger to everyone, including yourself."

"He is a boy, Raegar," said Aylaen, and her voice was tinged with scorn. "He will be safe with me."

"You are blinded by ignorance, Aylaen, and therefore Aelon forgives you for your defiance," Raegar said. "I don't want to have to harm you—"

"Enough!" said Zahakis. His face grim, he walked over to Aylaen, seized hold of Wulfe, and wrenched him from her grasp. When Aylaen started to protest, two of the soldiers drew their swords. She stood by helplessly as the warrior-priests walked off, dragging Wulfe with them.

Wulfe twisted around to look over his shoulder. "Skylan, don't let them take me! He's going to kill me!"

"Torval," Skylan prayed grimly, "I need your help."

Zahakis was standing directly in front of Skylan, his back turned. Zahakis was weary, or he would have never made such a mistake. Skylan's right arm still burned like it was on fire. Using his left hand, Skylan reached for the Tribune's sword.

It seemed to Skylan as if every bone in his right arm shattered. He could no longer feel his hand. Nausea wrung him. He fell to his knees, retching.

Zahakis bent down.

"I'm going to give you some advice, young man," Zahakis said softly. "Quit fighting. You cannot win."

"Would you?" Skylan demanded hoarsely. His face was bathed in sweat.

"Yes. Because I am a man of sense. You might even grow to like it here," Zahakis added. "You and your people will fight in the Para Dix, which means you will be treated far better than most slaves. You might earn your freedom—"

"Rot in hell," Skylan said through gritted teeth.

Zahakis shrugged and walked off, motioning his soldiers to come with him.

The priests hauled Wulfe to the carriages. The boy had gone limp in their grasp and Skylan wondered if he'd passed out from fear. Raegar cast a lingering look at Aylaen, who turned away. Raegar went back to the carriages. He would not permit Wulfe to be taken into the carriage, but ordered the priests to walk back to the Temple. The carriages rolled off, the soldiers walking on either side. The priests with Wulfe between them trailed behind.

The pain in Skylan's arm eased. Aelon had decided he'd been punished enough apparently. Skylan walked on shaking legs toward the *Venjekar,* which remained on the wheeled conveyance. He felt the eyes of his friends on him. Bjorn said something to him, but Skylan ignored him.

He had spoken defiantly to Zahakis, but now Skylan wondered: What good was defiance? What good was courage? There was no escape. No way home. Even his proud ship was a prisoner, bereft of the Dragon Kahg whose spirit sent it skimming over the waves. Skylan rested his hand lovingly on the hull of his broken ship, and he bowed his head and felt tears trickle hot onto his cheeks.

I am scared, Skylan admitted.

He had not felt fear like this, not even standing in the shield wall facing ogres, outnumbered two-to-one. He had fought giants and their bone-smashing stones and he had not known fear like this—gut-wrenching, bowel-shredding terror.

He was a slave with no control over his fate. If Acronis decided to starve him, Skylan would starve. If Acronis decided to whip him, Skylan would die under the lash. Raegar was probably going to kill Wulfe, and Skylan was helpless to protect the boy he had come to love.

I failed Wulfe, like I failed so many people—my father, Draya, Garn. I failed Aylaen. I failed Torval and my gods.

Skylan looked back at the mistakes he had made—mistakes that had led him and his people to this place—and he wished with all his soul that he could live his life over again. His arm burned and throbbed, but the pain in the limb was nothing to the pain in his heart. If his father, Norgaard, had been there, Skylan would have sunk to his knees and sobbed like a child.

"How is my fish knife?" said a voice.

Skylan raised his head and saw Torval standing over him. The god carried a cracked shield. His battle axe was notched, his helm dented. His clothes were torn, his face bruised and battered. His eyes were bright and glittered like a steel blade beneath a winter sun.

Skylan burned with shame.

"Do not look at me, Lord," he said. "I cannot bear for you to see me like this. I have failed you."

"No," said Torval, after a moment's brooding silence. "It is we gods who have failed you."

"No, Lord! Never!" Skylan said, shocked.

Torval gave a weary smile. "Well, well. We won't argue over it."

"How goes the battle in heaven, Lord?" Skylan asked, profoundly respectful.

Torval shrugged. "About as well as it goes for you here on the ground. Still, so long as you keep fighting, so will we."

"Fight," Skylan said bitterly. "How can I fight when their foul god, Aelon, has cut off my sword arm?"

"Gods may control the spinning of the wheel," said Torval. "But the thread the wheel spins is your own."

A slow and steady rain began to fall. The soldiers who had been left behind to guard the prisoners sat some distance away, huddled over a fire that sputtered in the rain.

Skylan pulled himself up and over the hull, onto the deck of his broken ship. The dragonhead prow lay on the deck, empty eyes staring into the rain. Finding a blanket, Skylan spread it out and lay down.

The cold rain drummed on his head, soaking the blanket so that it was worse than useless. Then he heard the sounds of other footfalls on the deck. He heard voices—Erdmun complaining about the rain and whining that his arm hurt, Bjorn telling his brother to shut up. He heard Sigurd gruffly order Aylaen down into the hold where it was dry. He heard Aylaen say defiantly, "I will sleep on the deck with the rest of you."

The tents the soldiers had erected for the slaves would provide shelter from the storm. The Torgun made their beds on their ship.

Skylan smiled in the rain-soaked darkness.

What good was courage? What good defiance?

Maybe no good at all. Maybe we will die slaves with tattoos burned into our flesh. Maybe we will be captives of Aelon until death frees us.

Until that time, we will sleep on our ship.

The Temple of the New Dawn was located at the entrance to the enclave housing the Church of the New Dawn. The Temple was not to be confused with the Shrine of Aelon. The Temple was open to the public. The Shrine was not. The Temple had been built some forty years ago by an ambitious Priest-General, a man named Saat-sakis.

The Temple was a beautiful structure, simple and elegant, open to the air, admitting the light of the sun by day and the light of the moon and stars by night. The building was constructed entirely of white marble striated with black. One could enter from any direction, ascending broad marble stairs and passing through the columned portico to the shaded interior.

In the center of the Temple stood an enormous statue of Aelon. Carved out of marble, the statue portrayed the god as a youthful, vigorous man, clad in golden armor. Aelon held a flame in one hand and a sword in the other. At his feet a dragon lay dying, pierced by the god's sword. The flame that burned in Aelon's marble hand had been miraculously kindled, brought to life by the prayers of the Priest-General on the day the Temple had been consecrated. The flame had never died.

The Temple was crowded, day and night, with supplicants bringing gifts and asking for Aelon's blessing. Aelon's priests maintained that the god was generous with his largesse, but then they would always hint that it was wise to give if one expected to receive. The priests transported gifts from the altar to their storehouses.

The wealth of the Church was divided up, much going to operating costs and maintaining the buildings, supporting the priests and priestesses of Aelon, and charitable works.

The mendicant priests and priestesses of Aelon worked among the poor. The warrior-priests of Aelon were the highest in rank and most respected. They maintained security and order and confidently and secretly looked forward to the day when the Church would supplant the Imperial family and rule Oran.

Many people did not know this, but the New Dawn was represented by a pantheon of gods. In the Temple were statues to the lesser gods, who had come to this world with Aelon. These were much smaller and, over time, they had been shoved off to one side, stashed in out-of-the way niches or backed into corners. Few people, even in the Church, could tell you the names of all the gods of the New Dawn.

Treia stood in the Temple of Torval's enemy, Aelon, gazing up at the youthful, handsome face of the god, which was, to her weak eyes, a white marble blur. She could see the dragon lying dead beneath his feet much more clearly, and she was reminded of the wooden statue of Vindrash that had split into two pieces in the poor and shabby little temple honoring the goddess. She looked again at the huge face of the god and saw him bold, strong, confident, powerful. He reminded her of Raegar, and she smiled.

Raegar had told her about Aelon, describing the god as ambitious, determined to allow nothing to stand in the way of achieving his goal, which was to rule all of creation. Treia could understand and admire such a god, but not worship. Treia had not yet met the god she could worship.

Raegar had talked about Sinaria, and Treia had eagerly looked forward to seeing its wonders. When the *Light of the Sea* had finally docked, Raegar had told Treia he was to be part of the triumphant parade. He had handed her over to the Temple guards (low-ranking warrior-priests). They had assisted her into something Raegar termed a "sedan chair"—a chair mounted on sturdy poles carried on the shoulders of slaves.

Treia was alarmed at riding in such a conveyance, but Raegar assured her it was perfectly safe. She sat stiff and tense inside the vehicle, terrified of moving lest the slaves should drop her. After a time, she relaxed enough to take a peep out of the silken curtains that guarded her privacy. She was excited by the vast number of people. She noticed the stench, but she had smelled worse during her years tending the sick. She found the city enthralling.

Raegar had ordered the guards to take Treia to a private room in the Temple, where she was provided with food and refreshment. She was to remain there until he came to fetch her. She did not find the wait tedious. She strolled through the beautiful gardens, watching the people come and go, gazing in wonder at the clothing worn by the women—which consisted of long, loose-fitting gowns attached at intervals along the shoulders with pins of gold. Over the under-gown some of the women wore a plain woolen gown held at the shoulder by two straps, which Treia would later discover meant the woman was married. Some wealthy women wore cloaks over this, draped gracefully over their arms.

She wandered from room to room. In one, scribes sat at desks, copying the teachings of Aelon onto papyrus scrolls. Treia had no idea what they were doing and was not interested enough to ask.

Raegar was in an ill humor when he finally returned to her, meeting her in the Temple's private room. After his triumphant return from a perilous voyage, he had expected the Empress to invite him to dine. She had invited the Legate Acronis and the Priest-General, but she had not chosen to include Raegar.

"Someday she will take notice of me," he raved. "My time is coming."

Treia blinked, confused. "What do you mean by that, my love?"

Raegar shook his head. "All your questions will be answered tomorrow, my dear. You are tired and I have work yet to do this night. I will take you to your sleeping quarters."

Treia was disappointed. She had been alone all day and she had looked forward to spending time with her lover. He led her from the Temple into the enclave, which was walled off, closed to the public. The gates were guarded by Temple guards in segmented armor similar to that worn by the Legate's soldiers. Their helms were different, lacking the cheek flaps, and they wore short caplets adorned with serpents and suns. The guards saluted Raegar, who gravely returned their salute.

Inside the wall, she could no longer hear the noise or smell the stench of the city. All was quiet. Priests and priestesses walked paths of crushed stone that connected the various buildings to each other. They sometimes spoke quiet greetings to Raegar, but for the most

part people went about their business in silence. The sunlight reflected from the top of the shrine of Aelon caused it to seem to glow
with holy radiance.

"What work do you have to do?" Treia asked.

"Aelon wants me to bring his light to our benighted people," said
Raegar. "The Priest-General believes these men are a danger. He
spoke to the Empress about putting them to death, saying it was
Aelon's will. Legate Acronis had already talked to her of fighting
them in the Para Dix. She refused to heed the Priest-General's advice.
He needs the means to control them."

Raegar described the tattoos, the crushed gemstones that were
mixed with the ink and then ground into the arms of the Torgun
warriors. "The gemstones embedded in the flesh allow the god to
communicate his thoughts to his priestesses. They, in turn, can
speak directly to the god. They are most blessed!"

"And Aelon intends to do this with Skylan and Sigurd?" Treia
asked. She almost laughed, but then realized Raegar might be offended.

"Of course not," Raegar assured her. "As if they would be so
honored!"

Treia noted that some of the priestesses smiled at Raegar, and she
wound her hands around Raegar's arm, walking closer to him. She
saw, too, that some of the women were staring at her strange clothes
and whispering and giggling.

"I am sorry Aylaen has to undergo such pain and humiliation,"
Treia said, "but the discipline will be good for her."

"You need not worry, my dear. Aylaen will be spared," said Raegar. "Despite the fact that the Legate has insisted on retaining her as
his slave, I have hopes that she will yet come to us."

A certain tone in his voice caused Treia to cast him a sharp glance.
"What you mean is that you hope Aylaen will come to *you*," she said
coldly. She withdrew her hands from his arm.

"I am certain we both hope she will stand in Aelon's blessed
light," said Raegar in reproving tones.

"You don't deny it," said Treia, overcome by jealousy. "You are in
love with her!"

"I love you, Treia," said Raegar, and he stopped in the middle of
the path to take hold of both her hands, bringing them to his lips. "I

want you for my wife. As for Aylaen, she is your sister. I care for her as for family."

Treia didn't believe him. Even with her weak eyes, she could see his admiration for Aylaen. All her life, Treia had been jealous of her sister, who was not only more beautiful, but whose life had been far easier than Treia's. That Aylaen, already so fortunate, should have now attracted Raegar's regard and affection was more than Treia could bear.

"I am sorry to have to tell you this, my love," said Treia coolly. "I love you so much. But I know that Aylaen does not have the slightest regard for you. In truth, I have heard her say many times how much she despises you."

Raegar frowned. "Perhaps I can find a way to change her opinion."

"Tell me about our sleeping quarters," Treia said, changing the subject. "I hope you will not be out late tonight. It has been far too long since we lay together."

She hoped to win a smile from him. Instead, he shook his head and quickened his pace.

"You will be given a room in the nunnery. Aelon permits only married couples to spend the night together."

Treia was not pleased. She could have pointed out to Raegar that his god had not objected to them making love aboard the galley, but she did not want to further annoy him. She waited for him to say something to the effect that this separation was only temporary, that soon they would be together forever as husband and wife. But Raegar went on to extol the beauty of the Temple grounds, pointing out various buildings as they walked together.

Treia smiled outwardly; inwardly she gnashed her teeth.

At last they came to the building he termed the "nunnery," a large stone structure that reminded Treia of the buildings where the Vindrasi housed their cattle during the winter. He gave her into the care of a sharp-eyed, dark-haired woman known as the Priestess-Mother, who looked askance at Treia's foreign attire and did not seem to know what to do with her.

The Priestess-Mother and Raegar held a whispered consultation. Treia stood off to one side, feeling her face burn when three young novices, passing by on their way to evening prayers, stopped to stare at her.

The Priestess-Mother sent two of them away with a sharp word. She ordered the third to take Treia to her room.

Treia looked pleadingly at Raegar. "Must you leave me?"

"You know what I have to do. I will meet you tomorrow after morning prayers," he said curtly.

He walked off, going to the Torgun, going to see her sister.

Treia's cell was one in a row of cells. The room was small and furnished with a bed, a desk, a chair, and a chamber pot. A small window cut into the stone wall near to the ceiling let in light and fresh air. Treia had no candle. The light shining from the dome of the Shrine of Aelon was so bright she did not need one.

The novice gave her a loose-fitting gown in which to sleep and waited for Treia to undress. The novice took away her clothes, telling her she would bring her suitable clothing in the morning. Treia wanted to keep the brooches pinned to her apron dress. The brooches were gold and part of her dowry.

"No personal possessions," the novice said. "Everything belongs to the god."

Treia let the brooches go without a murmur. She would have continued to wear her undergarments, but the novice insisted on taking those as well, saying in disparaging tones that they were likely crawling with vermin and would have to be burned.

Treia was offended and insulted, for she judged by the smell that she bathed far more often than did this young woman. Treia held her tongue, fearing that if she said anything to offend the priestess, Raegar would hear of it and be angry with her.

The novice finally left, saying that Treia would be expected to wake when she heard the morning bells calling her to worship. Treia had nothing else to do, and even though the sun was just starting to set, she lay down on the bed. She was tired, but she could not sleep. The light from the dome glared through her eyelids. Having spent weeks aboard ship, she had the strange and sickening impression that her bed was heaving up and down.

She lay in bed, thinking about Aylaen, about Raegar.

She rolled over, miserable. She woke to the sound of bells.

———

The Priestess-Mother herself brought Treia a gown such as she had seen the other women wearing and a cloak. To Treia's surprise, the Priestess-Mother, who had been cold and insulting last night, was warm and ingratiating this morning. Treia belted the thin woolen gown around her waist as she was instructed and draped the cloak over her shoulders, wrapping the cloth around one arm.

Accustomed to wearing several layers of clothing for warmth, Treia felt half-dressed as she joined the other women who were going to morning prayers.

The Priestess-Mother took Treia by the arm, acting as her personal escort to the Shrine of Aelon. The sun was yet only a pink glimmer in the sky.

Treia had thought they would be returning to the Temple, but the Priestess-Mother informed her that the Temple was where the "children" of Aelon worshipped.

"The common people, Sister," she explained in response to Treia's questioning look. The Priestess-Mother sniffed. "Those of us who have dedicated our lives to Aelon are privileged to come together for his worship in the Shrine of Aelon, a most holy place. No one is permitted inside except his faithful servants."

The Priestess-Mother smiled. "Raegar tells me that you have been converted to the true faith, that you have given your heart and soul to Aelon."

"I have, Priestess-Mother," said Treia.

The Priest-Mother cast her a shrewd glance. "Aelon can see into your heart, Sister. If you are lying, he will not permit you to enter this holy place."

"How would the god stop me?" Treia asked uneasily.

"If anyone who does not believe in Aelon dare to enter his shrine, a mighty wind will lift the heretic up to the heavens, that he may see the face of the god and tremble."

"And if this person persists in his unbelief?" Treia asked.

"Death is the fate of the unbeliever," said the Priestess-Mother sternly.

They followed winding paths across the grassy slopes. The paths were thronged. Everyone from the youngest novice to the eldest priest was required to attend morning prayers.

The Shrine was the strangest building Treia had ever seen. The large structure was built of brick and it was round in shape, looking like a kettle turned upside down. The top of the dome was covered in gold and gleamed brightly, making the sun goddess, Aylis, who was just rising, seem dull and shabby by contrast.

The Priestess-Mother said she was needed inside for the ceremonies and hurried off, leaving Treia alone to stare at the arched entryway of the domed Shrine. Treia could just barely make out carved symbols of the suns, held in the mouths of serpents. She recalled the Priestess-Mother's words.

Death is the fate of the unbeliever.

Treia considered what to do. She was not a convert to Aelon. She thought well of him, but she did not put her faith in him or in any other god. She had given her heart to Raegar, but her soul was her own.

That said, Treia saw no reason to fear Aelon. To her way of thinking, the God of the New Light expended a lot of time and effort to bring her here. He must have a reason.

Aelon would be nice to her.

Treia walked confidently through the door of Aelon's shrine.

The god did not disturb a hair on her head.

5

Treia gazed about the Shrine. A large hole in the roof, like an eye, stared down at the people crowded inside. The Priest-General conducted the service, which was extremely long. He stood on a spiral wooden staircase that placed him above the heads of the crowd so that everyone could see and hear him. His voice was loud and carrying. His exhortations roared through the building, his voice reverberating off the stone wall and rumbling down like thunder from the ceiling. The worshippers around her paid close attention and would often raise their voices in glad shouts.

Treia asked someone if they knew where she might find Warrior-Priest Raegar and was told he was near the altar, which was at the front of the hall. The warrior-priests served as honor guards to the Priest-General. Treia was in the back, near the door, wedged in among a flock of novices.

Her head began to ache from the noise and the heat of all these bodies packed together. She stopped listening to the sermon and thought about her sister.

Aylaen, always Aylaen! Beautiful, free-spirited, temper-blazing Aylaen. Not Treia the weak-eyed, Treia the dried-up virgin, Treia the homely.

Before Raegar had come into Treia's life, no man had ever loved her. No man had so much as looked at her. The thought of losing Raegar filled her with dread. She could not bear life without him. She had to think of some way to make him keep loving her. Some way to make him give up his desire for Aylaen.

Treia looked up at the eye in the ceiling staring down on those below. Aelon had permitted her to enter his sacred shrine. He needed her. Well, now she needed him.

She fixed her eye upon his eye and waited. As if in answer, the words of the Priest-General rang clear, as if he were speaking directly to her.

"None of the other gods, certainly not the gods of Raj or the worn-out gods of the Vindrasi, have the power of bringing the dead back to life," said the Priest-General. "Only Aelon!"

"Praise to Aelon!" cried the worshippers.

Raise the dead, Treia repeated to herself. She smiled. If that was truly possible, her problem with Aylaen was solved.

After what seemed an eon, the service ended. The faithful filed out, their faces glowing, basking in the light that shone on them from above. Treia kept near the entrance. Time passed and Raegar did not come. Eventually she was the only person in the building, which seemed immense now that it was empty.

At last, she saw Raegar come striding across the floor toward her, tall and imposing and handsome in his priestly robes. His bald head gleamed in the light; his eyes glistened with excitement.

"My love!" he said, and he greeted Treia with a kiss on the cheek and took her by the arm.

"What happened last night?" Treia asked. "With Skylan and the others. The tattoos of Aelon," she added, seeing Raegar looking blank.

"Oh, that." He snorted and made a dismissive gesture. "Skylan tried to fight the god's will, of course. He paid dearly for his rebellion. Over time, he will learn. Or the god will kill him," he added with satisfaction.

"What of Aylaen?" Treia asked.

"She tried to defend that daemon spawn, Wulfe, but gave up in the end when she witnessed Aelon's power. As for the boy, my priests took him into custody. I have not received their reports this morning, but presumably the boy is being held in a prison cell especially designed to resist the foul magicks of the fae. I will deal with him later today, after our meeting with the Priest-General."

Treia forgot about Wulfe and Aylaen. "We are meeting with the Priest-General?" she asked, as shocked as if he had said they had been invited to meet with Aelon himself.

"The Priest-General does us both a great honor," said Raegar.

Treia looked up at the eye as she walked beneath the hole in the domed ceiling. The light shone steadily and she was reassured.

They walked past the altar, which was probably beautiful. She had no idea. She was too nervous to pay heed to it. Behind the altar, double doors made of bronze on which was engraved the winged serpents led to the offices of the Priest-General. Two Temple guards stood in front of this door. Other guards ranged along either side. At Raegar's approach, the two guards crossed their spears to block his entrance.

"The Priest-General is expecting me," said Raegar.

One of the guards told them curtly to remain where they were and entered. Another guard immediately took his place. Treia had her hand upon Raegar's arm and she could feel him trembling with excited anticipation. She trembled, too, but not with anticipation.

The guard returned and told Raegar they could enter. He and his fellow stepped aside. Treia expected some magnificent chamber to lay beyond it. Instead, they entered a long and shadowy passageway lined with rooms, at the end of which was another set of double doors, these made of steel.

Treia looked curiously at the rooms as they passed. Inside one, priests sat upon tall stools writing on wax tablets or scrolls of papyrus. In another, several priests sat cross-legged on the floor. In front of each was a large silver bowl, plain and elegant, filled with water. Each priest concentrated fixedly on his bowl. Occasionally a gout of flame would rise up from the water, and when this happened, the priest leaned closer; he seemed to be listening.

"Those are the Watchers," said Raegar. "Any priest of Aelon anywhere in the world may send a message through fire and water to the Watchers, who will send it on to its destination."

As he spoke, one of the Watchers rose to his feet and glided silently over to a priest who sat in a chair in the center of the room. He spoke something in the priest's ear. He listened, ruminated, then nodded. The Watcher returned to the bowl and began to speak. The gout of flame wavered and danced as his breath touched it.

"Have you done this?" Treia asked in a whisper.

"Of course," said Raegar. "How do you think the Legate knew where to find the *Venjekar*?"

Treia was impressed, even awed. She began to think more highly of this god, Aelon, who could perform such wonders.

They continued on and eventually reached the set of steel doors at the end of the passage. These were not as imposing as the bronze doors, being plain and unadorned. A warrior-priest stood in front, not Temple guards. The warrior-priest raised his hand in formal greeting.

"Aelon is pleased. You may enter," he said.

"Aelon himself guards this door," said Raegar. "Inside is the treasure vault. The priests must pray to the god for access."

The vault was vast and resplendent with light that shone from a ball of fire hanging suspended from the ceiling, as if Aelon had captured the sun and tethered it to the roof. The light gleamed off gold and shone on silver and sparkled in the myriad jewels with a brilliance that hurt the eye. Treia was dazzled. Beautiful, valuable objects were jumbled together, piled on tables or stacked on the floor or spilling out of wooden chests. Statues (some life-size), chalices, bowls, necklaces, rings, belts, arm bands, coins, and more—all made of precious metals, many encrusted with gems—filled the room.

"Here you see proof of Aelon's greatness," said Raegar with a proud gesture.

Raegar was watching her eagerly, waiting for her reaction. Treia would not disappoint him. She knew what to say. She had known what to say all those years kneeling on the wood plank floor, bruising her kneecaps, chanting prayers to a block of wood carved into the shape of a dragon goddess.

"Blessed is Aelon and those who worship him."

"Well said, Sister."

A man entered the room through the steel doors. At his command, the doors closed behind him.

"Priest-General Xydis," Raegar said, "this is the woman of whom I have spoken. Treia Adalbrand, Bone Priestess of the Vindrasi."

"Your servant, Worshipful Sir," said Treia, having been told in advance the proper form of address. She bowed low.

Zyprexa Xydis was short and well-built, with muscular arms and a thick neck and body, appearing as strong and enduring as boulder, as if the waves of life might crash into him and never wear him down.

His complexion was swarthy, his shaved head covered with tattoos and with jewels embedded in the skin. His face was clean-shaven. The blue shadow of his beard outlined his jutting, squared-off jaw. His eyes were dark and keen.

Xydis stood straight as a spear shaft and wore an air of command; he had been a soldier before he became a warrior-priest. He wore a purple robe, the border trimmed in gold. He radiated power like the sun radiates heat, and Treia could feel Raegar tense and quiver in the man's presence.

Xydis studied her for long moments without speaking, shrewdly taking her measure. She met his gaze, refusing to quail before him, enduring his scrutiny with cool aplomb. He liked this, apparently, for he gave her an approving smile.

"Raegar said you were a remarkable woman," said Xydis in his deep, booming voice. "He was right. Come with me."

He walked off, moving rapidly. Treia was startled and a little alarmed by his abruptness. Xydis was a man of few words. He found mindless "palaverings," as he termed them, annoying and had been known to rudely cut short the vague ramblings of the Empress. He was blunt and pugnacious, preferring action to talk.

The Priest-General led the way through the fabulous clutter to a wooden table near the back of the vault. He stood in front of the table and, clasping his hands behind him and rocking forward on his feet, he gestured with his head and regarded her expectantly.

"Well, what do you think, Bone Priestess?"

The table held two objects. The gleam of gold came from one, but, with her weak eyesight, Treia could not make out precisely what she was looking at. The other was plainer, simpler.

"I must . . . look more closely, Worshipful Sir," Treia murmured apologetically. "My eyes . . ."

He nodded and stepped aside, crowding near her, dividing his gaze between her and the prizes. Raegar remained standing behind, looming over her.

Treia looked first at the object of gleaming gold and her heart stopped beating. She knew immediately what it was. She pretended she did not, however, for her mind was in turmoil. She must have betrayed her emotions, however, for she was acutely aware that Xydis's eyes narrowed. To cover her confusion and to give herself time to think, she concentrated on the other object.

"This is a spiritbone, the bone of a dragon," she said.

"So Raegar told us," said Xydis. "He said you are a Bone Priest-ess. Can you summon this dragon?"

"I know the ritual to summon the dragon," said Treia cautiously, not wanting to commit herself.

"Could this ritual be taught to another?" Xydis asked. "Suppose, for example, I wanted to summon this dragon myself. Could you teach the ritual to me?"

"I could," Treia said. "The ritual is not difficult to learn. But that does not mean you could use it to call the dragon, Worshipful Sir. The summoning is a pact made between the dragon and the sum-moner and the Goddess Vindrash. Even then, the dragon has free will. The beast must want to answer."

Xydis picked up the spiritbone, the plain one. The bone seemed to nestle in his hand.

"This dragon will answer," he said. "This dragon came to us of her own accord."

Treia stared, astonished. "This dragon is a follower of Aelon?"

"She is fond of jewels, it seems," said Xydis dryly.

Treia thought of the Dragon Kahg arrogant and smug and self-satisfied like all of his kind, considering themselves so superior. It seemed dragons were susceptible to what they would term human weaknesses.

"I could teach you the ritual, Worshipful Sir," said Treia. "Or the dragon could teach you herself."

"Excellent," said Xydis. He watched her closely and said softly, his gaze going to the other spiritbone, the one adorned with gold, "What about this one? Tell me about it."

Xydis had brought her here to see this, Treia realized. He already knew about the other spiritbone. He needed only her confirmation that it would prove useful. This was the prize.

Treia's mouth went dry, and her lips felt brittle and rough. She moistened them with her tongue and wondered desperately what to do, what to say. She was tempted to pass this off as nothing, merely a spiritbone adorned with gold. She glanced at Xydis and saw that he knew this object was extraordinary, that there was something special about it.

"Where did you get this?" she asked.

"Never mind—" Raegar said impatiently.

Xydis frowned at Raegar, who flushed, chastened, and kept quiet.

"Is it valuable?" Xydis asked, not answering.

"Oh, yes," said Treia, her voice tight.

"It is the bone of a dragon—"

"Not an ordinary dragon," Treia interjected. She felt smothered, unable to draw enough air into her lungs. "This is the spiritbone of one of the Vektan Five."

Raegar sucked in an astonished breath.

Xydis looked from one to the other and he frowned. "What does that mean?"

Treia marveled at the beautiful object. Golden bands twined around the bone like the tail of a dragon. Golden wings spread from the bone with a golden chain attached to the tips of each of the wings. The head of the dragon reared up from the bone. The largest emeralds Treia had ever seen adorned the spiritbone, placed above the head. Two smaller emeralds were embedded in the wings.

"How did you come by this, Worshipful Sir?" she asked again.

"The bone was a gift from one of your gods," Xydis replied.

Treia nodded. She was not surprised.

"Was it Hevis?" Treia asked, naming a god known to be rebellious, one who chafed under Torval's rule. One who had, long ago, seduced a Kai Priestess into summoning one of the Vektan Five—with disastrous results.

"I believe the name of the god was Sund," said Xydis, offhanded. The names of gods slated for destruction didn't much matter to him. "It seems this god, Sund, looked into the future and saw that Aelon would be victorious. Sund feared his own destruction and he traded the spiritbone for survival."

Sund, the God of Logic, of rational thought, of far-sight. If Sund had switched sides, he must have seen the old gods were doomed. Treia was not surprised at Sund's betrayal. The gods of the Vindrasi were known to be self-serving, caring only for their own pleasures and concerns, little for the mortals they ruled.

"Tell me what is so extraordinary about this dragon," Xydis said.

Raegar hastened to answer. He was excited, beaming and rubbing his hands. "The Vektia dragon is an immensely powerful dragon, Priest-General. Such a dragon can set entire cities aflame with a single breath."

Xydis looked at Treia, leaned toward her, drew nearer, talking to her as if this was confidential between the two of them.

"Does Raegar speak the truth, Sister?"

"Yes," said Treia.

"But there is more to this dragon than the ability to burn cities, isn't there? You are a Bone Priestess. You tell me about this dragon."

Treia hesitated. Not because she was wondering which side to take. She was as coldly calculating as Sund, and though her vision might be blurred, she could see the battle was going poorly for the old gods. Like Sund, she planned to be on the winning side. Treia hesitated because she was trying to figure out how much to reveal.

Treia had been expecting Xydis to ask her to summon an ordinary dragon, such as the Dragon Kahg. Instead, Xydis was going to want her to summon one of the Vektan Five! This was the reason Aelon needed her. Treia had to figure out how to take advantage of this unbelievable opportunity to further her own ambition. And Raegar's, of course.

"The Vektan Five are not ordinary dragons. They are made of the crest of the dragon, Ilyrion, the Creator of the World. Her essence is embodied in these five dragons."

Treia paused, waiting for Xydis's reaction to her words. He gave a perceptible start. His brows raised. His eyes widened.

"You are saying that these dragons are made of the essence of the Creator. These dragons are . . ." He stopped, thunderstruck, and stared at Treia.

"The Vektan dragons are not true dragons. They merely take the form of dragons. They were born of creation," said Treia. "They are the embodiment of creation. Whoever controls the Five gains the power to create whatever he wants—life, moons, stars, suns . . ."

Raegar was not impressed. "What does Aelon need with a dragon for that? He is all powerful."

"No," said Treia, "he is not."

"You speak heresy—" Raegar began, his face red.

"Oh, shut up, Raegar," said Xydis impatiently. "Proceed, Bone Priestess."

"One day Aelon will be worshipped by every person on this world," Treia said. "But even then, Aelon will never be the true ruler of this world. The old gods, the Gods of Vindrasi, will always rule."

"These old gods are too weak to rule a dunghill!" said Xydis, scoffing.

Treia shook her head. "You may weaken them. You might even

manage to slay them, as you did the Goddess Desiria. But the old gods can never be destroyed so long as they still control the Vektan dragons—the power of creation."

"Aelon is all powerful!" Raegar repeated angrily. He looked to Xydis for confirmation, and when Xydis did not respond, Raegar faltered. "Isn't he?"

Xydis remained silent.

He knows the truth, thought Treia. He doesn't want to admit it. The truth is that these wandering gods such as Aelon and the Gods of Raj are trying to take over this world because they lack the power to create worlds of their own.

Xydis took out his frustration on Raegar. "You should have told me this bone was of such immense value!"

"I did not know, Priest-General," Raegar said.

"He could not have known, Worshipful Sir," said Treia, coming to her lover's defense. "Not many of the Vindrasi know the truth about the Vektan dragons. One person knows the secret to the ritual used to summon the dragons into being. That person is the Kai Priestess. She keeps her secret until she passes it on to her successor when she is on her deathbed. At that time, she tells the new Kai Priestess the ritual."

Xydis regarded her intently. "Where is this Kai Priestess now?"

"She is dead, Worshipful Sir. She died before she could tell anyone the secret of the ritual."

Xydis eyed her shrewdly. "Then how do *you* know so much about the Vektan dragons?"

"Draya talked to the Goddess Vindrash," said Treia. "They had a very close relationship. She took all her problems to the goddess, talked to her incessantly. And I was there with her, a novice, for servant."

Treia did not conceal the bitterness in her voice. Even after all these years, she remembered the bone-numbing cold, the mind-numbing boredom.

"I was forced to wait on the Kai Priestess, forced to listen to her discussions. I had to kneel beside her on the floor, shivering, my knees bruised and aching. I heard everything she said. She talked often of the Vektan Five; of the great dragon, Ilyria; of the power of creation. She wanted to know if there was some way to use this power to ease the suffering of our people."

"And you heard all this," said Xydis. "Even though it was supposed to be secret."

"I was just a child," Treia said, shrugging. "Draya probably thought I wouldn't understand. But I did understand. I often imagined, as I knelt there on the hard floor, that I was the Kai Priestess and I had control of one of the Vektan dragons. The first thing I would have done was order it to kill Draya."

Raegar coughed and frowned. Treia thought she had perhaps gone too far and she cast a nervous glance at the Priest-General. He was gazing intently at the spiritbone and seemed not to have heard.

"You say there are five of these dragons and each had its own spiritbone," Xydis said abruptly. "We have one. Where are the other four?"

"I know where to find two of them," said Treia. "You have one. The ogres have another."

"Ogres!" Xydis exclaimed, aghast.

"Blessed Aelon!" Raegar said in a low tone. "I had forgotten about that. This is a calamity."

Xydis stared intently at Treia. "You are saying, Priestess, that the ogres have one of the Vektan bones?"

"Yes," she said. "They stole the bone . . . It is a long story. . . ."

"The ogres worship our foes, the Gods of Raj. And now the ogres have one of these powerful dragons in their possession." Xydis glanced at Raegar. "You are thinking what I am thinking."

"Now we know the reason why the ogre army is sailing to invade Sinaria," Raegar said grimly.

Treia was appalled. "Ogres? Coming to Sinaria?"

"We have been wondering why the ogres would think they are powerful enough to attack Sinaria," Xydis explained. "Now we know: They have a Vektan dragon."

"They are coming here?" Treia asked. "How do you know?"

"We have spies in the ogre kingdom," Xydis said. "They reported to the Watchers that the ogre fleet set sail over a fortnight ago. There was great celebration. Their shamans spoke openly of attacking Sinaria, made sacrifices to their gods."

Xydis held his hand over the spiritbone, as he might have held his hand over a fire to warm himself.

"Would the two Vektan dragons fight each other?" he asked.

Treia shivered at the thought. "The only time a Kai Priestess tried to summon one of these dragons, Worshipful Sir, she could not control it. The dragon went on a rampage, killing any living thing in its path. Hundreds, maybe a thousand Vindrasi died. Entire clans were wiped out."

"That does not answer my question," said Xydis, displeased.

Treia trembled, not at his displeasure. She knew what was coming and she was braced for it. "These dragons are forces of nature, Worshipful Sir. Does the hurricane care about the ships it sinks? Does the volcano weep for those who die in its fiery lava flows? These dragons have no care for anything, much less each other. The thought of two of them battling—"

"We must chance it," said Xydis. He clasped both hands behind his back. "You heard your Kai Priestess talk of these Vektan dragons. Therefore I assume you know the ritual to summon such a powerful being."

Treia shook her head. "I fear I do not, Worshipful Sir. The ritual is a secret the Kai Priestess guards very closely. Draya never spoke of it."

"But you know the ritual to summon other, lesser dragons," Xydis argued. "They must be the same."

"Even if the ritual is the same, which I doubt, there would be secret parts to it that only the Kai Priestess would know."

Xydis pondered this, then smiled. He had a solution.

"You are a Bone Priestess. Go to your goddess, pray to her, convince her to tell you."

Treia said nothing.

"You can do this, my love," said Raegar, prodding her.

Treia remained silent.

Xydis drew close to her, spoke to her softly, intimately, using her name. "You must discover the secret, Treia. We need the Vektan dragon to fight the ogres. Here is the spiritbone. Imagine yourself summoning the dragon, sending it to do battle with our foes. Imagine yourself, the heroine of Sinaria. All of Oran would be at your feet!"

Treia could imagine. She saw herself lauded, showered with wealth such as what was in this treasure vault. She would have a palace, every comfort. She saw the Priest-Mother and those giggling novices bowing before her. She saw, most importantly, Raegar as her adoring husband. She would achieve this, but she had to do it her way.

"It would be my honor to serve you, Worshipful Sir," said Treia in regretful tones, her heart beating fast. "But I cannot do what you ask. I cannot pray to Vindrash."

"Of course, you can!" said Raegar angrily. "Priest-General, let me talk with Treia. She can be stubborn, but I will convince her—"

Xydis raised his hand. He did not take his eyes from Treia. "Why not?"

"During the time Raegar and I have been together, Worshipful Sir, he has told me of the glories and blessings of Aelon. The god has shed his light upon me. I am a devoted follower of Aelon. The dragon goddess will not heed my prayers. Vindrash has turned her back on me."

Xydis almost smiled. Poor Raegar was gulping and floundering and flopping about, trying to find some way out of this predicament. He had done his job of converting her well, far *too* well.

Treia came to her lover's rescue. Before she was finished with Raegar, he would be deeply in her debt.

"The goddess *will* speak to my sister, Aylaen," said Treia.

The same morning Treia had been awakened by the bells to attend morning prayers, Skylan also woke early. The sun reddened the eastern sky, but the sunlight would be short-lived this day. The storms of last night had moved out, but rain clouds again gathered on the horizon. He wondered what had become of Wulfe and was determined to find out. Meanwhile, the Torgun had work to do. Ignoring the burning pain of the wound on his arm, he walked the deck of the *Venjekar*, yanking off blankets and ordering the warriors to wake up.

"My arm hurts," Erdmun grumbled, snatching back his blanket. "At least if I'm asleep I can forget the pain."

"I don't want you to forget it," said Skylan grimly. "I don't want you to forget the pain or who is responsible. This day may bring a chance for us to escape. And if not this day, tomorrow. If not tomorrow, the day after. Whenever that chance comes, we need to take advantage of it. So on your feet, sluggard. We are going to see to it that our ship is in readiness."

Bjorn grabbed hold of his brother's blanket and gave it a tug, rolling Erdmun out onto the deck. The others laughed and yawned and grimaced at the pain and stretched. Aylaen rose and went off alone to perform her ablutions.

"Repairing the ship is a good plan," Sigurd said. "I was going to give the order myself."

"Of course you were," said Skylan.

Clouds rolled in, obscuring the sun. Morning dawned cool, gray, and drizzly. The villa that stood on the hilltop was blotted out by the

mist rising from the river. Sigurd stood on the deck, gazing northward.

"I think about my two sons," he said suddenly. "They are of an
age to stand in the shield wall. I was training them for war. They are
good boys, but they are not ready. And now who will teach them?"

He sighed deeply and shook his head.

Skylan was startled. The dour Sigurd was never one to share his
feelings. Sigurd saw Skylan's sympathetic look and the older man's
expression hardened. He was clearly sorry he had spoken.

"I am the one in charge," he said harshly. "You will follow *my* orders, not give orders of your own."

Skylan shrugged. Sigurd seemed disappointed that Skylan had
given way so easily. Perhaps he was hungering for a fight. Perhaps,
like Skylan, he felt the need to lash out.

"I am Chief. I drew first blood. Someday, you must accept that,"
Sigurd said.

"Someday," Skylan said, and then he grinned. "But not this day."
He looked at Sigurd and, to his astonishment, Sigurd grinned back.

The first task of the Torgun would be to reattach the dragonhead
prow. The Legate's carpenters had failed, but they did not know this
ship. Skylan and Sigurd and Aki, who had worked for some time as
a carpenter and shipbuilder, studied the prow and discussed ways to
mount it.

The prow had been carved from a single piece of wood. The
break was clean, as though the beast's neck had snapped off at the
shoulders. Aki conceived the idea of carving a peg into the bottom
of the "neck," drilling a hole into the "shoulders," and then fitting
the peg into the hole.

This would be a temporary repair. When they returned to their
homeland, they would build a new ship to honor the Dragon Kahg.
When Erdmun said something about the dragon being dead, Sigurd
set him to scrubbing the decks.

The soldiers had hauled away the sea chest containing the weapons,
but they had left behind the tools. The Torgun set to work. Aylaen
brought food: bread (soggy from the rain), goat cheese, and the
olives that were a part of every meal.

At about midday, with the work on the prow going slowly, Sigurd
decreed they should stop. They needed to keep in training for the day
when they would have to fight.

The Vindrasi warriors did not generally train as a unit, not like the Southlanders, as Skylan had learned from talking to Zahakis. Skylan had listened with considerable skepticism to the Tribune explaining how he drilled his soldiers, taught them to march and fight in formations that could wheel and shift upon the battlefield to match the flow of the action. He talked of siege towers filled with men rolling up to the walls of great cities, machines that could hurl globs of fire.

He had thought Zahakis was making most of this up until he had seen the city of Sinaria and the wall that surrounded it and the walls within the walls that guarded the palace and the Temple. He had watched Zahakis's soldiers march in lockstep, performing complicated maneuvers, showing off their skills in the parade. At one point they had closed ranks to form a compact square. Those on the outside of the square locked their shields together, while those in the center raised their shields over their heads, forming what Zahakis called the "turtle."

"Protects from spears and arrows," Zahakis had explained, and Skylan had watched and marveled.

Skylan took his place alongside Bjorn and waited to hear what Sigurd had planned. Since the Torgun had no weapons and could not practice with sword and shield, Sigurd proposed wrestling matches between the men. Sigurd paired them off and had them practice throws and holds. At first, their participation was half-hearted.

But soon, as the matches started, the blood warmed and spirits rose. The warriors began to enjoy the competition, though it soon became apparent that the long period of forced inactivity aboard ship had taken its toll. Their muscles had grown flabby and weak, their skills diminished. Erdmun, who had never before been able to beat anyone in wrestling, took down Grimuir, much to Erdmun's elation.

Sigurd bullied and harangued and shamed them. He and Skylan fought a few rounds. Some Skylan won and some Sigurd won. The fight ended in a draw. No one cheered for Skylan, but he had the feeling that was because no one wanted to offend Sigurd. The cheers came at the end, when both men stood up, sweating and breathing hard, and shook hands.

Aylaen held herself apart, watching with an envious expression. Vindrasi women often held wrestling matches among themselves, and Aylaen had always enjoyed the sport. A woman wrestling a man was considered unseemly. She was the one who saw the soldiers approaching, and she called out a warning.

Skylan looked up the hill to see Zahakis, accompanied by four archers and eighteen soldiers, all of them armed. By the grim expression on the Tribune's face, something was wrong.

Zahakis gestured to his soldiers. "You men, search the ship and those tents."

The archers stood in front of the Torgun with bows raised, ready to shoot. Skylan wondered what this was about. The soldiers entered the tents and almost immediately came back out. They took more time searching the ship, going down into the hold, opening up the sea chests.

"The boy!" Zahakis said, staring around at the warriors. "Where is he?"

Skylan was startled. "I was going to ask you the same thing. The last I saw, Raegar's men were hauling Wulfe off to prison."

"They never made it," said Zahakis. "If you have the boy, Skylan, hand him over."

"He's not here," said Skylan. "I have not seen him. What do you mean, 'they never made it'? What happened to Wulfe?"

Zahakis turned to the rest of the Torgun. "If you men are lying or trying to hide him, it will go bad with you. With all of you."

The men glanced at each other and said nothing.

Zahakis eyed them, then turned to Aylaen. "Have you seen him?"

Aylaen shook her red curls. "I saw Raegar take him away. I have not seen him since."

Skylan was growing exasperated. "I tell you that Wulfe is not here. What has happened to him?"

Zahakis was watching his soldiers. The two who had gone into the hold came back up, shaking their heads.

"The two guards were found dead," said Zahakis grimly. "Weltering in their own blood. Their throats had been slashed, their faces mauled so that it was hard to recognize them. One of the men had his arm torn off at the shoulder."

"And the boy?" Skylan asked in fear, his heart constricting. He had not realized until now how much he had come to care for the waif he'd found on that ill-fated voyage to the Druid Isles. "What about him? Was he hurt?"

"The boy is missing. Raegar accuses Wulfe of murdering his guards."

Skylan stared at the man. He looked back at the other Torgun, who were slack-jawed in amazement. Then the warriors gave a great roar of laughter.

"You know our secret. Wulfe is our most valiant warrior," said Skylan. "When we go into battle, we send the boy out first to do the killing. We men just come along behind him to mop up."

Zahakis was not amused. "I saw the bodies of those men, what was left. I have seen men hacked to pieces on the field of battle and not blenched. But I will remember this horror to the day I die. It was not some gang or roving band of thieves murdered those men. It was some fiend of hell. Or rather, some beast from hell. We found bloody paw prints all around the bodies."

"Because his name is 'Wulfe' you have let your imagination run away with you," said Skylan. He was starting to grow angry. "The boy may be lying dead somewhere and you waste time accusing him of murdering two grown men, ripping off their arms!"

"What do you know about this boy?" Zahakis asked.

"He is an orphan I took in," said Skylan. "I know nothing about him except that he claims to be the son of a faery princess."

"The boy lived among us for a long time," said Aylaen. Her red curls straggled around her face in the damp. The flaring fire of her green eyes seemed the only light in the gray, bleak dawn. "He never harmed anyone."

The warriors added their avowals to Aylaen's. The Torgun considered Wulfe strange. He could cause the birds to come down from the trees, light on his hand. He claimed he could speak to animals and understand them. He spent a great deal of time with Owl Mother, an old woman many thought was a witch. Still, Wulfe was one of their own. The very fact that the detested traitor Raegar hated the boy was a mark in Wulfe's favor.

Zahakis looked very grim. "I tell you this for your own good, Skylan. If the boy returns, hand him over to me."

Skylan stood stubbornly silent, his arms crossed defiantly over his chest.

Zahakis eyed him, then said, "Meantime, the Legate wants to speak to you."

"Hang the Legate!" said Skylan angrily. "I need to find Wulfe—"

One of the soldiers jabbed Skylan in the gut with the butt of his spear and Skylan doubled over, clutching his belly.

Zahakis looked at the others. "I am in no mood to play games. I see you men want exercise. I am happy to accommodate you. There is a field that needs to be cleared of stones."

He rounded on his heel and walked off. The soldiers seized hold of Skylan and shoved him along, prodding him in the back with their spears if he slowed. The other soldiers rounded up the Torgun, including Aylaen, and ordered them to start marching.

Skylan glanced back to the see the *Venjekar* adrift on a sea of mist, and he was reminded suddenly and unpleasantly of the ghostly voyage he had made aboard the ship returning from the ill-fated trip to the Druid Isles. The Goddess Vindrash had been steering the vessel. She had taken the body of his dead wife, terrorizing him, forcing him to play, night after night, games of dragonbone. Only at the last, on the Dragon Isles, had the goddess revealed herself to him in her true dragon form.

Skylan's skin tingled, the hair prickled on the back of his neck. The goddess stood at the ship's stern. He stared, amazed. She raised her hand, palm outward, in what might have been a salute. Then, deliberately, she spread her fingers and made an emphatic gesture. The number five.

"Get moving, lout!" said the guard, giving Skylan a shove. He slipped in the wet grass and stumbled, almost losing his footing. He regained his balance and walked on. He glanced back. The goddess was gone.

In the villa, in the largest and prettiest of the bedrooms that looked out upon the atrium, Acronis paced back and forth, his hand rumpling his grizzled hair.

"Chloe, are you sure about this?" he asked.

The Legate was one of the most powerful, most influential men in the nation of Oran. He commanded his own private army. He was known as a brave warrior who bore proudly the scars of battle. He was a scholar, an inventor, a scientist and philosopher. The Empress often sought his counsel.

And one fifteen-year-old girl, slender and small for her age, had only to look at him with her winsome smile and brown eyes and say, "Oh, Papa, please!" and he was helpless as a newborn lamb.

Chloe lounged on her bed, propped up by pillows, holding a bronze mirror while Rosa, one of the female house-slaves, arranged the girl's curly hair into the latest style. Rosa first wound the hair into a bun at the back of Chloe's neck and then encircled the bun with a length of braided hair. She finished by twisting tendrils of the hair to hang loosely about the girl's face.

"There, Papa, how do I look?" Chloe asked, laying down the mirror and lifting her face to her father.

"As beautiful as the dawn," said her fond parent.

"That is to say that I am gray and dismal," said Chloe with a pert glance out into the atrium.

Her father had ordered the atrium doors to be shut, fearing she would be chilled. Chloe had insisted on having them open, however, saying she felt suffocated when the room was closed up.

And so, of course, the doors stood open.

Acronis said hurriedly he had not meant she was gray and dismal. He meant that she was beautiful as dawn when it wasn't raining, a clear dawn, a rosy dawn. Chloe laughed at him and laid down the mirror.

"Father, I am teasing you." She patted the side of her bed and scooted over to make room for him. "Now come and sit here and tell me all the reasons I am not to have what I want."

Acronis did as commanded. He was armed to the teeth with logic and common sense and he was firmly prepared to withstand the enemy onslaught.

Chloe immediately outflanked him.

"You *did* promise you would bring me a gift, something special to make up for the fact that you were gone so long," she said in wheedling tones. "Where is the necklace you promised me?"

Acronis's shield splintered, his sword broke off at the hilt. "My dear, we were not on a pleasure cruise. I could not go shopping for you in the markets because there were no markets in which to shop. We were in pursuit of dangerous men."

Seeing a breach in her defenses, he charged in and briefly rallied. "And it is precisely because these men are dangerous that I will not permit you to have one as a pet."

"I don't want him as a pet, Papa," said Chloe, pouting. "I am not a child. I want him for my manservant."

"You have Kakos—"

"I am sick to death of Kakos," said Chloe impatiently. "He is fat and lazy and smells of garlic. When I ask him to do the slightest littlest thing, such as carry me into the garden, he groans and claims his back aches. When I insisted and made him carry me, he whined that he threw his back out and took to his bed for a week."

Kakos had been in the Legate's service since birth. His mother was the cook and his father the groundskeeper. And though Acronis knew his daughter was exaggerating, he could not argue with the fact that Kakos was overweight and inclined to feel sorry for himself.

Acronis decided it was time to launch a counteroffensive. "This slave you want—I will make you this offer. I am going to be training him for the Para Dix, Chloe. This man will be your champion! There, what do you say to that? Not many fifteen-year-old girls in Sinaria have their own champion."

Chloe clapped her hands. "That is wonderful, Papa, thank you! He can do both. When he is training, I will be at my studies. When he is finished, he can attend me."

Chloe nestled her cheek on her father's arm and looked at him, her eyes shimmering with tears, and said softly, "You know how long my days are, Papa. You are so very busy with all your important work. I hardly see you. I ask for so little. . . ."

Acronis was routed, foot and horse. "I will consider it," he said reluctantly.

"Oh, Papa, thank you!" Chloe flung her arms around him and kissed him on the cheek. "What is my champion's name? You told me, but I forgot."

"Skylan," said Acronis.

"Skylan," Chloe repeated, lingering over the name with a sigh. "Bring him to me. I want to meet him."

"I'm not promising anything," said Acronis.

"I know that, Papa," said Chloe demurely, but she knew as well as he did that she was riding off with the honors of the day.

"You cannot be serious, my lord!" said Zahakis when Acronis told him. "You must change your mind. Tell her no."

"You do not have children, do you, my friend?" Acronis said with a smile. "Saying no is not that easy. And Chloe's life is so hard. This man is a barbarian, but he is not a savage. He has a rough code of honor. He could have killed me when the slaves revolted, but he did not."

"My lord, Skylan kept you alive out of expediency, not out of mercy," said Zahakis. "He and the rest of his men are filled with rage and determined to escape. To say nothing of that wretched boy who apparently slaughtered two grown men—"

"You don't believe that any more than I do, Zahakis," said Acronis.

"I don't know what to believe, my lord. All I know is that if I had a daughter, I would not let her within a mile of these brutes."

Acronis rumpled his hair with his hand, clearly disturbed. Then he brightened. "I have an idea. I promised Chloe I would bring Skylan to meet her. When she sees this barbarian—and hears him talk—she will not want anything to do with him. Where is he?"

"He is in the atrium, my lord, waiting your pleasure," Zahakis said.

"Bring Skylan to Chloe's room. I will meet you there. We will spring him on her without warning."

Chloe sat in her bed, propped up by pillows. The bed, one of the most beautiful in Sinaria, was carved of wood, highly polished and embellished with gold and seashells. The coverlet was of damask embroidered with flowers. Bowls of fresh-cut flowers from the garden, roses and lilies, perfumed the air. The day might be gray, but her room was always filled with light.

Chloe was reading the journals her father had written during the voyage. She loved reading his journals. They provided her a glimpse of the world that lay beyond her bedchamber, a world she would never see.

Acronis's writing style was didactic, the work of a scientist. The fifteen-year-old girl took the dry words and made them live, embellishing the scenes he described with her own romantic notions. She saw the Dragon Kahg in his words and longed with all her heart to see a dragon for real. She laughed out loud when she read about Zahakis with the jellyfish wrapped around his hand, and her heart beat fast when Skylan and the captives made their bid for freedom. She was moved to tears when she read of the prow snapping off, how the brave men had given way to despair.

Chloe was in the middle of Acronis's description of a Vindrasi battle, reading an account of how they formed a shield wall, when her father and Zahakis brought the slave Skylan into her room.

Skylan was taller than her father and Zahakis. His fair complexion was tanned. His hair was the color of the sun. His eyes were blue as the sky. She had never seen such blue eyes before and she was charmed by the intensity of their color. He was broad through the chest and shoulders, the cut of his muscles visible beneath his leather tunic, and she could understand why her father had chosen him for the Para Dix. What she found most fascinating was that he stood tall and proud, his head held high, his eyes boldly, even defiantly, meeting her gaze. He might have been some proud and noble lord, except for the horrid tattoo on his arm that marked him a slave.

His clothes were the worse for wear and stained with what she thought might be blood. He smelled of saltwater and wet leather and something indefinable. . . .

"Life," Chloe said softly to herself. "He smells of life."

He did not smell of *her* life, of perfume and scented oils and oranges and cut flowers and garlic and whatever Cook was fixing for dinner. Smells that were always pleasant, always the same, smells that never seemed to dissipate even when Rosa opened the doors to let in the air. Even the air smelled the same to Chloe, day after day after day.

Skylan was different. His smell made her want to inhale deeply and, at the same time, wrinkle her nose. He was danger, the unexpected. He was life, the life she had never known. The life she never would know.

He was a warrior. Men had died by his hand. Chloe felt a qualm of fear and was forced to admit that perhaps her father had been right. She shouldn't be in his company. And then she looked more keenly into the blue eyes.

He stood unmoving beneath her scrutiny. Yet she saw in the blue eyes that wanted to appear so impassive and cold a flicker of uncertainty. Chloe had read her father's descriptions of Skylan's people, his way of life, and she suddenly realized how strange and unfamiliar this world was for him. He must be feeling confused, overwhelmed, desperately unhappy.

"Skylan will suit me, Father," Chloe said. She saw Acronis raise his eyebrows. He seemed about to argue and she raised her small hand to forestall him.

The young man had shifted his gaze and was now staring, narrow-eyed, at her. Probably he didn't understand. She smiled at him.

"You will be my manservant, Skylan," Chloe explained. "Your duties will not be onerous. You will be required to read to me—"

"He cannot read," said Zahakis. "Nor can he write."

Chloe was startled by this, but, on reflection, found that made him more intriguing. "Indeed. Well then, Skylan, you will entertain me by telling me stories. As to your other duties, when the weather is fine, you will carry me to the garden—"

"Carry you!" Skylan's voice was sharp and loud and went off like an explosion in her room where all sounds were muted, only the softest music was played. Chloe jumped, startled and a little frightened. The feeling was thrilling.

The young man glared at her. "I carry shield and sword. Not spoiled brats. You have feet. Carry yourself."

"How dare you?" Acronis said angrily. "I will have you whipped—"

"Oh, Papa, don't be silly," said Chloe in crisp tones. "He is my slave and I won't allow him to be whipped. He meant no harm."

She gazed at Skylan and smiled. "You are right. I do have feet." Chloe drew back the damask coverlet to reveal her limbs and gave a little shrug. "But my poor feet do not work. They have not worked in many years."

Skylan stared at her, frowning, not understanding.

"My daughter had an illness when she was five," Acronis said. "She survived, but she lost the use of her legs."

"I would love to walk into the garden myself," Chloe said. "But I can't. I am forced to lie here in this room, day and night."

She looked at Skylan and added gently, "So you see, I, too, know what it means to be a prisoner."

Zahakis escorted Skylan from the bedchamber. They walked through vast and echoing rooms decorated with statuary and furniture the likes of which Skylan had never seen. There were even pools of water inside the house. Skylan was astonished to see golden fish swimming about. A great many people were coming and going, working about the villa. He and Zahakis passed by several women on their hands and knees, scrubbing the floors.

"Which one is the Legate's wife?" Skylan asked.

Zahakis glanced at him in amazement, almost laughing.

"The Legate's wife is dead. And she would not be on her knees, scrubbing floors. These are slaves."

Skylan stared at them. The women kept their eyes on their work, not looking up. He saw two men rubbing the wooden furniture with sweet-smelling oils. Going through one room, on their way to the atrium, they came across a small boy of about six years cleaning out one of the fish pools.

"Is the child a slave?" Skylan asked.

"He is the son of a slave and so, yes, he is a slave."

"But . . ." Skylan sought for words. "These people are your own people! How can they be slaves?"

"Some are born to slaves and as such they are slaves themselves. Some are sold into slavery and some sell themselves to pay off a debt."

"I live only for the day I escape this land," said Skylan.

Zahakis stopped walking. Reaching out, he caught hold of Skylan. The two were alone in a hallway of black marble that led to the atrium.

"Remember that you are a slave, the Legate's property. You and this bit of fruit have that in common."

Zahakis lifted an apple from a bowl that stood on a small table. With a sudden motion, he flung the apple against the wall with such force that it split apart. Juice and pulp slid down the wall and dribbled onto the floor.

"The Legate will do that to your head, Skylan Ivorson," said Zahakis, "if you so much as think of harming that child."

"His daughter? I don't want anything to do with his whelp!" said Skylan emphatically.

"If it were up to me, you would not be allowed near her. But it is not up to me," said Zahakis grimly.

"So I must do this," said Skylan.

"Chloe's wish is her father's command. And you are her father's slave."

Skylan watched bits of pulverized apple slide down the wall.

"You need have no fear," he said. "His daughter is safe with me. He is my enemy and I would kill him without hesitation, but I do not make war on children. I don't enslave them, either."

Zahakis barked an order. Two women hurried in with a bucket and rags. They would do the same if that had been his head split open on the floor, spilling blood and brains. Just another mess for the slaves to clean up.

BOOK TWO

Zahakis took Skylan into the atrium and left him standing near a flowering hedge with two guards and orders to await the Legate's pleasure. Skylan could see Acronis a short distance away on the other side of the hedge, which was a mass of green leaves and pink flowers. The Legate was pacing up and down on a path made of crushed pink marble. He caught sight of Zahakis and motioned for him. The two walked back and forth, discussing something with intense interest.

The rain had passed. The sun had come out, spattering the water-spangled leaves. Skylan stood where he had been told to stand, fuming and frustrated. He was not accustomed to being ordered about by anyone. He had always done what he wanted to do, and now he was sent here and told to go there and he did not think he could stand it.

Skylan eyed the bored soldier standing guard over him and considered attacking him. Or perhaps he would attack Acronis, who was not three paces from him. He and Zahakis were separated from Skylan only by the blooming hedge and a marble statue of a half-naked man leaning upon a spear. He would not stand a chance. The guards would cut him before he got near Acronis, but at this point, Skylan considered death preferable to this life, which was growing more intolerable by the moment.

Skylan was seriously considering carrying out his resolve when his attention was captured by something Acronis said. Skylan quickly forgot his self-pity and began listening.

"The Empress was told by the Priest-General that an ogre fleet is sailing toward Sinaria. A hundred ships or more, all crammed with soldiers."

"And how does the Priest-General know this?" asked Zahakis.

"His spies—priests who permitted themselves to be captured and enslaved by ogres so they could spy on them."

Zahakis shook his head.

"I know. I thought the same. These spies transmit their messages through the Watchers, those wretches who sit in the Shrine of Aelon day and night staring into bowls of water."

Skylan glanced sidelong at his guards to see if they were watching him. He was having trouble keeping his facial muscles from betraying his astonishment. He had heard about the ogre fleet from Wulfe, who claimed to have heard it from his oceanaids. Skylan had not believed such a ridiculous tale. But now it seemed the Southlanders did.

His guards were paying scant attention to him. Skylan remembered something Raegar had told him when his treacherous cousin had been pretending to be his friend. Raegar had been a slave in the Southland. He had lived many years as a slave.

"Slaves are held beneath contempt in Oran. They might as well be just another stick of furniture. Their masters think they are deaf, dumb, blind, and witless. Women entertain their lovers while their slaves stand at the side of the bed. Men plot to murder a rival as their slaves pour their wine. I could have ruined half the people in Sinaria with what I overheard when I was a house-slave."

Having never expected to find himself in such a situation, Skylan had laughed at the stupidity of the Southlanders. He was not laughing now. Being a slave in the household of Acronis could have advantages. Skylan touched the amulet he wore around his neck as an apology to Torval for doubting him.

"Ogres are poor sailors," said Zahakis. "They will never reach here. Their ships will all be sunk before they are halfway across the ocean."

"Do not underestimate them. Remember that year after year, these 'poor sailors' have managed to cross the sea to raid our northern colonies," said Acronis dryly.

Skylan could have provided confirmation of that. The ogres had sailed after him, following the *Venjekar* back to his homeland.

Acronis added something about the Priest-General having assured the Empress that Aelon would raise the seas to swallow up their foes.

Zahakis interrupted him. "Best change the subject, my lord."

"Ah, yes, quite right, Commander," said Acronis. "Thank you."

Skylan at first feared they had caught him eavesdropping, but then he saw them both looking at something on the other side of the garden. Sighting the newcomer, Skylan understood why the two had abruptly ended their discussion.

An ogre was walking toward them. The ogre had a tattoo on his arm like Skylan's.

Like all his kind, the ogre was immensely tall, standing head and shoulders over Skylan, which meant that he towered over the Southlanders. The ogre was in excellent physical condition; unusual for ogres, who disliked strenuous exertion of any kind and tended to run to flab. This ogre wore the customary ogre garb: leather breeches, held in place by a wide leather belt, stuffed into leather boots laced over massive calves. His well-muscled and hairy chest was bare, crisscrossed by a leather harness that, under normal circumstances, would have held the ogre's weapons. In this instance, the harness was empty.

And, as with all ogres, the hulking body was topped by a bald head and a face that was soft and round and guileless as that of a human babe. His cheeks were plump, his mouth small, his eyes bright. Aware that their faces tended to inspire laughter, not fear, ogres made themselves look more ferocious by painting their heads, a practice that also denoted the ogre's rank and place in society.

This ogre's head was painted white with a black stripe running from the neck to the chin and another black stripe crossing the nose and cheeks. Skylan thought back to the time not long ago (though it seemed a hundred lifetimes) when the ogres had entered his village to tell them the gods of the Vindrasi were dead. Skylan had seen only two ogres with faces painted like this and they were the ogre commanders, known as godlords.

Skylan was consumed with curiosity, wondering what an ogre godlord was doing in Oran and how he had come to be a slave. That the godlord was a slave was obvious, not just from the tattoo on his arm, but by the way Acronis and Zahakis treated him. They waited for the ogre to come to them, instead of going to meet him, and even when he was standing next to them, they finished their conversation (which had turned to something inconsequential) before acknowledging the ogre's presence.

The ogre stood patiently, looking about. Skylan had once considered ogres to be stupid brutes, lazy and dull-witted. He had learned to his sorrow that ogres were crafty, cunning, and intelligent. Heavy of girth and large-boned with broad shoulders and big bellies, ogres were of a naturally sedentary nature, which other races often mistook for laziness. They were not particularly skilled with weapons, having no need to be. They counted on their weight to overpower smaller foes.

Skylan recalled with painful clarity the hard-hitting ogre warriors smashing into the front lines of his shield wall. The wall had disintegrated, men crushed to bloody bits.

As he was thinking this, the ogre suddenly saw Skylan. He stared fixedly at him, plainly taking Skylan's measure, eyeing him up and down. The ogres and the Vindrasi were ancient foes. Skylan scowled and stood straighter, making himself taller, and thrust out his chest and crossed his arms. He met the ogre's gaze and looked *him* up and down.

The ogre chuckled, amused. Skylan burned with resentment. Zahakis and Acronis looked back at him, then the three began to discuss Skylan as though he was deaf. They spoke of him as a "hothead" and "youth." Then Zahakis said, "He has some skill with a sword."

"Some skill!" Skylan cried, blazing. "Give me a sword and we'll see how much skill I have!"

Acronis gave a commanding gesture, and Skylan's guard gripped him by the arm and led him around the hedge, down a path that ran beneath a trellis covered with grapevine. Skylan walked proudly, keeping his gaze fixed defiantly on the ogre.

"This is the leader of the Para Dix team. His name is Keeper of the Fire," said Zahakis, performing introductions. "He will be your trainer for the game. Keeper, this is Skylan Ivorson."

The ogre grunted and shook his head. "I trust he is smarter than he looks."

Skylan tweaked his nose between his thumb and finger. "And I hope you are smarter than you smell."

Keeper swung his arm. He could move quickly for an ogre. Skylan had no time to duck the huge fist that smashed into his jaw. He crashed backward into the flowering bush, snapping twigs and limbs. The thick foliage broke his fall and he sagged forward onto his hands and knees, spitting blood. He remained on the ground a moment, shaking his head groggily.

Keeper shook his head and opened his mouth to make another disparaging comment. Skylan leaped to his feet and drove his elbow deep into the ogre's gut.

Keeper doubled over with a groan.

Dimly, through the buzzing in his ears, Skylan heard lilting, girlish laughter.

"Hah! Keeper, he got you good! He's my champion!" Chloe called out. "My Skylan is going to be the best player in the city!"

The crippled girl had been moved from her bed to a couch in the atrium.

Skylan felt his skin burn in embarrassment. He glared at the ogre, expecting to see Keeper sneer in derision.

To his surprise, Keeper was eyeing Skylan with more respect. The ogre turned to the girl and made a clumsy bow.

"I will train this one and the others to be worthy of you, Mistress Chloe."

"I know you will, Keeper," said Chloe, smiling. "And though he is my new champion, you will still be my friend."

The face paint made it difficult to tell, but Skylan could have sworn the ogre's plump cheeks flushed in pleasure.

"And now, my dear," said Acronis, going over to her, bending over her fondly, "you have had quite enough excitement for one day. Back to your bed."

"Oh, but Papa, I want to watch!" Chloe protested.

"Perhaps tomorrow." Acronis motioned to a fat, pasty-faced fellow with numerous chins. "Kakos, take Mistress Chloe to her bed."

"Kakos, I am sure I heard a leg of lamb calling your name. You'd best go to the kitchen to see if you can find it," said Chloe. She gestured at Skylan. "My new champion will carry me."

"Absolutely not," said Acronis, frowning. "Kakos, do as you are told."

"Kakos, if you touch me with those clammy hands of yours I will give Cook orders that you are to be fed nothing but bread and water for a week," Chloe countered.

Kakos, caught between his master and his diminutive mistress, did not know which to obey. Wringing his hands, he appeared to be on the verge of tears.

"He is covered in blood," said Acronis in a low voice, remonstrating with his daughter.

"He can wash off in the fountain," Chloe ordered, and she lay back on the couch and folded her hands in her lap. She obviously considered the matter settled.

Skylan thought nothing more could add to his shame. He could not look at the ogre. He was certain Acronis would never accede to his daughter's demand and that was his only comfort.

"Get him cleaned up," said Acronis.

Zahakis, his jaw tight with disapproval, hauled Skylan over to a pool. A statue of a boar spewed water from its mouth.

"Wash," said Zahakis grimly, and when Skylan didn't move fast enough, the Tribune roughly thrust his head under water and held him there just a bit too long.

When Zahakis finally released, Skylan, half-drowned, gasped and snorted and rose dizzily to his feet. He stood there dripping. The slave, Rosa, came running to him with a towel and mopped him dry, dabbing carefully at his bruised jaw and split lip.

"Remember the apple," said Zahakis, and he shoved Skylan over to where Chloe reclined demurely on her couch, her useless legs covered with a silken cloth.

Skylan stood next to the girl, who was thin and frail, fragile as a baby bird, and did not know what to do with her. He was terrified that he would hurt her just by touching her. He stared down at her in helpless confusion, not knowing what to do.

Chloe looked up at him, unafraid, and laughed at his discomfiture. "I won't break. I'm stronger than I look." She reached up her arms to him, trusting as a child.

He awkwardly slid one arm around her back and his other arm beneath the lifeless legs and gathered her up, silken cloth and all. She clasped her hands around his neck and smiled at him. She was skin and bones and weighed next to nothing. He lifted her with ease.

"Keeper is a good trainer," she told him as he carried her through the door, into the room to where her bed stood against the far wall. "He has been with my father for three years now and he is an expert Para Dix player. You will be the best, though. I know it. All the women in the city will envy me."

He eased her down among the pillows.

"I am a little tired after all," Chloe said. "I will rest now. Tell Rosa to shut the doors."

As Skylan drew back, she caught hold of his hand. "You will

come to me tomorrow morning. I want to hear how your training goes."

Skylan mumbled something. Turning with relief to leave, he almost knocked over Zahakis, who had been standing right behind him. Rosa was shutting the doors that led outside, darkening the room. She ushered them out. Skylan glanced back to see Chloe nestling down among her pillows. She smiled at him, her gaze following him.

Skylan escaped into the atrium and drew in a deep breath, realizing only then that he'd been too afraid to breathe.

"You were gentle with her," said Zahakis. He sounded surprised.

"What did you expect?" Skylan asked, rounding on him angrily. "Did you think I would strangle her? She is a child and she is sick. This may be hard for you to believe, but we barbarians have children and we love them as you love your children. I myself have buried three of my little brothers."

He thought back to those little brothers. The babies had been born too soon and were too small to survive. He had held each of the tiny waxen bodies in his hands, commending their souls to Freilis, then laying them to rest. The last had been buried with Sonja, his stepmother, who had died in childbirth.

"I was going to help raise the little boys," Skylan said, thinking back. "I was going to teach them to wield their swords. One day, they would stand beside me in the shield wall. My brothers. Their valor would make me proud."

He sighed softly and shook his head. Seeing Zahakis staring at him, Skylan realized suddenly he'd spoken his thoughts aloud and he clamped his mouth shut.

His head throbbed, his jaw ached. He had not slept in many nights. He was worn out and he had an afternoon's grueling training for this Para Dix. He had the feeling the training was going to be brutal. The ogre, Keeper, was rubbing his hands and grinning.

BOOK TWO

At first, listening to Keeper's explanation, Skylan thought the Para Dix was similar to a child's game he and his friends had played as children known as Torval's Mountain. One of them was the god Torval. He selected warriors from the Hall of Heroes and arranged them in a shield wall at the top of the hill. The other children played the Dragon Ilyrion, who formed her own shield wall to try to push Torval off his hill.

The game had been a favorite with Skylan and had usually ended in a general free-for-all with small boys and girls rolling down the hill, ending up dirty and tired and happy, with scraped knees.

The Para Dix involved ten warriors on one side and ten on another. The goal of each team was to seize the sacred fire, which blazed in a pit in the center, then protect it from the other team.

The game was immensely popular in Sinaria. The Para Dix was played in the large new arena—a gift from Aelon to the people. Wealthy men, such as Acronis, sponsored their own teams. The common people crowded onto the concrete benches that circled the arena. The nobility, shaded by umbrellas and cooled by feather fans, watched from boxes furnished with cushioned chairs.

The Para Dix had been played for centuries and, like Torval's Mountain, symbolized the eternal battle waged by the gods for the world. Philosophers had once made the symbology of the game the subject of lectures, but that was prior to the coming of Aelon's priests, who saw no need for philosophers or their lectures or the game. Aelon reigned supreme, unchallenged. There could be no doubt about that. No game must dare depict Aelon as weak.

Many years ago, the priests of Aelon had tried to shut down the Para Dix. The people of Oran did not much care about the loss of the old gods, but they cared passionately about the loss of their sport. Faced with rioting in the streets, the priests had resumed the game, bringing the Para Dix under the auspices of the Church. Aelon was now the hero god, valiantly defending the fire of creation from evil interlopers.

Aelon might have saved himself the trouble. Few Sinarians knew or cared about the religious symbology. All they cared about was whether their team won or lost. The Church had abolished the practice of gambling on the games; it was unseemly to be gambling on a god. The only change this brought about was that the gambling was taken over by the street gangs.

The Legate had built a replica of the playing field on his estate, and this was where Keeper took Skylan to begin his training. He explained that eventually all the Torgun would be players, but that Skylan, who had a crucial role to play in the game, would require extra training. Keeper explained the rules as they walked, an explanation to which Skylan paid little attention.

He heard the ogre say the game involved fighting and that was all Skylan needed to know. He paid no heed to the rest, something about moving from one square to another and how certain pieces could only move to certain squares and how the Legate would dictate his movements. All Skylan knew was that he was going to be given a sword.

"You say the training involves fighting," he said, interrupting the ogre in midsentence.

"Yes," said Keeper, eyeing him as though he knew what he was thinking.

"Then my people do not need training, especially from the likes of you," said Skylan. "We know how to fight. I myself have been wielding a sword in the shield wall since I was fourteen. I once killed an ogre godlord."

He cast a significant glance at this ogre godlord and added, "Single-handed."

Keeper shrugged, not impressed. "You and your people are such great warriors, yet now you are marked with the tattoo of a slave."

"Because of a damn traitor!" Skylan said angrily. "We were ambushed. My men were not even armed! If we could have fought these bastards, there would not have been one left standing!"

He glanced at the soldiers walking behind him and raised his voice so they would hear. "The Southlander whoresons are cowards, afraid to meet true warriors in battle!"

The soldiers were talking together and they continued their conversation, paying no heed to him.

"You are wasting your breath. They don't even hear you," said Keeper. "To them, you are a dog barking in the night."

"A dog, am I?" said Skylan grimly. "Some day this dog will rip out their goddam throats!"

"I felt that same anger once," said Keeper. "You'll soon get over it. You are a Para Dix player. You will be well-treated. They will kill you with kindness, as the saying goes."

Skylan recalled Zahakis's words: *You might even get to like it here.*

"I don't want to get over it! I don't want to be like you, fat and content," said Skylan. "You like being a slave. The Legate takes care of you, feeds you, clothes you—"

"I hate it!" Keeper ground out the words. His passion startled Skylan. The ogre looked far off in the distance and pointed. "In that direction lies my homeland. I have been a slave for many years. My mate must think me dead. She has likely found someone else to warm her bed. Another man may be raising my children."

He sighed. "Yet I have no fire in my belly."

Keeper glanced ruefully at Skylan. "Once I was like you. For a year after my capture, the fire burned hot. Then one morning I woke to find that the fire had gone out. I didn't care anymore. Strange, because my name is Keeper of the Fire, a name I was given in my vision quest when I was a youth. I thought it had meaning. I guess it didn't."

They arrived at what the ogre termed "the playing field." Several circles within circles were painted white on the clipped grass. In the center was a fire pit with no fire. A great many boulders, also painted white with black runes, stood scattered about the circles, seemingly at random. Two platforms constructed of wood on the rim of the outer circle faced each other on opposite sides.

"This is where the game is played and where we will train," said Keeper.

Skylan cast a bored glance at the field. He had only one interest. "When do we fight?"

Keeper chuckled. "You must first learn the rules. You are the only Vindrasi I have ever trained to play the Para Dix. I have fought your people, but I do not know much about you. In my land, we play a game on a wooden board marked off in squares, using stones that hop from square to square. Do your people have something similar?"

"Nothing as stupid-sounding as that," said Skylan. The thought of his homeland made his heart ache. The fire in his belly burned. He intended to keep it that way.

He saw, out of the corner of his eye, Acronis coming onto the field to watch.

Skylan folded his arms across his chest and said loudly, "We play a game called 'Screw the Ogre.' "

Keeper quirked an eyebrow. Skylan decided that this ogre must be the stupidest ogre in the world since he obviously did not know when he had been insulted.

Keeper made a sweeping gesture. "Think of that as the game board. Think of yourself and your men as the game pieces."

He poked Skylan in the chest with a thick finger, then called to the Legate, "He is ready, lord."

"Tell him move to boulder number ten," said Acronis. "He can't read, so you're going to have to teach him how to recognize which that is."

"The boulder with the X is number ten," said Keeper. "The Legate has moved you to that area on the board. Go stand beside it and wait for further instructions."

"Tell the Legate he can go piss on the boulder with the X on it," said Skylan. "And if you touch me again with your filthy finger, I'll break it off."

"The Vindrasi slave says he finds the rules difficult to understand, lord," Keeper yelled.

"Then make them simple for him," said Acronis, smiling.

Keeper kicked Skylan in the gut. While he was groaning, the ogre lifted Skylan with one arm, slung him over his broad shoulder, and carried him to the boulder. With a heave, Keeper threw Skylan to the ground.

"And that is how you play the game," said the ogre.

BOOK TWO

While Skylan was learning the intricacies of Para Dix, the other Torgun warriors and Aylaen were picking up rocks in a field. The field was covered with stones of various shapes and sizes, some buried deep in the ground. The soldiers ordered the Torgun to dig out the stones that were about the size of a man's fist and pile them in heaps to one side of the field. The work was laborious and pointless, as far as Aylaen could see. She had worked in the farm fields since she was old enough to know a weed from a bean sprout, and she recognized that the ground was too rocky to be good for planting. Only when the Torgun were ordered to load the stones into wagons did she realize that the stones were the crop they were harvesting. According to one of the guards, the stones would be hauled away, crushed and used in the making of concrete.

Aylaen was accustomed to hard labor in the fields. She enjoyed farming, watching crops grow, tending to the seedlings, gathering in the harvest. This was different. She came to hate this work. The constant stooping and bending and carrying the rocks to the cart made her back ache. Her fingers were torn and bleeding from scrabbling to pull the rocks out of the ground.

The sun was hot, the air damp from the rain. The men stripped off their tunics. The soldiers taunted Aylaen, told her to do the same.

The soldiers who had treated her with respect while under the stern eye of Zahakis now felt free to insult her. They leered at her and made crude remarks. She pretended not to hear. Her stepfather heard, however, and he and the other Torgun were growing increasingly angry.

At some particularly unsavory remark, Sigurd threw the rock he had been carrying at the soldiers. The rock missed. The soldiers put their hands on their sword hilts, though they were in no danger. The tattoo on his arm was already starting to burn. The soldiers laughed and jeered. Aylaen wanted to sink into the ground with the rocks.

She was afraid and she was angry, and her anger began swallowing up her fear. She was angry at the soldiers for the ugly things they were saying. She was angry at her stepfather for feeling he needed to protect her.

The soldiers ordered all the Torgun to sit down with their backs against the cart. Aylaen was glad to rest, though she knew she would regret the inactivity when she tried to stand up. She could already feel her muscles stiffening.

Sweat rolled off her, dripping from her wet red curls. The man's shirt she wore clung to her body. She was ravenous and desperately thirsty, and when the soldier handed her a mug filled with water, she took the cup and brought it to her lips, tilting her head to drink.

The soldier grabbed hold of her breasts.

Shamed and outraged, Aylaen slammed the pottery mug into the man's face. The mug broke, the shards cut into his flesh. He swore and, touching his face, drew back fingers covered in blood.

"Whore! You should be grateful for my attention!" He struck her with the back of his hand.

She was furious, suddenly, at men—all men—for making her feel weak and vulnerable and afraid.

The Madness of Torval, the holy fire sent by the god that burns away fear and pain, swept over her. Aylaen grabbed a stone from the cart and flung it at the soldier who had hit her.

She grabbed another stone and threw it at Sigurd, who yelped in pain and stared at her in astonishment. Blinded by the madness, Aylaen threw stone after stone, hitting friend and foe alike. There was no need to aim, for the men were bunched together, and she could not fail to hit someone. Aylaen shrieked curses at them and hurled stones.

A man grabbed her from behind. Strong arms wrapped around her, pinning her arms to her side. She could not see who had hold of her. She had no idea if he was friend or foe. All she knew was that he was stopping her from hurting those who had hurt her, and she kicked him in the shins and tried to bite him and fought to free herself. The man refused to let go.

"Stop, Aylaen! They'll kill you if don't!"

"Good!" she said viciously, and stamped on his foot.

He kept hold of her.

"We will have our revenge one day, Aylaen," he said into her ear. "But not today. Today we must stay alive."

The madness receded. The bloody mist that had obscured her vision receded. Men held their heads, groaning, their faces bruised and bloodied. Aylaen was fiercely glad to see the soldier who had accosted her holding his hand over his cracked head.

"I'm all right," Aylaen mumbled. "You can let go now."

Skylan let go of her. Aylaen was startled. She had no idea Skylan was the one who had been holding her. Everyone was staring at her. She felt tears sting her eyes. She realized in dismay she was going to cry in front of all these men and that would make her look even weaker.

Skylan stepped in front of her and began to talk, telling the Torgun about the Para Dix, about how they were going to be fighting in this game. The men turned their attention to him, giving Aylaen a chance to avert her head and hastily wipe her eyes.

Zahakis had no need to ask what had happened to cause the fight. He could guess. He ordered the soldier with the broken nose to get himself patched up. Zahakis ordered the Torgun to go back to work, then walked over to Aylaen.

"I have orders to take you to the Temple," he said.

"You sent Wulfe to the Temple and he never made it," said Skylan dourly.

"Don't start trouble," Zahakis said grimly. "You won't win."

"What about the Para Dix?" asked Skylan. "Keeper says she is to be one of the team."

"She is only going to the Temple for a visit," said Zahakis. "She will be back for training."

"It's all right, Skylan," Aylaen said. "I want to see to Treia."

"See what you can find out about Wulfe," Skylan said to her in a low voice.

Aylaen nodded. Her eyes were swimming. She couldn't see him very well.

"You routed two armies," he said to her. "Single-handed. Well done."

Aylaen wiped her running nose with the back of her hand and walked off with Zahakis, holding her head high.

Zahakis rode to the Temple on horseback, with Aylaen riding behind him. She paid little attention to the crowds or the people in the streets who stared at the two of them. She was so weary it was all she could do to keep from falling off the horse. Zahakis brought her to the Temple and sent a messenger to summon Raegar.

He came swiftly, accompanied by Treia.

"I will send an escort for her tomorrow to commence her training," said Zahakis.

Raegar frowned, displeased. "Perhaps she will not want to leave. Aelon might call upon her to serve him as a priestess."

Zahakis glanced at Aylaen. Her face was flushed and filthy, her clothes torn and sweat-stained, her hair straggling into her face, her fingers and arms scratched and bloody. He thought about the trouble she had caused and would continue to cause.

"I wish Aelon luck with that," said Zahakis.

Treia and Raegar took Aylaen into the Temple. Raegar showed her the wonders, the huge statue of Aelon, the gifts people were leaving. Aylaen yawned and stumbled and almost fell asleep standing up. Treia, seeing her fatigue, suggested that she take her back to her room.

Aylaen accompanied them, too tired to pay any attention to where they were going. She did note that Treia had donned what was apparently the garb of a priestess of Aelon, for all the other women walking the Temple grounds were dressed in the same long, white flowing gown, belted at the waist.

They reached the nunnery. Raegar gave Aylaen a smile and, taking her hand in his, squeezed it affectionately, and then left. Treia had noticed, Aylaen saw.

"You look as though you have been in a brawl," said Treia, regarding her with disfavor. "And you need a bath."

Treia took Aylaen to the small cell and made her lie down on her bed. Aylaen argued a little, but not much. She let her sister strip off her clothes and bathe her in cool water. Aylaen fell asleep during these ministrations and knew nothing more until she woke to find that it was night.

Light shone through the tiny window and she could see her sister quite clearly. Treia was seated in a chair beside the bed.

"You took a little nap. How are you feeling?" Treia asked solicitously.

"Sore," said Aylaen, wincing at the pain in her lower back and her arms. "And hungry."

Treia provided food—bread and honey, dried apples and olives.

"Sister," Treia began.

"Don't call me that," said Aylaen, annoyed. She dipped the bread in the honey.

"Call you what?" Treia asked, startled.

"Sister. You only call me sister when you want something from me," said Aylaen.

Treia flushed an ugly color and rose to her feet. She stalked over to the window, her back to her.

Aylaen was suddenly ashamed.

"Treia, I'm sorry. I didn't mean to hurt you. I don't know what I'm saying or doing anymore. I'm so tired. I can't sleep. And yet . . . I can't seem to wake up either!"

Treia turned to her. She regarded her sister silently for a moment, then came to sit by her side. Treia's eyes were wide and coated with a moist sheen that glimmered in the light. "I want to help, Aylaen. And so does Aelon. That's why I needed to talk to you. The god wants to give you your heart's desire."

Aylaen regarded her sister in perplexity. "Aelon? He is the god of our enemies, Treia. Why are you praying to him?"

"Why not pray to him? Our gods took away my childhood. Our gods made me half-blind and made me a spinster for people to mock. Our gods bring nothing to our people but hardship and pain. Why should I worship them?"

She drew nearer, resting her cold hand on Aylaen's.

"Why should you worship them, Aylaen? They let Garn die. . . ."

The thread is twisted and spun upon the wheel. Then I snip it and he dies. The little song ran through Aylaen's head.

"Aelon wants to ease your pain, Aylaen. He wants to give you a gift."

"Have you seen the tattoos on our menfolk? Your god inflicts pain. He does not ease it."

Treia shook her head. "Our god does not want to harm them. He grieves when he is forced to punish them, just as our mother grieved when she had to punish us."

"Sigurd was never sad when he punished us," said Aylaen. "He enjoyed hitting us. Perhaps your god is the same."

"Stop it, Aylaen," said Treia tersely. "I'm trying to help you. Aelon is not like Sigurd. The god wants you to know that he loves you. That is why he wants to give you a gift."

"And what is this 'gift'?" Aylaen asked warily.

"Aelon can bring Garn back to life."

Aylaen stared. "I don't believe you. This is a cruel jest."

"No, my sister," said Treia. "I am in earnest."

Aylaen stood up, dragging the bed linens with her to cover her nakedness.

"I won't listen to this. I want to leave. Where are my clothes?"

"I threw them out. They were bloodstained and they stank. Don't you want to be with Garn again?"

"This is a lie," said Aylaen, trembling. "I don't believe you."

"Raegar assures me—"

"Raegar!" Aylaen gave a bitter smile. "So he is the one behind this. I might have guessed."

"Please listen to me, Aylaen!" Treia tried to take hold of her sister's hand, but Aylaen drew back from her. "I know you don't like Raegar, but he is fond of you"—her lips twisted when she said this—"and he is sad to see you suffer."

"You are telling me that this god can bring Garn back to life," Aylaen said. "How is that possible?"

"Aelon is a powerful god, Aylaen," said Treia. "Far more powerful than the gods of the Vindrasi, which is why they are going down in defeat."

"Garn would be with me, living, breathing. He could touch me, talk to me . . . ?"

"Through the blessing and wonder of Aelon, Garn will be with you."

Aylaen sat back down on the bed. She thought of loving Garn again, of holding him in her arms, of telling him how much she loved him. Tears filled her eyes.

"I don't believe it," she said again.

"Raegar will prove it to you, Aylaen," said Treia. "Tonight you will sleep here with me. You will have all day tomorrow to think about this. If you are willing, Raegar will take you to the Spirit Priestesses tomorrow night. Now sleep. You must look your best. For Garn."

Aylaen lay down on the bed, but she could not sleep. She was bewildered, confused, her mind in turmoil. She wanted so much to believe that she and Garn would be together again. But restoring the dead to life was impossible. Not only impossible, but wrong. Garn would be in Torval's Hall with the other heroes. He would be angry with her for dragging him away.

But I can bear his anger, Aylaen thought. I can bear anything so long as he is with me again!

"Treia, what does Aelon want of me?" Aylaen asked. "The god must want something."

"Aelon wants you to love him, Sister. As he loves you."

"And nothing else?"

"Well . . ." said Treia with a smile hidden by the shadows, "perhaps Aelon does want a *little* something. . . ."

BOOK TWO

The sky was clear the next day, the sun shone brightly, strong and powerful. The day would be hot. Raegar basked in the sun's warmth as he walked to the Shrine to meet Treia early, as the crowds were gathering for morning prayers. When he had first come to Oran as a slave, he had detested the summer's heat. He had thought he would die of it, the breathless nights lying in bed, bathed in his own sweat; the relentless sunshine that beat on him like a hammer during the day, making him light-headed and giddy.

He had grown used to the heat, and now came to relish it. He recalled the cruel, killing winters of his homeland, of toes that turned black from frostbite and had to be cut off, of enduring bleak months of snow and wind, half-starved, half-frozen. He looked back on his life with distaste, wondering how he could have ever longed to return to it.

Aelon was his life now. Sinaria and its people were his life. He wanted, more than anything, for them to accept him, respect him. He had the spiritbone of the dragon. Treia would teach him the ritual or the Dragon Fala would teach him.

He had not yet attempted to summon the dragon, but he was certain she would answer. Her spiritbone had all but leaped into his hand during the raid on the temple. Though he had not yet met her or spoken to her, he seemed to know her. Her image came into his mind whenever he touched the spiritbone. Fala was a young dragon, eager and ambitious. Young dragons have a difficult time surviving and bringing children into the world, for the older dragons, like Kahg, have first pick of the jewels that in some instances are not jewels at all, but unborn dragons.

The Dragon Fala was not a follower of Aelon. She wanted treasure and in return, she agreed to help Raegar sail the seas in search of jewels. A war galley was being secretly rebuilt and refitted to accommodate the dragon.

Now all Raegar had to do was to convince Treia that she must learn the secret to controlling the Vektan dragon. He would be savior of his people. He would ride through the streets in a chariot. The crowds would praise his name and throw flowers in his path. The Empress would crown him with laurel leaves. She might well make him Priest-General.

He found Treia seated by herself on a bench in the shade of an oleander. She sat with her accustomed stiff-backed rigidity, her hands in her lap. He could not tell from looking at her whether she had been successful convincing Aylaen or failed utterly. One could never tell what Treia was thinking or feeling.

When he had first met her, he had thought her frigid, a woman born to die a virgin. Even when it became obvious that she was in love with him, she had grown stiff and cold in his arms whenever he had tried to make love to her. He had taken others to his bed during those months, so he did not feel the lack of female companionship. Yet he was surprised to find that he wanted Treia. He wanted to break through her shell of ice and make her his own.

He still remembered how she had come across him in the Hall of Vindrash on the Dragon Isles. She had feared he was dead and she was overjoyed to find him still alive. In the transports of her joy, she had given herself to him with abandon, not once, but several times. And their lovemaking had been like that ever since, passionate and fiery. He felt his blood burn at the memory. He saw her sitting on the bench, cold to all the world, and he thought of her sweating in his arms, moaning and digging her nails into his flesh.

He wondered if Aylaen would be like her sister in that regard. With her red curls and fiery temper, he imagined that she would be like a catamount in his bed.

He looked around.

"Where is Aylaen?" he asked.

"Zahakis came to fetch her. She is in training for that silly game.

Don't worry," Treia added, seeing him frown, "I told Zahakis she must return to the Temple tonight. She has agreed to go to the Spirit Priestesses."

"Excellent," said Raegar, his good humor restored. "In truth, I'm glad she's gone." He grasped hold of her arm and pulled her close. "Come with me."

"Where? We will miss morning prayers."

"No, we won't. We have time. This won't take long."

He led her to a small shrine located on the grounds. The shrine was small and shabby, one of the first built to Aelon when he was newly come to this world. The Priest-General had rededicated it to one of the lesser gods of Aelon's pantheon.

The priests and priestesses went to this shrine, though not to worship. Surrounded by a thick stand of pine trees, the shrine offered one of the few places on the Temple grounds where lovers could find some privacy. Most couples came here by night. Raegar could not wait for night, however.

The shrine was small, more like a mausoleum. He pushed open the heavy door and drew Treia inside and slammed the door shut, leaving them in darkness. She knew immediately what he wanted and she gave a fierce cry and clasped him in her arms. He lifted the skirts of her robes and shoved her up against a wall. He fumbled and grunted and she moaned with pleasure and in moments, their lovemaking was over.

A bell began to ring, summoning the faithful.

Treia shook down her skirts and combed her fingers through her tousled hair. Raegar smoothed his robes and caught his breath. When they were both seemly, they left the shrine, walking back toward the Temple.

"You know I love you, Treia," Raegar said.

"I know," she said softly. "I love you. I adore you."

"I want us to be happy together always. I want us to be married."

"I spoke to Aylaen," said Treia. "She will do what we ask. Or rather, she will do what *Garn* asks."

Raegar nodded. "I understand."

"She expects him to be alive, living and breathing."

"The Spirit Priestesses are accustomed to such expectations. They know how to handle people. She will be disappointed at first, but speaking to him, talking to him will whet her appetite. They will give her hope . . . hope that someday there will be more."

They were drawing near the Temple, merging with other people coming to pray. Treia lowered her voice.

"How will the Spirit Priestesses know to get this right? She must think she is talking to the man she loved. The man she's known since they were both children together."

"You forget the power of Aelon," said Raegar confidently. "He will work his holy magic. You will see."

"And these Spirit Priestesses know what 'Garn' must tell her to do? What he must say to her, ask of her?"

"Both the Priest-General and I have spoken to the Spirit Priestess who will be undertaking the ritual. She is venerable, experienced. She understands."

They had reached the Shrine. The doors remained closed. People were gathered in groups, laughing and talking. They had some time yet.

"Tell me about these Spirit Priestesses. What do they do? You say they communicate directly with Aelon. How? Do they talk to the god, like Draya talked to Vindrash?"

Raegar explained. "The Spirit Priestesses of Aelon live and work apart from the warrior-priests and the Mission-Bringers," he told her, "because the Spirit Priestesses need quiet to hear the voice of the god. The numbers of the Spirit Priestesses are relatively low. Few could meet the qualifications and, of those who do, fewer still agree to undergo the procedure that will bind them to Aelon for the remainder of their lives.

"Spirit Priestesses are required to lay bare their hearts and souls to Aelon and be obedient to his will in all things. Spirit Priestesses are not permitted to marry or take lovers," Raegar said. "Their lives are dedicated to the god and his holy works. Spirit Priestesses are in direct communication with the god, but Aelon does not speak to them on a personal level, not as Vindrash spoke to Draya.

"Aelon communicates with his Spirit Priestesses through the gemstones embedded in the flesh of their cheeks or, with those of higher rank, on their foreheads."

Treia found this difficult to believe.

"The embedding of the gems is known as the 'gift of enlightment,'" said Raegar, "and it is a most holy ceremony, performed in secret, with only Spirit Priestesses in attendance. Not even the Priest-General knows what transpires during these ceremonies."

"Does the crystal powder the women poured into the tattoo in Skylan's arm allow slaves to communicate with the god?" Treia asked.

"No, no," Raegar said. "The crystal powder allows the god to communicate his will to his slaves, let them know of his displeasure. A slap on the hand, such as a mother gives a naughty child."

"I see. Then why didn't you do that to Aylaen?" Treia demanded, confronting him. "Why didn't you tattoo her? Then Aelon could have forced her to reveal the secret."

"I have hopes that she will come to Aelon of her own accord," said Raegar.

"You have hopes she will come to your bed," Treia muttered.

"You wrong me, Treia," said Raegar, drawing himself up. "Aylaen is your sister. I love her for your sake. Nothing more."

Not precisely true, but Raegar was biding his time. Once he and Treia were married, he could do what he pleased. Aelon knew that men have needs, that it took more than one woman to satisfy these needs. Many men kept female slaves in their homes for that very reason. He did not try to explain it to Treia. She would never understand.

He turned his back and walked off by himself, letting Treia feel the full weight of his displeasure. After a few moments, he heard her come running after him. He smiled inwardly.

"I am sorry, my love," she said meekly. "Please forgive me."

He forgave her with a kiss and they walked to the Shrine of Aelon together.

The doors to the Shrine swung open. Raegar drew Treia close and said softly, "Bring Aylaen to the Spirit Priestesses at sunset this night. Remember, my love, if we summon the Vektan dragon to defeat the ogres, we will be the saviors of Sinaria. Nothing will be too good for us!"

After the service, the Priest-General summoned Raegar to meet with him in his office. Raegar waited a short time for Xydis to conclude a previous appointment, then he was ushered inside.

Xydis gestured to a chair. Raegar had barely seated himself when Xydis said, with his customary abruptness, "We must do something about Acronis. The Empress informed him of the threat posed by the ogres, how they intend to attack Sinaria. I sent a request that due to the emergency, he hand over command of his triremes and his private army to me, as the law of Aelon requires in time of crisis."

"And he refused," said Raegar.

"Not only did he refuse, he had the unmitigated gall to tell me that his men would refuse to serve under my command! I told him they would be under your command. He said that his men had even less respect for you than they did for me."

Raegar flushed in anger. "Tell the Empress he flouts the law. Have him arrested."

"I cannot," said Xydis. "I will need his army in this battle. His soldiers are better trained, better equipped than ours. If I had his wealth, the men would fight for me."

He made an impatient gesture. "Acronis sails off on voyages fraught with danger, yet never fails to return unscathed. Sometimes I wonder what Aelon is thinking."

"I don't see that we would gain much if Acronis died," said Raegar. "His estate would go to his daughter and, from what I hear, she is as obdurate as her father."

Xydis was amused. "Unlike you barbarians, women cannot inherit property in Oran. And since Acronis has no male heirs, the estate would come to the crown. And from the crown, to the Church."

Raegar was angry at the insult. He let it go, however, as he let go a thousand others. He considered Xydis's words and wondered, suddenly, if the man was hinting at something.

"Acronis does not need to sail the ocean to find danger," Raegar said, feeling his way forward tentatively. "He could easily fall victim to a thief or run afoul of one of the city's gangs."

"We are working hard to find a way to rid our city of such criminal elements," said Xydis mildly. Then he added, "But, yes, the Legate falling victim to a murderous gang would be a shame. We should pray to Aelon to keep him safe."

Xydis paused, then added, "Especially tonight. The Legate and that cousin of yours, Skylan, and the ogre, Keeper, have been invited to the Palace for the celebration of the opening of the Para Dix games. He will be returning to his villa well after darkness falls. . . ."

"Let us pray," said Raegar, with a smile.

12

BOOK TWO

The first training session for the Para Dix took place the morning
that Raegar and Xydis met. The Torgun were marched to the
playing field by the Tribune's soldiers, who ordered them to sit on the
ground and keep quiet. Aylaen arrived shortly after, escorted by Zahakis. All Aylaen could think about was Garn and the claim that
Aelon could bring her lover back to life. Garn had attained what every
warrior longed for—he had died a hero's death. He would be in Torval's Hall. If she dragged him away . . . Unhappy and troubled, war-
ring between doing what she longed to do and doing what she knew
she should do, she sat apart from the others, her head bowed.

Skylan, keeping an eye on the guards who were talking to Zahakis, managed to slide closer to Aylaen.

"Did you find out anything about Wulfe?" he asked.

Aylaen gave a start and stared at him as if she had no idea who he
was.

Skylan eyed her. "Are you all right?"

"Yes, of course," she said shortly.

"Are you sure? You don't look well."

"I'm fine!" she said, glaring at him.

"Did you ask about Wulfe—"

Aylaen flushed guiltily. "I didn't . . . have a chance. I'm sorry."
She hunched her shoulders and turned away from him.

The ogre came into view, lumbering across the playing field. The
day before, Skylan had told his men that an ogre godlord was going
to teach them how to fight. He told them what he learned about the
Para Dix, which was, in truth, next to nothing because he hadn't

been paying attention. At first Sigurd and the others refused to believe him, and then, when he swore an oath on Torval's beard that he was telling the truth, they were outraged—at him.

"We are supposed to fight and bleed while these goat-fornicating Southlanders jeer at us!" Sigurd said angrily.

"You can always go back to picking up rocks," Skylan said. "You were good at that, I hear. I, for one, want the chance to hold a sword in my hand."

Sigurd glowered, realizing he'd put himself in a bad position. Given manual labor or the chance to fight—no matter if it was for show—the other Torgun would side with Skylan. Even Sigurd's most loyal supporter, Grimuir, was looking uncertain.

"I will fight in this Para Dix," said Sigurd grandly. "The men will need their Chief to lead them."

Once, not so long ago, Skylan would have leaped down Sigurd's throat. He had come to the realization that rainy night on the *Venjekar,* when he had almost given way to despair, that the Torgun's greatest strength lay in each other. To win this battle, they would have to stand together, shoulder to shoulder, as in the shield wall.

Keeper ordered the Torgun to stand, the tattoo of Aelon keeping them under control. The Torgun obeyed, sullenly, glaring at the detested ogre. Keeper looked them over, eyeing them up and down.

He walked over to Sigurd. "You call yourself a warrior, Graybeard? I am not surprised you ended up as slaves."

Keeper clenched his large fist and punched Sigurd in the face. Sigurd went down in a heap, his face covered in blood. Grimuir leaped on the ogre's back, wrapping his arms around Keeper's neck. The ogre reached behind, grabbed hold of Grimuir, and flipped him up and over his head. Grimuir landed flat and lay there staring stupidly at the sky. Zahakis and his men were lounging on the sidelines, watching, grinning.

"Get up, both of you," Keeper ordered.

Grimuir heaved himself to his feet. Sigurd muttered a curse and spit a gob of saliva mixed with blood on the ogre's boot. Keeper walked over to Sigurd and, using the maltreated boot, kicked him in the head, knocking him out cold.

Keeper looked around at the others.

"Any of the rest of you want to test me? Or maybe you just feel like hitting someone. Come on." The ogre beckoned. "Go ahead.

Give it a try. No? Then we will start practice. Our time is limited. Your first game is tomorrow afternoon."

He glared at Aylaen, who was standing with her arms crossed over her chest, staring at her boots.

The ogre looked sourly at Zahakis. "I have never trained a female. Does the Legate insist on putting her in the game?"

Zahakis nodded. "He believes she will be an attraction. The crowd will love her."

Keeper scowled.

Zahakis shrugged.

Keeper heaved a sigh and asked Aylaen sourly, "Have you been tested in battle, Female?"

Aylaen was somewhere else. She didn't even seem to hear him.

"You, Female!" Keeper said loudly.

Aylaen blinked and lifted her head.

"Are you battle-tested?" Keeper asked.

"She has been tested," said Skylan. "She fights well."

Keeper was puzzled. "Is it the custom of your people for females to fight?"

"Aylaen was chosen by the Goddess Vindrash to fight for her. The goddess gave her a blessed sword to use in battle."

The ogre was regarding Aylaen with new respect. "You know that the Para Dix is dedicated to Aelon, Female. Will fighting for a god of the Southlanders offend your goddess?"

"Of course it will," Aylaen said coolly. "The rage of Vindrash will strengthen my arm."

The Torgun glanced at each other and nodded.

"Tribune Zahakis," said Keeper, "see to it that the female's sword is returned to her. And give the males their weapons, as well."

The Torgun wondered if they had heard him right. Their eyes widened, their jaws dropped. They looked at each other. They looked at Skylan for confirmation. He kept his face straight, giving away nothing of his feelings.

Sigurd, who had been lying unconscious on the ground, started to groan, putting his hand to his ringing head. Grimuir went to help his friend stand. He muttered something.

"Huh?" Sigurd grunted. "Our weapons? The fools are giving us back our weapons?"

Skylan could have kicked him in the head again. Sigurd shook off Grimuir's aid and staggered off to join his fellows.

"Don't get your hopes up." Keeper grinned at them. "You will be armed, but only during the game. And you will use your weapons with Aelon's sanction. Try attacking me, for example, and you will feel Aelon's wrath."

Skylan glanced down at his bandaged arm. When the tattoo didn't sting and burn, it itched. He could attest to Aelon's ire and he had to concede that the god knew how to make his presence felt. Still, Skylan's heart soared. He would be armed. His men would be armed. Someday, somehow, with Torval's blessing, they would find a way to use their swords to escape this place.

Keeper launched into an explanation of the game. The ogre pointed to the center of the playing field that consisted of a circle blocked out in concentric squares, large on the outside, becoming smaller and more numerous in the center. Six enormous boulders, equidistant from each other, stood around the circle's outer boundary.

"The priests light a bonfire in the center of the field. The object of the game is simple. You must capture the fire. As I say, the object of the game is simple," Keeper repeated. "The playing of the game is not."

The Torgun shook their heads. How difficult could it be to capture a fire?

"I am your chief—" Keeper began.

"Like hell you are," Sigurd said, his words muffled by blood from his broken nose.

"—whether you pissants like it or not," Keeper continued. "I am your chief because I have been a participant in this game for many years.

"Many years," Keeper repeated, his voice hardening. He glanced at Skylan, perhaps recalling their conversation of yesterday.

The ogre was silent, his face shadowed. Then he shook himself, like a wet dog, and went on to describe the rules of the game.

He is thinking of what I said, Skylan realized, smiling inwardly. He can no longer eat his dinner with the same enjoyment. Every time he chews a mouthful, he remembers that he is eating his master's table scraps.

An elbow jabbed Skylan in the ribs.

"Are you listening to this bullshit?" Bjorn asked.

"I heard it yesterday," said Skylan.

All about each player being able to move so many squares at a time, in one direction at a time. Each player could move only when told to move, each could fight only when told to fight.

"Bullshit, as you say, my friend," said Skylan loudly.

Keeper stopped talking.

"All we have to do is capture the fire, right?" Skylan said. He gestured. "Give us shields and swords, and while our foes are dancing from one square to another, we will capture the goddam fire."

The Torgun laughed their agreement.

Zahakis left off lounging and stepped forward.

"That was how the Para Dix was played long ago," he said. "Men killing each other, blood covering the playing field. The spectators quickly grew bored with what was little more than an organized brawl. Now we have the rules as Keeper explained them."

"I think this young man finds it hard to play by the rules," Keeper said, eyeing Skylan.

"You obey their rules," Skylan said. "And you have grown fat and happy in the land of your enemies."

Keeper's plump cheeks quivered in anger, his small eyes narrowed. He clenched his fist and took a step. Skylan braced himself for the blow. Slowly and with an effort, the ogre regained control.

"You will find the game demeaning," Keeper said, his gaze on Skylan though he spoke to all of them. "You will find it hard to bear. You will hear the audience jeer and call you names. They will laugh when you are writhing on the ground in pain and applaud when a foe jabs you in the gut with a spear. They will cheer as you lay dying. And for what? For a stupid game, you say.

"You say wrong. We Para Dix players, we do not fight for the stinking crowd. We do not fight for the Empress or for our master or even for their god."

Keeper drew himself up proudly and now he looked at each of them, gathering them up, bringing them together. "We fight for honor. Not for the honor of winning, because sometimes we will not win. We fight for our honor and that of our people. And to gain honor, we must fight by the rules, even if we don't like them." He looked back at Skylan and there was a glint in the small eyes. "We may be slaves. They may have taken away our freedom. They may take our lives. But our honor is in our hearts and that they cannot take away."

The words seemed burned into Skylan's brain, like the tattoo on his arm. It was only an ogre who spoke, but it seemed to Skylan that the voice came from the gods.

The Torgun spent the rest of the afternoon hopping one square up and back three or leaping over one square and landing on another or doing mock battles with swords made of wood. When any of them made a move they shouldn't have, as when Aki went forward one square instead of back two, Keeper made sure Aki learned his mistake by knocking him on his arse. And if any tried to retaliate, as when Aki took a swing at the ogre, Keeper knocked him down again and again until he got it right.

Only one of the Torgun was not punished for making a mistake and that was Aylaen. If she moved to the wrong square or if she stood staring at nothing and forgetting to move at all, he would thunder "Female" until she looked at him.

Skylan thought at first Keeper was being easy on Aylaen because she was a woman, but he soon realized he was wrong.

"You, Female, you fight for the honor of your goddess," said Keeper angrily. "Yet you make your goddess look the fool."

"This is a stupid game," said Aylaen sullenly.

"It may be a stupid game, but if you make a mistake, you are not the only one who will suffer. You will let down everyone on your team, your comrades, your fellow warriors."

Aylaen shrugged, uncaring.

"When you stand in the shield wall, Female, do you use your shield to protect only yourself?" Keeper asked. "You overlap shields, so that your shield protects your body and that of the warrior next to you. Think only of yourself and another will suffer."

Aylaen paled. She looked so ill and unhappy that Bjorn said angrily, "Leave her alone. She is doing the best she can. We all are."

"The gods help you," Keeper growled.

Aylaen was careful to pay attention after that.

There were ten players on a team and only eight Torgun; the Legate brought in two veteran players from another one of his teams to train with them. Keeper explained that often "unblooded" players were put in with veterans so that they would learn what to do. These men were slaves; they all had the tattoos, but they were Southlanders, and, as Skylan was soon to learn, they were proud of the fact that they were players in the Para Dix.

The veterans laughed loudly at the stupidity of the barbarians, and there would have been trouble, despite the presence of the soldiers, if the Legate himself had not come strolling onto the field to see how the practice was progressing. The Southlander slaves were different men in his presence. Meek and servile, they groveled and fawned over him.

"Makes you want to vomit, doesn't it?" Bjorn said grimly.

Keeper had given them time to rest, drink some water, wipe away the sweat and the blood.

Skylan was surprised to find that Bjorn was actually holding a conversation with him, no longer ostracizing him. He was more surprised when Bjorn added, awkwardly, "I'm sorry for the way I've treated you, Skylan. I was punishing *you* for Garn's death. It wasn't right."

"I'm the one who is sorry, my friend," said Skylan. "I let Garn down. I let you down. I let all my people down."

Bjorn stared, amazed, then he said with a half smile, "That's the first time I have ever heard you say you were sorry for anything. When the real Skylan comes back, tell him I was asking for him."

"Skylan Ivorson has grown up, my friend," Skylan said quietly. "Torval willing, the other will never return."

Keeper blew a whistle and the practice started all over again.

It was late afternoon before Keeper called a halt. The Torgun sank to the ground, limp with exhaustion from standing and jumping and running and fighting in the hot sun.

"You must get used to it," Keeper told them. "In the arena, you will be fighting on the field, with a roaring fire burning in the center."

They were too tired to give a damn. Zahakis had orders to take Aylaen back to be with her sister. She had gained some color in her face during the practice, but the moment she saw Zahakis walking toward her, she went livid.

"Refuse to go back," said Skylan.

Aylaen cast him a desperate, fearful glance. Then she shook her head and went off with Zahakis.

Skylan had never been so exhausted, not even after fighting in the shield wall. Every muscle ached and burned. His head throbbed from the heat. He was bruised and bleeding. Every step required an effort and they had a long walk back to the slave compound.

He made no complaint, however, nor did any of the Torgun. Grimuir had stepped in a gopher hole and twisted his ankle. Sigurd had to stop on the way to throw up. Young Farinn's breath came in pain-filled gasps and he held his hand pressed against his ribs. Aki stifled a groan as he walked through the tall grass. Bjorn had to practically carry Erdmun. But they felt better than they had picking up rocks. *Our* honor is in our hearts. . . .

Skylan was looking forward to collapsing, when Keeper called out to him.

The ogre, bathed in sweat, gave off a rank odor. He walked slowly, his massive shoulders sagging. Ogres have very little stamina. Keeper was in better shape than most ogres, but even he must be as weary as Skylan.

"Haven't you tortured me enough today?" said Skylan, annoyed. "What do you want?"

"To thank you," said Keeper. He kept his voice low, his eyes on the soldiers.

"For what?" Skylan thought the ogre was jesting. "Not puking on your boots? Oh, I forgot. I *did* puke on your boots."

Keeper smiled, then grew serious. "You were right. I *have* grown too comfortable here. I have brought dishonor on myself and my people."

Skylan came to a sudden halt and stared at Keeper, an idea forming in his mind. He stared at the ogre so long, without saying a word, plans fomenting, that Keeper grew annoyed and the soldiers suspicious.

"What's the matter? Have I suddenly grown one eye like a Cyclops?" Keeper demanded.

"No talking, you two," a soldier yelled. "Keeper, the Legate wants you back at the villa. Don't keep him waiting."

"Go bugger yourself," Keeper muttered, but he obeyed.

Turning his back on Skylan, he walked off, heading in the direction of the villa.

Skylan ran soft-footed over the grass after Keeper. The soldier gave a warning shout, but it was too late. Skylan jumped on the ogre's broad back. Keeper roared in anger and, beneath Skylan's weight, fell to the ground.

"Listen to me!" Skylan smashed the ogre's forehead into the dirt and spoke into his ear. "Ogre warships are sailing to attack Sinaria."

Keeper managed to twist his head. One eye peered up at Skylan.

"It's true," Skylan said, grinding his knee into Keeper's back. "I overheard Zahakis and Acronis talking about it."

Keeper got his hands planted and heaved himself up off the ground, sending Skylan flying. He rolled out of the way just as Keeper's boot slammed down, barely missing his head, and scrambled to his feet. He and Keeper glared and circled each other, ignoring the soldier's orders for them to stop.

"Are there more of your people in the city?" Skylan asked.

"Yes," said Keeper.

"Can you get the word out?"

Keeper nodded. They had no time for more before the soldiers came.

"All right, break it up. Haven't you savages had your fill of blood enough for one day?"

Keeper wiped dirt and blood from his face.

"Not nearly," he said.

Skylan smiled. The fire burned.

It was only later, when he was half-asleep, that he realized his arm had not burned when he had attacked Keeper. Apparently Aelon had no problem with slaves killing each other.

Raegar sent a messenger to Treia, saying that he would meet her and Aylaen at the fane of the Spirit Priestesses at moonrise. The messenger gave Treia directions to the building, which was located in a distant and isolated part of the enclave. Treia made her way along the winding paths, stopping often to ask others if she was on the right path, and they reassured her. With her poor eyesight, Treia was often nervous being in strange places and she insisted on holding Aylaen's hand, saying she needed someone to serve as her guide. In truth, Aylaen was so nervous, her hand was so cold, that Treia feared her sister might bolt.

When they reached the garden and could see the walls of the Temple beyond, Aylaen stopped. She felt her legs go weak and she leaned against the wall.

"I am afraid," she said, trembling. "I don't know if I can, Treia. This is not right. Garn is with Torval, in the Hall of Heroes. I am selfish—"

"You are in love," said Treia, wondering impatiently what had become of Raegar. She needed his help. She did not know how much longer she could keep hold of Aylaen. "There is no Hall of Heroes. It is all a lie. Garn's spirit is lost, abandoned. You will find him and show him the way."

"Show him the way where?" Aylaen asked, puzzled.

Treia checked an annoyed remark. How was *she* supposed to know? She was only repeating what she'd heard Raegar say. Hearing footsteps, she breathed a sigh of relief to see Raegar coming toward them. Treia lifted her lips to be kissed. Raegar brushed her cheek, then turned to Aylaen.

"You do not look well, my dear," he said gently. "Your grief is making you ill."

"I am not 'your dear,' " said Aylaen, pulling away from him when he tried to take her hands. "I do not want to do this. I . . . want to go back."

"The choice is yours, of course," said Raegar smoothly. "No one is forcing you. Standing on the threshold of Death requires courage. Only those whose love is strong dare make the attempt. You are young. Time has passed. It is natural that your love for Garn has waned—"

"My love has not waned. I love him more than ever!" Aylaen cried. "I want to see him, to be with him. But he is in the care of the gods. . . ."

"At least, you should make the attempt. If, as you say, Garn is in Torval's Hall, carousing with the other warriors, he will not come and you will know that he has forgotten you. You need no longer grieve for him."

Aylaen was silent, stung by his words.

"I will see for myself," she muttered.

Raegar started to give his arm to Aylaen. She disdained it and walked off on her own. Treia, casting him an angry look, seized his arm and the two walked together.

"She will never have anything to do with you," said Treia.

"We will not speak of it," said Raegar coldly.

The Fane of the Spirit Priestesses was a small structure, cubic in shape, constructed of limestone blocks fronted with marble. The fane was simple and elegant in design. Columns on all four sides supported the roof. The building had no windows. A single door at the top of a flight of stairs provided entry.

Unlike the Temple of Aelon, which was decorated with all manner of symbols and runes, this building was plain and unadorned. The magic worked by the Spirit Priestesses was delicate and sensitive as a strand of gossamer in an intricate web. The Spirit Priestesses had to be attuned to every quiver of every strand and could not be distracted by any other magic, even though it was the holy magic of their god.

The Priest-General met them at the entrance to the fane. He glanced once at Raegar, a questioning look, and received a nod in return. Xydis smiled and greeted Aylaen kindly, expressing sorrow for her loss. He could see she was frightened and uncertain. He pressed her hand and spoke words of reassurance.

Xydis rang a small bell and the bronze door opened.

Aylaen hung back, shivering.

"The ceremony is not horrible or terrifying. It is sacred, blessed. You will soon be reunited with the man you love."

Xydis put a fatherly arm around Aylaen and led her over the threshold.

Treia and Raegar were about to follow when Treia tightened her grip on Raegar's hand and pulled him close.

"You are sure this will go the way we want?" she said in an undertone.

"The Spirit Priestesses know their business. And so does Aelon," said Raegar in a whisper. He squeezed her hand in warning. "Now we must be silent."

They entered cool darkness perfumed with incense and the smell of melting wax. Tall, slender, wrought-iron candlesticks formed a large circle in the middle of the floor. A Spirit Priestess stood in the center of the circle, gazing at them without expression.

She was an older woman of perhaps fifty years. Her face was seamed with the marks of age and was an odd contrast to the skin of her shaved head, which was smooth as a babe's. Her eyes were large and calm and mild. She was there and not there. She saw them and yet she didn't. Or rather, she saw them and was not much interested.

"After one hears the voice of the god," the Spirit Priestesses were wont to say, "all other voices are as the cawing of crows."

She had no snake tattoo. Instead, three large diamond crystals were embedded in her flesh—one in her forehead and the other two on her cheeks. Raegar's eyes opened wide when he saw her. He drew in an awed breath.

"We are highly honored. She is Semelon, the Head of the Order," Raegar whispered.

The diamonds marked Semelon's high ranking. Those of lower rank were given semiprecious gems. Slaves, like Skylan, made do with pulverized quartz. Semelon wore a plain white tunic that fell from thin shoulders and was belted around the waist. Her feet were bare, and she gestured to all of them to remove their shoes and leave them at the entrance.

She did not speak, but made a gesture of welcome, extending her hands as if she would embrace them. A sense of peace stole over everyone, a quieting of the soul, an inner calm. Aylaen quit shivering and drew in a deep breath and closed her eyes. Xydis gave a slight inclination of his head to indicate their readiness.

Semelon looked from one to another. She asked no questions, spoke no words. Gliding forward, she took hold of Aylaen's hand and drew her into the circle of light. Aylaen went without hesitation, no longer fearful, no longer doubting.

Semelon lifted two of the lighted candles from one of the candlesticks. She handed one candle to Aylaen, kept the other candle for herself. Semelon knelt on the floor in the middle of the circle and tilted the candle, causing the molten wax to drip onto the floor and form a small pool. She placed the end of her candle into the pool and gestured for Aylaen to do the same, indicating she was to place her candle about twenty paces from Semelon's. She took two more candles and, giving one to Aylaen, put these on the floor at right angles from the others, forming a square within the circle.

Semelon led Aylaen out of the square and, keeping hold of Aylaen's hand, touched Aylaen's fingers to the diamond in the left cheek and held it there. Semelon closed her eyes. Her lips moved in an incantation. They could not hear her words.

A ghostly figure appeared in the square formed by the four candles. Treia sucked in her breath between her teeth and dug her nails into Raegar's hand. He swallowed and backed up a step.

"Garn!" Aylaen murmured.

Tears filled her eyes. Semelon placed her hand on Aylaen's mouth, cautioning her not to speak. The ghostly figure was wispy, wavering, like morning mist rising off the water. Semelon strengthened her incantation; they could hear her words. Her tone was insistent, commanding.

The ghost became more substantial, flesh and bone. Garn's wrists were chained, as were his feet. His face was bloodied and bruised, as though he had been struck repeatedly.

Aylaen gasped and put her hand to her mouth.

Xydis cast a sharp, questioning glance at Semelon. She remained calm, impassive.

"You may speak to him," she said.

"Why are you in chains, my love?" Aylaen said, agonized.

"You keep me here," said Garn and his voice was filled with sorrow. "Because of you, I am a prisoner."

Aylaen gave an anguished cry and started to walk toward him into the square of light. Semelon detained her.

"He speaks to us from the realm of the dead. The living may not enter."

"Forgive me. . . ." Aylaen said brokenly. "They said Aelon would bring you back to life!"

She reached out a trembling hand. "I love you so much, Garn. I miss you. . . ."

"If you truly love me, you will find a way to set me free," said Garn. He held up his chained wrists. "Do not let them keep me a prisoner throughout eternity."

"How can I free you? I will do anything!"

"You must tell your sister the secret of the Vektan dragons," said Garn.

Treia gave an audible gasp. Raegar stared at the ghost with wide eyes.

"But . . . I don't know anything about the Vektan dragons!" Aylaen faltered. "How could I? Only a Kai Priestess knows such things!"

"Vindrash speaks to you, Sister," Treia said harshly, "as she once spoke to Draya. If you ask the goddess, she will tell you."

Aylaen looked at her sister in bewilderment. "But why would you want to know such a thing?"

Treia said nothing. The Priest-General was stone-faced, glaring balefully at Semelon. Raegar swallowed. He was finding it difficult to look at the dead man. The fane was silent except for the hissing of guttering candles.

It was Garn who answered. "The priests of Aelon have one of the five spiritbones of the Vektia. The god, Sund, gave it to them. Treia plans to use it to summon the dragon."

"The god, Sund . . . Is this true, Treia?" Aylaen cried, dismayed. "Are you working for our enemies now? Are you a traitor, too?"

"Do not judge me, Aylaen," Treia said. "You have no idea what you are talking about."

"Give your sister the secret and Garn will go free," said Xydis. He added more gently, "As Treia says, events are transpiring in the world, important things are happening that will affect you and your people and everyone in Sinaria. Your sister is not a traitor and neither is your god. They both do this for the good of your people."

Aylaen clasped her hands in anguish. She looked at Treia and then she looked back at Garn. She covered her face with her hands. Her body shook with sobs. She sank to her knees.

Garn drew near her. He did not leave the circle. He made a motion as if to embrace her. The chains prevented him, held him back.

"You do not need to ask Vindrash, Aylaen. Someone else knows the secret to the Vektan dragons. Skylan knows. Ask him."

"Skylan!" Raegar repeated hoarsely. He frowned. "How could Skylan know? It is a trick. The ghost lies."

"The dead cannot lie," said Semelon.

Treia drew close to Raegar and whispered, "Draya must have told Skylan. The fool woman adored him. She would have told him all her secrets. Skylan loves Aylaen. He will tell her."

Raegar sucked in a breath and said in a mutter, "He lies."

"Talk to Skylan, Aylaen," Garn urged her. "Ask him for the secret. He will tell you."

Aylaen regarded Garn sadly. "If I tell Treia, will Aelon set you free?"

"Ask Skylan, Aylaen," Garn said.

A warm breeze wafted through the fane. The candles wavered. The breeze strengthened and the candles went out. The ghost vanished. Aylaen's strength failed her. She fell to the floor, insensible.

"She has fainted," said Semelon, kneeling beside her. "She is overcome with the spirit. This often happens."

Semelon took Aylaen in her arms and, holding her close, began to rock back and forth, murmuring soothing words.

Xydis walked out the door, giving Raegar a commanding look to follow. Raegar hastened to obey him.

"That did not go as anticipated," Xydis said, once they were outside and the door had shut behind them. "Still, we got what we came for and that is all that matters. This Skylan . . . will he tell her?"

Raegar said nothing. His face was livid. Sweat covered his brow.

"He will tell my sister, Worshipful Sir," said Treia, wondering what was wrong with Raegar. He looked extremely ill. "He is besotted with her."

Xydis grunted his satisfaction and hastened off. Raegar groaned and slumped back against a stone wall.

"What is the matter?" Treia asked in perplexity. "The news is good. Skylan knows the secret—"

"*That* is what is the matter!" Raegar shouted, rounding on her in a fury. "Skylan knows the secret. And I arranged to have him killed!"

B O O K   T W O

Zahakis brought Aylaen back to the Torgun slave compound early the following morning. She was wan and upset and refused to talk to Bjorn when he asked her what had happened. She brushed past him.

Skylan did not make an attempt to try to talk to her, knowing he would be rebuffed, as usual. He was therefore astonished beyond measure when Aylaen walked up to him.

She did not speak. Her gaze was searching, pleading. If he had said something to her, she might have told him everything, but he was so startled he was tongue-tied and paralyzed. Aylaen sighed, lowered her eyes, and walked away.

Skylan came to his senses and started to go after her, only to feel Zahakis's hand on his shoulder.

"Mistress Chloe wants you."

"Not now," said Skylan brusquely, forgetting where he was, who he was. Forgetting everything. Aylaen wanted him, needed him.

"I beg your pardon, my lord," said Zahakis. "I will tell Mistress Chloe to wait until you are at leisure."

The next thing Skylan knew he was rolling around on the ground, groaning from a jab to the kidneys from the butt-end of a spear.

"Ah, my lord, I see you are at leisure," said Zahakis, and he hauled Skylan to his feet.

Skylan stood in the opulent bedroom shifting from foot to foot to try to ease the pain in his back. The female house slave, Rosa, spread a silken coverlet over Chloe's legs and placed a bowl of chilled grapes within the girl's reach. Rosa opened the doors to the atrium, filling the room with sunshine. A gentle breeze carried with it the perfume of a multitude of flowering plants.

"Leave us, Rosa," said Chloe to the slave.

The slave bowed and took her place in a shadowy corner.

Chloe frowned at her. "I said leave us."

Rosa seemed uneasy. She did not move.

"In a minute, I shall grow angry," said Chloe severely.

"She can't leave," said Skylan. "Your father told her to stay here to see that I don't harm you."

Chloe laughed bubbling, gurgling laughter. "And if you were going to hurt me, Skylan, would Rosa be able to stop you?"

"No," said Skylan, smiling in spite of himself. "But she could scream. And then the twenty armed soldiers Zahakis has posted outside your door would come rushing in and kill me."

"And would you fight for you life?"

"Of course," said Skylan.

A dimple flashed in Chloe's cheek. "I'd like to see that. Perhaps I'll scream. Should we try it?"

"Twenty Southlanders to one Torgun warrior is hardly a fair fight," said Skylan. "Your father would be angry at me for slaying his soldiers."

Chloe laughed. "Rosa, go tell my father that he is a simpleton."

Rosa shook her head, terrified.

Chloe heaved an exasperated sigh and raised her voice. "Zahakis!"

There was silence, then the inner door that led from the main house into the bedroom opened. Zahakis stepped inside.

"Yes, Mistress Chloe."

"I'm sure you and your men have better things to do than stand guard outside my door. Go away. And take Rosa with you."

Zahakis might have said he was not accustomed to obeying orders given to him by fifteen-year-old little girls, but he knew he would only be putting off the inevitable. Chloe would next appeal to her father and her dimpled smile would bring Acronis to his knees and he would end up ordering Zahakis to remove the guards. Zahakis might as well save them all time and effort and humiliation.

"I can scream quite loudly myself, Zahakis," Chloe added mischievously. "Do you want to hear me?"

Zahakis was not amused. "I will remain within earshot," he told her. He gestured to Rosa, who skittered out after him and shut the door.

"Now, that is better," said Chloe. She pointed to a chair. "Sit down. You are fighting in the Para Dix tomorrow and you must keep up your strength."

Chloe clasped her hands together and said eagerly, "I am going to the Para Dix to watch you fight! And tonight I am going to the palace for the celebration given by the Empress! My father has said I could go. You and Keeper are to come, too! I am so excited. You are my first champion. Now, you must tell me how your training went. What position are you? The woman, the beautiful one with the red hair. What is her name? My father says she is also going to be on your team. He will dress her as an Ogressa. Do you know what that is? What is *her* position? Now, I'll be quiet. Tell me everything."

Skylan thought of Sigurd on his knees puking up his guts. Bjorn bashing headlong into a boulder. Grimuir always in the wrong place and Aki and Farinn backing into each other. He did not know what to say.

"I'm sorry. I ask too many questions," said Chloe. "My father says I chatter like a magpie. What is your position?"

"I am a . . ." Skylan hesitated, stumbling over the unfamiliar word. "I am a thing called a pradus."

Chloe clapped her hands again. "Pradus! Perfect! The most powerful piece on the board. And the most difficult to play. That's the right position for you. And the woman . . ."

"Aylaen," said Skylan.

"Aylaen is a loris, right? Of course! The piece of mystic power. My father told me she fights for the honor of her dragon goddess."

Chloe asked another question and another and Skylan soon realized that she was truly knowledgeable about the game. She knew far more than he did, that was for certain, and she explained the reasoning behind the pieces and the movements that Keeper had not bothered to tell them.

After they had exhausted Para Dix strategy, Chloe asked Skylan about his home and his family, the Vindrasi people, and their dragons.

"My father told me he saw your dragon. I am so jealous of him I could spit," said Chloe. "But since I will never see a dragon for myself, you must tell me about them."

Skylan had always enjoyed an audience. He was a good story-teller, and Chloe was an appreciative and attentive listener. Telling stories about the Dragon Kahg made him recall his battle with the ogre godlord. He related to Chloe how the ogres had come to his village and told the Torgun their gods were dead. How the Torgun had tried to trick the ogres by roasting the boar he had slain, using the smoke as a signal fire to summon their clansmen. How the ogre godlord had arrived at the feast wearing the sacred Vektan torque and how the Dragon Kahg had come to fight in the battle and how Skylan had killed the godlord, only to have the ogre shaman put a magical curse on him and steal the torque from his hand.

Chloe listened in breathless excitement and sighed when the story came to an end.

"I wish *our* god was dead," she said. "I like your gods better. Tell me more about Torval."

Skylan told her about Torval, the god of battle, to whom every warrior dedicated himself. He told her about Torval's Hall, where the heroes went after they died to spend eternity drinking and carousing and fighting each other if there was no one else to fight.

"Are there no women in Torval's Hall?" Chloe asked.

"A woman who is wife to a hero meets him there when she dies," said Skylan. "There is singing and dancing and the telling of tales. Warriors meet the heroes who have gone before us, such as the great Thorgunnd. We meet our friends there and our families."

"Do you have friends there?"

"My best friend is in Torval's Hall," said Skylan. "His name is Garn. He died fighting giants on the Dragon Isles."

"Fighting giants on the Dragon Isles!" Chloe drew in a soft breath. "How wonderful that sounds. I mean, not wonderful that he is dead. I am sorry for that."

"You must not be sorry," said Skylan. "Garn died a hero and he is with Torval. It is what all of us wants."

"But you miss him?" said Chloe.

"I miss him," said Skylan.

He stood up and began to roam around the room. He wasn't used to sitting for so long and his muscles had stiffened.

"Would Torval mind if I prayed to him?" Chloe asked suddenly. "I know I'm a girl and I can't walk and I'll never be a hero, but sometimes I can't sleep at night and I lie awake, staring into the darkness, and I think this is what death will be like—silent and dark. So very dark. I don't like the dark. When I think about death, I get so frightened I can't breathe."

She paused, then said softly, "It's not dark in Torval's Hall. It's not silent, either. There's singing and dancing. If Torval was with me, standing beside me, I don't think I'd be afraid."

Skylan started to tell her that women did not pray to Torval. Women prayed to Vindrash or Aylis or one of the other female goddesses who protected women during childbirth and guarded the home. Then he saw the fear in her eyes.

"I cannot speak for Torval," he said gruffly. "But you could try. If the god does not want you to pray to him, he would tell you so himself."

Chloe's eyes brightened. "He could speak to me? What would he do?"

"Torval would tear the door to your villa off its hinges and come stomping into your room with a sound like thunder, raising the roof with his anger. He would demand to know why a grown-up young lady comes whining to him that she is afraid of the dark. And then he would slam his hammer down on your fine bed and smash it to bits."

Chloe laughed. Her room rang with her laughter and the house slave, Rosa, poked her head in the door.

"And if Torval doesn't come?" Chloe asked, her dimple flashing.

Skylan shrugged. "Then he is not angry with you."

Rosa glided timidly into the room. "My lady, your honored father reminds you that you must rest if you are going to the palace with him this night."

"Yes, Rosa, very well. Go tell my father I will take my nap."

She held out her hand for Skylan to shake.

"Come, you may touch me. I won't break."

He kept his distance, not sure what to do. He knew quite well that Acronis would have seven sorts of apoplectic fits if he saw the barbarian near his beloved daughter. Chloe understood his hesitation and waggled her fingers insistently.

"I am accustomed to being obeyed," she said with mock sternness.

Skylan took her hand, which was small and thin and fragile in his calloused, rough palm. Yet her grip on his was firm. He gave her hand a gentle squeeze in return.

"You will do well in the Para Dix," she said.

Skylan shook his head. "I will be lucky if I don't fall in the fire pit."

Chloe laughed and snuggled down in her bed. Rosa fussed around her, plumping pillows and arranging the silken coverlet.

Skylan bowed and turned to leave. He was fumbling at the door, unable to figure out how it operated, when the door slid open of its own accord and he came face-to-face with Acronis.

The man's face was grim, stern. He made a sign that Skylan was to keep silent, not give away his presence. Skylan walked out of the room. The slave, Kakos, closed the door softly behind him. Skylan thought he was in trouble, until he saw tears glimmer in Acronis's eyes. The Legate motioned to Zahakis, who stepped out of the shadows.

"Make Skylan presentable," Acronis said. "We leave for the palace at sundown."

He turned on his heel and stalked off.

"He was listening," Skylan said.

"Of course," said Zahakis. "What did you expect?"

"He heard her ask me about praying to Torval. Was he angry?"

Zahakis shook his head. The two men walked through the long hallway, past the fish ponds and the fountains, across the marble floors, through the atrium and into the yard, heading for the out-buildings. Zahakis seemed to be trying to make up his mind to say something.

Glancing around to make certain they were alone, he said, "There is something you should know, Skylan. Chloe doesn't have long to live. The physicians all say so. They've done everything they can for her, but there's no hope."

Skylan felt an ache in his throat and he was angry at himself. A crippled child like her would have never survived in his land. The harsh winters would have killed her. Pampered and showered with wealth, she was lucky to have lived this long.

"Has her father told her she is dying? Does she know?" Skylan asked.

"Of course not," said Zahakis, shocked. "Only a monster would do such a thing. Acronis tells her she is getting better."

Skylan remembered Chloe saying she saw death in the darkness.

She knows, he realized. She knows.

Zahakis took Skylan to the men's bathing house, then to a barber, who shaved him and trimmed his hair. All the champions would be wearing the armor they would wear in the game. Skylan and his team had specially designed clothes and armor made to look like their own.

"Only without the bloodstains," said Zahakis dryly.

Skylan wore a fur-trimmed leather tunic that left his arms bare, tight leather breeches, and leather boots lined with fur. He was told to wear his own chain-mail armor, since the armor for the tournament had been delivered to the arena in preparation for tomorrow's game, and his own helm.

Keeper was also going to be in attendance, as team chief. Skylan asked Keeper what would happen at this party. Keeper told him they would be kept in a holding area, then paraded about the dining hall for the amusement of the Southlanders.

"They make us dress the part. We wear our armor, but you note that they do not let us carry the weapons," said the ogre. "All for the spectacle."

"A man puts on armor to do battle," Skylan said, scowling. "Not to be gawped at."

Keeper shrugged. "You can go before the Empress looking like a peasant or you can go before her looking like a warrior. The choice is yours."

Keeper was wearing the traditional leather harness in which ogres carried their weapons, leather breeches, boots, and nothing else. Ogres did not wear metal armor. Equip an ogre with a breastplate of a size to cover his massive chest, an equally large chain-mail shirt, metal helm, greaves, bracers, and other accoutrements, and the armor could end up weighing almost as much as the ogre. He would be worn out before he ever reached the field of battle.

Keeper painted his head and face and he wore an animal skin cape that marked his rank as a godlord. The Legate had given it to him, he said. The cape was made from the skin of a bear, complete with paws that dangled down from Keeper's neck. He looked fierce and formidable. Skylan took extra care polishing his armor.

He thought about the other times he had worn his armor, worn it with pride, taking his place in the shield wall, facing an ogre godlord alone in single combat. He wore it with the idea of making Torval proud. Now Skylan hoped that Torval was off fighting somewhere and would not be witness to his shame.

They left before sunset, the Legate and his party forming a small procession. Acronis rode to the palace on his horse. Chloe was carried in a contraption the likes of which Skylan had never seen—a couch covered by a canopy mounted on two long poles. Once she was settled inside, four strong house-slaves lifted the couch, settling the poles on their shoulders. Curtains hung from the canopy to protect Chloe's modesty. Wellborn women did not permit strangers to gawp at them.

Chloe disliked the curtains, complaining that they were hot and suffocating and prevented her from seeing anything. Her father insisted she keep them closed, however, and Chloe ostensibly did as she was told, though Skylan saw as he took his place in the procession that she opened them a crack and peeped out at the people as they passed. Her maidservant, Rosa, scurried alongside the litter.

Skylan and Keeper walked behind Acronis. Zahakis and six soldiers followed behind them. People stopped to watch and applaud. The Para Dix was popular with the citizenry, and Para Dix players were highly respected. Several shouted to Keeper, whom they recognized, yelling encouragement or jokingly asking if they should place money on his team.

At the palace walls, Acronis and Chloe entered one gate, Skylan and Keeper and the soldiers another. The soldiers took Skylan and Keeper to an area behind the palace, which Keeper said was where the Empress's team trained. The arena was ablaze with torchlight. A fire burned in the pit. There was roast pig and fresh baked bread, olives and cheese and apples. Each of the players was given wine (only a cup per man and that was watered down). Guards surrounded the arena, but they were relaxed and at ease. Many spent the time chatting with the slaves they were supposed to be guarding.

Some of the men were free men who had chosen to play in the Para Dix. Many were slaves, like Skylan. Or rather, they were slaves like Keeper. They had grown comfortable, even come to enjoy their captivity. They were given good food, treated well, cheered by the masses. Skylan stared at the well-fed slaves in their shining armor and he wondered, with a qualm of cold fear in his belly, if this would be him in a year. Would he grow complacent? At ease? Would he come to enjoy having someone telling him what to do, what not to do? Skylan shuddered.

The evening for him was a long stretch of boredom, waiting with the other players in the arena until they were formed into a line, marched to the palace, and paraded in front of the Empress. Skylan was aware of a blaze of light, the cloying smell of perfume, men and women reclining on couches, twittering flute music that was drowned out by loud, drunken voices. Most of the players were herded into the room and herded out again. Some of the more famous players, those whose skill in the Para Dix had earned them fame and in some cases fortune, were invited to stay.

No one paid any attention to Skylan except Chloe. He saw her waving to him from where she lay on her couch. The excitement had brought some color into her pale face. Her eyes were shining; she was having a wonderful time. Skylan recalled his talk with Zahakis about Chloe, the fact that she was dying.

Skylan remembered vividly the fear of death he experienced every time he took his place in the shield wall—a fear he could never quite overcome, though he told himself repeatedly that when he died, he would be where he longed to be—with Torval. Skylan tried to imagine living with the knowledge day in and day out that death was only days away. Of going to sleep with that fear every night. He smiled at Chloe and stood a little straighter. He was glad he had polished his armor.

Back in the arena, the players talked about the Para Dix or went to sleep or started gambling. Skylan settled down next to Keeper. He nudged the ogre, who was napping. Keeper belched loudly and opened his eyes.

"Did you talk to your people?" Skylan asked. "About the invasion."

"Keep your voice down," Keeper grunted.

Skylan glanced around. "No one's paying any attention." Still, he moved closer to the ogre and spoke in an undertone. "Well, did you?"

"I talked to some," said Keeper, keeping his eyes on the other players. "Meeting together is dangerous. We tend to stand out in a crowd."

Skylan pictured a group of ogres chatting together on a street corner in Sinaria, and he nodded in understanding.

"None of my fellows had heard anything about it." Keeper shook his head gloomily. "They did not believe me."

"Acronis told Zahakis the news was being kept secret so as not to start a panic. You believe it, don't you?"

Keeper shrugged. "I tried escaping once. A friend and I made plans. We found a boat. It turned out to be a trap. I managed to get away. My friend dove in the water. Ogres are not such great swimmers. He drowned."

"I'm sorry, but what does that have to do with the invasion?" Skylan asked impatiently.

"I was excited when you told me the news, but then I thought it over. I'm not sure I do believe it. It's too good to be true."

Skylan was about to say that Wulfe had told him the same thing, but he remembered in time that Wulfe had his news from his friends the Oceanids. The thought of the boy, who was still missing, gave Skylan a pang.

He sighed and said in a low voice, "I believe it. I *have* to believe it!"

Keeper eyed Skylan. "You know that if my people *do* invade Sinaria, you will be just another pisspot human to them. They'll kill you same as the rest of these whoresons."

"They can *try* to kill me," said Skylan grimly. "And at least then I'd die fighting."

Keeper yawned and belched again. He'd eaten three times as much roast pork as Skylan. "If the invasion happens, wake me," he said, and laid back down.

Time passed slowly and Skylan eventually fell asleep. He was awakened by a stir and bustle. The party was breaking up, time to go home. One of the Legate's soldiers came to fetch him and Keeper. They joined Acronis in front of the palace walls outside the gate. He was carrying a slumbering Chloe in his arms. He placed her gently in the waiting litter.

"She fell asleep right after the parade of champions," Acronis was telling Zahakis, who was holding aside the curtains of the litter. "I was going to leave early. You know how I despise these feasts. But Xydis insisted on talking to me. Nothing would do but that we had to speak in private. He hauled me out of the hall and off to some secluded room."

Acronis tenderly drew a silken coverlet up over Chloe's shoulders.

"What did the Priest-General want?" Zahakis asked.

Acronis glanced around. One of the soldiers was bringing his horse from the stables. The others were holding blazing torches, preparing to light the way back to the villa. Skylan and Keeper happened to be standing on the opposite side of the litter. The curtains blocked Acronis's view of them. Skylan raised his finger to his lips, warning Keeper to be silent.

"He wanted to talk about the ogre invasion. He has word that the ogre fleet made landfall at Argon and spent three days there hunting for food and taking on water. Then they set sail again, heading this direction."

"Argon," said Zahakis, considering. "That's forty days sailing with a good wind. What does Xydis plan to do?"

"Pray to Aelon for a bad wind," said Acronis dryly. "Xydis told me about the defenses he's planning for the city. Adequate, so far as they go, though it is going to take every one of those forty days to get the job done and they have yet to start! He wants me to block the entrance to the harbor with two war galleys when the ogres are sighted. I almost laughed in his face. Two triremes facing a fleet of over a hundred ships! The man is mad."

"How did he take your refusal?"

"He took it well," said Acronis, marveling. "I thought he would be furious, but he admitted that he did not understand naval tactics, said the decision was mine, and so on. He asked me for proposals on how the triremes could be used. He asked my opinion on his plans for the city. He was friendly to the point I couldn't get away. Whenever I tried to leave, he insisted on detaining me to continue our discussion."

Zahakis shook his head. "He's up to something."

"Oh, yes," said Acronis. "I just can't figure out what."

"Perhaps this ogre threat is a lie."

"To what end? No, he's telling the truth about the ogre invasion. He wouldn't be spending the Church's gold on building walls and so forth if he didn't think it was real."

Zahakis muttered something, then said, "What will you do, sir?"

"First I must make arrangements for Chloe to travel far inland to our country estate. She will be safe there. Then I suppose it will be up to me to find some way to defend the city. I don't plan to put my trust in Aelon . . ."

The two walked off and Skylan could hear no more. He really didn't need to hear anymore. He looked triumphantly at Keeper.

"What do you say now?"

"About what?" Keeper asked.

"About what we just heard! About the invasion!"

The ogre shrugged. "I'll believe it when I see it."

He walked off to take his place behind Acronis, who was mounting his horse. He raised his hand and the small procession moved out, moving slowly and quietly so as not to wake Chloe.

The night was dark. The new moon gave only a feeble light. A thin layer of clouds obscured the stars. The guards were watchful and alert as the procession moved through the empty streets. No light shone anywhere. The taverns had closed for the night. The glare from Aelon's dome illuminated the rooftops of the buildings but did not descend to street level. Delivery wagons would not be making their rounds until closer to dawn.

The silence was thick and oppressive, and when it was broken by the sudden, screeching yowls of two tomcats doing battle in an alley, the men jumped and Rosa stuffed her hand in her mouth to stifle a shriek that might have awakened her mistress.

They could travel only as fast as the litter-bearers could walk the streets, and they went slowly and cautiously. The streets were paved with large, fitted stones laid over a layer of rock, and although the roads were kept in good condition, sometimes a stone would crack or shift, causing the unwary pedestrian to stumble. No slave wanted to bring down the wrath of Acronis by tripping and dropping Chloe's litter.

They were deep in the heart of the city when Skylan became aware that they were being followed. He hadn't been certain at first. It was hard to hear the sounds of running feet over the tromp of the soldiers, the jingling and clanking of their armor, and the horses' hooves ringing on the stone. He'd first heard the sounds soon after they left the palace, and though the feet stopped sometimes, they always kept coming.

Skylan looked around to see if anyone else had heard. Acronis was riding with his head bowed, deep in thought, probably mulling over the news from the Priest-General and wondering how he could defend a city that, in Skylan's view, was indefensible. Keeper plodded along at the horse's side, shaking his head groggily, trying to stay awake. Ogres required a lot of sleep and he was not used to staying up late. Neither Zahakis nor the soldiers gave any sign that they noticed anything out of the ordinary.

Skylan continued to hear the footfalls, and he began to keep a lookout, hoping to catch sight of this person who was taking such an interest in them. Skylan was more curious than concerned. A single person would hardly attack well-armed, well-trained soldiers.

He heard the footfalls coming from side streets, moving parallel to them. The times he couldn't hear them, he came to realize the person was taking a circuitous route or circling around a building, yet always coming back to find them again.

The procession was coming up on the intersection of two major thoroughfares. Both streets were wide and Skylan calculated the person dogging their steps would have to move out into the open. He watched closely, hoping their pursuer would be near enough to be seen in the torchlight.

To Skylan's surprise, the person not only drew near; he jumped deliberately into the torchlight, becoming a head of shaggy hair, a thin body, eyes that flared yellow-red, and a frantically waving hand.

"Wulfe!" Skylan cried, and ran after him.

Seeing Skylan suddenly flee into the night, Zahakis shouted orders. He left two men with the litter while he and two other soldiers dashed after Skylan. Acronis reined in his horse and shook his head over the young firebrand, who was apparently making a bid for freedom. The slaves bearing the litter came to a halt that jolted the occupant. Chloe woke up with a start. She was confused, with no idea where she was. She called for Rosa, who was too terrified to answer.

Skylan had a jump on the soldiers and he reached Wulfe before Zahakis managed to reach him. Skylan didn't know whether to hug the boy or punch him for having caused him so much worry. Before he could do either, Wulfe grabbed hold of Skylan's arm with pinching fingers.

"They're coming for you!" Wulfe cried shrilly. "They're coming!"

Skylan was opening his mouth to ask who was coming when he saw.

Wolves, the largest wolves he'd ever seen—the size of mountain lions. And these wolves were not only the largest, they were the strangest and most terrifying. Their fur was dark, blending in with the shadows. Their eyes burned with a fiery yellow-red glow that lit the alley. Their tongues lolled, their fangs gleamed. Saliva flew from their mouths. The wolves were grinning with the joy of the hunt.

Skylan caught hold of Wulfe around the waist and turned and almost ran headlong into Zahakis and the two soldiers. Due to a slight curve in the road, they could not see what was coming.

The soldiers latched hold of Skylan.

"Look behind me, you fools!" he cried.

The wolves bounded into sight and the soldiers, startled, let go of Skylan, who kept on running.

Sighting prey, the wolves began to growl and bark, one to another, almost as if issuing orders.

"Don't run," said Zahakis to his men. "Use your torches."

The wolves were on them now. Zahakis and the soldiers lowered the torches and thrust the flaming brands at the wolves in the lead, thinking to use the fire to frighten them, drive them back.

Ignoring the flaring torch, the lead wolf leaped at Zahakis and knocked him flat on his back. Zahakis cried out and struck at the wolf. His men tried to help him, shouting at the wolves and waving the torches. More wolves emerged from the shadows. The soldiers guarding the litter drew their swords and ran to the aid of their fallen comrades. The lead wolf bounded off Zahakis and kept running. The other wolves circled around the soldiers to follow the pack leader.

"Skylan, listen—" Wulfe cried, squirming in his grasp.

"Shut up," said Skylan.

He ran to the litter with Wulfe tucked under his arm. Flinging the curtains open, Skylan dumped the boy inside. Chloe was wide awake, more startled than afraid. Wulfe kept yammering about "man-beasts."

"No time!" said Skylan sharply, and he yanked the curtains shut, not so much as to protect the youngsters, for the silken fabric would hardly do that, but to prevent both of them from witnessing what he feared was going to be a gruesome and deadly confrontation.

He confronted the litter-bearers, who were standing stock-still, staring in terror.

"Get moving, you fools!" Skylan shouted at the slaves. He waved his hands. "Go! Now! Fast as you can."

The slaves obeyed him, but not as he expected. They dropped the litter to the ground and fled.

Skylan cursed them for cowards, even as the thought came to him that he could use this opportunity to make a dash for his own freedom. He spent one brief second considering the notion and then sneered at himself. He had finally found Wulfe and was not going to lose the boy again, and he was not about to leave a crippled girl to be torn apart by wolves.

"A weapon, I need a goddam weapon!" Skylan called out.

"Skylan—" Wulfe stuck his head out from the curtain.

"Shut up!" Skylan yelled.

A horse screamed, and Skylan swung around to see the wolves converging on Acronis. Two were attacking his horse, who was half crazed with fear. The wolves nipped at the horse's legs and raked his flanks with their claws.

The horse bucked and plunged and twisted, striking out with its hooves and kicking with its hind legs. Acronis fought to keep his seat, trying to brace himself with his thighs. More wolves came running to surround the horse. Zahakis and his men were trapped in the alley; the wolf pack was between them and Acronis.

He heard a sharp cracking sound and turned to see Keeper wrenching loose one of the posts that supported the litter's canopy. The post snapped off in the ogre's strong hands. The canopy sagged a little, but did not fall.

"I'll guard the young ones," Keeper said tersely. "You go to the Legate."

Skylan looked at Keeper, both of them thinking the same. This was the man who had enslaved them. They had no reason to save his life.

"He should die by my hand, not in a wolf's belly," Skylan muttered and broke into a run, coming up on the wolves from behind.

Skylan sucked in a lungful of air and bellowed as he ran, "Sword! I need a sword!"

Zahakis hesitated. But Skylan was close to Acronis and Zahakis was not and, at that moment, the horse reared. Acronis lost his grip and slid off, landing in the midst of the wolves. Zahakis flung his sword through the air.

The sword landed on the pavement and slid toward Skylan, who grabbed it while he was still on the run. He couldn't see Acronis, for the furry, heaving mass on top of him, but he could hear his cries. The horse galloped past Skylan, its flanks bloody, eyes wide with terror. The wolves paid no heed to the horse. They were intent upon Acronis, until they heard Skylan roar.

The lead wolf glanced around. Seeing Skylan, the beast's eyes flared. The wolves stared at him. Their eyes glinted with a humanlike intelligence that unnerved him. The lead wolf snarled and growled and two of the other wolves broke off the attack on the fallen Acronis to charge at Skylan.

He caught a glimpse of Acronis, saw him lying unmoving on the pavement, and then the wolves were on him.

Skylan slashed at the wolves with his sword. At the sight of the gleaming steel, the wolves shrank back, staring at the weapon with hatred in their glittering eyes.

Fire doesn't affect them at all, but they are afraid of the sword.

Skylan didn't have time to follow where that thought might lead him. Hearing a warning shout, he glanced over his shoulder to see Keeper pointing at a wolf dashing up on him from behind, as another wolf attacked from the front. Skylan yelled and lunged with his sword. The wolf leaped nimbly away. The other wolf jumped on Skylan's back and bore him to the ground.

Skylan smelled the stench of rotten meat on its breath. He felt hot breath and burning pain as the wolf sank its teeth in his flesh, trying to clamp its jaws on the back of his neck.

Skylan fought to heave the beast off him, but the wolf was heavy and he could do nothing but strike frantically and blindly at the wolf's head with his fist and the sword's hilt. He could hear snarls and growls. The other wolves were coming in for the kill.

And then he was bathed in an eerie light and from somewhere close beside him, he heard Wulfe singing. The wolf on Skylan's back gave a yelp of pain.

Skylan raised his head. Wulfe stood over him, holding a torch in his hand. Red-hot cinders rained down from sky, landing on the wolves like fiery snowflakes. The wolves howled in pain as the cinders set their fur on fire and burned into their flesh. The wolves snapped at the burning cinders or ran around in panic or rolled around on the ground, trying desperately to put out the fires.

Wulfe continued singing and waving the flaming torch in the air.

A cinder landed on Skylan's head. He smelled singed hair and quickly brushed it away.

Zahakis and his men moved in, attacking the wolves, who were now caught between bright steel and magical fire. The wolves gave up the fight and with parting snarls ran off into the night, some of them still smoldering.

Skylan heaved himself to his feet. The wolf bite hurt worse than a sword thrust. The soldiers were tending to Acronis, trying to staunch the flow of blood from his wounds.

"I'll take that now," said Zahakis, wresting the sword from Skylan's hand.

Zahakis hesitated a moment, then gave Skylan a curt nod that might have been gratitude, then thrust the sword into his belt and went to see to Acronis, who was conscious and asking frantically about Chloe. Zahakis assured the Legate his daughter was safe and advised him to lie still. Acronis insisted on seeing for himself and tried to rise. He fell back with a groan and then doubled over, vomiting.

"I have to talk to you!" Wulfe said urgently, latching hold of Skylan.

"Later," said Skylan, stifling a groan.

"It can't be later," said Wulfe. "I can't stay. Raegar will come for me."

"No, he won't," said Skylan. "I won't let him. Not this time."

The soldiers were helping Acronis back to the litter. Zahakis stood staring, frowning, at the blood on the pavement. Hearing the boy's voice, he looked up and seemed to see Wulfe for the first time. Zahakis's eyebrows shot up.

"Where the devil did he come from?"

Wulfe gave a leap, preparing to flee. Skylan grabbed hold of the boy. "He was in the alley. He warned me the wolves were coming."

Zahakis's eyes narrowed. He looked back down the alley, to where the wolves were disappearing into the night.

"I've fought wolves before and I've never seen the wolf who wasn't afraid of fire. Or wolves that pick and choose their victims, let a horse go to get at a man. I've never known wolves to come into the city, either, not in the middle of summer when food is plentiful."

He looked back at Wulfe. "Skylan said you warned him. What do you know about this?"

"Nothing," said Wulfe sullenly.

Zahakis walked over to Wulfe. He squatted down in front of the boy, looked him in the eyes or tried to. Wulfe ducked his head, his shaggy hair falling over his face.

"The two men who took you to the Temple looked as though they'd been attacked by a wolf. What do you know about *that*?"

Wulfe dug a toe into a crack between the paving stones.

One of the soldiers shouted at Zahakis and the commander rose to his feet.

"I'll want to talk to the boy later," he told his men. "Take him back to the compound. And see to it that the brat stays out of sight. I don't want Raegar hauling him off again."

Zahakis walked off. One of the soldiers had gone after the Legate's horse, which had not run far, and brought it back. Zahakis tried to persuade Acronis to ride in the litter, but the Legate angrily refused. His men assisted him onto the horse.

The soldiers and Keeper lifted up the broken litter with its sagging canopy and bore it off. Zahakis walked beside Acronis, in case he should fall. Skylan and Wulfe joined the procession.

As they walked past the litter, Chloe drew aside the curtains. Her eyes shone with tears. Her lips quivered and formed the words, "Thank you!"

"She's pretty," said Wulfe. "Like a dryad."

"Yes," said Skylan, "she is."

He was nervous, uneasy. He found himself staring hard into every dark alley they passed. When a dog barked, he nearly leaped out of his skin.

"Those were very strange wolves," said Skylan.

"That's because they weren't," said Wulfe.

"Weren't what?"

"Weren't wolves," Wulfe said. "I tried to tell you. You wouldn't listen."

"If they're not wolves, what are they?" Skylan asked the question reluctantly, knowing he was going to hear some wild tale.

"They are evil fae, bad fae," said Wulfe in a low voice. "We call them man-beasts. Men who can turn into animals. Raegar hired them."

"Raegar!" Skylan repeated, startled. He gave a snorting laugh of disbelief. "Raegar hired wolves! To do what?"

"To kill you and him," said Wulfe, pointing to Acronis. "He hired the man-beasts to kill both of you."

Skylan eyed the boy. He remembered how the wolves had been afraid of the sword, not of the fire. He remembered the intelligence in the eyes and how their growls had sounded very much like speech. He remembered how they had drawn off Zahakis and the soldiers and penned them up into the alley. He remembered, too, how Wulfe had told him that his father and his family had been cursed, turned into wolves. He remembered the cinders raining down from the torch Wulfe was holding, remembered the boy's song.

"Did those . . . man-beasts of yours kill the guards who were taking you away?" Skylan asked.

"No," said Wulfe, and he added softly, after a pause, "I did."

BOOK TWO

The dawn glimmered in the sky by the time they reached the villa. Lights blazed from the windows. The entire household was roused by the return of their injured master. Slaves rushed about with hot towels and cold, salve and bandages. The physicians were summoned. Chloe was carried off, against her will, to her bed. She refused to go to sleep until she knew her father was going to be all right, and she insisted on sending the physicians to treat Skylan's wounds.

The physicians stated that Acronis had suffered no major injuries. He was lucky. His armor had prevented the wolves from tearing out his throat. He had suffered a mild concussion from hitting his head on the pavement, however. He was ordered to rest, but warned not to fall asleep. Slaves were posted at his bedside with orders to rouse him if his eyes closed.

The physicians then went to examine Skylan, who had been taken to the kitchen along with Wulfe. They gave the boy food, which he ate ravenously. The Cook and her female slaves fussed over Skylan, washing away the blood and cleaning the bites, doing more to aid him than the physicians, who glanced at the wound, told Skylan to pray to Aelon, and left.

Assured that her father and her champion were both going to survive, Chloe was at last persuaded to sleep.

Zahakis ordered his men to escort Skylan and the boy back to the slave camp. Before they left, Zahakis tried to talk to Wulfe, who hung his head and shuffled his feet and pretended to have gone deaf and dumb. Zahakis eyed him, then drew Skylan to one side, leaving

Wulfe in the custody of the soldiers. The boy was fidgety and uneasy and did not take his eyes from Skylan.

"What did the kid say to you in the alley?"

"He warned me the wolves were coming," Skylan answered.

Zahakis's eyes narrowed. "Those wolves were like no wolves I've ever seen, Skylan. He knew they were coming, which meant he knows something about them. He's dangerous. I've told you that before."

Skylan glanced over at Wulfe. His hair was uncombed and flopped over his face. He was dressed in rags that hung off his thin frame. His eyes darted about. He kept shifting nervously from one bare foot to the other, poised for flight.

"He's just a boy," said Skylan, but he sounded unconvincing, even to himself.

Zahakis grunted. "He knows what happened this night. Find out what it is."

He started to walk off, then turned back and said grimly, "And keep him away from Chloe! She likes him."

Skylan was thoughtful as the soldiers escorted him and Wulfe to the compound. His friends were still asleep on board their ship when they arrived, for which blessing Skylan was grateful.

"We need to talk," said Skylan, and he took Wulfe into one of the empty tents and sat the boy down on a cot.

Skylan lit one of the crude lanterns made from a rag dunked into a dish of oil and placed it on the dirt floor. The light wavered in the breeze from the opening in the tent, the oil smoked.

"I want to know what's going on," said Skylan, sitting on the cot opposite. "You warned me the wolves were going to attack us. How did you know—"

"I'm still hungry," said Wulfe, interrupting. "Can I have something to eat?"

Skylan had the feeling the boy was stalling, but Wulfe did look thin and underfed. Skylan brought back food and gave it to Wulfe, who ate ravenously, tearing at the bread with his teeth and swallowing chunks of it whole. Hunger assuaged, Wulfe slowed down, but he kept eating.

"You've wasted enough time," said Skylan. "Start talking."

Wulfe pointed to his mouth that was filled with bread.

"I can sit here all day," said Skylan.

Wulfe sighed and, after a struggle, managed to swallow the large wad of bread.

"I don't know where to begin," he said.

"How about when the guards took you to the Temple."

Wulfe made a face. "Do I have to tell you?"

"If you want to stay with me, you will."

"The guards took me away," said Wulfe. "I was afraid. I knew they were going to kill me. You knew it, too," he added, with an accusing glance at Skylan. "You let them take me."

Skylan pointed to the tattoo. "I tried to stop them. You saw what happened. Raegar's god nearly burned off my arm."

The thought occurred to him, suddenly, that the god had not tried to stop him from defending himself against the wolves. Strange, if Raegar wanted him dead, why hadn't Aelon prevented him from fighting? Skylan tucked the thought away, planning to return to it later.

"Don't try to change the subject. Obviously you escaped from the guards. How?"

Wulfe ducked his head. He started to stand up, but Skylan grabbed him and yanked him down. Wulfe flinched. He kept his eyes on the ground.

"I have something bad inside me. The druids called it a daemon. My daemon tries to make me do bad things. Most of the time I don't pay any attention to it, but sometimes I do because I like what the daemon says."

His voice was soft and mumbling; Skylan had to lean closer to hear him.

"The daemon told me that the guards were going to kill me," Wulfe said, barely speaking above a whisper. "The only way to stop them was to kill them first. I was afraid. And so I did."

"Did what?" Skylan asked, wanting to hear Wulfe say it.

The boy looked up at him. "I killed them."

"Two grown men, both armed," said Skylan. "And you killed them. How?"

"I turned into a man-beast." Wulfe grinned suddenly, a feral grin that showed all his teeth. "When I did that, *they* were the ones who were afraid."

Skylan's mouth was dry. He told himself he didn't believe a word Wulfe said, but the boy's grin unnerved him.

Skylan had to moisten his lips to speak. "What happened after . . . ?"

"I don't remember," said Wulfe. He gave a deep sigh. The worst was over and the words spilled out. "I never remember. All I know is that when I woke up I was in a rickety old house. I was covered in blood and tied to a chair. I didn't know where I was or how I got there and I was frightened. A woman was with me and she said, 'You're one of us. Don't bother to lie. I saw what you did.' I said I didn't do anything, but she knew better. She washed the blood off me and when I said I wouldn't try to go anywhere, because I didn't have anywhere to go, she untied me and gave me something to eat. I slept for a long, long time. I always sleep a lot . . . after . . ."

"You've done this before," said Skylan, his throat tight.

Wulfe nodded his head. "When I was living with the druids."

"What about when you were with me in our village?"

"No!" Wulfe said emphatically. "You were nice to me and the daemon never talked to me. I thought he'd gone away. I guess he didn't."

"You know I don't believe you," said Skylan.

Wulfe shrugged. "I can't help it. It's the truth."

Skylan considered asking Wulfe to prove his tale by turning into a wolf on the spot, but he thought better of it. If the boy did turn into a wolf, Skylan would be forced to believe him. As it was, he could still harbor a tiny sliver of comforting doubt.

"So you stayed with this woman?"

"And the man who lived with her. They're both man-beasts."

"I was worried about you," said Skylan, ignoring that last part. "So was Aylaen. Why didn't you come back to live with us?"

Wulfe was quiet a moment. His lip trembled. His eyes filled with tears. "I killed those men. I knew you'd be mad at me."

"Torval help me," Skylan muttered. The sliver of comforting doubt vanished. He believed Wulfe. He couldn't help but believe him. Raegar was right. Zahakis was right. Wulfe was fae, as he'd claimed. Skylan remembered the boy standing over him, singing an eerie little song, and the cinders from the torch falling like rain. Wulfe was a danger to Skylan and everyone around him. The boy could never be trusted. He should be killed. Skylan gave a deep sigh and reached back to gingerly touch the bite mark.

"You believe me now, don't you," said Wulfe.

"You don't give me much goddam choice!" Skylan said angrily.

He jumped to his feet and hit his head on the roof of the tent, nearly bringing it down on top of them, frightening Wulfe, who crawled on all fours into a corner. Skylan resumed his seat on the cot.

"You said Raegar hired these man-beasts. How did you know that?"

"The man-beasts gather in this tavern in the part of the city down by the river. I was there one day and I saw Raegar, but he didn't see me. I hid under a table. He seemed to know these people. He said he had another job. He wanted some men killed and he would pay well. He said that the men would be coming back from the palace late in the night. Raegar gave the man-beasts money and said there would be more when the job was done."

"If you knew this was going to happen, why didn't you come warn me?" Skylan demanded.

"I didn't know it was you!" Wulfe said defensively. "I couldn't hear the names. When I did find out you were one of the men they were going to kill, I did come. Only I was too late. The wolves were right behind me."

"How did you find out they were after me?"

"Raegar came storming into the tavern tonight. He was red in the face and sweating. He looked scared. He said he had to cancel the job. It was all right if the man-beasts killed Acronis, but they couldn't kill a man named Skylan. The man-beasts asked if they would still get paid and he said yes. But after he left, they left, too. I asked the woman where they went and she said they were going to do the job anyway. Raegar wanted you alive but someone else wanted you dead and was paying them more money. I didn't hear, because I ran off to warn you."

Skylan shook his head. "That doesn't make any sense. First Raegar plots to kill me and then he tries to keep me from being killed. And then someone else tries to kill me! I wonder why I'm suddenly so valuable?"

Wulfe yawned a huge yawn, cracking his jaws. "I don't know. Can I go to sleep now?"

Skylan nodded. Wulfe curled up in a corner of the tent and closed his eyes. Skylan started to leave him, then thought better of it, and lay down on the cot. It occurred to him that he could never leave Wulfe by himself again.

The light still flickered from the oil lamp. Skylan was too tired to get back up and blow it out. Besides, he didn't feel like being left in darkness. Not after what he'd heard. He was closing his eyes when a voice softly calling his name sent a lightning bolt through his body.

"Skylan?" Aylaen said from outside the tent. "Are you in there? I need to talk to you."

Skylan jumped to his feet and flung open the tent flap.

"I'm sorry if I woke you . . . ," Aylaen said.

The sky was starting to turn gray in the east. She looked worn out. Her clothes were disheveled. Her hair was rumpled, her eyes sunken in her head.

"I wasn't asleep. Look," said Skylan. "It's Wulfe. He's back."

"Oh, thank goodness!" Aylaen said. She crept over to him, gently smoothed the hair from his face. "He's so thin. Is he all right? Where has he been?"

"It's a long story. I'll tell you later. What did you want to talk to me about?"

She stared at him. "You're bleeding! What happened?"

Before Skylan could answer, she saw the bloody marks on his neck. "Did a dog bite you?"

"A wolf," said Skylan.

"But you were at the Palace with the Legate. . . ."

"Again, long story. Please, tell me, why did you come?"

"I will get some of Treia's potion," Aylaen said, and she was out of the tent before he could stop her.

Skylan waited, his heart beating so rapidly he was having trouble breathing. When she didn't return, he wondered if the potion had been an excuse for her to leave. He was almost sick with disappointment, when she opened the flap.

"It took me awhile to find it. Someone moved the chest it was in. Sit down. This will sting."

Aylaen sat down beside Skylan on the cot. He was aware of her closeness, of her scent. Love and desire burned inside Skylan. She began to rub the potion on the wound. Her touch was chill, her fingers trembling. He felt her hand shake.

"I have to ask you something," she said.

"You can ask me anything," said Skylan. He turned to face her. "You know that."

Aylaen flushed and lowered her eyes. "I need to know the secret for summoning the Vektan dragons."

Skylan wasn't sure he'd heard her correctly. "What?"

"I know Draya told you the secret," Aylaen said desperately. "You *have* to tell me. You have to!"

Her voice softened. She reached out to him.

"Please, Skylan!" she said tremulously. "Please tell me! You must! Or else . . ."

"Or else what?" Skylan asked, puzzled.

Aylaen bit her lip and shook her head. The flush had gone from her face, leaving her pale and shivering. "Nothing. I need to know. That's all. You have to trust me."

Skylan began to pick up the pieces. Raegar summoned Aylaen to the Temple and paid to have me killed. Raegar suddenly tries to stop his hired killers and is extremely upset when he's told that it's too late. Aylaen now comes asking me about the secret of the Vektan dragons.

"Raegar has one of the Vektia spiritbones," said Skylan.

Aylaen gasped and drew back from him. "How did you know?"

How did he know? He saw again the Goddess Vindrash standing on the ship holding up her hand. The five fingers spread wide.

Wulfe stirred on his cot and gave a little whimper.

"Come outside," said Skylan.

Aylaen ducked beneath the tent flap. She stood outside the tent, her arms tightly clasped, her face tense and strained in the pale light of the coming morning.

"Why does Raegar want to know the ritual?" he asked.

"He claims something dire is about to happen, an attack or invasion or something. He says he wants Treia to summon the dragon to protect their people."

"You don't believe that," said Skylan.

"It doesn't matter what I believe. I have to tell them what they want to know."

"And you won't tell me why."

"You have to trust me, Skylan," Aylaen said in a low voice. "You do trust me, don't you?"

"You know I do—"

"Then tell me the secret."

Skylan wanted to think, an idea was gnawing at his mind. "Have you seen this spiritbone? Do you know where it is being kept?"

"Treia knows," said Aylaen. She stared off into the east where the faint light of the rising sun was causing the stars to fade. "She has seen it. Treia told me the spiritbone is in a vault in the Shrine protected by Aelon. No unbeliever can enter that shrine. Aelon will strike him down."

But anyone wanting to summon the dragon would have to take the spiritbone out of the Shrine. Skylan's excitement grew. He could see the hand of Vindrash bringing all the threads together. There was just one problem.

"I do trust you, Aylaen," said Skylan slowly. "I would trust you with my life. And I would tell you the secret of the Vektan dragons—"

She turned to him with an eager smile, her green eyes shining.

Skylan shook his head. "But I don't know it."

Aylaen glared at him. "Don't lie to me, Skylan. Of course, you know the secret! Garn told me you know it!"

"*Garn* told you?" Skylan repeated, amazed.

Aylaen flushed and bit her lip.

"I don't remember Garn and I ever talking about Vektan dragons," Skylan said.

"Well, you must have," said Aylaen irritably. She avoided his eyes.

And then it all came back to him.

After his return from the disastrous confrontation with the druids and the death of his wife, Draya, her corpse had come to Skylan and forced him to play the dragonbone game. She had begun her turn by throwing down five bones, an unusual move. Skylan had spoken of it to the old wise woman, Owl Mother, who had said perhaps the number itself was significant. Skylan had asked Garn if he knew why the number five should be special.

"All he could think of was that there were five Vektan dragons," said Skylan. "That was the only time we ever spoke of it. I never said anything to him about knowing the secret to summoning the dragons."

"Then Draya must have told you," Aylaen said. "Wives tell their husbands everything."

"Draya and I . . . weren't really husband and wife," said Skylan, ashamed.

"You have to know, Skylan! You have to!" Aylaen said desperately. "Garn said you knew!"

"I'm sorry, Aylaen," said Skylan earnestly. "For your sake, I wish I did."

Aylaen studied him intently, and then gave a low moan and buried her face in her hands. "What am I going to do?"

"Aylaen, I know you're in some sort of trouble. Let me help you. Tell me what Raegar has done to you," said Skylan. "I'll confront him. I'll make him talk. We'll find a way to take the spiritbone, to steal it back—"

"No!" Aylaen cried, terrified. "No, you mustn't! You don't know what would happen if you did! And I can't tell you." She seized hold of his arm, dug her nails into his flesh. "Don't do anything or say anything about this, Skylan, please! This is my problem. It's my fault. I'm the only one who can fix it. Promise me you won't say a word to anyone. Swear by Torval, Skylan. Swear!"

Skylan hesitated. "You can tell me, Aylaen."

"Not this," she said in hollow tones. "You would hate me forever!"

"That's not possible," said Skylan gently. "I love you, Aylaen. I have always loved you—"

"Then if you love me, swear," Aylaen said in ragged tones. "Give me your promise."

She took hold of his hands. Her fingers were colder than the fingers of the draugr. "Swear by Torval that you will tell no one what I have told you. Swear by Torval that you will forget everything I've said to you!"

"Aylaen, I can't—"

"Swear!" she said, her voice grating.

"I swear by Torval," said Skylan, and he put his hand to the amulet. "But you must swear to let me help you."

"You can't," said Aylaen. "No one can help me. You don't know the terrible thing I have done. Even the gods have turned their backs on me."

She started to walk away, then looked back at him. "If you remember anything about the Vektia, come tell me."

She walked off. Skylan considered going after her, trying to persuade her, but he feared he would only make matters worse. At least, he reflected, she had come to him when she was in trouble. She had talked to him as a friend, almost like the old days.

Skylan went back inside the tent and lay down on the cot. He had a lot to think about.

What struck him as truly odd was that Raegar and Treia, Aylaen and apparently Garn all believed he knew the secret to the Vektan dragons.

Skylan began to wonder uneasily if he did.

BOOK TWO

Chloe did not send for Skylan the next day. He guessed that she was worried about her father. Acronis could not leave his bed, but he insisted that they hold Para Dix practice.

That turned out to be a mistake.

Keeper was grumpy and irritable from lack of sleep. Aylaen walked about in a daze, distracted and unhappy. Sigurd and the others were sullen and rebellious. Skylan worried about Wulfe, afraid that Raegar would find him, and spent half his time trying to remember everything Draya had said to him about Vektan dragons.

Keeper yelled at them until he was hoarse and used his fists freely on everyone except Aylaen, telling her balefully that he was leaving her to her goddess.

The end came when one of the Southlander players called the Torgun "stupid savages." Sigurd knocked the man to the ground. The other Southlander jumped him. Grimuir and Skylan both went to his aid and the fight was on. They were reveling in a glorious brawl when Skylan heard Zahakis call his name.

Skylan was tempted to ignore the summons, but sometimes the only way to get information was to give it.

Zahakis spent a moment looking out at the playing field where the soldiers and the Torgun and the Southlanders were beating the crap out of each other. Only Aylaen was not involved. She sat slumped on the grass, her arms resting on her knees, her head in her arms.

"What's wrong with Aylaen?" Zahakis asked.

"Female trouble," said Skylan, knowing that would end the questioning. No man ever wants to talk about female problems. Zahakis quickly changed the subject.

"You were going to talk to that boy of yours. Did you?"

Skylan had gone over what he would say, trying to juggle how much of the truth to reveal and how much to keep to himself. "This is the boy's story. You can believe it or not. He claims that the wolves weren't wolves. He says they are fae, what the boy calls man-beasts. He's always claiming to know the fae. He talks to dryads and Oceanids. . . ."

"Like I said last night, these wolves didn't act like any wolves I've ever seen," Zahakis said, nodding his head. "What else did the kid say?"

Skylan was startled. He hadn't expected Zahakis to believe him. He wasn't sure he wanted to be believed.

"According to Wulfe, these man-beasts look like ordinary humans when they want to," said Skylan. "They work as hired killers, using their beast form to murder people, making it seem as if their victims were torn apart by wild animals—"

"Like the guards who were taking the boy to the Temple," Zahakis said, interrupting.

Skylan pretended he hadn't heard and kept talking. He knew this next bit of information would capture the Tribune's attention.

"Someone hired these man-beasts to kill the Legate. Raegar."

"Raegar?" Zahakis repeated, staring. "Are you sure?"

"The boy saw him talking to the leader of these man-beasts and recognized him. Raegar told the man-beasts where to find the Legate. He told them Acronis would be on his way home from the Palace—"

"Where the Priest-General kept him talking until late into the night," said Zahakis softly. "It all begins to make sense."

"Priest-General?"

"Raegar's only an arse-licker toady. He's not allowed to think for himself. He's acting on orders from above. Do you want proof? Those four yellow-bellied litter bearers fled into the night. They have the same tattoos that you have on your arm. Apparently they never felt a twinge when they ran off. Your arm burned, didn't it? When you tried to defend the Legate?"

No, his arm hadn't burned. But that was because Aelon wanted him alive because of the secret of the Vektan dragons. Skylan kept that bit of information to himself.

"I don't suppose that boy of yours remembers the name of the tavern or could show us where it is," Zahakis said. "I'd like to get a look at these man-beasts."

Skylan shook his head. "If he does, he won't tell me. He's terrified of them. Afraid they'll come after him."

"Is he?" said Zahakis. "Who killed those Temple guards, Skylan? Ask yourself that. And then ask yourself if you want to keep that boy around."

"Wait a moment, Tribune," said Skylan, as Zahakis was about to walk off, "why would the Priest-General want to kill the Legate?"

"If Acronis dies, his wealth and property go to the Empire. And we all know who is really running the Empire these days."

"What would happen to Chloe?"

"She would become a ward of the Empress."

"What will the Legate do?" Skylan asked. "Will he leave Sinaria?"

"Acronis is no coward. He is needed here. Especially now. He won't leave the people to the mercies of —"

Zahakis stopped, clearly having said more than he intended.

"Aelon?" Skylan finished for him.

Zahakis grunted. He started again to walk off, then turned back. "You Torgun are going to disgrace yourself in the Para Dix. You know that, don't you?"

"Ask me if I give a rat's ass," said Skylan.

"You will." Zahakis smiled. "Because you can't stand to be beaten. At anything."

That night, when darkness fell and the soldiers on guard duty around the compound were involved in their gambling games, the Torgun sat on the deck of the *Venjekar* and talked in low voices about the possibility of escape. They would have their weapons and their shields. But they also had Aelon's hated tattoo on their arms. Every warrior was strong in the belief that he could overcome the pain with an effort of will.

Sigurd wanted to form a plan, but, as Skylan pointed out, they were venturing into the unknown. They had no idea what this arena was like or where it was located, how many guards there would be, how many people. There were a myriad questions and no answers.

"All we know for certain is that we are Torgun," said Skylan. "We stand together and if, by the blessing of Torval, a chance to escape arises, we will take it."

The Para Dix was held once a month in an arena built especially for the game. Almost every person of noble rank, including the Empress, sponsored a team and entered that team in the contest. Acronis, as well as other members of nobility, actually participated in the game themselves, directing the movements of the game pieces. The Empress hired players, who directed the game play for her.

The entire day was devoted to the game. The people of Sinaria were given a holiday from work. The morning began with the dedication of the players to Aelon, a ceremony held in the public Temple. Aelon, through his priests, informed the players that they were fighting for his glory and he bestowed on them his blessing.

Acronis, foreseeing trouble from Skylan and his Torgun if they were forced to participate in this ceremony, kept his players from attending, pleading as his excuse that they were barbarians and might behave in an unseemly manner that Aelon would find offensive.

Priest-General Xydis officiated at the ceremony. The Temple was crowded, though most people had come to see their favorite champions, not to hear the prayers.

At the conclusion of the ceremony, Xydis sent word to Raegar to meet him in his private office. When Raegar arrived, Xydis made certain no one was in the hallway, then pulled the door shut and locked it. He rounded on Raegar.

"Legate Acronis came to me with a complaint. It seems several nights ago, after he left the Palace, he was set upon by a pack of wolves."

I told the man-beasts that they were to kill only the Legate. I assured them they would still get paid. They must have decided to kill Skylan on their own," said Raegar defensively.

"Relax," said Xydis. "This isn't your fault. The man-beasts were following the orders of another. Someone who does *not* want the secret of the Vektan dragons to be revealed. I have a spy among the man-beasts, a woman named Rea. She said someone else hired them to kill Skylan."

"But who could possibly—"

"I don't know, nor does it matter," said Xydis impatiently. "The Bone Priestess, Treia, must talk to her sister, find out Skylan's secret this morning before the game commences. Whoever tried to have Skylan killed once will try again. What better place for a murder than in the arena?"

Treia traveled the distance to Acronis's villa in a covered conveyance provided by the Church. She entered the slave compound and, after same searching, found her sister in one of the tents. Aylaen was regarding with dismay and outrage the outlandish armor she had been given to wear in the game—a skirt of tooled leather that barely covered her hips and a leather chest protector that barely covered her breasts. She would wear metal greaves and bracers, but no helmet, so that the spectators could admire her beauty, so Keeper told her.

Hearing someone enter, Aylaen looked around. She was too angry to be surprised to see her sister.

"Look at this! Look what they are making me wear!" Aylaen gestured to the armor.

"You have dressed like a man for months. You should be used to making a spectacle of yourself by now," said Treia.

Aylaen flashed her an irate glance. Belatedly Treia remembered that she was here to persuade her sister to tell her Skylan's secret.

"I'm sorry," said Treia with a stiff smile. "I didn't mean that. It's just . . . ever since the night in the shrine, I've been so worried about you. Did you talk to Skylan?"

"No," said Aylaen shortly.

She kept her face averted and Treia knew she was lying. Aylaen was a terrible liar.

"Why not? You've had time."

"I'll wear this armor if I must, but I'm going to wear breeches underneath it," Aylaen said, trying to change the subject.

Treia was not to be deterred. "You must talk to Skylan today, Aylaen. Ask him today to tell you the secret of the Vektia."

"Why today particularly?" Aylaen asked, glancing curiously at her sister.

"The Para Dix is dangerous," Treia said. "Something might happen to him. If Skylan is the only one who knows the secret of the Vektan dragons, you must get him to tell you. Otherwise it might be lost forever."

"*I'm* playing in the game," said Aylaen. "Aren't you afraid something will happen to me?"

"I am not worried about you, Sister," Treia said with a made-up smile. "Aelon will keep you safe."

Aylaen frowned at her sister.

"Then why won't Aelon protect Skylan?"

Aylaen's eyes widened with alarm. "Something bad is going to happen to Skylan. What? What is it?"

"I know I am being overcautious," said Treia, sitting on the cot. "Raegar assures me the Para Dix is perfectly safe. No player has died in months. But accidents *do* happen and the secret of the Vektan Dragons is so very important that we dare not take any chances. You must talk to Skylan today."

Aylaen was silent a moment. She sat down beside Treia and asked in an altered voice, "What would happen if Skylan didn't know this secret?"

"Of course, he knows it!" said Treia. "Garn told you he knows it." She reached out her hand and smoothed Aylaen's rampant hair. "Skylan loves you, Sister. He would do anything for just a smile—"

Aylaen's eyes flared. "I won't play the whore with him, if that's what you're asking me to do!"

Treia lost patience. "Just find out the damn secret!" she said, and stormed out of the tent.

Following the dedication ceremony in the Temple was a parade through the streets of Sinaria known as the Procession of the Players. Each team marched down the street in the order of their ranking. As a new team—"unblooded"—the Barbarians, as the Legate called them, marched last.

The Torgun dressed in their own armor, all except Aylaen, who wore the fancy armor Acronis had provided for her, with leather trousers beneath it. She would dress like this or she would not participate, she told Keeper, and the ogre had assured Acronis that she meant it. The Torgun carried their own shields, though not their own weapons. Swords and axes would be distributed to the players in the arena. The reason for this, according to Keeper, was that in the old days, players who brought their own weapons had resorted to cheating, such as smearing the tip of a sword with foxglove or nightshade.

Though he was facing his foes in a game, not in a shield wall, Skylan was surprised to feel a pulsing of excitement as he put on his helm, buckled on his breastplate, and took his place in line with his comrades, standing directly behind Keeper, who, as captain, walked in front.

The Barbarians were at the back of the parade, the very end, the last to march. The preeminent team this year belonged to the Empress. Her players were dressed in rich panoply with feathers in their helms. Their bronze skin glistened with oil. Their long black hair was plaited and braided. They wore gold armbands and specially tooled boots. They had their own drummer and trumpeter, their own colorful standards. Their captain rode in a chariot festooned with the team colors, and as they set out along the parade route, the crowd went wild. Men called out well wishes and shouted for their favorites. Women blew kisses and tossed flowers. Children ran after them, hoping for candy, which slaves of the Empress were tossing to the crowd.

The rest of the teams moved out. Skylan and his team waited, growing hot and weary in the bright sunshine. Keeper had warned him that few people stayed to the end of the parade to see the "unblooded" teams.

"Those who do will be wondering how much money to risk on us," the ogre predicted. "Or they will stay to laugh."

The crowds had thinned by the time the Barbarians started along the parade route. People watched quietly, not cheering. But no one was laughing either.

Skylan and the Torgun walked on proudly because they were a

proud people. He could hear the ring of their armor, the thud of their feet, and the ogre's grunt of astonishment.

"Look at them, Skylan," said Keeper in a low voice. "They are slaves."

The slaves of Sinaria—slaves to masters or slaves to poverty—remembered the strange foreign slaves who had valiantly hauled their broken ship through the streets of their captors with a song of defiance on their lips. The other teams had slaves on them, but these were slaves who wore golden armbands and smelled of fragrant oils; their children were fat. The slaves who waited for Skylan and the Torgun were thin and gaunt, with the pinch of hunger in their cheeks. Their children played in the gutters with the rats and died of starvation.

These slaves dare not cheer. Their masters might be watching. Perhaps they were not even supposed to be here and would face a beating when they went back to their duties. The city guards, standing on the corners to keep the crowd in order, were keeping a baleful eye on the gathering, always on the watch for signs of rebellion, always quick to put it down.

One man began to clap his hands. Others followed his lead. Skylan heard the applause and he thought of their last practice session, which had been a fiasco. His face burned. He began to wish he'd paid more attention to Keeper's attempts at training them. Perhaps, as Zahakis had said, Skylan couldn't stand to be beaten at anything. Or perhaps, looking at the pot-bellied, scrawny children, he didn't want to let these people down.

"We are going to make fools of ourselves," Keeper muttered, echoing Skylan's thoughts.

"Maybe not," Skylan said.

Keeper snorted. "Are you joking? Sigurd can't count. He's always moving too many squares. Grimuir keeps facing the wrong direction, and yesterday young Farinn tripped over his own feet and cracked his head on a boulder."

Skylan had to admit the ogre was right, but his warriors were failures because they hadn't taken the game seriously. He could see by grave expressions on the faces of his men that they were taking it seriously now.

"How do you think we will do this day?"

Keeper gave a grunt and rolled his eyes. "With luck, no one will get killed. With *luck*." He laid gloomy emphasis on the word.

The champions of the Para Dix trod on sweet-smelling flowers and heard the people sing their praises. Skylan and his team trod in manure and heard the forbidden applause of slaves.

Skylan put his hand to the amulet he wore on his neck. He felt a slight twinge of conscience for making what the gods might view as a frivolous request, but his honor and the honor of the Vindrasi was at stake.

"Torval, I have asked that you find a way for us to gain our freedom. I still ask for that, of course," Skylan added hastily, "but now I ask something else. First, help us win the Para Dix!"

BOOK THREE

The teams to fight in the afternoon were the unblooded teams. Most sponsors had a champion team, a second-rank team, and an unblooded team. The sponsors used the unblooded teams as a way to train players. The good ones were promoted to the second-rank team. Players advanced to champion team only if they were considered outstanding.

Unblooded teams fought each other. The victors of these games advanced to play against the second-rank teams. The people who came to the afternoon games involving unblooded teams were those who took the sport seriously, coming to watch the new players in order to discover the next rising star or to study the competition.

Skylan and his team members marched into the arena and onto the playing field. He stared about in wonder. This was the first time he had been inside the arena when it was set up for the game. Naively, he had assumed it would be like the practice field Acronis had built on his villa. The famous Para Dix arena of Sinaria was as far removed from his practice field as the palace was removed from a hovel.

The builders of the arena had chosen to place it in a small, shallow valley located a short distance from the city. The floor of the valley had been smoothed and grated to form the playing field. The common folk sat on tiers of wooden benches that had been cut into the valley's rim and encircled the playing field.

The nobility occupied grandstands built along one side of the arena. The Empress and the Priest-General and other notables were sheltered from the elements by a wooden roof. They sat in the best position for viewing the game, directly across from the fire pit in the middle of the field.

All the teams stood on the playing field while priests performed the ceremony of lighting the sacred fire and dedicating the games to Aelon. The ceremony was long and few people were paying attention. They were filing into their seats, talking to their neighbors, opening baskets of food, and getting themselves settled. Skylan had never seen so many people gathered in one place at one time, not even when he was fighting in the Vutmana and all the chiefs and many hundreds of the Vindrasi had come to watch.

He and Sigurd and the others looked at each other and grimly shook their heads. He and the others had talked excitedly about trying to make a bid for freedom. All were thinking the same thought. The Torgun were not going to escape this day.

Skylan fought down his bitter disappointment and took the opportunity to study the other teams, trying to guess which players were the best, which team they would go up against.

Only a few members of the nobility had arrived. Most would not venture out to see the afternoon games. They would wait until the champion teams staged their matches in the evening. Those who were here, like Acronis, would be managing their teams. Skylan, squinting against the bright sun, tried to find where Chloe was sitting. He had promised he would wave to her.

When the religious ceremony finally ended, people cheered. A ripple of excitement ran through the crowd, for the Para Dix was about to begin. Keeper and the captains of the unblooded teams came forward to draw lots to see which team they would fight. The lots were clay disks marked with the team colors and placed in a bowl. Each captain averted his eyes, reached in, and plucked out a disk.

The teams left the field and lined up on the edges. Most watched the drawing with keen interest. Skylan was worried about Aylaen. She was nervous and unhappy.

He edged his way over to her. "I saw Treia come to camp this morning. She was asking about the Vektan dragons, wasn't she?"

Aylaen nodded and pressed her lips together. She did not look at him, but stared, unseeing, at the playing field.

"Treia is worried that something might happen to you in the game."

Skylan almost laughed out loud. "Treia—worried about me?" He started to add, "When pigs fly," but then he understood. "This sudden concern of hers is because she thinks I know the secret and she fears I might take it to my grave. Well, I might, just to spite her."

"Don't joke about it, Skylan," said Aylaen miserably. Tears glimmered on her eyelashes. "You don't understand."

He felt wretched for having made her cry. "I'll keep thinking, Aylaen. I promise. And look at it this way: So long as I know this secret, or they think I know it, Treia and Raegar will work hard to keep me alive."

Aylaen managed a smile and brushed away her tears. The captains dispersed and came back, telling their players which teams they would face. Soon teams began shouting insults and challenges at each other.

Keeper, returning to his team, looked very grim. Acronis and Zahakis were there to meet him.

"I was afraid of this," the ogre said. He opened his palm to show a lot marked with red. "We play against the unblooded team of the Empress."

Acronis and Zahakis exchanged glances. Zahakis raised his eyebrows and rubbed his jaw.

"What's wrong? Is her team that much better than we are?" Skylan demanded.

"A herd of donkeys is better than you lot!" Keeper said scathingly. "Have you heard the rumor, Legate?"

"It is all anyone is talking about," said Acronis.

"This is against the rules, my lord!" Keeper stated angrily.

"She is the Empress," said Acronis. He turned to face his players and raised his voice so all could hear over the noise in the arena. "It seems the Empress has a new player she is going to test today. A player said to be one of the fae."

"One of the faery folk? Like a nymph or a dryad?" Skylan said, grinning. He had never encountered a nymph or a dryad, but Wulfe had described them to him, and he did not think they had much to fear.

"No," said Acronis coolly. "More like the wolves you fought the other night."

Skylan's grin vanished.

"The Empress is said to have captured a fury," Acronis continued. "She has trained this fury for the game."

The Torgun stared at him blankly.

"What is this thing—a fury?" Bjorn asked.

"Furies take the form of beautiful human females. They are said to be drawn to people who commit murders or acts of violence by the suffering and terror of the victim, much like sharks are attracted by blood in the water," Acronis explained. "Some believe that the furies avenge the victim by tormenting the killer until they drive him mad. Others believe that these evil faery folk simply enjoy inflicting pain on humans and that they choose murderers because the gods have turned their backs on them."

"I served in the legions with a man who was tormented by a fury," said Zahakis. "He had murdered his wife. He went mad and jumped into the river and drowned."

The Torgun appeared skeptical, all except Skylan, who remembered the torment he had endured from the draugr of *his* dead wife.

"What sort of fighter is this fury?" Sigurd asked, always practical. "How does she attack? What weapons will she use?"

Acronis shook his head. "I had hoped to see the fury during the procession, but the Empress considers the creature too dangerous to risk parading it among the people. She is being transported to the arena under armed guard."

If Wulfe had been here, he could have told Skylan everything he wanted to know about furies. Or at least made up a good story. Skylan hoped Wulfe was obeying him and staying hidden in the ship. Wulfe had promised that he would, but Skylan didn't put much faith in Wulfe's promises. Thinking of the boy gave Skylan an idea, however.

"We should withdraw," Keeper was saying.

Skylan gestured at the people in the stands. "You want them to mock us and call us cowards? No! Besides, there is no need. This fury is one of the faery folk. She will not be difficult to fight. The fae are afraid of iron. She will run at the first sight of a sword."

"How do you know this?" Keeper was skeptical.

Skylan could not very well say that Wulfe had told him, that he'd seen the boy's fingers blistered and burned from touching a sword.

"It is common knowledge among my people," he said.

He looked around at Bjorn and Grimuir and Sigurd and the other Torgun for support. They looked a bit startled, for they'd never heard of this particular quirk of the fae. But they wanted their swords in their hands and they all loudly voiced their agreement.

"We will play," Skylan added. "For the honor of the Vindrasi."

"The Empress doesn't give a damn about your honor," said Acronis. "She is doing this to please the masses who like the blood and gore. She breaks the rules. This is an insult."

"Then we will insult her by defeating this evil creature," said Skylan.

"Speaking of evil creatures," said Sigurd, spitting on the ground. "Look who's coming to pay us a visit."

Raegar and Treia were walking toward them, moving in considerable haste. Raegar had participated in the dedication ceremony and was wearing his official robes and his armor. His bald head gleamed with sweat. Treia was wearing the robes of a priestess of Aelon. This was the first time the Torgun had seen her dressed like this, and they glared at her and scowled.

"You know the rules, Raegar," said Zahakis, moving to halt them before they could reach the team. You should not be here."

"This is important," said Raegar. "You drew the Empress's lot. I have just heard she is bringing in one of the fae folk to fight in the game."

"We've heard the same," said Zahakis. "Thank you for the warning, but now you must go—"

"Then, of course, you are planning to withdraw, Legate," said Raegar, peering over Zahakis's head, talking to Acronis. "Do not worry about your ranking. I will undertake to mention this serious infraction of the rules to the Priest-General—"

Acronis looked questioningly at Keeper, who said loudly, "Skylan is right. I do not like to be branded a coward."

"I will not withdraw." Acronis added with a sly smile, "If, as you say, the rules have been broken, Raegar, then I trust Aelon will look with favor on us and give us his blessing."

Raegar knew quite well Acronis was mocking him, but he had come here for a reason.

"I am worried about the Torgun. I am one of them. They are my kinsmen—"

A rock struck Raegar on the forehead. Raegar glared angrily around for the culprit, but the Torgun stood bunched together, and Raegar could not see who threw it.

"I know you will never believe it," Raegar told them angrily, "but I brought you here for your own good. I want to save you from

gods who are old and useless and bring you to the knowledge of
Aelon, who is young and powerful."

The usually quiet and taciturn Farinn gave a growl of contempt
and lunged suddenly at Raegar, his hands reaching for the man's
throat. Skylan and Bjorn caught hold of Farinn and dragged him
back.

"I think you had better go, Raegar," said Acronis.

"We will," said Treia, who had been watching in silence. "But first
I want to speak to my sister. Alone."

"I am sorry, Mistress," said Acronis. "As Zahakis told you, that is
against the rules."

"I don't understand," said Treia, blinking. "Why should talking
to my sister be against the rules?"

"No one is permitted to speak to the players before the game except trainers and owners. The rule is an ancient one, Mistress, insti-
tuted to prevent gamblers from cheating by trying to persuade
players to throw the game or slipping players opiates or giving them
tainted water."

"But gambling is forbidden by Aelon," said Treia.

"True," said Acronis in solemn tones, with a wink for Zahakis,
"but you know as well as I do, Mistress, that there are bad people in
this world. People who would do anything for money."

Treia was clearly upset. "I *must* say something to my sister."

"Say it so we may all hear," said Acronis. "And then take your
leave."

Treia looked at Raegar.

"He is right," Raegar said. "It is against the rules."

Treia turned to Aylaen.

"Sister, is there anything you want to tell me?" Treia asked.

"Only that I love you, Sister," Aylaen said, her eyes lowered.

Treia's lips tightened. "Nothing more?"

Aylaen shook her head. Skylan longed to ask Treia and Raegar
about the spiritbone of the Vektia, but he had sworn an oath to Aylaen, invoking Torval's name, that he would keep what she had told
him secret. He'd broken too many oaths to Torval to break any more.

Raegar saw the referee glaring in his direction and, taking hold of
Treia's arm, he tugged at her. They walked reluctantly off the field.

Skylan tried to catch Aylaen's eye, but she ignored him. She
looked very well in her outlandish armor. Her skin was brown from

the sea voyage, her red hair flamed in the sunlight. She stood with her head tilted back, her arms crossed over her chest, her eyes gazing out at the playing field, as though her thoughts were centered on the game. Skylan was willing to bet a herd of fine cattle that she was not thinking about the game at all. He wished he could persuade her to share her troubles with him, but he knew her well enough to know that pressing her would only make her more stubborn. She had come to him once. She would come to him again.

Zahakis and Acronis were talking earnestly together. Pretending that he wanted to get a better view of the playing field, Skylan wandered over to where he was within earshot.

"Just to be safe," Acronis was saying, "you will take Chloe home."

Zahakis gave a wry smile. "How should I do that, sir? She will not go quietly. And may I remind you, sir, she is the guest of the Empress. She is sitting in the Empress's box. Perhaps if *you* spoke to her—"

Acronis shook his head. "I do not have time to argue with her. Ours is the first game of the day and I am already late taking my place on the field. There, you see the stewards are coming to look for me. Zahakis, stay with my daughter. Guard her. No matter what happens to me. Understood?"

"Yes, Legate," said Zahakis, and, clapping his hand over his sword's sheath to prevent it from banging against his leg, he broke into a run, heading for the royal boxes and the diminutive figure who was even now being carried to her seat by the fat slave, Kakos.

Skylan looked out at the playing field, the six large boulders standing in a circle, the squares painted on the grass, the bonfire burning in the center of the pit. Across from them, the opposing players were gathered around their captain. They were glum, angry.

"I'm guessing those poor bastards don't want to be on the field with the fury any more than we do," Skylan said to Bjorn.

"None of this makes sense. Especially Raegar's sudden surge of brotherly love for us." Bjorn glanced over his shoulder. "And something is wrong with Aylaen. Ever since she came back from her visit to the Temple. What did that foul god do to her? Do you know?"

Skylan knew, but he couldn't tell. Fortunately he was spared from answering by Keeper, who summoned his players and began laying out the game plan.

The Torgun warriors listened to their captain in extreme confusion.

The royal box was unusually crowded for an afternoon game.
People were taking their places, ordering slaves to unpack food
baskets and pour wine. They hailed friends, laughing and talking
and exchanging the latest gossip. Raegar had been ordered to report
back to Xydis. The two had to leave the box and move down to the
ground level, beneath the grandstands, to find some privacy.

"Aylaen refused to tell us. She is being perverse and stubborn,"
Raegar told his superior. "I believe she knows, but she is deliberately thwarting us."

"We hold her dead lover's spirit hostage," said Xydis. "She would
do anything to free him. It is this Skylan who is refusing to talk. Did
you warn Acronis about the fury?"

"I did," said Raegar.

"He will withdraw, of course."

"No, Worshipful Sir, he refuses."

"The man is an arrogant fool!" Xydis stated.

"The Empress is breaking the rules," Raegar said, his voice so low
Xydis had to strain to hear. "Couldn't we do something to stop the
game from proceeding?"

"She is the Empress," said Xydis. "For her, there are no rules.
Speaking of the Empress, I must be on hand when she arrives to
welcome her. We will speak later. Pray to Aelon."

"Well," said Treia eagerly when Raegar returned to their seats, which
were near the fire pit. As a warrior-priest, Raegar would guard the

sacred fire during the game. "Is the Priest-General going to stop the game?"

"He can't," said Raegar. "She is the Empress. There is nothing he can do."

"But what about the secret of the Vektan dragon?" Treia asked, dismayed.

"Xydis says we must have faith in Aelon. Our god knows best," said Raegar. "Aelon has us in his care. Now I must go attend to my duties."

He hurried off, leaving Treia on her own.

"Piss on Aelon," she muttered.

She stood thinking a moment, then, turning on her heel, she shoved her way through the crowd.

Wulfe was determined to keep his promise to Skylan. The boy was glad to be back with his friends, glad that he was free of at least one burden of guilt—the murder of those two guards. Skylan had assured him that he wasn't angry with him.

"Though some of the others would be very angry," Skylan had warned him. "Even to the point of wanting to get rid of you. You must keep the secret that you . . . uh . . . have this daemon inside you. Promise?"

Wulfe promised. One promise he meant to keep.

The Torgun had been glad to see the boy return. Wulfe had been touched and astonished by their obvious affection for him. Which made the second secret he knew harder to bear. Skylan and his friends were slaves and Wulfe had the means of setting them free. Or at least the means of giving them a fighting chance.

After the Torgun left for the Para Dix and Wulfe was alone to do what he pleased, he first went to find something to eat. Then he made the long trek to the river and back for a bath.

He played in the water awhile, hoping to find some river sprites to talk to, for he was lonely and bored. There were no river sprites, however. No dryads in the trees, exchanging gossip. The fae in this land had fled or been driven out by Aelon.

After his swim, Wulfe was sleepy and he went back to his tent to take a nap. He woke, terrified, from a dream that a fury was trying to kill Skylan.

———

The driver of one of the Church carriages had been extremely annoyed when Treia had accosted him and told him to drive her to the
villa of Legate Acronis, saying she was going to treat an ill slave. He
didn't want to leave the game. Treia insisted, however, telling him
that she was acting on orders from Warrior-Priest Raegar.

Muttering imprecations, the driver obeyed and they rolled off
through the streets that were relatively empty, since most people were
attending the game. A few children and half-starved dogs roamed
the alleys, searching through piles of garbage for food. Slatternly
women with babies on their hips looked wearily out of doorways or
sat in the shade. The carriage passed a man either dead or dead drunk
lying in the gutter.

When they arrived, Treia told the driver not to wait for her; she
didn't know how long she would be. He was glad to go, eager to return to the games.

Treia walked down the hill toward the slave compound.

When Wulfe woke, he remembered clearly the frightening dream.
His friends were in danger in this horrible place. They would always
be in danger. He had the means to save them and he was going to
do it.

Wulfe left the tent and made his way across the compound to the
Venjekar. The ship had been removed from the cart and now lay wal-
lowing on the grass like a beached whale. Wulfe pulled himself up
and over the side. He felt happy and glad to be home, a feeling that
vanished when he saw the dragon-shaped prow propped up against
the hull.

Wulfe had always been in awe of the Dragon Kahg—awed and
afraid. The dragon's red eyes glared disapproval, at least in Wulfe's
mind.

Wulfe knew the dragon's secret. He knew the spiritbone on the
Venjekar was not lost. It was hidden away safely in the niche Wulfe
had cut into the ship's hull.

He was going to retrieve the spiritbone and give it to Skylan, but
there was the dragon's head, propped up against the hull right over
the hiding place.

Wulfe wavered a moment in his decision, then, getting a firm grip on his courage, he approached the dragon, taking care not to come too close to the mouth with its newly painted white fangs.

Wulfe recalled with a shudder the time the head had broken off and swooped down on him. The head, resting against the hull, had only one red eye visible. That eye was glaring at the boy.

"I don't mean to bother you, Kahg," said Wulfe politely. "I would just like to check to make certain the spiritbone is safe. If you could move a bit to the left . . . ?"

The dragon did not move. Wulfe could have shoved the prow to one side, but he would have sooner thought of shoving a real dragon. He was going to plead, when he noted that the red eye was no longer looking at him. Wulfe followed the dragon's gaze and saw someone walking toward the ship, walking fast and purposefully.

Wulfe gulped. "Treia!"

He knew at once she was coming for him. If she caught him, she'd hand him over to Raegar and that would be the end.

Wulfe muttered a word of thanks to the Dragon Kahg for the warning and raced for the hold. He pulled open the hatch and dove down the stairs, searching frantically for a place to hide.

His usual hiding place was the wooden chest where Treia and Aylaen kept their clothes. But Treia knew that he always hid there. That would be the first place she'd look.

A pile of blankets was more inviting. He pulled the blankets over his head, curled up among them. When he heard steps on the deck, he froze, hardly daring to breathe. His heart thudded as the footsteps came nearer and nearly leaped out of his chest when the footsteps descended the stairs. Treia was going to search the hold.

Wulfe huddled among the blankets, waiting fearfully for her to find him. His daemon began clawing at him, urging him to attack her and rip out her throat. Wulfe considered this, but he was fairly certain the Dragon Kahg would not approve of him murdering Treia and he didn't want to anger the dragon.

Wulfe kept firm hold on his daemon and, after a moment, he was glad he did, for Treia didn't come over to the pile of bedding. He heard her rummaging about and he peeped from under a corner of the blanket. Treia had opened the lid to her chest and was looking for something inside. Wulfe went limp at the thought that he'd very nearly hidden in there.

———

Treia began to undress, taking off the gown of a priestess of Aelon and tossing it to the deck. She took from the chest the ceremonial robes of a Kai Priestess, put them on, and then knelt down awkwardly.

The interior of the hold was dark, the air cool and moist. Treia thought she heard a sound coming from a pile of blankets and she turned to stare in that direction. Her weak eyes saw nothing. The sound was not repeated.

Probably a rat.

Treia clasped her hands together, her fingers pressing against the knuckles. She was nervous. She had never before spoken to the god, Hevis, but she knew the ritual prayer.

Once a year, the Kai Priestesses dedicated a day to Hevis, not so much to honor as to placate him. Hevis was the god of fire and smoke, deceit and hidden acts. The son of Volindril, the goddess of spring, and the five dragons of the Vektia, Hevis was devious and dangerous, treacherous and destructive. He was also necessary to the very survival of the Vindrasi. His fire cooked their food and kept them warm in the harsh winters of their land.

"Hevis, creator and destructor, I bring to you my prayer of supplication." Treia unclasped her hands and traced on the deck a rune symbolizing fire. "I beg you come to me, Hevis. I am in need."

Treia waited in the darkness. The wooden floor of the deck bruised her knees and she thought back to the many times she had been forced to kneel on the floor of the Hall of Vindrash during Draya's prayers.

The voice, when it answered, burned her soul.

"You are a woman of few words, Treia Adalbrand. I like that. You can't imagine how the other Bone Priestesses used to bore me."

The face of the god blazed in the darkness like a lump of charcoal with orange and red and yellow flame flaring through the cracks, shooting from the mouth, and glowing in the eyes. His hair was fire. He had no body, no limbs, no trunk. His heat beat on her, seemed to suck the air from the hold. She gasped and shrank away to keep from being burned.

"I find it strange that you pray to me, since your allegiance is now to another god." Hevis paused. The flame eyes seared her heart. "A god whose foul name will not pollute my mouth. A god who is my enemy."

Treia trembled. A god of lies and deceit might be won over by the truth. Or he might destroy her. She had to take the risk. Sweat beaded on Treia's forehead and ran down her face and trickled down her breasts.

"My allegiance is not to Aelon or any god, great Hevis," said Treia in a voice that was barely above a whisper. She raised her eyes. "My allegiance is to myself."

His fire flared.

"A truthful response. What do you want of me?"

The god was detached, uncaring. He was here out of curiosity, nothing more. He would soon grow more interested, of that she was certain.

"I know a secret," Treia said. "A valuable secret. I am here to share it with you."

Hevis scoffed. His heat scorched her. "You, a mortal, claim to know something we gods do not?"

"I do," she said with more confidence than she felt.

"Tell me and I will be the judge," said Hevis.

"I risk my life bringing this secret to you. I want something in return."

Fire raged around her and Treia feared she would die. She smelled the sickening odor of burnt hair, her own hair, and saw flaming ash dropping on her robes, burning holes in the cloth.

"I must first decide if this secret is worth the price of your miserable life," said Hevis. "What do you know?"

Treia cowered before him and gasped out, "The god, Sund, has given Aelon one of the spiritbones of the Five Vektia, one of the spiritbones of your fathers!"

The flaring light of Hevis dimmed, the hold cooled. Treia sighed in relief. She was right. The gods of the Vindrasi did not know that Sund was a traitor.

"How do you discover this?" Hevis asked.

"The priests of Aelon showed the spiritbone to me. I have seen it, touched it."

"How do you know it is one of the five?"

Treia described the spiritbone, its golden setting, its beautiful emeralds.

"Yes," said Hevis, and his voice was bitter. "That is the spiritbone given to Sund for safekeeping. You say that Sund gave it to Aelon? Voluntarily? What was his reason?"

"Sund looked into the future and saw that Aelon would win the war. Torval and the rest of you would be defeated. Sund gave the spiritbone to Aelon in exchange for his own survival."

Hevis's flames hissed and crackled, but not in anger. He seemed to be laughing. "Torval loves Sund. This will break his heart and is indeed valuable information. What do you want in return, Treia Adalbrand? Request what you will. I am in a generous mood."

"Teach me the ritual to summon the Vektan dragon."

"Why do you want to know?" Hevis asked, flames flickering.

"So that I may use it to command the dragon to destroy the ogres, who are coming to invade this land," said Treia.

"Perhaps I do not know this ritual."

"You know it," said Treia. "Long ago you helped a Kai Priestess summon the dragon."

"You are not a Kai Priestess."

"Draya is dead and left no successor," said Treia. "In this time of turmoil, it may be long before a Kai is chosen, if ever."

"You know the history of the Kai Priestess. You know she could not control the dragon. The Vektan went berserk and destroyed entire villages, killing many hundreds of your own people. You must prove to me you can control the Vektan dragon, Treia Adalbrand. I dare not risk teaching you otherwise."

"Tell me what I must do," Treia said.

"You must prove to me that you are strong-minded. You must show me that you will not let emotions sway you. Only then will I deem you capable of controlling one of the Vektia. You must sacrifice to me a person you hold dear."

"You mean I must kill someone," Treia faltered. "Someone I love. . . ."

Treia's first thought was of Raegar and she knew she could never make such a bargain. He was everything to her. More than life itself. She was devastated. All this trouble for nothing. And then a thought occurred to her.

"This could be anyone?"

"Anyone at all," said Hevis. "So long as you hold this person dear."

Treia's palms were clammy. Her stomach twisted. A horrid taste filled her mouth. She recoiled from herself in horror at the very thought, but she recalled what was at stake, what she stood to gain. She swallowed the bitter taste and said firmly, "Teach me the ritual. You will have your sacrifice."

Hevis looked into her heart and was satisfied.

Wulfe dove down among the blankets the moment the god appeared. He could not see the face of the god, nor did he want to. He could feel the heat and he lay shivering and quaking, afraid the dread god of the Uglies would find him.

Wulfe could hear the discussion between Treia and the god quite clearly, but the boy was frightened half out of his wits and the words made no sense to him.

Just when Wulfe thought he would die of terror beneath the blanket, the god left, taking his horrid heat with him. Treia sat for a long time in the dark. Wulfe lay beneath his blanket hating her and wishing she would leave.

Finally he heard her stirring about at the other end of the hold, and he shoved aside a corner of the blanket and was finally able to draw a breath of fresh air.

Treia was taking off the ceremonial robes. She bundled them back into the chest and put on the gown of a priestess of Aelon. She took one final look about the hold. Wulfe held very still. Then Treia left, climbing up the ladder and walking swiftly across the deck.

When Wulfe was no longer able to hear her footsteps, he scampered up the ladder and saw her hurrying across the compound. He kept watch until she was gone, then he went back to look up at the dragon's head, which was still blocking his way to the hiding place of the spiritbone.

"Please, can't I give it back?" Wulfe asked plaintively.

The dragon's red eye glittered fiercely.

Wulfe sighed and wandered off to find something to eat.

A rumor that the Empress was bringing in a new player to fight
in the Para Dix spread about the boxes of the nobility, rippling
among them like wind across a field of barley. People leaned into
their neighbors to hear the exciting gossip, then they turned to im-
part the information to those seated beside them.

Chloe heard the rumor from Rosa, her house-slave, who had
heard it from a slave belonging to a nobleman, who had heard it
from a friend of a noble lady, who was currently a favorite with the
Empress. Rosa was agog with excitement when she told her young
mistress and talked so rapidly Chloe had trouble making sense of
what she was saying. Well aware of Rosa's tendency to exaggerate,
and also somewhat suspicious of Rosa's sources, Chloe longed to
ask someone more reliable.

Although she was seated in the Empress's royal box, Chloe was a
small moon compared to the glorious sun that was Her Imperial
Majesty—allowed to bask in the light and feel the warmth, but only
from a distance. And, as of now, the royal box was still benighted,
for the Empress had not arrived. Generally she came to the games
only in the evening, to watch her champion team. Today, word flew
that the royal party was on their way to the arena. The Empress was,
of course, taking her time, for it was fatiguing to travel in the heat
of the day. The game would be delayed to await her arrival.

The delay and the fact that the Empress was going to be in attendance added credence to the rumor. Chloe wished someone would
visit with her, but though the noble lords bowed to her and their

lady wives blew kisses from the tips of their fingers, no one came to sit beside her and chat.

Chloe understood. Her father was a wealthy man and, as such, the members of the nobility were polite to her, for no one wanted to offend him. Acronis was still on good terms with the Empress, which was why she had invited Chloe to sit in the royal box. But Acronis was also known to be cynical and outspoken, particularly in regard to his religious views, and that made people uncomfortable. There had been a time, back in the early days of the new religion, when the nobility looked down upon Aelon, deeming him an upstart young god, a god of the lower classes, popular among the unwashed and the uneducated, but hardly suitable for polite society.

As Aelon's Church increased in wealth and gained followers, the attitudes of the nobility changed. When the Empress became a fanatic follower, Aelon's priests, who had formerly been admitted to noble villas only through the servants' entrance, were now invited to dine with the royal family. Acronis did not change his views on Aelon, however, and the Priest-General and the Empress's friendship for him was starting to cool. She could not afford to anger him, for he had his own army and paid for two triremes. She could make her displeasure known in other, more subtle ways, such as reducing the number of invitations to dinner.

Acronis never noticed. He disliked dining out, preferring to share his meals with his daughter and those who were his true friends. Acronis came from an ancient noble family, one of the founding families of Sinaria. He was an intelligent man, but he was short-sighted. He had honestly believed the worship of Aelon was a fad, a passing fancy. He was starting to realize he had been wrong. If he had seen the treasure room and knew the vast amount of wealth being secretly amassed by Aelon's priests, he would have been appalled.

Chloe felt and believed exactly the same as her father. She thought the Empress a silly, vain woman. Chloe cared nothing for the haughty nobles and their snooty wives. She didn't care where she sat, so long as she had a good view of the game. But being a social outcast had its disadvantages, and she'd never felt that more than now, when she longed to find out the truth of what was happening and no one would tell her. Then, at last, she saw Zahakis and she waved to him wildly and sent Rosa to fetch him.

Zahakis was known to all as the commander of her father's army, and as such he had no difficulty being admitted to the royal box. He came straight to Chloe and said quietly, "Your father has ordered me to take you home."

Chloe laughed at him. "Be serious, Zahakis, and sit down and tell me if this rumor I've heard is true."

"I am serious, Mistress," he said gravely. "Those are your father's orders."

Chloe saw the way the Tribune's eyes roved about the crowd and how he kept his hand conspicuously near his sword and she knew he *was* serious. She also knew she wasn't leaving.

"Sit down and talk to me," Chloe said, patting the silk cushions. She smiled at him and the dimple flashed. "Those are *my* orders and you know that I outrank my father."

Zahakis was well aware of that. He sat down beside her.

"I've heard a rumor that the Empress is bringing in some sort of monster to fight against Father's team," said Chloe eagerly. "Is that true?"

"Keep your voice down, child," said Zahakis.

The Empress and her party were entering the royal box. She was accompanied by her little dog, who had its own slave, and slaves with pillows, slaves carrying baskets of food, slaves with large ostrich-feather fans. All was noise and confusion as she greeted friends and the nobles crowded around to fawn over her.

"Your father wanted to withdraw from the game," said Zahakis, under the cover of the loud greetings and laughter, "but your barbarian insisted on fighting."

"Skylan!" Chloe said, her eyes shining. "He did? He is so brave!"

" 'One man's hero is another man's fool,' " Zahakis said, repeating the old quote.

Chloe made a face at him and playfully slapped his hand.

At that moment, heads turned, conversation ceased, people all over the arena stood up to see.

A chariot entered the main gate, driving onto the dirt track that circled the arena. Word spread excitedly through the crowd that this was the new player, a creature known as a fury. Nothing like this had ever happened in a Para Dix game. Players left the benches and came out on the field, as did the referees, the Game Masters, and even the warrior-priests, who were supposed to be tending the sacred fire.

A shocked buzz spread through the crowd. A child screamed, a woman fainted, the buzz faded out, and silence fell. People stared, struck dumb with shock.

The fury was as beautiful as she was awful. Her eyes, large and deep blue and luminous, dripped with blood that ran down her cheeks like dreadful tears. The hand that waved to the crowd was delicate, the fingers slender and fine-boned, ending in long, rending, bloodstained talons. Her hair was long and black and adorned with snakes that sprouted from her head, writhing and coiling and biting at each other. Wings of black feathers thrust out from her shoulder blades.

The fury was naked from the waist up. Her breasts were large and swayed and jiggled as the chariot jounced over the uneven surface of the track. A long skirt made of red silk was belted around her waist and draped provocatively over her legs. No one in the stands felt any sort of sexual attraction, only a cold, creeping horror.

The chariot was drawn by slaves, not horses, for the horses had gone into a panicked frenzy at the sight of the fury. The slaves had not undertaken the task willingly. The six men eventually chosen for the task had been driven to obey by the pain of Aelon's displeasure. Sweating with fear and exertion, they dragged the chariot by its traces, and though the load was heavy, they were running to escape the terror of being in such close proximity to the chariot's passenger.

Most people in the stands were staring in shock and horror at the fury, who appeared to be enjoying the attention, and few noticed the man who walked at the chariot's side. He was a tall man, well built, with a smooth face, high cheekbones, and a strong chin. His long brown hair flowed down his shoulders. He wore gray robes, plain and unadorned. He was not afraid of the fury, for he kept close to her and every so often he would turn to say something to her.

The crowd was amazed. The people of Oran believed in the fae, knew that they were a part of their world—an evil part, as Aelon's priests often told them. People took the usual precautions: avoiding rings of mushrooms, nailing strings of garlic bulbs to the door, wearing clothes backwards if they had to venture into the woods, and so forth. These were pleasant superstitions, and apparently they worked, for most people in Oran had never encountered any of the fae.

The idea of one of the faery folk brought in as a player had seemed good fun at first, something out of the ordinary to brighten up the dull routine of everyday life. Now the curtain between their well-ordered world and the chaotic world of the fae had been torn aside. They could picture the fury trailing after her victim, coming to him in the night, gazing at him as he tried to sleep, shedding tears of his victim's blood, rending his soul with her talons until all he wanted to do was end the torment.

The warrior-priests shook off their own horror, and, fearing a stampede, moved among the crowd, reminding everyone that they were under Aelon's protection. People settled down, and a modicum of calm returned, though the crowd remained tense and uneasy.

The slaves dragged the chariot to a halt in front of the royal box. The Empress rose to her feet and was about to make a speech. She was interrupted by the fury, who threw back her head and shrieked in laughter. The Empress smiled upon her fury and glowered around at the crowd. The Empress had expected applause and cheers for her "pretty pet" and she was angered by the reaction of the crowd. She was about to speak out, make her anger known publicly, when one of her attendants whispered that since the game was already late in starting, perhaps she should not try the patience of the audience any further. The Empress shrugged and, wrapping the folds of her cape around her in magnificent displeasure, sat back down and held out her goblet to be filled with wine.

Chloe was frightened, but unlike many of the other girls, who were shivering and covering their eyes, she only gave a little gasp and reached out to Zahakis. Her first concern was for Skylan, and she looked over to where he was standing in the player's area. She spotted him easily by his blond hair. He stood with his arms crossed, his shoulders back, studying the fury with narrow-eyed concentration as he might have studied any foe he was to meet on the field of battle. Chloe leaned close to Zahakis.

"Do you know any prayers to Torval?" she whispered.

"I don't know any prayers to any god, Mistress," Zahakis said. "Why do you ask?"

"I want to ask Skylan's god to protect him," she answered. "And I don't know how to pray to Torval. I don't want to offend him."

"From what I have heard, Torval is not a god to stand upon cere-mony," said Zahakis, hiding his smile. He added hurriedly, "Just don't let anyone hear you!"

Chloe nodded and, folding her hands, she whispered, "Torval, you don't know me, but I know you. Skylan told me about you. He's my champion. I hope you don't think I'm being too presumptuous. I want to ask you to protect him from this monster. Thank you."

Hoping Torval could hear her over the carousing in his Hall, she put her chin on her hand and stared intently at the fury, who was stepping down out of the chariot.

"If she is fae, she must be very strong," said Chloe. "I wonder how the Empress's people managed to capture her? And who is that man who is with her? The one in the gray robes."

Zahakis had been regarding this man with interest. "He is a druid."

"A druid!" Chloe drew in an excited breath. "I've never met a druid. Do you suppose he would come to dinner? You must tell my father to invite him, Zahakis."

"You are your father's daughter," said Zahakis, continuing to keep an eye on those around him. He was startled to see his interest returned. Xydis, the Priest-General, was looking at him. The Priest-General rose to his feet and began to descend the stairs.

"The Priest-General is coming," Zahakis said in a warning undertone.

"Don't worry," said Chloe. "I'll be good. I won't say anything to embarrass you."

Zahakis rose to his feet and stiffly saluted. Xydis acknowledged the Tribune with a cool glance. The Priest-General bowed to Chloe and said he was glad to see her looking so well. Chloe shifted among her pillows and smiled politely. She was mistress of the household, in the absence of her mother, and she asked the Priest-General if he would take some wine and a honey cake. He politely declined, then indicated, with a look at Zahakis, that he wanted to speak to him.

"Walk with me, Tribune," said the Priest-General.

Zahakis accompanied the man to one of the recessed entrances leading into the royal box. People here were milling about, talking excitedly about what they had just witnessed. The hubbub was such that the two men did not have to bother to lower their voices.

Xydis did not look directly at Zahakis as he spoke. The Priest-General stood with one arm crooked, holding the folds of his robe, gazing out onto the playing field as though he were discussing the game.

"You will be interested to know, Tribune, that the Empress received this monster as a gift. She has no idea who sent it or where it came from. The messenger who delivered it stated that the creature was trained to fight in the Para Dix. The Empress cannot confirm this because her trainers were too terrified to have anything to do with the monstrous thing. You might want to inform Legate Acronis."

Zahakis frowned, not sure he understood what Xydis was saying and less sure as to why he was saying it.

"In addition, the drawing was rigged, Tribune," said Xydis, smiling and bowing to an acquaintance. "The gift-giver specified that the fury was to fight your team."

The Priest-General walked away, going off to join friends. Zahakis stood in the entryway, mulling over what he'd heard. He took only a moment to make a decision, then returned to Chloe.

"I have to go speak to your father." Zahakis added earnestly, "I would take it as a personal favor, Mistress, if you would return home."

"Don't be silly, Zahakis," said Chloe. "I'm going to see a fury fight in the games."

"I could command my men to take you—"

"And I would sulk for a week and make everyone's life miserable. Come now, Zahakis, stop fussing over me. You are worse than my old nanny." She pulled him close to whisper, "You know very well that if anything bad is going to happen to me, it will happen whether I am here or at home. And I would much rather be here with you and my father. At home, I would be alone."

She looked at him, making certain he understood her.

"I am not afraid, Zahakis. I'm not."

"You are, in truth, your father's daughter," said Zahakis. "I will send one of my soldiers to stay with you."

"Not Manos," said Chloe, wrinkling her nose. "He farts."

Acronis was walking on the field, side-by-side with the opposing player, taking part in the opening ceremony, which involved determining which "Mirchan," as the players were known, was to have the first move. (In ancient times Mirchan was the name of a goddess of the Oran the Vindrasi knew as Mirchana, one of the Norn who controlled the fates of men. The name had since come to mean something akin to "puppet master.") The fury had gone to join the Empress's team meekly enough and the crowd was starting to relax. After the initial shock had worn off, the people were enjoying the excitement. A rustle of anticipation swept through the stands.

The fury had passed close by Skylan in her triumphal circuit of the arena. The blood-oozing eyes stared directly at him, seemed to pay particular attention to him. The beautiful lips parted in a smile made hideous by the crimson tears that rolled down her cheeks and dribbled into her mouth. Her snakes hissed, uncoiled.

Skylan felt his stomach clench. He clasped the amulet of Torval and averted his eyes. He saw Sigurd's face go rigid. He felt Bjorn, standing beside him, shudder. Erdmun made a sound that might have been a whimper, and Farinn gave an audible gasp. Aylaen stared at the ground, twisting her hands. Keeper was holding some sort of charm, rubbing it and muttering to himself. Skylan had thought Owl Mother's wyvern a fearsome beast. The wyvern was a tame crow compared to the fury.

"Who is that man with her?" Aki asked, his voice harsh with fear. "Is he one of the foul faery folk, as well?"

"No," said Skylan. "He's a druid."

Wulfe had told him that of all the Uglies, the druids were the only humans the fae trusted.

The druids Skylan had encountered on the Druid Isles feared the Southlanders, who were threatening to take their beautiful island home away from them and cut down their sacred trees to build cities of stone. So what was a druid doing here in Sinaria? Was he a slave, a prisoner? And what was he doing in company with the fury?

The druid turned to look directly at Skylan, almost as if he could hear his questions and wanted to answer them. Skylan had no idea what the druid might be trying to say. Skylan tried to remember if he had seen this man before. He didn't think so. The druids he had encountered had been elderly graybeards. This man was young, in his twenties.

The druid kept his gaze on Skylan. Obviously, although Skylan did not recognize him, the druid recognized Skylan. Remembering how shamefully he had treated the druids, Skylan felt his heart sink.

"The creature looked straight at me!" Grimuir was saying in a shaking voice. "I saw in her face the face of that old woman I killed in a raid. Her death was an accident. I was aiming for a warrior and the old woman got in the way. My spear went clean through her! I saw her face. . . ."

Acronis and the other Mirchan were climbing up the stairs to the platforms that overlooked the field of play. Keeper thrust his charm in a pouch and told Skylan and the other players it was time.

The Para Dix was about to begin.

Skylan and his friends would be walking out onto the field to fight in a game they did not understand. They were going to have trouble enough and they needed their wits about them, especially Aylaen, who was a "loris," one of the key players, or so Keeper kept telling her. Aylaen could move in any direction and take any path on the game board, whereas Skylan's movements and those of the others were restricted.

Skylan was a "pradus," which Keeper had described as a kind of chief. Being pradus, Skylan was the only "piece" permitted to fight the opposing pradus for control of the fire in the center of the field. Unfortunately, getting to the center was no easy task. Skylan could not simply walk over there (as he had tried yesterday and been knocked on his butt). According to the rules, he could not move to any square without being accompanied by another "piece." And for some reason, if an opposing piece came between him and the fire, he had to move back to the "touchstone," one of the six boulders.

Skylan had only the vaguest idea what he was doing and why he was doing it. The other Torgun were equally bad, equally confused. And instead of standing firm, concentrating on the foe.

All he could see was Garn's face and the faces of all those men who had died because of him. Like vipers, they uncoiled, hissed at him. . . .

The clang of metal on metal broke the spell. Slaves hauled hand-carts filled with weapons out onto the field. Keeper ordered his players to choose a weapon and a shield.

Skylan gazed glumly at the collection of swords the slaves placed on the ground. All the weapons were designed to be used in the game, which meant—according to Keeper—that they were made for show. They looked well to the audience, but the blades were of poor quality with blunted edges.

Skylan picked up a sword—the best of a bad lot. All players were supposed to use the same type of weapons, but Keeper had explained that the champion players were permitted to fight with weapons of good quality, which they had specially made for them. The referees turned a blind eye.

Skylan hefted his sword, noting the poor balance, and was about to turn away when he stopped to stare at the pile of weapons more closely. He had seen one of the weapons before. The sword was Aylaen's, given to her by the Goddess Vindrash. He looked at Keeper in astonishment.

"She fights for her goddess," Keeper said. "It is right that she should use the sword the goddess gave to her."

Aylaen stared straight at the sword, but made no move to pick it up. The sword had been long neglected when Aylaen had found it in the Hall of Vindrash. She had been proud of it. Skylan remembered her cleaning it with loving care, spending days rubbing the blade with oil and sand to remove the rust, polishing it with a soft cloth.

"What is the matter with the female?" Keeper asked, scowling. "I took a great risk smuggling that sword from the storage room for her."

The ogre picked up the sword and tossed it into the ground at Aylaen's feet. The blade struck point first in the dirt and stood there, quivering.

"A fine sword," he said loudly. "Suited to a female's hand." He lowered his voice. "Take it! Do not offend your goddess."

"I have already offended the goddess," Aylaen said. "I will not further offend her by using her sword."

Aylaen picked up an axe. She was good with the sword, not nearly so good with an axe.

"Say something to her!" Keeper told Skylan.

"Don't waste your breath," Aylaen warned. "I won't use the sword. Vindrash would curse me if I touched it. You don't know, Skylan. You don't know what I have done!"

The trumpet sounded, calling the players to the game.

Keeper, shaking his head, picked up the goddess's sword and flung it back onto the pile.

At Keeper's direction, the players lined up on the sidelines. He was about to describe to them the opening moves when Sigurd, hearing the trumpet, hefted his axe and ran onto the field.

"Arsehole, get back!" Keeper yelled, and stormed out after him. "Back to the sidelines, you dolt!"

Sigurd stopped and looked around.

"Me? What the hell is wrong?" he asked, astonished.

"It's not our move!" Keeper cried, seething. "Get off the field, you bloody idiot, before we have to forfeit a turn! And next time wait until I call the play!"

The crowd needed a break in the tension generated by the fury, and they found this hilarious. The players on the Empress's team grinned and jeered, asking if the Barbarians wanted to forfeit the game now and spare themselves humiliation.

Sigurd realized everyone was laughing at him. His face flushed dark with shame and he slouched off the field. Reaching the sidelines, he flung down his axe, muttering and swearing that he would die before he'd participate in the "stupid, bloody game."

Keeper summoned Aylaen, Bjorn, and Farinn. He told them the play. The three stared at him blankly and he patiently repeated his instructions, ignoring the boos from the audience. Acronis, as Marchin, called the plays, giving his players a goal to achieve this turn. Keeper told the players the goal and sent them onto the field of play. It was up to the players to determine how to achieve that goal, always keeping in mind that each could move only according to the nature of his or her piece.

Bjorn, as a chaveus, could move as many as four spaces, the final move being toward the fire pit. Farinn, as a kovas, could move an equal number of spaces, but his final move had to be away from the pit. Aylaen, the loris, could move as many spaces in any direction as she wanted. Skylan, the pradus, could not even come out onto the field during the first turn.

They all knew this. They had all practiced it. But not one of them could make any sense of it.

The game started with one player from each side advancing onto the playing field. Keeper sent Aylaen out first, telling her to go to the middle square on the outer ring.

Aylaen stared in dismay at the crowd. The noise they were making seemed to shake the ground. All she could see were gaping mouths. She shrank back.

"I can't go out there!" she said. "I feel sick. . . ."

"It's only stage fright," said Keeper. "You'll get over it."

He gave her a shove that sent her stumbling and staggering onto the field amidst roars of laughter from the crowd.

Skylan tensed. The player sent out by the Empress's Marchin was their loris—the fury. The fae creature walked with sensuous grace onto the field, her gown wafting around her, the black feathers in her wings ruffled by the hot afternoon breeze. People saw her and their laughter ceased. An uneasy silence fell.

"You can't send Aylaen to fight that thing!" Skylan said angrily. "Send me out there instead!"

Keeper shook his head. He looked grim, worried. "You're the pradus. You're not allowed to move this turn. Don't worry, they will not fight. This is a classic opening gambit. The loris of the Empress will move one square—"

The fury made her move, but it was not one square. Spreading her wings, she rose into the air and took flight.

Her lips parted in a hideous grin. She extended her clawed hands and, folding her wings, dove down on Skylan.

He heard Aylaen cry out and Bjorn shout a warning.

Skylan remembered what he himself had said about the fae being afraid of iron, and he raised his sword to block her attack.

The fury screeched in anger. Flapping her wings, she hovered over him. Her gaze fixed on the sword. A beam of light, hot and white, flared from her bleeding eyes. The light struck Skylan's sword. The iron began to melt. Steel dripped like an icicle to the ground.

The fury struck Skylan before he had recovered from his shock, hitting him with the weight of her body, knocking him to the ground. She perched on top of him, driving her knees into his stomach. Her stench was foul, like a week-old corpse. Her wings beat. The vipers on her head hissed and struck at him. Her lips parted in a screech showing bloodstained teeth. She dug her nails into Skylan's throat.

Skylan choked, tasting blood. He grabbed hold of her wrists trying to break her hold. She was immensely strong, and she only laughed horribly at his efforts to save himself. He could not breathe. Pinpoints of light burst in his eyes. He was starting to lose consciousness when suddenly the fury's hands released their grip.

Bjorn and Keeper and Grimuir had thrown themselves on the fury and managed to wrestle her off Skylan. He drew in gulping breaths and rolled over, too weak to do anything except watch as the three men fought her.

Bjorn let go with a howl of pain and fell back, clasping his arm where blood was starting to well up out of two puncture marks on his skin. One of the vipers had bitten him.

Sigurd yelled for the others to get out of his way. Keeper and Grimuir fell back and Sigurd ran at the fury, his axe raised. She turned her white-hot gaze upon the weapon and the axe head dissolved into a lump of molten metal and fell off. Swearing, Sigurd struck at the fury with the wooden handle. The fury seized the axe from him and smashed him on the temple with such force that the wood splintered. Sigurd fell to the ground. He heaved himself up, groaned, and collapsed. He did not get back up.

Farinn picked up a spear and was about to fling it. The fury saw him and spewed a glob of spit into his face. Farinn screamed and dropped the spear. He dug the balls of his hands into his eyes and moaned with pain.

Keeper snatched up a sword from the pile of weapons on the ground and tried to stab the fury from behind. One of the fury's beating wings touched the iron. There was a strong smell of burnt feathers and she shrieked and whirled on him. Drops of blood flew from her eyes, striking his blade. The sword began to glow red-hot and Keeper dropped it with a cry.

The fury shifted her gaze to the pile of weapons. Axe heads melted. Sword blades started to bubble and dissolve. Satisfied that her foes could no longer attack her, the fury turned her blood-dripping eyes again on Skylan.

Wings beating, the fury rose up into the air. Skylan grabbed a wooden shield wrapped in leather and held it in front of him while he searched frantically for something to use as weapon. He looked at the smoldering mass of metal and saw Aylaen's sword, un-touched. The steel had not melted.

He made a lunge for it. The fury dove at him and he had to duck behind the shield, holding it braced as the fury struck the shield with her fist.

The wood splintered. The shield was covered in leather and re-mained intact, at least for the moment. He looked back at the sword and yelled and pointed. His warriors were focused on the fury, hov-ering near, wanting to help, but uncertain what to do. No one was looking at the sword except him. He shouted again and jabbed his finger at the weapon.

Aylaen saw and understood. She ran to the pile, snatched up the sword, and came to stand by Skylan's side.

The fury glared at the sword in hatred. The magical white light beamed from her eyes. The sword caught the beam of light and re-flected it back, striking the fury in the face. She screeched in anger and flapped away, staring balefully at the sword.

"Why didn't it melt?" Aylaen gasped.

"Because Vindrash blessed it? I don't know!" Skylan raised the shield. "I'll cover. You strike."

Aylaen was ready to thrust the sword into the fury's body when a gray-robed figure darted in front of her, his hands raised.

"Don't hurt her!" the druid cried.

At first, Skylan thought the druid meant that the fury was not to hurt Aylaen, and then he realized he was talking to Aylaen about the fury.

He cast a glance around the field, where Sigurd lay in a pool of blood, Farinn had his hands over his eyes, and Erdmun was suck-ing the poison out of his brother's snake bite.

"Get out of my way," said Skylan grimly. "I don't want to kill you, too, but I will if I have to."

"Please!" the druid begged. "Let me talk to her. I have been searching for her throughout Oran. I finally found her here. Unfortunately, I was too late."

He turned to face the fury and began speaking to her in some unknown language. His voice was calm. He seemed to be trying to placate her.

The fury pointed at Skylan and her lips curled back from her bloodstained fangs.

Skylan kept his shield raised, not taking his eyes from the fury.

The druid spoke to the fury again. His voice was stern. The fury grew angry. She screamed something in reply and pointed with hatred at Aylaen's sword. The snakes on her head writhed and hissed.

The fury snarled something and spit at Skylan. The saliva struck his shield, burning a hole through it. The fury spread her wings and leaped into the air. She flew over the heads of the spectators, laughing shrilly. Her flight was swift. She soared into the blue sky, winging her way northward.

No one dared moved, fearing she might return. When she was a distant speck, chaos erupted.

Soldiers swarmed onto the field.

"I believe they are going to arrest me," the druid said with a smile.

"Lose yourself in the crowd," Skylan told him urgently. "We'll cover you."

The druid folded his hands over the front of his gray robes, calmly assessed the situation, and gave a nod. "A good idea. But before I go there is something I must tell you, Skylan Ivorson. You have made a very bad enemy. The fury was sent to kill you."

Skylan stared in shock. The druid bowed and walked without haste toward the stands. Five soldiers were hot on his heels within arm's length and were about to nab him, when both the soldiers and the druid were swept to the side by a throng of spectators rushing the playing field.

Skylan feared the mob was going to attack, and he grabbed Aylaen and pulled her behind him, raising his shield to protect them both. Hands reached out and he braced himself, only to find that the people were pounding him on the back or trying to shake his hand or simply wanted to touch him.

A woman tore Aylaen from his grasp, but it was only to embrace her. People began cheering them, hailing the Barbarians as heroes.

A group of men seized hold of Skylan and lifted him onto their shoulders. Several tried to pick up Keeper, but that proved impossible; the ogre was far too heavy. Men commandeered the handcart in which the weapons had been stored and hoisted Keeper up over the side.

Fearing Aylaen would be trampled, the ogre pulled her up with him. She stood beside Keeper looking dazed, holding on tightly as the young men began to drag the handcart around the field. People followed after them forming an impromptu parade. Another group of men grabbed the chariot in which the fury had ridden and lifted Legate Acronis into it and drove it in triumph.

Watching from the royal box, Chloe had been almost suffocated with terror and now she was crying from relief. She shouted herself hoarse and clapped her hands. When the men carried Skylan past the royal box, she waved at him and called out his name. She waved at her father and he smiled back at her.

Chloe followed her father's gaze and looked around to see the Empress rising angrily to her feet and stalking out. Her slaves tumbled over each other to gather up fans and wine jugs, pillows and food baskets, and the lap dog. Her courtiers, caught by surprise, scrambled to follow her, and the box soon emptied out until the only other person remaining was the Priest-General. He sat at his ease, watching the tumult on the field without expression.

Now even the players on the opposing teams were crowding around the Torgun warriors, vying with each other for a chance to shake their hands.

"You better go rescue my slaves!" Acronis shouted, leaning over the side of the chariot to speak to Zahakis. "I fear they're going to be killed by kindness."

He tossed Zahakis the winner's purse, having been given the victory by default. "You may find this useful."

Zahakis summoned his men and led them onto the field. He and his soldiers went among the people, handing out the coins from the purse and suggesting that they celebrate the team's victory in the taverns. The crowd cheerfully dispersed. Zahakis found that Skylan had managed to keep the Torgun together. The only three missing were Sigurd and Farinn and Bjorn and they were safe in the handcart, under the care of Keeper, being treated for their injuries and snake bite.

"So what god did *you* piss off?" Zahakis asked Skylan as they were walking out of the arena.

After the people had departed and the arena was empty, Raegar and the other warrior-priests were tasked with the job of cleaning up the playing field. Treia found Raegar supervising a group of slaves who were tying ropes around one of the touchstones that had been knocked over.

"Where were you?" Raegar asked testily. "Where did you go?" He added, scowling, "You weren't with the other priestesses. I tried to find you—"

"I went to pray. So much is at stake for us, my love," Treia answered. "I felt the need to take my cares to the god."

Raegar opened his mouth and then closed it again. He couldn't very well chastise her for praying.

"Tell me what happened," Treia said. "What did I miss?"

Raegar was glad to have a chance to talk about the episode. He explained how the fury had attacked Skylan, how the fiend could melt iron with a look from her bleeding eyes, how she possessed the strength of twenty men.

"It was our prayers to Aelon that drove the creature away," he said angrily. "But did the rabble notice that? No! They swarmed onto the field, lauding Skylan and the Torgun as heroes! They are now the darlings of Sinaria."

The slaves heaved on the ropes and the boulder started to rise. One of them slipped, however, losing his grip on the rope, and the boulder crashed to the ground. Raegar kicked the offending slave and ordered them all to start over. He walked back over to where Treia was standing, observing the proceedings.

"Some god must love that whoreson Skylan," Raegar continued in low and bitter tones. "He survives assassination, not once, but twice."

Treia wrapped her hands around his arm, snuggled up against him. "He won't survive a third."

Raegar snorted. "There won't be a third. The Priest-General is already furious with me as it is. Skylan must live! He is the only one who knows the ritual—"

"Not the only one," said Treia. "Not anymore."

Raegar looked down at her, startled. He was about to ask her what she meant, then he realized that the center of the Para Dix field was probably not the best place to be holding this conversation.

The slaves managed to haul the boulder into position and looked to Raegar for further orders. He curtly ordered them to start picking up refuse from the field. He led Treia to a shadowy, secluded area beneath the grandstand.

"Did Aylaen find out the secret?" he asked.

"We no longer need Aylaen," said Treia calmly. "We no longer need Skylan."

"Then who knows the ritual?" Raegar demanded.

"I do, my love," said Treia.

He stared at her, amazed.

"I can summon the Vektan dragon," Treia continued. "I can repel the ogre invasion."

"But how did you find out?" Raegar asked, bewildered. "Who told you?"

"Aelon, my love," said Treia. "Who else?"

"Aelon! Of course! A miracle!" Raegar cried fervently, embracing her. "Praise Aelon's name!"

"Praise Aelon's name," Treia repeated. She nestled into his arms. "You no longer need to keep Skylan alive."

"We'll get rid of the whole bloody lot of them," said Raegar. "Except Aylaen, of course."

Treia put her arms around her lover and pressed her head against his chest so that he could not see her smile.

Practice for the Para Dix was called off the next day to allow the players to recover. Skylan was up early checking on the wounded. He was particularly worried about Farinn, who had been blinded by the fury, and was relieved to find that the quiet young man was slowly recovering his eyesight.

They shared a meal of bread and dried meat, all except Bjorn, who was still ill from the effects of the snake's poison. Sigurd and the others discussed the fury, speculating on where she might have gone, hoping it was a far distance away. Skylan said nothing to anyone about what the druid had told him, about someone powerful wanting him dead.

The warriors were strong in their praise of Aylaen and talked of the sword she had used to drive the fury away. A magical sword, they said, blessed by Vindrash. Too bad the priests had taken it from her, but not surprising.

Aylaen responded to their praise with a wan smile and left the group as soon as she could, saying she was going to make Wulfe take a bath. As they watched her walk away, Grimuir voiced what they were all thinking.

"She ate almost nothing. Something is wrong with her."

"The same that is wrong with all of us," Sigurd said. "We are slaves."

"We may be slaves, but the people love us now," said Erdmun. "They cheered us yesterday. A girl kissed me."

"His first," said Bjorn.

The men laughed, but the laughter was half-hearted. Sigurd did not laugh at all. His nose was swollen. His eyes were blacked, he had a lump on the side of his head. He tossed his half-eaten bread to the deck of the ship in disgust.

"Torval wasn't cheering. If we had come to his Hall, he would have planted his boot in our rear ends and kicked us out the door."

He rose to his feet and glared around at them. "It was a *game*! A goddam game! We are *slaves* playing a goddam *game*! Where is the honor in that?"

"You wanted to win yesterday as much as any of us," said Erdmun.

"That's how they trap us," said Sigurd. "They treat us as if we were important." He cast a dark glance at Skylan. "And some of us fall for it. We should have tried to escape in the melee. What has happened to Vindrasi honor?"

"Torval does not honor those who throw away their lives foolishly." Bjorn pointed at the tattoo. "What should we do about this? Cut our arms off?"

"If that's what it takes, maybe we should," said Sigurd with a snarl. "What I said goes. You're all a bunch of sniveling pukes. Especially you, Ivorson. You like it here, and why not? You saved the Legate's life. You're his pet. Four slaves escaped the night the wolves attacked. Why didn't *you* try to escape? Why didn't you make a break for it?"

"You are saying I should have run off and left you and my friends behind?" Skylan asked. He shook his head. "We are Torgun. All escape or none."

"And when will that be?" Sigurd demanded.

Skylan was tempted to tell his men about the impending invasion of Sinaria by the ogres. That was the time to escape, when the city was under assault, the people panicked, the soldiers occupied in fighting the ogres. Even Aelon might be preoccupied, might not notice a handful of slaves sneaking out of their compound, carrying their ship to the river and sailing away. That was his plan and knowledge of his plan would give his people hope.

The words were on the tip of his tongue. In the end, he did not speak them.

"When the time is right," he said.

The answer was weak. The men looked disappointed. Sigurd

sneered in disgust and Skylan turned away. It was not that he didn't trust his friends. All of them, even Sigurd, had come together to fight the fury yesterday. His men would never purposefully reveal the secret. But they would be excited when they heard the news, and their excitement would be hard for them to conceal. Cheerful slaves. Slaves in a good mood. Slaves exchanging grins and conspiratorial whispers. The guards would be sure to notice and suspect something was amiss.

Skylan found it hard enough to keep his knowledge of the invasion to himself. He had to set a continual watch on his tongue, make certain not to blurt out what he knew.

And then, what if the invasion did not happen? Any number of things might go wrong. A horrific storm might send the ogre fleet to the bottom of the sea. Raegar and his priests must be praying nightly for such a storm, and Aelon might be powerful enough to cause the winds and water to rise against his foes.

Then there was the spiritbone of the Vektan dragon. How could he leave that in the hands of their foes? He was still trying to think of some way to steal it back. An enormous task, he conceded. Some would say impossible. He glanced at the dragon's head, propped up against the rail. His men believed fixing the broken prow was impossible, but Skylan didn't accept that either. He remembered his vision of the goddess standing on the deck of the *Venjekar*.

He went in search of Aylaen. He found her by following the sounds of Wulfe shrieking. The two were in the creek; Aylaen was holding Wulfe by the arm while she scrubbed him vigorously with lye soap. Wulfe was screaming that she was trying to poison him.

Catching sight of Skylan, Wulfe begged for help. Skylan shook his head and stood with his arms folded, watching, until Aylaen finally decreed that the boy was as clean as he was ever going to be and let him loose.

Wulfe cast Skylan a bitter glance as he dashed past him. Skylan walked over to Aylaen, who was climbing out of the creek, as wet as the boy.

"I need to ask you something about the spiritbone—"

"Did you remember the secret of the Vektan dragon?" Aylaen asked eagerly.

"No," said Skylan, "but I have been thinking about it and I believe I *do* know the secret. I don't know I know it."

Aylaen shook her head. "That doesn't make sense."

"Did Treia tell you how the Southlanders managed to find this spiritbone?" Skylan asked. "This isn't the Vektan spiritbone the ogres stole from us, is it?"

"No, it is a different one. I was told"—Aylaen paused, seemed to be choosing her words carefully—"that the god Sund gave the spiritbone to Aelon. I didn't believe it at first, but I've thought about it, and I fear it's true."

Skylan was silent, waiting for her to continue.

"You know how I have visions sometimes," Aylaen said awkwardly. "Visions of the gods . . . Treia always scoffed at my visions. She said they were only dreams. But they're not dreams, Skylan."

Aylaen glared at him defiantly, daring him to challenge her. He remained silent, and after a pause, she went on, sounding defensive.

"Dreams are rambling. Everything is gray and black and nothing makes sense. But my visions are bright and filled with light and color. I remember them clearly. I can hear every word. I was with the gods in Torval's Hall. The gods had returned from battle. They carried their shields and weapons. And one of them was missing. The God of Stone, Sund."

Skylan interrupted. "The druid told me that someone powerful sent the fury to kill me. Perhaps it was Sund."

Aylaen thought this over. "But that doesn't make sense. If Sund gave Aelon the Vektan spiritbone, he must want the priests to be able to summon the dragon. Which means he would want to keep you alive because you know the secret."

"You're right," Skylan admitted, stymied.

"Unless . . ." Aylaen paused.

"Unless what?"

"Unless there's something about the secret itself. Sund is the only god who can see into the future. That's what Vindrash meant when she said the other gods were now blind. What if Sund gave our enemies the Vektan bone for a reason, but not for the reason we think. Not for the reason *they* think . . ."

Aylaen grabbed hold of Skylan and gave his arm a shake. "You have to remember, Skylan! You *have* to! When we know the secret, we'll have the answer to this mystery."

"A mystery that belongs to the gods," said Skylan gloomily. "Perhaps there is no answer." He sighed, then said, with a rueful smile, "At least one good thing has come out of this. You are talking to me."

Aylaen flushed crimson and hurriedly let go her hold of him.

"I know you can never forgive me for Garn's death," he added. "I don't deserve your forgiveness. I can never forgive myself. But I hope you don't hate me—"

"I was angry, Skylan," said Aylaen with a bleak sigh. "I was filled with rage. I hated you. I hated the gods. I hated Garn because he died and left me. Now I hate only myself. I've done something terrible, Skylan. Worse than you can imagine."

Drowning in misery, she was reaching for help. She was on the verge of telling him. He waited, not moving, scarcely daring even to breathe lest he frighten her.

"Skylan Ivorson!" Zahakis's shout rang through the camp.

"Damn!" said Skylan.

"You better go," said Aylaen.

"We'll talk later," he said, and she nodded, but he knew she wouldn't.

Zahakis had brought Treia along with him. Skylan was leaving the compound when Treia entered it. She did not look at Skylan, but swept past him.

"What is she doing here?" Skylan asked.

"She said she wanted to speak to her stepfather and the others," said Zahakis.

"What about?" Skylan was suspicious, alarmed.

Zahakis shrugged. "I neither know nor do I give a crap."

"I should stay, hear what she says—"

Zahakis looked at him and then looked at the six soldiers marching behind them. Skylan heaved a sigh.

"What does the Legate want with me?" he asked irritably.

"Not the Legate. Chloe. She has asked for you. She's not well, Skylan," Zahakis added abruptly. "Too much excitement, the physicians say. They also say we should do whatever she wants. Give her anything she asks for."

"She's dying?" Skylan asked, shocked.

Zahakis shook his head.

Skylan was filled with a sorrow that startled him. He had only known Chloe a short time, but her wyrd had wrapped closely around his in a knot that could not be broken without pain.

Treia was no longer important. He forgot about her.

Seeing Treia approaching their ship, the Torgun warriors rose angrily, even Farinn, who was still half-blind from the fury's attack. Their expressions dark and grim, they stood together in a line, shoulder to shoulder. Aylaen cast the warriors a nervous glance and hurried to intercept Treia, draw her away.

"I am glad to see you, Sister," said Aylaen. "We should talk in my tent—"

Treia pulled free of her grasp.

"I came to talk to all of you," she said loudly.

"Next time, bring along your traitor lover," said Sigurd. "I'd like the pleasure of 'talking' to him."

"Where is Skylan?" Treia demanded.

"I am Chief now," said Sigurd. "As for Skylan, he's a slave like the rest of us. He has to obey his master."

"And who's responsible for us being slaves, I wonder," said Grimuir, folding his arms across his chest.

"*I* am not, if that is what you are implying," Treia said sharply. "As for Raegar, he did what he did for your own good."

"If you are here to preach at us—" Bjorn began.

"I am here to help you escape," said Treia.

The Torgun regarded her in startled and distrustful silence.

"And why would you do that?" Sigurd asked, frowning. "You have made it clear you despise us."

"And what about me?" Treia cried. Her face was pale, pinched with bitterness. "My mother as good as sold *me* into slavery when I was a child, giving me to the Kai so that Vindrash would spare her husband's life. And then he died anyway. No, I did not weep to see the rest of you made slaves."

"If that's how you feel about us, why would you want to help us?" Sigurd asked, still suspicious.

"I know you will never believe this, but Raegar brought you to Sinaria to try to make you see reason. He believed in the old gods as you did. He was taken into slavery and he found Aelon, and since then his life has been blessed. He wanted the same for you."

"I'll give him a kiss next time I see him," Erdmun said, and the men laughed.

Treia gave a shrug. "I told Raegar that you will never give up your barbaric ways. He sees now that I was right. But he does not want your blood on his hands and neither do I."

"Blood?" Sigurd asked. "Who's going to kill us? The people love us—"

"The Empress doesn't," said Treia bluntly. "She is furious. You made her look ridiculous before the people. Never mind that she broke the rules or that the fury could have easily turned on the crowd if you had not stopped her. The Empress cares nothing about that. She cares only about appearance. She was angry to see the crowd make heroes of you at the expense of her players. And so, she has arranged for you to die."

The Torgun stared, amazed.

"Her soldiers can try to kill us," said Grimuir. "They may not find it that easy. We will fight—"

"Fight!" Treia scoffed. "Her Imperial Majesty won't let her soldiers soil their hands by fighting slaves! She has far cheaper and easier means of destroying you. The bread you ate this morning. Did it have a strange flavor? Perhaps the ale was more bitter than usual."

"You mean she'd poison us?" Erdmun looked queasy.

"Poison is one means. She has many others. Aylaen is my sister. You are my kinsmen," said Treia. "You are Raegar's kinsmen. Neither he nor I can stand by to see you foully murdered. We have devised a plan for you to escape."

"What is this plan?" Sigurd asked. "Let us hear it."

"There is an ancient shrine in the old part of the garden. Beyond that shrine are catacombs—they are like tunnels," she explained. "The catacombs are very old and were created to allow the inhabitants of the villa to escape should they ever be attacked. These tunnels lead from the villa to the sea where, in the event of an emergency, the Legate would have a ship waiting to carry him and his household to safety. I can tell you how to find the shrine. The Legate has the key to open it."

"It's not likely he'll just hand it to us," Sigurd said.

"That is true," said Treia calmly. "You will need to kill the Legate and his guards and take the key from him."

"Give us weapons and we'll deal with the Legate. But what about this?" Sigurd pointed to the tattoo. "How do we stop your foul god from burning off our arms?"

"Aelon would not weep if the Legate were to meet an untimely demise," said Treia.

"In other words, we do the god's dirty work for him and the god allows us to go free," said Bjorn.

"Not such a bad bargain," said Treia. "The Legate enslaved you, remember. Our men died because of him."

Most of the men glanced at each other and shrugged, ready to go along with the scheme. Farinn looked doubtful; Bjorn shook his head. Aylaen had said nothing the entire time. She regarded her sister with a puzzled frown.

"Once you have entered the catacombs," Treia continued, "all you have to do is follow them to the sea."

"Will there be a ship for us?" Erdmun asked.

"Raegar cannot do everything for you," said Treia tartly. "In the matter of a ship, you must fend for yourselves."

"We could steal a fishing vessel," said Aki. "I saw hundreds of them docked in the bay when we sailed in."

"It sounds simple," said Sigurd.

"*Too* simple," said Bjorn. "I don't trust Raegar or his god. I think we should wait for Skylan, talk it over with him."

"If you want to do so, that is fine with me," said Treia. "Although you know he will be opposed. I have heard that the Legate has promised Skylan his freedom if he serves him. I don't suppose he has shared that news with the rest of you. . . ."

"Skylan wouldn't do that," said Bjorn.

Sigurd grunted and shook his head. Treia turned to Aylaen. "Let the men discuss it. You and I need to talk privately."

Aylaen agreed and while the men conferred, she and Treia walked some distance away.

"We need to talk about the Vektan dragon," said Treia.

"I don't know the secret," said Aylaen. "Skylan doesn't know it."

"Say rather he refuses to tell you," said Treia.

"I believe him, Treia. He wants to help—"

"You didn't tell him about Garn, did you?" Treia asked, alarmed.

"No, of course not. How could I? I am too ashamed. . . ."

Treia breathed a sigh and took her sister's hand, gave it a gentle squeeze. "You do not need to be, Aylaen. You acted out of love. I understand. I would do anything for Raegar."

"But I *don't* understand, Treia," said Aylaen. "If you help Skylan escape, the secret of the Vektan dragons will go with him."

"It doesn't matter now," said Treia. A flush of pride mantled her cheeks. "I know the ritual."

"You do?" Aylaen was astonished. "How did you find out?"

"I prayed to Vindrash," said Treia. "She has no love for Aelon, that is true. But our goddess hates and fears the Gods of Raj more than she does Aelon. 'The enemy of my enemy is my friend,' as the saying goes. Vindrash has granted me the power to summon the dragon to destroy the ogre fleet."

"But what about Garn?" Aylaen said, dismayed. "I cannot leave his spirit bound in chains."

"You need not worry. Garn has been set free. I promised Vindrash that I would help all our people gain their freedom. That included Garn's spirit. Vindrash would not teach me the ritual otherwise. What's wrong? I thought you would be glad."

"I am," said Aylaen slowly. "I want to speak to Garn. See for myself."

Treia was hurt. "You don't trust me."

"I trust you, Treia," said Aylaen. "But this is too important. Please, take me to the shrine, let me talk to him. I want to ask him to forgive me—"

"Impossible," said Treia. "The Spirit Priestesses would be certain to suspect something. You would jeopardize the escape plan, put the lives of our men at risk."

Aylaen was troubled. "I would not want to put the others in danger."

"Garn is with Torval, Aylaen," said Treia. "He wants you to be free yourself now. I swear, Aylaen, by my love for Vindrash and for you, my sister. You must leave with our friends and kinsmen and you must make certain Skylan goes with you. The Legate is not to be trusted. If Skylan stays here, he will die."

"I wish *you* would come with us, Treia," said Aylaen, relenting. "I only just found you. I can't bear the thought of being separated again. Maybe forever."

"I love Raegar as you love Garn," said Treia. "I would sacrifice anything for his sake."

Aylaen embraced her, pressing her wet cheek against her sister's. Treia returned the hug stiffly.

The conference among the men did not last long. Sigurd had proclaimed himself Chief of Chiefs and he was in favor of the escape plan. Bjorn wanted to wait to hear what Skylan said, but Sigurd reminded them that Skylan had led them into disaster, which was why he was no longer Chief. When Aylaen returned and said that she was prepared to go along with the plan, Bjorn gave way.

Treia told them where to find the shrine.

"What about the Legate's soldiers?" Sigurd asked. "He posts guards on our compound and he must have fifty men standing guard around his villa at night."

"You do not need to worry about the soldiers," said Treia. "All is arranged. Only a few will be standing guard and you can deal with them easily enough. A wagon will come this evening to deliver supplies. Your weapons will be hidden inside."

"We'll have to find somewhere to hide them," said Sigurd, rubbing his jaw.

"No need," Treia remarked coolly. "The escape is set for tonight."

"Tonight?" Sigurd repeated, displeased. "That's too soon. We have to make plans. Farinn is half-blind—"

"Everything is arranged for tonight," said Treia. "Do you think the Empress is going to wait to kill you? Either you go tonight or"—she shrugged—"you stay here and die. The choice is yours."

They agreed to go. Aylaen embraced her sister again and bid Treia goodbye. Treia kissed her sister and bid the rest of them a cold farewell.

As she was walking across the compound, Treia glanced up into the heavens.

"I have done what you required of me, Hevis," she said softly. "This night you will have your sacrifice."

BOOK THREE

Skylan and Keeper stood outside Chloe's bedchamber, waiting to be summoned. The house was unnaturally quiet. People crept about, speaking in whispers. Death walked the halls, and everyone, from soldier to slave, was hushed with awe in that dread presence.

"Where is Acronis?" Keeper asked in a subdued voice.

"With her," Zahakis answered. "He won't leave her side."

"Is she . . . in pain?" Skylan asked gruffly.

"The physicians gave her poppy syrup. To ease her suffering, so they say." Zahakis gave a thin smile. "I think the true reason was to keep her from pestering them."

The door opened and Rosa came out. Her eyes were red from weeping. Flute music played softly somewhere. The room was dark and stuffy, the doors to the atrium shut. The time might have been night instead of mid-morning.

"She is not dead yet, to be sealed up in a tomb," said Skylan. "She loves the fresh air, sunlight. The doors should be open."

"So she kept insisting," said Zahakis dryly. "One reason for the poppy syrup."

Chloe lay in her bed, looking very small and frail beneath her silken coverlets. Skylan could not see Acronis from this angle, but he guessed her father was not far from her. She seemed to be asleep, but, hearing Skylan's voice, Chloe roused and opened her eyes. She smiled to see him and Keeper and called weakly, "I want to talk to my champions. Bring them in."

A physician hastened to her side, clucking and fussing. "No visitors. You must rest." He held a cup to her lips.

"Oh, go away, you old fart," Chloe said crossly. "And I won't touch a drop of that horrid stuff." She knocked the cup from the man's hand. Syrup spilled over the coverlet. "I won't drink it anymore, do you hear me! The only pain I feel is in my backside and you're the cause of that."

Acronis could be heard trying to remonstrate with her. Chloe raised her voice.

"I want to see them. My champions. They were wonderful yesterday, weren't they, Father? They were all wonderful. My Para Dix team. I want all of them here. I told you, Father, send for all of them, right now."

The physician's eyes widened. He seemed likely to pass out from shock. Zahakis turned away, his hand over his face, either to hide his laughter or his tears, or perhaps both. Keeper shook his head. Skylan swallowed and was about to enter when a shocked voice sounded behind him.

"What are those heathens doing here?"

Skylan turned to see a short, stocky man wearing ceremonial robes striding importantly toward the door. The man eyed Skylan and the ogre with disgust, then said to Zahakis, "Tribune, remove these slaves."

Keeper growled dangerously. Skylan gripped the ogre's arm, silencing him.

"Priest-General Xydis," said Zahakis, amazed. "What are you doing here?"

"I am here at the request of the Legate," said Xydis. "Ask him, if you don't believe me."

Acronis stood in the door. He was grim-faced, his skin gray beneath his tan. He had not slept. His chin was dark with a day's growth of beard.

"Let him in, Tribune," said Acronis.

Chloe gave a shrill cry.

"Send him away! I don't want him!"

She tried to sit up in bed, but she was too weak. She dragged the coverlet over her head. The physician came hurrying forward, another cup in his hand. He pulled off the coverlet and held the potion to her mouth, forcing her to drink. Chloe gagged and spit most of it out, but some of it must have stayed down, for her head drooped.

She sank back on the pillow. Her defiance dwindled to an incoherent murmur.

"Legate," said Xydis, "I passed a large contingent of soldiers on my way to the villa. You should send them away. This sweet child should be surrounded by nothing but the love and peace of Aelon."

"Dismiss the household guard, Zahakis," said Acronis. "Give the men a seven-day furlough."

"You can't be serious, my lord!" Zahakis said.

"That is an order, Tribune," said Acronis in hollow tones. He glanced at Skylan and Keeper. "And take these men back to camp."

"Chloe wants to see us, Legate," said Skylan.

"My daughter is asleep," said Acronis, and he shut the door.

"What is he doing?" Skylan asked Zahakis as they walked through the silent house.

"He is desperate," said Zahakis, shaking his head in sorrow. "He will try anything to save her—even praying to a god he hates."

The moment Skylan entered the compound, he knew something was wrong. His friends stood together, talking in low tones.

"What's happened?" Skylan asked tensely. His first thought was that the soldiers had found Wulfe.

Conversation ceased. Everyone, including Aylaen, looked to Sigurd to be their spokesman. Sigurd was smug, pleased with himself. Skylan was immediately wary.

"Where is Wulfe?" he demanded.

"Who gives a crap?" said Sigurd.

"He's here, Skylan," said Aylaen. "He's safe. Don't worry."

"Then what's going on?" Skylan asked, relieved.

Sigurd glared at Keeper. "Send the ogre away."

"He's a slave like the rest of us," said Skylan. "And he's our friend. You can trust him."

Sigurd looked the ogre up and down and shrugged.

"Very well. He might come in useful at that. We're getting out of here. We're going to escape."

"Escape . . ." Skylan looked from one of his friends to the other. He would have expected them to be jubilant. Instead they were watching him distrustfully. They were expecting him to oppose this. By his half smile, Sigurd was *hoping* Skylan would oppose it.

"What's your plan?" Skylan asked.

"It's not our plan," said Bjorn with a dark glance at Sigurd. "It's Treia's plan."

"Treia!" Skylan said, shocked. "Treia has a plan to help us to escape?"

Sigurd heard the disbelief in Skylan's voice and glowered. "It doesn't matter whose plan it is. It's a good one."

He explained how Treia had discovered the Empress's plot to have them killed and she was going to help them escape. They would storm the Legate's villa, kill him, and take the key to the shrine. The hidden tunnels would lead them to the sea.

"You're going to break into the villa," said Skylan. "What about the soldiers?"

"There won't be any soldiers there tonight," said Keeper. "Remember? They were given leave."

"By the Priest-General," Skylan said, thoughtful.

"No soldiers?" Sigurd grinned. "This is perfect!"

"Isn't it," said Skylan. He shook his head in disbelief. "Treia came up with this scheme. How can you trust her? She is Raegar's lover!"

"And she is my sister," said Aylaen. "I trust her. She cares about us."

Skylan appealed to his friends. "Think what you're saying. For the Empress to murder someone she has to first acknowledge that the person exists. We are *slaves*. We are beneath contempt, lower than ants in the honey jar! Raegar, on the other hand, has said more than once he'd like to see us dead."

"Treia would never let us come to harm," cried Aylaen angrily.

"What if Raegar lied to her, Aylaen? He's lied to her before this."

Even as he spoke, Skylan could tell he was wasting his breath. His friends had seen the dazzling light of hope. They would not go back to the darkness.

And what if they are right? he asked himself. What if, for some strange reason, Raegar is giving us the gift of freedom? Treia might be a cold and callous bitch, but she loves Aylaen. Treia would not send her sister to her death.

"What do you think?" Skylan turned to Keeper.

"I know of these catacombs," said Keeper. "I have been inside. I was there when Acronis laid to rest the body of his wife. His family is buried there, going back for many generations. They are sacred places."

"Buried?" Erdmun's voice quavered. "You mean, the catacombs are filled with corpses?"

Sigurd cast him a scathing glance. "Don't tell me you're afraid of a few moldy old bones?"

"I'm not," said Erdmun defensively. "But such places are sacred, like he said. The gods might not like it. . . ."

"Sacred or not," said Sigurd, "do these catacombs lead to the sea?"

Keeper shrugged his massive shoulders. "I suppose it is possible. I don't know."

"We'll find out soon enough," said Sigurd. "We leave tonight."

"Tonight!" Skylan shook his head. "Impossible."

"Why?" Sigurd asked.

"We need weapons—"

"We have them. Swords and axes. Treia told us they would be hidden in a cart filled with supplies and they were."

"Well, then, what about the guards at the entrance to the compound? Acronis didn't give them leave."

"The wine with their meal tonight will be drugged."

"And these tattoos? Won't Aelon have something to say about our escape?"

"This Aelon is a weak-stomached god, it seems. He doesn't sanction murder. He's letting us go. If you want proof, we unpacked the weapons and none of us felt so much as a twinge."

Skylan didn't like it, but he didn't know what to say. It *was* perfect. All too perfect.

"Our plans are made," Sigurd added. "Either you are with us or you're not."

Skylan looked for help to Aylaen. *He* could not tell them about the Vektan spiritbone. He had taken his vow to Torval. But she could.

Aylaen understood him. She stood with her arms folded, her lips compressed. She met his gaze with a blank stare.

"I am with you," said Skylan reluctantly. "But we cannot attack the villa tonight."

"Why not? You want to have time to warn your friend, the Legate?"

Skylan regarded them grimly. "Acronis is a soldier. He can take care of himself. It is his daughter. The girl is gravely ill. She is dying. She should die in peace."

"That's true," said Farinn. "I heard one of the soldiers talking. The girl is not expected to live through the night."

"We have our own children to think about," said Aki dourly.

Skylan had lost and he knew it.

"I said we would all escape or none of us. Will you come with us, Keeper?"

"He doesn't have a choice," said Sigurd. "He knows too much for us to let him go. Maybe we should kill him—"

"Don't be an idiot. He knows where to find the shrine," said Bjorn. "He can show us."

"I can show you," said Keeper. He shook his head. "But I won't help murder the Legate. He has been good to me. Maybe too good," he added sorrowfully to Skylan.

"I don't like this," Skylan said. "It's happened too fast. No one has time to think. I still believe it's a trap. You shouldn't go, my friend. You should wait here until your people come."

"You lit the fire in my belly," said Keeper. "As for my people, I've heard nothing. They're not coming."

Skylan needed to talk to Aylaen about the spiritbone. But she saw him coming and offered to help pack the supplies they would need. She disappeared down into the ship's hold with Grimuir and Aki.

Skylan caught sight of the dragon's head leaning up against the railing. The dragon seemed to be regarding him with anger.

Wulfe came wandering over. "Treia was on the ship yesterday," he said. "While you were fighting the fury. I had a dream about that. Did I tell you?"

"Treia was on the ship?" Skylan eyed the boy. "What was she doing here?"

"She was talking to a god," said Wulfe. "She went down into the hold and put on her robes and talked to a god."

"Treia was here, praying . . ." Skylan said softly. "Maybe I have misjudged her. Maybe she really does want to help us."

"I don't think so," said Wulfe. "The god was a very bad god. But then," he added on reflection, "the god is a god of the Uglies and, according to my mother, all your gods are bad."

Skylan shook his head and walked off.

The Torgun waited impatiently for the sun to set. The Sun Goddess, Aylis, was in no hurry, however. She shone bright and hot and long. The day dragged. The warriors surreptitiously polished the weapons and polished them again. Aylaen packed some of the precious healing salves in a bag. Skylan worried about Chloe. Keeper thought about his mate, his children, and the invasion that might lead to his family being reunited. Farinn sat off to himself, murmuring words to a song he was making about their journey, a song that might or might not have a happy ending.

Everyone was tense, nervous, fearing that at any moment the plot would be discovered and the Legate's soldiers would come swooping down on them.

But the afternoon passed without incident. The guards at the gates dozed in the sun or walked moodily about the compound or groused about the fact that they had to work when their comrades had been given leave.

At last, Aylis dipped behind the hills, trailing red and purple scarves of fire as she left the world. When the shadows slid down the hillsides and washed over the compound, the Torgun entered the hold of the *Venjekar* and handed out the weapons. Keeper was watching the guards. The men ate their meal and drank from the wineskins. When they slumped over, heads on their chests, the ogre gave the signal. The Torgun left their ship, all except Skylan.

He remained on board the *Venjekar*, running his hand fondly along the wooden rail, remembering everything the two of them— he and this ship—had been through together. He had fought ogres on this ship. He had sailed in triumph to the Vutmana. The *Venjekar* had carried away the body of the disgraced Chief Horg, never to be seen again. The *Venjekar* had taken him and Draya on that ill-fated voyage to the Druid Isles and had brought Skylan back, alone, with the draugr of his dead wife forcing him to play dragon bones. The *Venjekar* had survived a storm hurled at them by a furious goddess, only to fall victim to a powerful new god.

It hurt him to have to leave his ship behind. He wondered what would happen to the *Venjekar* after they were gone. He had no idea, but he made a vow to Torval that he would come back for her.

Leaving the rail, he walked over to stand in front of the dragon's head. He placed his hand on the dragon's carved snout to bid farewell. The wood seemed warm and quivered beneath his fingers.

"He doesn't want us to go," said Wulfe.

"He left us," said Skylan. "He doesn't get a say."

Still he stood there, eyeing the broken prow, the peg that had been carved into the bottom, the slot into which it fit.

"I may have to leave the *Venjekar* behind," Skylan muttered. "But I will not leave my ship broken."

"Ivorson!" Grimuir called in a low voice. "You better come. Sigurd is getting impatient."

Skylan picked up the dragon's head, lifted it, and mounted it carefully, fitting the peg into the hole. He felt the prow settle into place. He gave it a gentle shove. The prow did not move. He followed with his eyes the graceful curve of the neck, the fierce head that gazed, unafraid, into the future. Looking into the painted eyes, Skylan thought he saw a flicker of red flame.

A trick of the dying light, he said to himself, and he turned away. He climbed over the ship's hull, landing on the ground. Everyone was silent, staring at the dragon's head that stood firmly, defiantly, in his accustomed place.

"How did you do that?" Bjorn demanded. "We tried to fix it and it kept falling off."

Skylan shook his head. He had no idea.

"Maybe we shouldn't go," said Erdmun uneasily. "Maybe it's a sign."

"I'll give you a sign," Sigurd said grimly. He raised his fist and shook it under Erdmun's nose. "That's my sign. Now let's get out of here. Time's wasting."

Skylan started off after the others, then realized that Wulfe wasn't with him. Swearing softly beneath his breath, Skylan dashed back to the ship. It was hard to see in the failing light. The boy was over by the dragonhead prow.

"Wulfe!" Skylan hissed softly and urgently.

"I'm coming!" Wulfe called.

He stuffed something in the top of his leather breeches and then came racing across the deck. He jumped down beside Skylan, landing on all fours.

"What were you doing?" Skylan asked, helping the boy to his feet.

"Getting my treasures," said Wulfe, patting the bulge beneath his frayed shirt. "I had a special place where I hid things. The dragon guarded them for me."

"What things?"

Wulfe glanced back at the dragon. Then he shrugged. "Just things."

Skylan thought no more about it. The others had ranged far ahead of them and were now approaching the entrance to the compound. He grabbed hold of Wulfe and hustled him along.

Sigurd motioned for silence. According to Keeper, the guards had fallen victim to the drugged wine. Still, they might be shamming. Sigurd padded soft-footed to the iron gate and peered out between the bars.

"I see one man sleeping," he reported in a harsh whisper.

He motioned for Keeper to come forward. Their plan was for the heavy ogre to open the gate by brute force. Keeper planted his shoulder against the gate and gave a heave. The gate swung open easily, causing the astonished ogre to nearly fall through it.

Keeper drew back, suspicious. The others gripped their weapons. The thought crossed everyone's mind that this was too easy, going too well.

"They just forgot to lock the gate, that's all," said Sigurd. "Torval walks with us."

"So does Aelon," said Bjorn grimly.

He pointed down at the tattoo. The warriors felt no pain, not so much as a twinge.

Sigurd thrust the gate open and walked through. No one challenged him. No one stopped him. The others followed. The soldiers lay on the ground. Wine jars lay upended beside them, the Legate's wine spilling out onto the ground. The men lay very still, unusually still and quiet. Grimuir bent down, put his hand on a soldier's neck.

"This one is dead," he reported.

Bjorn squatted beside the other man and, grabbing his shoulder, rolled him over. The man's arms flopped on the ground, his eyes stared into the twilight. There was froth on his mouth; his face was contorted in pain. His dying had not been easy.

"Treia said there would be a sleep potion in the wine," Aylaen said, her voice strained. "Raegar told her it was a sleep potion!"

"This one did not drink a sleep draught," said Bjorn. "The wine was poisoned."

"Treia didn't know!" Aylaen said defensively, and then she repeated softly, to herself, "She didn't know. She couldn't have."

Skylan was standing beside her and he felt her shiver. He reached out his hand simply to touch her, to offer reassurance. Her fingers closed over his in a grip that was almost painful.

"Poison," Keeper was saying, shaking his bald head. "A bad way for a warrior to die."

The Torgun knew what the ogre meant. A warrior should die with his axe in his hand.

"We can stand here staring at corpses all night or we can escape," said Sigurd angrily. "What's done is done. Pick up those torches. We're going to need them in the tunnels."

Aki and Grimuir grabbed up torches. Sigurd took the lead, heading in the direction of the villa that was silhouetted on top of the hill against a pale purple sky. The villa was dark. No lights shone.

Aylaen let go of Skylan's hand. She walked past the dead men without looking at them. Skylan pondered the deaths of the guards and his sense of foreboding grew. His unease wasn't helped by Keeper, who fell back to walk with him.

"The Priest-General saw to it that the soldiers who guarded the house were sent on furlough," said Keeper softly. "But it would have been mad folly for the Priest-General to have given the same order for those who guarded the slaves. There is a reason these men had to die. Sleep potions wear off, leaving men groggy, but not too groggy to handle a sword. Whatever is going to happen at the villa this night, Raegar is making certain that none of the soldiers will be around to interfere."

"Raegar and his god are working hard to help us escape," said Skylan, frowning.

He had the sickening feeling that every step he was taking away from his ship was taking him in the wrong direction. His wyrd was bound to the *Venjekar* like the rope tied to the anchor.

Sigurd started the warriors moving at a run. The Torgun swept up the hill toward the dark villa. Wulfe dropped down on all fours to run faster. Skylan watched the boy dashing through the grass like a dog—or a wolf. The hair prickled on the back of his neck.

"Stand straight," he told Wulfe irritably. "Run like a human being."

Startled at the harsh tone in Skylan's voice, Wulfe stood upright.

"You're mad at me, aren't you?"

"I'm not mad at you," said Skylan. "I'm mad at Sigurd. I'm mad at myself. I should have refused to go. There's something all wrong about what we're doing."

He looked back over his shoulder. He could no longer see the ship in the darkness. But he could feel the dragon watching them.

"I said we would all escape or none of us. And now we're leaving one behind."

The Torgun climbed the steep hill that led to the villa. A broad, paved road—wide enough to accommodate two wagons traveling side-by-side—wound back and forth across the hillside. The road was made of crushed stone that glimmered white in the light of the stars and a round, fat, full moon that was a strange orange in color; the sort of moon one sees in autumn, not in the middle of summer.

The road was deserted, but the warriors kept to the shadows of the pine trees that grew alongside. Whenever they came to a curve in the road, they could see the villa, black against the stars.

Skylan noted that the tattoo on his arm had still not so much as tingled. He supposed this was good, though he did not find the notion that Aelon approved of what he was doing particularly comforting.

They reached the grounds in front of the villa and their pace slowed. No slaves bustled about attending to their duties. No soldiers kept guard. The villa was dark. The night was so quiet that a sudden, eerie wail made them all jump.

"Run!" Wulfe gasped, his eyes wide with fear. "It's a lemur!"

"A what?" Sigurd asked, raising his sword and looking about.

"Lemures are spirits of the family's dead ancestors," Keeper explained. "Some say they are good spirits who guard the house, protect the living from harm."

"We should leave," Wulfe insisted, trembling. "The lemures don't want us here."

The wailing grew louder and now they could hear broken words and blubbering.

"That's no ghost," said Sigurd, relieved and angry that he was relieved. He mopped his face with the back of his hand. "It's a woman weeping."

"The Legate's daughter is well loved," said Keeper, and there was a catch in his voice. "The house-slaves grieve for her."

The men glanced at each other, grim and uneasy. The sound of a woman sobbing in the night over someone about to die was unnerving, an ill omen.

"Lemures, you'll see," Wulfe muttered.

"Someone shut him up," Sigurd ordered irritably. "Where is the shrine that leads to these catacombs?"

Keeper pointed off to the east. "Over that direction. It is an ancient shrine dedicated to the old gods. Behind the shrine are the catacombs where the dead are laid to rest. We don't need to enter the house at all."

"Keeper has a good idea," said Skylan. "Let us go straight to this shrine. No one will know where we went. The Legate will wake to find us gone. By the time he figures out *where* we've gone, we will be far from Sinaria."

"Always one to take the coward's way out, aren't you, Skylan?" Sigurd said, sneering. "You forget we need the key from the Legate to open the gates."

"I remember a door made of bronze," said Keeper. "But it was not locked. We can enter as Skylan says, with no one the wiser."

"And I say we need a key," said Sigurd, glowering. "And the man who has it is the one who made us a slave and I, for one, do not want to leave without having my revenge."

"Would you jeopardize our escape to slit a man's throat?" Skylan asked, holding back his temper. "There will be others in the house besides Acronis. Zahakis will be there and he will be armed. There will be physicians, priests, the house-slaves. We can sneak into the tunnels with no one the wiser, or you can go inside and create an uproar and maybe some of us will die."

"Lemures or women mourning, the sound is an ill omen. The Goddess of Death, Freilis, walks that house this night," said the usually quiet Farinn. "I say we leave them at peace."

Sigurd gnawed his lip. "Torval will hold us to account. He will want to know why we did not take our revenge."

"We will take it," said Skylan. "When we return to our homeland, we will assemble the dragonships and come back here. We will free the *Venjekar* and have our revenge!"

Sigurd thought this over.

"Just do *something*!" Aki said nervously.

The wailing sound grew louder, harsh and piercing.

"Go ahead, Keeper," said Sigurd. "Take us to the shrine."

Skylan breathed a deep sigh of relief that caught in his throat when the door to the villa opened. Standing in the door, illuminated in the soft light of the flame from an oil lamp, was Acronis, or rather, what was left of him. His shoulders sagged. His head was bowed. His eyes were red-rimmed, his skin sallow. He blinked burning eyes, trying to see, and raised the oil lamp so that its light fell on the warriors.

"Skylan . . . I did not expect you so soon." Acronis glanced at the Torgun warriors. The weapons in their hands gleamed in the lamplight. "Thank you, men, for bringing him so quickly. I feared you would not . . . not get here in time."

"What the—" Sigurd began.

"He thinks we are his soldiers," said Keeper softly, awed.

"He'll find out different when I slit his gut!"

Sigurd raised his sword and started forward. He was stopped by Skylan's hand clamping down over his sword arm.

"The man is not armed," said Skylan. "His child is dying. Will Torval honor you for killing a man whose mind is overthrown by grief?"

Sigurd muttered something and wrenched his arm free. He kept his sword lowered, however.

"You men are dismissed," said Acronis sharply. "Return to your duties. Skylan, come with me now."

"Is the Priest-General still here?" Skylan asked.

"I sent the bastard away," said Acronis. "He told my daughter, my child, that because she would not profess her belief in Aelon, she was doomed to dwell forever in darkness."

He swallowed, brushed a trembling hand across his eyes, and said brokenly, "It was my fault. The Priest-General told me Aelon could save her. I couldn't let her go!"

"I couldn't let him go. . . ." Aylaen whispered. Tears glimmered in her eyes. "I'm sorry, Garn. I am so sorry!"

Skylan spoke in Sigurd's ear. "Go quickly before the Legate realizes he has made a mistake. Keeper will show you the way. I will stay here, cover your escape."

"We're not coming back for you," Sigurd warned. He turned, motioning. "The rest of you, come with me."

"I will stay with Skylan," Aylaen said.

Skylan tried to dissuade her. "Aylaen, there's no need—"

"There is need," she said calmly. She looked at him steadily, met his gaze for the first time since Garn's death. "I have to tell you the truth."

"I don't think we should leave anyone behind," said Bjorn.

"No one gives a crap what you think," Sigurd snarled. "Skylan, take that brat of yours with you. Keeper, you're with me."

Keeper looked uncertainly at Skylan.

"Go, my friend," said Skylan. "They need you."

"I will lead them to the shrine," Keeper promised. "Then *I* will come back for you."

"Make haste, Skylan!" Acronis said urgently. "We must hurry."

He raised the oil lamp to light the way into the house. He shut the door and there was a hollow, grating sound—the lock falling into place.

"You came dressed for the Para Dix," Acronis said, glancing at their swords. "Good. That will please her."

Acronis walked in front. They were alone in the entryway. Skylan could stab him in the back. He and Aylaen could catch up with their comrades.

The thought flitted into his head and was as quickly gone.

Acronis walked swiftly, and Skylan and Aylaen had to hurry to catch up with him. Wulfe kept close to both of them. The boy kept glancing fearfully into the shadows.

"The lemures are here," said Wulfe. "But they're not mad at us. They won't hurt us. They're waiting. . . ."

They hastened through the villa. Aylaen had never before been in the house and she slowed her steps, gazing in wonder. Oil lamps had been lighted in the living areas and she marveled at the large vases filled with cut flowers, the indoor ponds with the glistening, golden fish, the couches and chairs, the beautifully painted porcelain.

They reached Chloe's room. Acronis opened the door and ushered them inside.

The bedchamber was ablaze with light. Every oil lamp in the house had been brought in to drive away the darkness. The heat was stifling.

Chloe lay on her bed, grimly, stubbornly awake. She had refused to take any more of the poppy syrup, and the physicians left in offended ire, saying there was nothing more they could do. She had sent Rosa away for "blubbering." Her hands plucked at the silken coverlet, sometimes clenching the fabric when a spasm of pain shook her.

Her body was frail and weak, her spirit indomitable. Skylan first felt pity. He was soon moved to admiration. Zahakis stood beside her bed. His face was stern, his jaw clenched tight.

Hearing the sound of the door opening, Chloe turned her head.

"Father, did Skylan come?" she asked eagerly. "Is he here?"

"Yes, my dear. He and Aylaen and"—he glanced with some bewilderment at Wulfe—"a boy . . ."

Acronis stood aside for them to enter. Wulfe shook his head violently and pulled away.

"Lemures," he told Skylan in a whisper. "They're standing around her bed."

"Wait for me," said Skylan.

Wulfe nodded. "I'll wait. I promise."

Skylan walked inside and met Zahakis's piercing gaze. The Tribune either knew or guessed that the Torgun would be taking this opportunity to escape. Skylan unbuckled his sword belt and wordlessly handed over the weapon. Aylaen was about to do the same when Chloe stopped her.

"Is that the sword blessed by your goddess? The sword that frightened the fury and kept her from attacking? My father told me. May I see it, please?"

Aylaen looked stricken. The weapons Treia had delivered to them were not their own weapons. Aylaen had grabbed a sword and sheath and belt from the pile.

"Show her the sword. Make something up. She won't know the difference," Skylan whispered.

Aylaen drew the sword from its scabbard. Her eyes widened. She stared wildly at Skylan, then back at the sword. The hilt with its intricate pattern shone like the sun on the scales of a dragon in the lamplight.

"It is lovely," said Chloe, awed. "Tell me about your goddess. Is she beautiful? Does she know Torval, Skylan's god?"

"Her name is Vindrash," said Aylaen. She had to stop to clear her throat. "She is the goddess of dragonkind and the goddess of our people. We call ourselves 'Vindrasi' in her honor. She is Torval's wife and she is very beautiful."

"She must love you very much to give you her sword," said Chloe.

Aylaen's eyes filled with tears. "She used to love me. I have done a great wrong and I fear she is angry with me."

"I make my father angry with me sometimes," said Chloe. "But I know he loves me. Could I hold the sword?"

Aylaen rested the weapon on the silken coverlet. Chloe clasped her hand weakly over the hilt. Her small fingers tightened around it. She looked up at Skylan.

"If I die with a sword in my hand," she said, "then Torval will have to let me into his Hall."

Zahakis walked away, went over to stand in the shadows. Acronis's lips trembled. He clenched his fist behind his back.

Skylan thought of the heroes gathered in Torval's Hall. Heroes who had fought on despite their wounds, overcoming pain and fear, refusing to surrender, making Death come to take them by force.

"Yes," said Skylan, "Torval will welcome you into his Hall."

Chloe's voice trembled. Skylan saw the shadow of fear in her eyes.

"Torval's Hall is not dark, is it, Skylan? I won't be alone in the dark."

Skylan rested his hand on her hand that held fast to the sword.

"Torval's Hall is lit with a thousand torches that blaze for all eternity. In the great fireplace burns a log taken from the Life Tree that fills the hall with warmth and light. There is music and song, dancing and feasting. The heroes tell the stories of their battles. The tables are laden with food and the flagons never run dry."

"I would like to dance," said Chloe. "I've never danced before."

Her breath came short. She made a little grimace and gasped. Her hand clenched over the sword's hilt. She would not give in. She fought on.

"You and I will lead the dance," said Skylan.

"Will we? I would like that." Chloe gave another little gasp and, after a struggle for breath, she suddenly sat up in the bed. She stared at something far away, a vision only she could see. Her eyes shone with light, and who was to say the light did not come from Torval's Hall?

"A thousand torches blazing," Chloe whispered. "Banishing the darkness. And I will lead the dance. . . ."

Her eyes closed. She sank back among the pillows. Yet her hand remained holding fast to the sword.

Skylan unclasped her fingers from the sword. Lifting the limp hand, he pressed it to his lips. Aylaen wept silently. Acronis picked up the sword and handed it to her.

"Thank you," he said softly.

He sat down on the bed and gathered his daughter to him, holding her, wrapped in the coverlet. Burying his face in her hair, he gave a wrenching, shuddering sob and cradled her in his arms, rocking back and forth.

"You two should go," said Zahakis. "No one will stop you."

Skylan nodded, then glanced at Acronis and asked quietly, "What will become of him?"

"I don't know," said Zahakis. "I don't know."

An oil lamp flickered and went out. So they would all go out eventually. So will we all, Skylan thought.

Aylaen clasped hold of his hand and the two walked out together. They found Wulfe crouched behind a large vase. He jumped up and came pattering along after them.

The front entrance was locked. The rooms in this part of the villa opened onto the atrium. Skylan found a door that took them into the garden. He stood amidst the trees with their still leaves trying to decide which way to go. The night-blooming flowers filled the air with perfume. The day-blooming flowers had closed tight in slumber. A nightingale sang. Some small creature, fox or rabbit, hunter or hunted, made a rustling sound among the hedges. He had just decided which way to go when he saw Keeper.

The ogre was a dark hulking shape among the trees. Every so often, he would stop as though looking about. Skylan whistled softly. The ogre whistled back and began to walk in their direction.

"Wait, Skylan," said Aylaen, clutching his hand, holding him back. "I have to tell you something."

Skylan had been longing for her to talk to him. But now was not the time he would have chosen.

"If this could wait—"

"It can't," said Aylaen stubbornly. "If I don't tell you now I may never find the courage to tell you at all. It's about Garn. I was desperate." She echoed Acronis's words. "I couldn't let him go. I missed him so much I thought about . . . about going to join him."

"Aylaen, I understand," Skylan said, one eye on Keeper. "I feel the same way—"

"Let me finish!" she cried. She twisted her hands together, wringing her fingers. "Raegar promised me that if I would tell him the secret to the Vektan dragons, his god would bring Garn back to me. Aelon would bring Garn back to life."

Skylan felt his stomach clench, his mouth go dry.

"And did he?"

"Yes," Aylaen said, shuddering. "There are priestesses, Spirit Priestesses who can summon the dead. They brought Garn to me, only it was a trick. He wasn't alive. His spirit was in chains. He was a prisoner. The priestess said that Garn would be a prisoner for all eternity unless I told them the secret of the Vektan dragon. I said I didn't know it and that's when Garn spoke to me. He told me you knew the secret."

"Torval save us!" Skylan breathed.

Aylaen swallowed. "Treia told me she had freed him, Skylan, but I . . . I'm not sure I believe her now. When I asked if I could see him, speak to him, she wouldn't let me. I'm sorry, Skylan, but I can't leave Sinaria knowing that Garn's soul might still be a prisoner."

Skylan's skin prickled. Tiny jolts sizzled through his body, as had happened once when he'd been standing near a tree struck by lightning. He was playing dragonbone. He saw his opponent's pieces and where they were placed and suddenly he saw the pattern. He knew the strategy. The Torgun were playing a losing game.

He broke into a run, crashing through the flowering hedges, knocking down urns. He very nearly knocked down Keeper.

"Where are you going?" the ogre demanded.

"It's a trap!" Skylan cried.

The shrine was small and old and derelict. Predating the villa, the shrine had once been important to the people of the estate. This was obvious from the fact that it was built out of concrete faced with marble, at a time when the family home had been constructed of wood. The shrine guarded and honored the catacombs where the family laid their dead to rest. But when the old gods began to grow careless of their creation, and men began to lose their faith, the shrine fell into disrepair.

Dimitri Acronis, grandfather of the Legate, had, like his grandson, also been of a scientific turn of mind. He had small use for the gods and visited the shrine only when a family member died. A parsimonious man, Dimitri had wasted no money on the shrine's upkeep. His son, Theodoro Acronis, father of the Legate, was far more interested in increasing the family's wealth than in honoring gods. He heard about the new god, Aelon, and his worship, for it was becoming quite popular among the elite of Oran. He had no time for gods of any sort, however. He built his villa and enlarged his estate and bought and traded slaves. His only pastime, other than making money, was competing with his teams in the Para Dix.

Acronis was more like his grandfather than his father. He was an explorer, an adventurer, and a scientist. The day came, shortly after his marriage, when the priests of Aelon visited the Legate's villa to tell him about an edict that required he tear down his family's shrine. The priests decreed everyone was to now worship in the Temple of Aelon.

Acronis could have gone along with the demand. He had not

visited or even thought about the old shrine since he had buried his father. But when ordered to destroy it, he went to visit it and memories flooded back. As a young boy, he had heard stories about the old gods from his tutor and become enamored of them. He had made boyish sacrifices, bringing them oat cakes and once a small frog, which had kept hopping off the altar.

Perhaps it was his boyhood memories that prompted him to fight for the shrine or perhaps (his wife had said) it was a perverse desire to annoy the priests. He had refused, saying, quite rightly, that the shrine honored his ancestors. When the priests went to inspect the shrine to see if illegal worship was being carried on inside, they saw morning glory vines trailing around broken columns, marble slabs lying moldering on the ground, and bats hanging from the domed ceiling. In back of the shrine, in the hillside, was the bronze door—long ago turned green—that led to the cavern where the dead lay in repose.

The priests had informed Acronis that since the shrine was in such proximity to the burial site, they would not disturb the dead by tearing it down. Undoubtedly, the Priest-General of that time had considered it unwise to anger a man who could personally fund two triremes and his own private army. It was after this incident, however, that the Legate had been ordered to the outlying provinces.

Sigurd and the others followed Keeper over paths of crushed stone that wound through the pruned plants and ornamental trees leading to a wrought-iron gate. The full moon shone brightly. They had no trouble finding the way.

"Beyond the gate is the old garden," Keeper said. "The shrine is through those trees."

The gate was not much used; they had to beat on its rusted hinges to pry it open. Broken stones green with moss and overgrown with weeds led into a tangled wilderness of plants and trees.

Keeper told them to follow the path, then turned to leave.

"Where are you going?" Sigurd asked suspiciously.

"I told Skylan I would go back for him," said Keeper dourly. The ogre did not like Sigurd.

"And I think you are going to warn your master we are escaping," said Sigurd.

"Why would he do that?" Bjorn asked.

"For the reward? Because he is the Legate's toady? How should I know?" Sigurd muttered.

The men looked into the grove of tall trees. The overarching, tangled boughs would cut off the light of the moon and stars.

"Go on, Keeper," said Bjorn, casting an annoyed glance at Sigurd. "Go back to fetch Skylan and Aylaen. We will wait for you as long as we can."

"When you reach the shrine, go through it," Keeper instructed. "You will come to a bronze door. Push on the door and it will open. The catacombs are inside."

He walked off, trudging back up the path. The men entered the path that wound among the trees. The darkness was so thick they were forced to light the torches.

"There it is," said Bjorn.

Torchlight shone on a small round building with a domed roof and surrounded by a porch. Graceful columns, cracked and stained with time, supported the roof. The men eyed the building uneasily.

"We go through the shrine," said Sigurd. "Here, give me that light."

He seized the torch and walked into the shrine. The others trailed after him. Their uneasiness evaporated when they saw the floor covered with rodent dung and bat guano and spider webs dangling between the columns. If the gods had once been here, they were gone now.

As Keeper had said, a path led from the shrine to a bronze door set into the side of a hill. The door was closed, but, as Sigurd found out by giving it a shove, it was not locked.

Sigurd did not go inside. He stood staring at the door. Once buried, the dead of the Vindrasi were not disturbed. Sometimes it was the dead who disturbed the living by refusing to stay decently interred. Even then, the Vindrasi were patient with draugrs and specters and the like, rarely resorting to drastic measures such as digging up the body and cutting off the head unless the dead became a menace.

The idea that dead ancestors were kept in catacombs, subject to periodic visits whenever someone else died, was unsettling. Sigurd, glancing behind him, saw the men standing some distance away. They were all watching him, waiting for him to go in first. After all, he was Chief.

Sigurd drew in a breath and gripped his sword in one hand, the torch in the other. He started to open the door.

"I think we should wait for Skylan, Aylaen, and the boy," said Erdmun.

Sigurd glared at him. "You don't even like Skylan."

"I like him better than I used to," Erdmun stated, adding in a low voice, "I like him better than I like you."

"We are Torgun," said Farinn. "We stand together. There should be no talk of leaving anyone behind."

The others nodded their agreement.

"We will wait for *Aylaen*," said Sigurd, annoyed. "And while we're waiting, we might as well take a look around."

He shoved on the bronze door, and, holding the torch high and his sword tight, he entered the burial cave. The men came after him.

The first section of the catacombs was the oldest. Small niches had been carved into the rock walls. Inside the niches were porcelain urns. The Torgun had never heard of cremation, and they had no idea what these urns were for. Aki wanted to open one, but Grimuir told him it might be some offering to the dead and that he should leave it alone.

The catacombs extended on into the hillside. The niches grew larger. Burning the dead was no longer fashionable. Bodies were entombed in sarcophagi—receptacles carved out of stone. At first these were plain, but as the family's fortunes improved, the sarcophagi became more elaborate and were topped by life-size statues of the dead.

Marble matriarchs, their hands folded on their breasts, lay in repose beside soldiers, whose hands clasped the hilts of marble swords. The Torgun could not read, but they guessed that the words carved into the niches above the tombs or sometimes on the tombs themselves were the names of the dead.

The Torgun were hushed as they walked the silent catacombs. Every man could feel the thread of his wyrd stretch and quiver. At any moment, it could snap. Suddenly they came to a niche where the corpse had not been entombed. The men came to a halt, shaken by the sight of the ghastly figure.

The skeletal remains, draped in rotting cloth, reclined on the stone as though seated on a couch. The flickering torchlight caused the shadows in the eye sockets to stir. Sigurd stopped to stare in horror, like the others, then he feared they might think he was frightened. He steeled himself and marched on, saying he was going to investigate. He did not go far, however, for there was no place to go. The catacombs came to an end. He faced a solid rock wall.

Sigurd stared at the wall in teeth-grinding fury. He bashed at the wall with the hilt of his sword and beat on it with his hands. The wall did not move. Behind him, the Torgun were silent.

Sigurd turned to face them. "We have come the wrong way. There must be a place where the tunnels branch off, and we missed it."

"We didn't miss anything," said Bjorn.

"Go back!" Sigurd roared.

The men started to retrace their steps. Passing by the tombs had been bad the first time. Now it was worse. They seemed to see eyes, hear voices. They quickened their pace and a few started running.

"Keep watch!" Sigurd ordered. "You'll miss the turn-off—"

A blast of hot air doused the light of his torch, leaving him in darkness. Sigurd was not worried. He could see the flickering lights of the other torches some distance away and he yelled, "Erdmun, my torch blew out! Bring me a light."

Erdmun did not answer.

"Someone bring me a light! What is the matter with you pissants? Don't tell me you are afraid of a bunch of bones!" Sigurd called out.

Still no one answered him and his annoyance changed to anger. He was Chief and yet no one obeyed him. They were continually questioning his orders, arguing with him. *Wait for Skylan,* they said. To the daemons with Skylan. There were tunnels that led to the sea. There had to be.

Sigurd walked on, moving slowly, feeling his way through the darkness.

"Grimuir!" he shouted, calling upon a trusted ally. "Bring me a torch!"

Finally, someone obeyed him. He could see light shining on fair hair and a beardless face. Sigurd recognized Farinn and he let out a gusty sigh. He didn't like to admit it, but he had been starting to grow nervous.

"About damn time!" he said angrily.

Farinn came to a halt. He stood in a pool of light, a battle-axe in his hand. Sigurd snatched the torch from him.

"What's the matter with you? Why do you stare at me like that?" Sigurd demanded.

Farinn made no answer. Gripping his axe with both hands, he swung it.

Sigurd saw the flash of the axe blade and he leaped backward.

The blade whistled past his midriff. If he had not moved, it would have sliced him in half.

"Farinn, what the—"

Farinn swung the axe again. Sigurd dove to the ground, dropping the torch. The blade clanged on solid stone. Sparks flew, and Sigurd crawled backward on all fours. He did not go far before he bumped up against a wall. Farinn kept up the attack. Fortunately for Sigurd, Farinn fought like someone who had never before used a battle-axe. He swung wildly, without skill.

Sigurd knew the young man was generally silent, but it seemed he should be saying something, at least telling Sigurd why he wanted to kill him.

The torch lay on the floor, but it continued to burn. The light slanting upward cast leaping shadows on the walls. Sigurd jumped to his feet, holding his sword so that Farinn could see it, see his danger.

"I don't want to hurt you—"

He stopped, staring. Farinn's eyes had been a bright, vibrant blue. No longer. Now his eyes were white as an egg, with no pupil, no iris. Farinn tried once more to kill him.

Sigurd ducked the wild blow and then leaped at Farinn. Plowing straight into him, he carried him to the ground. Sigurd smashed the young man in the face with his fist and the horrible eyes closed. Sigurd wiped the sweat from his forehead and stood up and looked around.

A body, still and pallid as the stone faces on the tombs, wispy and ephemeral as smoke, floated toward him. A hand, like chill mist rising from a frozen lake, reached out to him.

Sigurd screamed and tried to flee, but the mist wrapped around him and his scream ended abruptly.

Semelon, the Spirit Priestess, watched from the darkness outside the ancient shrine. Enveloped in a dark purple stoa, she was part of the night. Raegar was beside her, keeping behind a pillar, his armor covered by a thick black cloak. Treia pressed against him, keeping hold of him. With her weak eyesight, she was effectively blind, and that always made her nervous.

They had been here when the warriors arrived. They had listened to the men argue about waiting for Skylan and Aylaen, watched Sigurd push open the bronze door, watched the warriors go inside.

"Where could Skylan and Aylaen be?" Treia wondered. "Why aren't they here with the others?"

"Don't worry. Skylan would never give up this chance to escape. He will be along shortly. As for Aylaen"—Raegar glanced at Treia, frowning—"you said she was staying behind. You said you had persuaded her to join us."

"I said I *tried* to persuade her," Treia returned in some confusion.

Raegar's frown deepened and Treia added hurriedly, "You know how stubborn she can be. I reminded her of the bright future you promised her. She spurned and mocked me. She will never worship Aelon. Let her go, my love."

"But if she enters the catacombs, she will die with the rest of them," said Raegar. "You don't want her to die!"

Treia started to speak, but he hushed her.

"Don't worry. I will find a way to rescue her. I know how much she means to you, how sorry you would be to lose her."

Treia clenched her fists in the darkness to keep her fear under control. Hevis required a sacrifice—someone Treia cared for. Treia could not sacrifice Raegar; that was out of the question. She loved him with a passion that sometimes frightened her. And it was because of her love for Raegar, her desire to make him happy, to promote his ambition, that she was willing to sacrifice the only other person she cared about—Aylaen.

Treia had not known how much she cared about her sister until that moment on the ship when Hevis demanded her promise. Treia had felt a pang of remorse and then she reminded herself that Aylaen wanted to die; she wanted to be reunited with Garn. Treia was granting her sister's wish. The fact that Treia would also be ridding herself of a lovely rival made her decision that much easier.

Treia had spent a sleepless night devising various ways to kill Aylaen and had at last been forced to admit that she could not do the deed herself. She could not stab Aylaen or give her a cup of poisoned wine. She could not watch her sister writhing in agony. She could not see the accusing look in her sister's dying eyes.

Hevis had not specified that Aylaen had to die by Treia's hands. When Raegar and the Priest-General devised their plot to kill Skylan and the other Torgun, Treia had simply added her sister to the mix. True, she had promised Raegar she would keep Aylaen from going into the accursed catacombs with the others. Treia would much rather break a promise to her lover than break a promise to a god.

Aylaen should be here with the others. But she was not, for some reason, and now Raegar was planning to save her.

Which meant that Raegar needed to be somewhere else.

Treia tried to think of a plausible excuse to send him away and could not come up with any.

Hoarse cries and screams of terror echoed from inside the catacombs. The Spirit Priestess shook her head and began to chant.

"What is she doing?" Treia asked, alarmed. "Why does she summon the dead? It is too soon! Skylan is not here!"

Raegar said something to the Spirit Priestess, who halted her chanting a moment to reply, then immediately resumed.

"She is *not* summoning the dead," Raegar said. "She is trying to calm them. Unfortunately, the lemures who guard the tomb are angered by the invasion and will not be appeased. The spirits of the dead have seized the men's bodies and are forcing the warriors to attack each other."

"All except Skylan and Aylaen," Treia said frantically. "Where are they?"

As if in answer, blobs of firelight gleamed in the night. Skylan's voice shouted out that this was a trap. He came crashing through the trees. The ogre, Keeper, pounded along at his side.

"Here he is," said Raegar with satisfaction. "Just in time to die."

"But where is Aylaen?" Treia asked, peering into the bright torchlight that hurt her eyes. "Is she there? I can't see her!"

"Here she comes! And that demonic boy is with her," Raegar said. "Go to her, Treia."

Treia ground her teeth. She had no choice. If she refused, Raegar would be furious. Even now, he was fuming at her hesitation. "What are you waiting for? Don't let her enter the catacombs!"

"Hevis!" Treia prayed in desperation. "You want this as much as I do! Help me!"

She felt Raegar's hand suddenly tighten on her shoulder. His fingers dug into her flesh. Afraid of his anger, Treia raised her eyes fearfully.

He was no longer paying attention to her. He stared into the darkness, his eyes unfocused.

"Raegar," said Treia, but he could not hear her. He was listening to another voice. The Watchers were speaking, summoning the faithful in Aelon's name. The Spirit Priestess ceased her chanting abruptly and turned her head in the direction of the Temple.

Treia watched the two in growing alarm. Raegar's jaw sagged, his face darkened. The priestess Semelon's customary calm was shaken. Her lips quivered, then tightened.

Raegar looked at Semelon.

"You heard?" he asked.

The Spirit Priestess nodded and said softly, "We must have faith in Aelon. We should return to the Temple—"

"What is wrong?" Treia demanded.

"We can't leave," said Raegar. "Not until we know the barbarians have been killed."

"What is going on?" Treia demanded loudly, annoyed at being left out of this conversation.

"The ogre fleet has been sighted rounding the point," said Raegar.

Skylan, Keeper, and Aylaen were pulling on the bronze door, shouting to the men trapped inside. Wulfe had apparently run off.

"But . . . that can't be!" Treia gasped. "The Priest-General said it would be weeks before the ogre ships arrived. His spies said—"

"His spies were wrong," Raegar said. "Instead of making landfall on Ardon, the ogres kept sailing. Their foul gods gave them a favorable wind and fine weather and now they are here, by the thousands, and our defenses are not ready!"

"But we are," Treia said in low, fierce tones.

Raegar turned to her with a puzzled look. She glanced sidelong at Semelon, and drew him away out of earshot.

"What are you talking about?" Raegar asked.

"The Vektan dragon!" said Treia, barely speaking above a whisper. "I can summon it."

Raegar stared at her, at first uncomprehending. Then he drew in a deep breath of exultation.

"You are certain?"

Skylan, the ogre, and Aylaen entered the catacombs.

They would all die. Aylaen would die. Treia breathed a sigh of relief. "I am certain," she said. "Tell Semelon we are taking the carriage back to the Temple. She should remain here to make certain that Skylan and the others do not leave the catacombs alive. If Skylan finds out about the Vektan dragon, he will try to stop us."

"But what about Aylaen!" Raegar turned back toward the catacombs. "Where is she? Did she go inside?"

"I am afraid she did," said Treia. "There is nothing we can do for her now, my love."

"But she is your sister," said Raegar, agonized. "We can't send her to her death. If I went after her, I could save her."

"There is not time!" said Treia, seizing hold of him. "How long before the ogres come ashore?"

"Ogres do not fight at night. They will attack with the dawn."

"Think of all we have to do before now and then! We must go to the shrine, tell the Priest-General, enter the storeroom, and retrieve the bone of the Vektia. Then we must find a suitable location and prepare for the ritual. We should leave now—at once."

Still Raegar continued to hesitate. "But, Aylaen . . ."

Treia dug her nails into the palms of her hand to keep from slapping him. She was offering him the chance to make history, to be the savior of his people, to gain esteem in the eyes of gods and men, and all he could think of was his own carnal desire.

"The god has given us this chance to save your people, my love," Treia said. "I know it is hard, but we must make this sacrifice."

Raegar looked down at her. "I am sorry, Treia. You are right. I will tell Semelon we are leaving."

Raegar went to speak with Semelon. While they were talking, Treia heard a noise, a rustling in the undergrowth. She turned and saw Wulfe standing there, staring at her with his yellow eyes. He had heard everything! She drew in a hissing breath and was about to make a grab for him when Raegar returned.

"Semelon will wait here. We will send the carriage back for her. What is it, my love?"

Treia looked back. The boy was gone.

It doesn't matter, she thought. He'll soon be dead. They'll all be dead.

Treia took hold of Raegar's arm and the two hastened from the shrine. He kept his hand on her elbow, guiding her through the tangle of vegetation, the full moon lighting their way. As Raegar lifted Treia into the carriage, she heard Aylaen scream—a shrill wail of pain and terror.

Treia shuddered, then said softly, beneath her breath, "Hevis, accept the sacrifice!"

B O O K   T H R E E

Skylan ran into the catacombs with Keeper at his side holding a torch in one hand and a war hammer in the other. They could hear in the distance the sounds of battle—the clank of metal hitting metal. But those were the only sounds. The cries and shouts of men under attack had ceased.

"Strange," said Skylan, and his steps slowed. He came to a halt only a short distance from the bronze door. "I can't see anything. Can you?"

"Nothing," said Keeper. "And you are right. It is very strange."

Skylan was not surprised when Aylaen arrived at his side, her sword in her hand. He had told her to stay behind with Wulfe, and, of course, she had disobeyed.

"Why are you just standing here?" she cried, gesturing into the darkness. "Our friends are fighting in there, maybe dying!"

"If so, it's a strange sort of battle," said Skylan.

"What are you talking about?" Aylaen asked.

"Do you hear Sigurd shouting commands? Grimuir yelling at Aki to watch his back?" Skylan stared into the darkness, frowning, then he glanced around. "Where's Wulfe?"

"He's outside. He kept yammering about lemures being angry at us." Aylaen shivered. "Maybe he's right."

"I never heard of ghosts wielding swords," said Keeper.

"We can't just stand here!" said Aylaen. "I'm going—"

Skylan caught hold of her. "We will all go. But we will go slowly. Whatever is down there, I want to see it before it sees me."

"You sound like your father," said Aylaen irritably. "What did you used to call him? An old granny?"

She is right, Skylan realized. Not so many months ago, I would have raced headlong into the fray. Now I go slowly, eyes and ears open.

He thought of Norgaard and the grief he had brought his father. There were many mistakes he had made, actions he had taken that he had come to regret. But few lay heavier on his heart than that.

"You pay me a compliment," Skylan said.

Aylaen looked at him startled, then her face softened.

"Yes," she said, after a moment. "I guess I do."

She reached out her free hand to him. Her fingers were cold, but her touch warmed him like hot spiced wine. He looked back into the past and saw what he had been—Skylan, Chief of Chiefs, brash, bold, arrogant, demanding her love, becoming angry when she loved another. He had never stopped to consider that love, like respect, must be earned. He was no longer Skylan, Chief of Chiefs. He was only Skylan, trying every day to make up for the past.

Hand in hand, they moved deeper into the catacombs. Then Skylan stopped, staring. Keeper jabbed him hard with his elbow, and Aylaen gasped.

A chill mist hung in the air near where they were standing. The mist flowed from the walls and drifted over the floor of the catacombs. Trapped in the mist, his friends were doing battle.

Not against a foe. They attacked each other.

As Skylan watched, Sigurd took a swing with his sword at Bjorn. Grimuir attacked Aki. Farinn hacked at Erdmun with an axe and Erdmun slashed at Farinn with his sword. The men fought in an eerie silence. None of them spoke. None cried out in pain, though Skylan saw blood running freely from their wounds.

"Have they all gone stark raving crazy?" Skylan said, watching in amazement. He raised his voice. "What do you fools think you are doing? Sigurd! Bjorn!"

His voice jarred the silence. Sigurd turned slowly toward him. Aylaen screamed.

"His eyes! Torval save us, Skylan, look at his eyes!"

Skylan could not take the time to look at anyone's eyes. Sigurd was running straight at him, his sword raised.

Skylan shifted his body sideways and thrust out his foot. Sigurd tripped, stumbled, and fell to the ground.

"Take him outside!" Skylan cried to Keeper. "Aylaen, go with him. Treat his wounds."

She hesitated, and he yelled at her, "Take him out. I'll try to save the others."

Keeper grabbed hold of Sigurd, lifted him by the scruff of his neck, and hauled him bodily out of the catacombs. He tossed him onto the ground and stood over him, ready to bash him with the war hammer if he tried to attack.

Aylaen bent over Sigurd. He was unconscious and, remembering the hideous eyes, she was loath to touch him.

"Ah, a lemur got him," said Wulfe, creeping up out of the darkness. "I told you so."

The boy sniffed at Sigurd and wrinkled his nose and gave him a poke in the arm with his finger.

Sigurd groaned and sat up. Wulfe scrambled away in terror. Aylaen jumped to her feet, her sword poised, ready to strike. Sigurd blinked his eyes and looked up at her. "Treia lied," said Sigurd. "It was a trap."

Inside the catacombs, Skylan was moving up on Bjorn, who had turned to attack his own brother. Bjorn's back was to Skylan, and he hoped to hit his friend on the head, knock him out. He paid no heed to the mist that curled around Bjorn's boots and began to slide toward him.

"The lemur!" Keeper thundered a warning. "Don't let it touch you!"

A ghostly figure rose before Skylan, ghostly hands reaching out for him.

Skylan's stomach clenched. The hair raised on his arms and prickled on the back of his neck. He backed away. The ghost glided toward him.

"How do I fight it?" Skylan called.

"You don't," said Keeper. "You run."

Skylan shook his head. "I won't leave my men."

"You can't help them if you end up like them," Keeper told him.

Swearing, Skylan turned and ran for the bronze door. He dashed outside with Keeper right behind him.

Once there, Skylan stopped, turned. The lemur did not follow him. The ghost wavered in the entryway like a curtain of fog. He was safe, but his friends were still in there, trapped in the catacombs, forced by the spirits to fight each other to the death.

"A dead end," said Sigurd. "Literally."

Skylan turned to see the older man sitting up, wiping blood from his face. His eyes were back to normal, except that they were dark, shadowed with terror.

"What happened?" Skylan asked. "How can I stop the ghosts?"

Sigurd shook his head. "All I remember is a pale hand touching me and the next thing I knew all I wanted to do was kill those who dared disturbed my rest."

"If it was a trap, it wasn't Treia's doing," said Aylaen defensively. "She didn't know!"

"She knew," said Wulfe. "She was here, watching. She and Raegar."

"Raegar? Where?" Skylan asked grimly.

"They're not here now. They both ran off. They left because of the ogres."

"Ogres . . ." Skylan said, startled. "What about the ogres?"

"They're coming in ships," said Wulfe. "Tonight."

"Keeper, did you hear that!" Skylan said, excited.

Keeper snorted and shook his head.

"You can ask the other woman," Wulfe said. "She's still in there."

"What other woman?"

"The one who is talking to the dead."

"It might be a Spirit Priestess," said Aylaen. "Like the one who summoned Garn. Raegar said they have power over the dead. Where is she, Wulfe? Can you see her?"

"She's hiding in the bushes," said Wulfe. He sniffed the air. "I can't see her, but I can smell her."

"We'll find her," said Skylan. "If she has power over the dead, she can stop this attack. Keeper, come with me. Aylaen—"

Searing pain tore through Skylan's arm. He felt as though someone had torn open his skin and reached inside to rip out the muscles and shatter his bones. His hand went into spasms. He dropped his sword and doubled over, moaning, pressing his burning arm into his stomach. Sigurd was screaming and rolling on the ground. Keeper clutched his arm and bellowed in pain and rage. Only Aylaen, free of the tattoo of Aelon, was unaffected. She hovered near them, helpless.

"What can I do?"

"Go with . . . Wulfe!" Skylan gasped. He had to fight the god for every word. Sweat rolling down his face, he said harshly, "Find the priestess, Wulfe. You know how."

Wulfe stared at him, then he started to tremble and shook his head violently.

"Find her," said Skylan, through gritted teeth. "Find her!"

Still Wulfe hesitated. He looked at Skylan, who was in pain, and the boy's lips parted in a strange, tight-lipped smile. He dropped down on all fours and began to run as Aylaen had seen him run many times before. Except that now, as he ran, the hair on his arms and legs began to grow long. His awkward and ungainly scrabbling on hands and feet changed into a graceful, ground-eating lope. His teeth sharpened to fangs; his mouth expanded, widened; his tongue lolled; his muscles hardened.

The wolf loped down the path. He went only a short distance, stopped, and put his nose to the ground. He ran about, sniffing, then raised his head. Ears pricked. He had found the trail. He bounded off into the darkness.

Aylaen could not move. She could only stand, staring.

"Follow him!" Skylan urged. He gave a ragged cry and sagged to his knees. "Don't let him . . . kill . . ."

The wolf came back, ran straight at Aylaen. The wolf was young, scrawny. He stopped short of her, growled and jerked his head, then turned and trotted off a short distance. Stopping again, he looked back at her and jerked his head again.

Aylaen understood. He wanted her to follow.

She forced her numb feet to move. Hampered by the tangle of undergrowth, she could not travel as fast as the wolf, or as silently. The wolf led her to the old shrine.

The floor was striped, black and silver, with moonlight and shadows. Aylaen tried to keep out of the light and hugged the shadows, but the woman must have seen something that alarmed her. Aylaen heard the woman's long skirts swishing through dead leaves.

The wolf lifted his head, growled softly, and dashed off in pursuit. Mindful of Skylan's warning, Aylaen ran after him. The wolf easily caught up with her. The woman cried out in terror, and Aylaen recognized her voice. Semelon—the woman who held Garn's soul captive.

The wolf's jaws gaped, tongue lolled. Semelon saw the wolf almost on her and screamed and raised her arms in front of her face. The wolf jumped, knocking her to the ground. Aylaen lost sight of both of them.

"Don't hurt her! Wulfe, don't hurt her!" Aylaen yelled frantically.

Aylaen found Semelon curled into a ball on the ground, her eyes squinched tightly shut. Wulfe, in boy form, crouched on his haunches a short distance from her, panting hard, his sides heaving.

"I did what you asked," he said. "I didn't hurt her."

Aylaen kept a nervous eye on him and knelt down beside the priestess.

"The wolf is gone. You're safe," she said.

Semelon shrieked and struck at Aylaen with her fists.

Aylaen grabbed her wrists. "You're safe! Open your eyes!"

Semelon's eyes flared open. She stared at Aylaen and then at the boy crouching in the weeds.

"The boy is fae! A man-beast. You must kill him, quickly, before he changes and kills us both—"

"He won't kill us *both*," said Aylaen. She took hold of the priestess and dragged her to her feet. "He will kill you. Unless you do what I say."

Semelon regarded her with horror. "You are in league with evil!"

Aylaen glanced sidelong at Wulfe, who was watching both her and Semelon. Swallowing her horror, Aylaen seized the priestess and dragged her through the garden back toward the catacombs. Moonlight glinted off the bronze door.

Aylaen feared Skylan and the others would still be caught in the grip of the god. She was astonished and pleased to find them on their feet, flexing their hands and looking confused.

Sigurd gave a grunt. "One moment Aelon is tearing off my arm and the next he is gone. What is going on?"

"The god has more pressing matters to attend to," said Skylan. "And so do we."

He turned his grim gaze on the priestess and pointed toward the catacombs. "Free my men!"

"Your friends angered the lemures by disturbing their rest," said Semelon. "There is nothing I can do—"

"She is lying," Aylaen said harshly. "I saw her work her magic. She summoned Garn. She holds his spirit prisoner—"

"I am not the one who keeps him bound to this world," said Semelon.

Aylaen went livid.

Skylan didn't have time for this. He pointed to the catacombs. "Use your power! Free my friends. Or I will set the boy on you."

Semelon cast a look of loathing at Wulfe, who grinned at her.

"The boy is fae," said Semelon. "He cannot be trusted. Mark my warning, he will turn on you someday."

"I'll worry about that when the time comes," said Skylan. "Do as I tell you."

Semelon shrugged and began to chant. The ghostly curtain remained, blocking the entrance. But inside the catacombs, the Torgun stopped fighting.

"The dead will let them depart," said Semelon. "But they must leave their weapons behind."

"Lay down your arms!" Skylan called to his friends.

The men hesitated, not happy.

"This is the only way the dead will let you go," he urged them.

Erdmun was the first to fling down his axe and run for the door. Grimuir and Bjorn took hold of Farinn and helped him outside. Aki walked out on his own. They were all bloodied and bruised, but none had suffered serious harm.

Once they were all out, Skylan walked over to the bronze door. He clasped hold of it. The mist brushed his arm with a chill warning.

"We are sorry we disturbed you," he cried.

Keeper came to help him, and between them, they pushed the bronze door shut. Skylan and the ogre walked back to where their friends had gathered.

"So much for our plans to escape," Bjorn said glumly.

"We are leaving Sinaria," said Skylan. "Tonight."

They stared at him. Skylan glanced at Keeper and said, "Ogres are about to invade the city. Their fleet has been sighted." He pointed to the tattoo on his arm. "That's why the god let us go. He has more important matters to worry about."

"How do you know this?" Sigurd asked suspiciously.

"Wulfe overheard Treia and Raegar talking. Aelon told them. Ask the priestess. Aelon speaks to her."

Semelon regarded them in stony silence.

"It's true," said Bjorn. "Look at her face."

"We will carry our ship to the river, hide it among the trees on the riverbank until night falls," said Skylan. "The ogres will attack Sinaria at dawn."

Keeper stirred and seemed about to say something. Skylan glanced at him, but the ogre apparently changed his mind, for he only shook his head.

"When the ogres are occupied in looting and burning and killing, we will set sail for home."

Home! In his mind, Skylan walked once more on the beach of Luda. He embraced his father and asked his forgiveness. He sat beside his friends during the long winter nights relating again the tale of their journey.

He was about to go on when he looked at Aylaen, who stood apart from the rest, pale and mute and motionless.

"I won't leave without Garn," she said.

12

G arn!" said Sigurd, amazed. "Garn's dead."
The wind rose. The branches of the trees creaked and swayed, leaves rustled. If there had been dryads in those trees, they would have been chattering excitedly about the coming of the ogres, for this wind had been sent by the Gods of Raj to fill the sails of the ogre ships and drive them toward their destination.

Skylan felt the wind blow on his face. He smelled the salt tang in the air. "I will stay with Aylaen," he said.

She told her story, keeping it short, mindful of time.

"Raegar promised me that Aelon could bring Garn back to life if I would tell him the ritual to summon the Vektan dragon. . . ."

The men stared at her in dazed shock. Garn's spirit a prisoner. A Vektan dragonbone. It was too much to comprehend. They looked at each other, troubled. Skylan knew what they were thinking because he was thinking it himself.

We don't have time for this. We must run to our ship now, make good our escape. The Torgun stand together. We leave no one behind. But Garn would understand. He would not want us to lose this chance for our freedom because of him. As for the spiritbone of the Vektia, what can we do? It is beyond our reach.

Skylan could see in his mind's eye the triangular sails of the ogre ships, white in the moonlight. Soon, the lookouts on the watchtowers along the harbor would see them and they would raise alarm.

The Vektan Five . . .

Five dragonbones. Every night, the goddess threw down five dragonbones. Five together. The Torgun stand together.

Understanding struck Skylan like a thunderbolt, bursting upon him in a shower of sparks and sizzling flame.

"Garn is right," he said to himself in amazement. "I *do* know the secret."

And he knew, horror-struck, the appalling danger. He knew what Treia and Raegar planned to do as surely as if they had told him. He knew why they had tried to force Aylaen to find out the secret to the summoning of a Vektan dragon. The secret!

Treia had told Aylaen she knew the *ritual*. Perhaps she did. But she didn't know the secret.

"Carry the *Venjekar* to the river and make ready to sail. Aylaen and I will free Garn."

"What about the spiritbone?" asked Bjorn.

"The less said, the better," Skylan replied, glancing at the priestess.

Semelon was watching them, listening to every word they said. She had the power to speak to her god, warn Aelon. Skylan supposed he could kill her, silence her permanently, but in a way he owed her. If it had not been for her summoning Garn, he would have never solved the puzzle.

"What's going on?" Erdmun asked. "What's Skylan doing?"

"Gods have ears," Sigurd said, jerking a thumb at the priestess. "Now get moving."

Skylan motioned to Sigurd as the men moved off.

"Aylaen and I will try to join you, but if we haven't reached the ship by the time you are ready to sail, you must leave without us."

To Skylan's surprise, Sigurd shook his head. "I will wait for you."

"The ogres will attack at dawn," said Skylan. "If we're not back by then, we won't be coming back. Take the *Venjekar* out to sea and put as much distance between this city and yourselves as you can."

Sigurd hesitated, then thrust out his hand. "Torval walk with you."

Skylan clasped the older man's hand. "You are my father's best friend. Tell him I am sorry for the trouble I brought him."

Sigurd grinned. "I will tell him that his brat finally grew up."

He began shouting at the others, who were moving slowly, berating them for laggards. The men set off at a run.

"Thank you for coming with me to free Garn," Aylaen said. "Maybe we could find Treia. . . ."

We *have* to find Treia, Skylan thought. He hoped they were going to save Treia. He didn't like to think what would happen if Treia didn't want to be saved.

"The priestess spoke the truth," said Aylaen with a sigh. "It's my fault. I forged the chains Garn wears." She glanced at Semelon and frowned. "What do we do with her? She'll warn her god—"

"Warn him of what? That a bunch of slaves are going to escape?" Skylan smiled and shrugged. "Aelon has his hands full. A few thousand ogres *and* their gods are about to descend on him. We'll take the priestess with us. She might be useful."

He was about to start off when he caught sight of Wulfe lurking about in the shrubbery. He had forgotten about the boy.

"You should go with Sigurd, back to the ship," said Skylan. His voice was cold and he knew it. He couldn't help himself. He found it hard to look at the boy and not see the beast.

"You're mad at me, aren't you?" Wulfe said, his lip quivering. "I did what you asked. I found the priestess. And I didn't kill her!"

"I know," said Skylan, sighing. "It's going to take time for me to get used to the idea of you being a . . . a man-beast. Like it took time for you to get used to living with Uglies—"

He paused. The word stirred a memory. He took hold of Wulfe by the shoulders, said swiftly, "You told me Treia was praying to a god on board our ship. A god of the Uglies. Do you know the god's name?"

Wulfe thought back. "No," he said. "But I smelled smoke and it was really hot."

"Hevis," said Skylan. "Hevis told Treia the ritual."

Wulfe slipped from his grasp and ran to Aylaen, hoping, probably, that if he kept clear of Skylan, he wouldn't be sent back.

"Where are you going?" Keeper asked. "What is your plan?"

Skylan had assumed Keeper had gone off on his own. He looked at him in wonder.

"What are you doing here? If my people were sailing their ships into the harbor, I would be halfway to the dock by now, ready to greet them when they land."

"And if I had a ship of my own I would be sailing away," said Keeper. "How long do you think you will survive in a city overrun by ogres?"

"I'm planning to be out of here long before they attack," said Skylan.

Keeper shook his head and thrust out his lower lip.

"Humans think ogres are stupid."

Having been guilty of that himself, Skylan didn't know what to say. He had no idea what Keeper was talking about.

"We chose this night to invade." Keeper tilted back his head, looked up into the sky. "Why do you think we did that?"

Keeper's eyes glittered in the bright moonlight, and Skylan understood.

"The ogres won't wait for dawn to attack!"

"Of course we won't," Keeper muttered, grumbling. "We're not stupid. They will gut you as they would any other human. Unless I am with you."

Skylan shook his head. "Thank you, my friend, but it's too dangerous—"

Keeper brushed that away with a wave of his large hand. "I owe you. You saved my life."

"No, I didn't," said Skylan, astonished.

"I was dead inside," said the ogre. "You made me see that. Now, again, what is the plan?"

13

The night air sparkled in the moonlight and seemed to crackle with power. Skylan caught of a whiff of brimstone though there was not a cloud in the moonlit sky. He felt himself in the presence of the gods—old gods and new—converging on this city in a fight that would turn the tide of battle.

They left the old part of the garden, and once they were out of the shadows of the trees, he could see the villa. The house was completely dark except for one room, Chloe's room. The flames of the oil lamps still burned.

Skylan pictured her entering Torval's Hall. She would be startled and overwhelmed by the noise, the raucous singing, the pounding of the ale mugs, the overturning tables and smashing chairs, the roaring laughter. She would stand in the great door, shy and abashed, small and brown, a sparrow among eagles. Torval would come striding up to her and he would be frightening in his glory, but his touch would be gentle. He would take her by the hand and bring her forward to stand before them, and he would say, "Here is a hero worthy of you all—"

Skylan and his companions cut through the atrium, taking the shortest route to the armory and the stables, which ran through a narrow passage that separated the kitchen and the bakery. Due to the risk of fire, the large ovens with their roaring fires were kept separate from the main house, yet close enough to the kitchen so that the cook had ready access. A stone archway covered the passage. They were beneath this archway, in its shadows, when both Keeper and Skylan came to a sudden halt.

Skylan's braced arm stopped Aylaen and Wulfe. Keeper grabbed the priestess, putting his huge hand over her mouth.

From this part of the villa, they had a good view of the paved road that led up the hill. The road was to their left. The barracks, the stables, and the armory ahead on their right. The main part of the villa and the atrium were behind them.

Six men wearing the uniforms of the Temple Guard came riding up the highway. They rode swiftly and brazenly, not bothering to keep to the shadows. Each man carried a naked sword, blades shining in the moonlight.

"Have they come for us?" Aylaen whispered.

Skylan shook his head. "Raegar thinks we're lying dead in the catacombs. They're here for the Legate."

The men galloped past never looking their direction. They were heading for the front entrance. They had nothing to fear. No soldiers would be there to stop them. Seeing them gave Skylan an idea.

"Aylaen," said Skylan, "stay here with Wulfe and the Priestess. Keeper, go fetch horses and weapons and enough armor to make us look like the Legate's soldiers. I'll meet you around at the front of the villa."

Aylaen caught hold of him. Her eyes were gray in the moonlight and bright with anger.

"You're going to save him, aren't you? You're going to risk your life to save him—the man who made us slaves!? Leave him to his fate."

"I would," Skylan said, "but I need him."

He ran off, retracing his steps through the atrium. As he ran, he calculated the amount of time it would take the soldiers to reach the front of the villa. They would have to dismount and gain entrance through a locked door. Once inside, they would lose time searching the large house for Acronis, whereas Skylan knew exactly where to find him.

He went to the lighted room and flung wide the door that led from the atrium. The flames of the oil lamps wavered and danced as the night air rushed inside with him. The still, pale figure lay on the bed. Chloe's body had been washed and perfumed. Her hair was brushed and arranged around her face. Her hands lay folded on her chest. Her eyes were closed. Her expression was peaceful, with even the hint of a smile.

Skylan looked about for Acronis and could not find him. He

knew he could not be mistaken. A father's loving hands had brushed her hair and composed her body. Then Skylan heard a sound coming from the far end of the room.

Acronis was attempting to position his sword so that the hilt rested against the wall and the point pressed into his breast. Once he had the weapon set, all he had to do was lunge forward to drive the blade into his chest.

"Would you shame her?" Skylan asked.

Acronis jerked. The sword slipped. He caught it as it fell.

"Get out," he said harshly. "Or better yet, hold this damn sword. You don't have to do anything. Just stand there—"

"I don't have to do that much," said Skylan. "Six men with six swords are coming to kill you right now. And if you survive them, you can always die fighting the army of ogres that is about to descend on your city. At least if you are murdered, your daughter would not be ashamed to know that her father is a craven coward."

"Ogres," said Acronis in astonishment.

"And assassins," Skylan reminded him.

Acronis waved that aside.

"The ogre fleet has been sighted?"

"Yes, Legate. Where is Zahakis?"

Acronis shook his head. "I sent him away—"

A bellowing shout thundered through the villa. The shout was accompanied by the clash of arms and more shouting. Zahakis was yelling a warning to the Legate.

"I think we've found Zahakis," said Skylan. "Or rather, your assassins have found him."

Acronis stood with his sword in his hand staring at it as though he was not quite certain what it was.

"Zahakis is a good warrior," said Skylan. "But he can't stand against six men alone."

Acronis's gaze shifted to the still figure on the bed.

"I can't leave her," he said.

"I will stay with your daughter," said Semelon.

Skylan turned, startled to see the priestess standing in the doorway. Aylaen came running up behind her, panting, "I tried to stop her—"

"Go help Keeper with the horses," Skylan ordered. "And find Wulfe. We can't have him running loose!"

Aylaen hesitated a moment, then ran off.

Semelon walked inside the room and looked down on the bed. She smoothed back the hair from the girl's cold, pale brow. "I see her spirit in a great hall filled with light and laughter and music. Somewhere, she is dancing."

Acronis and Skylan looked at each other in astonishment. But there was no time for wonder, or even for Skylan to thank Torval. The sounds of battle were growing louder. Zahakis continued to shout. Acronis bent to kiss his daughter.

"Don't worry," he said softly. "I will not shame you."

He flung open the door and ran out into the hallway, heading for the sound of clashing swords. Acronis looked extremely startled to find Skylan running alongside him.

"This isn't your fight," said Acronis as they ran down first one hall, then another. Moonlight streamed through the windows.

"Oddly enough, it is," said Skylan, making a hasty sidestep to avoid falling in the fish pond.

The clashing steel, more shouts, and a low, gurgling scream ended further talk. Acronis slowed his pace. He raised his hand, cautioning Skylan to keep to the shadows and move silently.

The door to the villa stood wide open. Steel blades flashed in the moonlight. Zahakis stood with his back braced against the wall, swinging his sword slowly back and forth, the tip shifting from one to another of his foes, who were ranged around him.

The marble floor was slippery with blood and gore. The screaming was coming from a man writhing on the floor trying desperately to keep his bowels from spilling out of his gut. He was the only man down, though not the only man wounded. One assassin had blood streaming down his face; another was limping from a slash mark in his thigh.

The five guards still standing exchanged glances. They were going to rush Zahakis. Skylan gave a shout to draw their attention and ran into the entryway with Acronis at his side. The two converged on the guardsmen, who were thrown into confusion by their new foes threatening death from behind.

One slipped in the blood and went down. Skylan kicked him in the head and drove his sword into the unprotected armpit of another. Skylan jerked his blade free and whipped around, sword raised, to discover that the fight was over. Three lay dead or dying. The other two were running for their lives.

Skylan pictured this cowardly lot facing seasoned ogre warriors. No wonder the Priest-General wanted Treia to summon a dragon to do his fighting for him!

"Are you all right, Legate?" Zahakis asked.

"Yes, thanks to you. And our pradus." Acronis smiled at Skylan. "I would grant you freedom in return for saving my life, young man, but you appear to already have it."

He paused, rubbed his eyes, and said softly, "The night seems a terrible dream. Did you tell me something about ogres invading our city?"

"What's this about ogres?" Zahakis asked, alarmed.

"The fleet has been sighted," said Skylan. "They may already be sailing into the bay."

"Legate," said Zahakis urgently, "you and I should go—"

"And do what, Tribune?" Acronis asked with a weary shrug. "The triremes are in the boathouses, being overhauled. They could never be made ready to go to sea in time. And even if they could, it would take days to round up the rowers. As for your men, I doubt you could find many sober at this hour. Face it, my friend, there is nothing we can do—"

"Yes, there is," said Skylan. "You saw the spiritbone Treia used to summon the Dragon Kahg. The Priest-General has one of these spiritbones hidden away. If we can find the spiritbone, we can save the city."

Skylan was not lying. He wasn't telling all the truth, but he trusted Torval would forgive him.

"The Bone Priestess can summon the dragon to fight for us?" said Acronis, amazed.

"But why would she?" Zahakis asked.

"Because it's the only way to save *my* people as well as yours," said Skylan. He didn't want them thinking about this too much and finding the holes in his story. He hurried on. "We don't have much time. The Priest-General thinks the ogres will wait for dawn to attack, but Keeper says that with the full moon to light their way, they will enter the gates as soon as their army is assembled. We need to reach the Temple grounds and gain entrace to find the spiritbone—"

"You can do that, Legate," said Zahakis. "They will let you in without question. I'm going to defend the city. I know where to look for the men, sir. And there are the street gangs. Most of them are better armed than our soldiers and they know how to fight."

"A good plan," said Acronis. "Go carry it out."

Zahakis saluted and started off.

"One more thing—" Acronis called after him.

"Sir?" Zahakis turned.

"I have named you my heir," said Acronis. "All this is yours."

Zahakis stared, dumbfounded. Then he shook his head. "No, sir. It's not right—"

Acronis turned and strode off, not looking behind him. Skylan was left with Zahakis, who was still staring after Acronis.

Zahakis roused himself. "Take care of the Legate. He means to get himself killed this night."

"We'll be lucky if any of us survive," said Skylan. The two walked out the door together.

Zahakis clapped Skylan on the shoulder. "Good fortune to you and those barbaric gods of yours."

"I still plan to kill you myself someday," Skylan said, grinning. "Don't let the ogres rob me of my victory."

Zahakis smiled and shook his head. Mounting one of the horses abandoned by the guards, he wheeled it around and galloped off.

Skylan had told Keeper to bring the horses around to the front. They should be here by now. Just as he was thinking he should go find them, he heard hoofbeats outside the entrance to the villa.

Keeper was seated on an enormous draft horse, and led another horse for Skylan. Aylaen rode at the ogre's side wearing the armor of one of Acronis's soldiers. Her face was concealed by the wings of the helm that fit closely to her cheeks. Hinged plates fit over her shoulders and her chest. The leather skirt with metal strips was too big and sagged at the waist. She wore braces on her arms and greaves on her shins. An ecstatic Wulfe rode behind her, his arms around her.

Keeper tossed a bundle to Skylan. It landed at his feet with a clanking sound. He ripped it open and began putting on the segmented armor, the leather skirt, and the winged helm. His hands were shaking with nervous excitement. Keeper dismounted and came to his aid.

"The Legate has agreed to help us," Skylan said as Keeper assisted him with the armor.

"You are putting a lot of trust in a man who enslaved us," Aylaen said, frowning.

"He is a man of his word," said Skylan. "And he has no love for Aelon."

Skylan mounted the horse. He looked around the villa, the grounds, the hills that fell away from him leading down to the river, and far beyond that, the sea. He stared intently at the bay, trying to see the ogre fleet. All he could see was a flat surface silvered in the moonlight. The ogre ships would look like black bugs crawling over the water. No sign of them yet. He could see the watchtowers silhouetted against the water.

Would the men in those towers light signal fires when the ships were sighted? Send swift runners to the palace? Whatever they did, it wouldn't matter. The Sinarians had been caught sleeping—literally.

I will never see this place again, Skylan thought. I was brought here in chains, a slave. And now I might die trying to save the very people who enslaved me.

Acronis came out of the villa, resplendent in his ceremonial armor. He wore the purple cape of a Legate thrown over his shoulder, his sword at his side. He was about to mount the horse of one of the men who had tried to kill him when he saw Keeper. Acronis blinked at him in astonishment.

"What are you doing here?"

"I am sorry for your loss, Legate," said Keeper. "I fear many more children will die this night unless we can stop this madness."

"Yes," said Acronis quietly. "You are right."

He motioned for his "escort" to fall in behind him. They kicked their heels into their horses' flanks and galloped down the highway.

They had not ridden far, however, when Aylaen reined in her horse.

"Skylan!" she cried. "Look! Look at our ship!"

At first Skylan could see nothing out of the ordinary. The *Venjekar* floated on an ocean of silvery grass that rippled in the wind, mocking the waves on which the ship should have been riding. Skylan fondly traced the ship's graceful lines, from the stern to the curve of the neck, the dragon's proud head, the burning red eyes.

Eyes that glared triumphantly.

"Kahg has come back!" Skylan breathed.

"Has he?" Wulfe asked eagerly, and he raised himself up on the horse's rump to see. The next moment, he burst into tears and buried his face in his hands. The moment after that, he began fumbling beneath his shirt.

"Here! Take it!" he cried.

He pulled out the spiritbone and, still blubbering, thrust it into Aylaen's hands.

She stared at it, then shook her head. "The dragon brought this to you, Wulfe."

"Kahg wants you to have it," said Wulfe. "I was only keeping it safe."

"You must keep it safe for a little longer," Aylaen told him. "Take it back to the ship. Tell Sigurd you found it."

"Sigurd hates me," said Wulfe.

"If you show him the spiritbone, he will love you like a son," Skylan said. He added, more seriously, "I'm trusting you with this, Wulfe. We need the dragon to escape."

"You're trusting me," Wulfe said. Tears flooded his cheeks. He blinked his eyes furiously and slid off the back of the horse. He clutched the spiritbone in a grimy hand. "No ogre will get this. I promise."

He ran off down the hill, yelling over his shoulder, "If one tries, I'll rip out his throat!"

Skylan and Aylaen sat on their horses, watching Wulfe bound on all fours through the grass.

"Do you think the Dragon Kahg brought us to this place?" Aylaen asked softly.

Skylan would have liked to say yes, to blame this fate on someone else: dragon, gods. But he had promised Torval there would be no more lies.

"My folly brought us here," said Skylan. He smiled reassuringly at her and added, "But the dragon can damn well get us home!"

They rode off. If they had waited a moment longer, they would have seen the first ships of the ogre fleet sail into the harbor. The city of Sinaria now lay dreaming, but she would soon wake to a nightmare.

CHAPTER

14

Acronis wended his way confidently through the maze of streets in which Skylan would have soon been hopelessly lost. A few carts and wagons were out making their nightly deliveries. Men had no need for torches; the bright moon reflecting off the white pavement outshone the light of Aelon that beamed from the dome of his shrine. Skylan thought once he caught sight of Zahakis entering a tavern, but they rode past too quickly for him to tell for certain. He forgot about Zahakis and concentrated on his own problems, which were numerous enough. Skylan had to talk to his dead friend.

As for Zahakis, he was going from tavern to tavern, spreading the news of the invasion and rounding up his men. He sent some home to fetch weapons and armor and to warn their families. Others had their weapons with them, and they swarmed out into the streets, commandeering the wagons and carts, turning them over in the street, and using them to form barricades. That would not stop the rampaging ogres, but might at least slow them down.

Zahakis warned the gang bosses, who left their haunts to man the barricades. While these preparations were under way, people began to shout and point. Those who had taken to the rooftops could see the flames of a signal fire blazing on one of the watchtowers.

Neighbor carried word to neighbor, pounding on doors and yelling underneath windows. Now the wails of children yanked from their warm beds blended with the sounds of pounding feet and shouted commands.

"If the ogres think they are going to be attacking a sleeping city," Zahakis said to himself with a grim smile, "they are going to be in for a rude awakening."

Far from the city, away from the commotion and the cries of children and the tramping of booted feet, the Temple of Aelon blazed with light. Warrior-priests and Temple guards had heard the calls of the Watchers and were reporting for duty, some of them struggling to put on their armor as they ran.

Priestesses, clutching their nightclothes around them, were being herded into the Temple where they were assured that Aelon would keep them safe. No one knew for certain what was going on. Terrible rumors flew about. But as terrible as the rumors were, they were not as terrible as the truth.

Raegar and Treia hastened toward the Shrine, where the warrior-priests and Temple guards were gathering. The place was in turmoil with men shouting orders and everyone running around in confusion. Raegar used his great height to see over the sea of heads in an effort to locate the Priest-General. Unable to find him, Raegar began to shove and bully his way through the crowd. He kept fast hold of Treia so that they would not be separated.

Guards stood before the doors leading to the inner offices. Raegar stated curtly that he had an urgent message for the Priest-General. The guard opened the door. Keeping a firm grip on Treia, Raegar entered. The guard shut the door behind them and they were suddenly engulfed in silence. The Watchers knelt before their bowls of fire and water, sending and receiving information. Sometimes one would rise to his feet and glide out, bearing news or asking for instruction.

The door to the office of the Priest-General stood open. He had called a hasty meeting with his officers and was just finishing.

"Get your men into position." Xydis was giving final orders. "The protection of the Church grounds is our first priority."

Catching sight of Raegar and Treia, Xydis motioned for them to come into his office and dismissed his officers. After that, a Watcher came with a message, which he delivered in a whisper. The Priest-General listened in silence, his brow furrowing. He looked at Raegar and frowned. The Watcher bowed and returned to his duties. Xydis shut the door and began to pace the room.

"This is a disaster!" he said. "We have been caught completely un-prepared. I am summoned to the Palace. The Empress is furious."

He fixed his piercing gaze on Raegar. "Tell me that I can bring her good news."

"You can bring her the best, lord," said Raegar, smiling expan-sively. "Her Imperial Majesty need have no fear for Sinaria. Aelon will save us. *And* the Vektan dragon."

Xydis quit pacing. "You can summon it?"

"I can summon the dragon, Worshipful Sir," said Treia. "I know the ritual."

This was Treia's moment of triumph. Her reward for the hard life she had endured, the sneers and slights and insults, the hardship and deprivation, the hours of kneeling on the wooden floor, shivering in the bitter cold, listening to Draya's interminable praying to a god-dess who had, in the end, forsaken her.

"The ritual must be performed in a large open area," Treia contin-ued.

"We were thinking the arena where they play the Para Dix would be suitable," Raegar suggested.

"An ideal location," said Xydis. "I will inform the Empress. She will want to be present."

Treia was annoyed. The summoning was a religious ritual, meant to be performed with solemn ceremony. This was not a game, not a spectacle. She could see Raegar was pleased by the thought of being noticed by the Empress, so Treia bit her tongue and said nothing. She was having trouble enough combating a flutter of fear in the pit of her stomach. She had failed before when summoning an ordi-nary dragon such as Kahg. She would not fail now; she *could* not. Hevis was with her.

She had given the god his sacrifice. Aylaen was dead. The Torgun were all dead.

"The first ships have been sighted sailing into the harbor," Xydis said. "We must wait to summon the dragon until the entire fleet is assembled; the dragon can destroy every ship in the ogre fleet and wipe out the ogre army. A great victory for Aelon. A great vic-tory."

He rubbed his hands, then frowned at Raegar. "It is fortunate you brought me this good news, my friend, otherwise you would be in my bad graces."

"What have I done to deserve your anger, Priest-General?" Raegar asked, startled.

"Legate Acronis is still alive. The attempt on his life failed. Several Temple guards were killed in the fight. He was warned by that kinsman of yours, Skylan."

Raegar's jaw sagged. "But . . . that's impossible, Worshipful Sir. Skylan and the other Vindrasi were trapped in the catacombs by the lemures. I saw them myself. They could not have escaped—"

"And yet they did," said Xydis testily. "This was the news the Watcher brought me when you arrived. Semelon reported that the barbarians threatened her life if she did not free his men from the lemures. At least"—Xydis turned graciously to Treia—"you will be glad to know your sister survived."

"Aylaen . . . alive . . ." Treia stared at him wildly. She had to grasp the back of a chair to keep from collapsing.

Aylaen . . . alive! Treia saw Raegar and Xydis talking. They were speaking to her. Their mouths moved, but she had no idea what they were saying. Raegar seemed concerned. He took hold of her by the elbow and escorted her out the door, following Xydis. She realized in horror they were taking her to the treasure vault.

Taking her to the spiritbone of the Vektia and an angry, vengeful god.

Acronis and his escort rode up to the fane of the Spirit Priestesses at a gallop. They could hear within the fane the voices of women chanting the name of Aelon, calling upon him to protect them from their foes. Acronis dismounted his horse practically before the beast had stopped running and strode swiftly to the door. Two of his soldiers accompanied him. Keeper remained in the shadows, holding the horses.

Acronis pounded on the door.

"I am Legate Acronis," he called impatiently. "Open this door!"

The chanting ceased suddenly. There was a brief wait and what sounded like voices hurriedly conferring, then a scraping noise as a bar was lifted. The door opened a crack. A young woman peered out. Seeing Acronis in his shining armor and purple cape, accompanied by two soldiers in their winged helms, she gave a sigh of relief and flung the door wide open.

"Legate, you are welcome. Please come inside."

"This is not a social visit," Acronis said. "The city is about to come under attack—"

"Yes," said the priestess calmly. "We were warned. We have been praying to Aelon."

"You are in danger here." Acronis pushed his way past her and walked inside the fane. His two escorts accompanied him. "The other priestesses are gathering in the main Temple. You are to join them there."

"We are not in danger," said the priestess with a serene smile. "I told you. We are praying to Aelon. He will protect us."

The other priestesses smiled and murmured their agreement. Acronis regarded the women with exasperation mingled with sorrow. The young priestess could not have been much older than Chloe.

"Ogres do not believe in Aelon," said Acronis harshly. "What do you think will happen when ogre warriors find this temple filled with women? They will give praise to their gods. Do you know what ogres do to human females? They rape the young ones and take them captive back to their homeland. The older ones, they rape and then kill."

The young priestess paled and cast an uncertain glance over her shoulder at one of the older women.

"I thank you for your care, Legate," said the priestess, coming forward. "Aelon will protect us—"

"Aelon protects those in the Temple, Priestess, by surrounding them with men carrying swords."

The women began to argue among themselves. Acronis glanced at his escorts and slightly shrugged his shoulders. They shifted impatiently, their armor rattling.

"Very well," said the older priestess at last. "We will come with you. Undoubtedly, Aelon sent you."

"Undoubtedly," said Acronis dryly. "And now, you must make haste. The signal fires are lighted. The enemy ships have been sighted in the harbor."

One of the younger priestesses gave a frightened cry. The older one frowned at her. As they started to blow out the lights and remove objects from the altar, one of the soldiers cast an alarmed glance at Acronis.

"Please, Priestess, you must leave now. My men will see to it that all the valuables are removed to a place of safety."

As Acronis spoke, he began to shepherd the women out the door, reassuring them in soothing tones that they had nothing to fear, keeping them moving.

"Be quick, you two!" he ordered Skylan and Aylaen as he gestured toward the altar. "We are going ahead. You can catch up with us on the road."

The two saluted and moved toward the altar that was ablaze with lights.

Acronis finally maneuvered his charges outside the fane and into the garden. The sight of Keeper, an ogre, caused a flutter of panic until one of the women recognized him from the Para Dix games.

"Get them started toward the Temple," said Acronis. "Hand them off to the first warrior-priest you see and circle back to us."

Keeper nodded. "What is Skylan doing?"

"He says he is going to talk to a ghost," said Acronis.

The Legate waited until he saw Keeper and his flock of priestesses heading off in the direction of the Temple, then walked quietly back to the Shrine. Acronis did not enter. He stood in the doorway, hidden in the shadows.

Acronis was a scientist. Invading ogres, assassins, even his soulwrenching grief for his daughter could not stop his pursuit of knowledge. Chloe would understand, he reflected.

He watched Aylaen walk to the center of the Shrine. She removed her helm and shook out her red hair. Her face was pale, luminous. Her green eyes were clear. Her voice was steady. She placed four candlesticks in a square, and four in the square to form a circle. Then, standing in the square, she spoke quietly to the empty air.

"Garn, I have come to ask you to forgive me. I was wrong to want you to return to this life when you have found glory with Torval. I forged the chains that dragged you back, kept you bound. I compelled you to remain in this world when your spirit wanted to go with the gods. I love you, Garn," Aylaen said, her voice gentle, but not faltering. "I will always love you. But I, too, must go with the gods. We will meet again in Torval's Hall and there we will embrace."

Acronis watched with interest, hoping to see a ghost as he had been promised. But no ghost appeared.

Skylan removed his helm and came to stand beside Aylaen. He was not as composed as she was. He had to clear his throat before he could speak.

"Garn, my friend," he said huskily, "I wish I could say the chains that I used to bind you were forged of love, but they were not. They were made of guilt. I blamed myself for your death. If I had listened to you . . ."

Skylan had to stop talking. He wiped his hand over his eyes and nose, then drew in a shaking breath and said quietly, "I listen to you now, my friend. Whenever I am about to do anything reckless or selfish, I hear your voice. You taught me patience, forbearance. You gave me the wisdom to understand what the goddess was trying to tell me. You have forgiven me and I forgive myself. We will meet again in Torval's Hall and there we will embrace."

Acronis, from the shadows, said softly, "Chloe, my own dear child, will you wait for me in Torval's Hall? I may have trouble finding my way. . . ."

"She will wait," said a woman's voice. "She waits to hear the stories you will tell her."

Acronis turned to see a woman clad in armor that gleamed in the moonlight like the scales of a dragon. Her helm was adorned with dragon wings. She smiled at him and then left him, trembling and shaken, to enter the Shrine.

She walked into the circle of candles. Seeing her, radiant and beautiful and awful, Skylan and Aylaen sank to their knees.

"Vindrash," said Aylaen, "forgive me for being in the house of your foe. I came to free Garn. . . ."

"You have already done so. His spirit has joined the heroes in Torval's Hall," said Vindrash. She glanced back over her shoulder at Acronis and smiled gently. "The last I saw, he was dancing with a new young friend."

Acronis sank to his knees. He did not believe in gods and he was in the presence of a goddess.

Vindrash turned back. "What about you, Skylan? Do you ask my forgiveness?"

"I have asked so often, blessed Vindrash," said Skylan. "I fear you must be weary of the sound of my voice. But I do," he added, raising his eyes to hers, "with all my heart."

Vindrash laid her hand upon his forehead. "Five dragonbones, Skylan Ivorson. Do you know the secret?"

"I believe so, Vindrash," said Skylan in a troubled voice.

"You do or you don't," she said.

Skylan paused, then said firmly, "I know the secret."

"Then you know what you must do. Fight well in the Para Dix, Skylan Ivorson," said Vindrash. "I have a wager with Torval on this game. My fish knife against his shining sword."

The goddess vanished, leaving behind the sparkling shimmer of dragon scales in Acronis's mind.

"The Para Dix?" Aylaen said, puzzled. "What does she mean? We have to find Treia—"

"We will find Treia in the Para Dix arena," said Skylan, rising to his feet.

"But why would Treia be there?" Aylaen asked. Her tone sharpened. "Skylan, tell me what's going on. This has something to do with the secret of the Vektan dragonbone. You told the goddess you know the secret. What is it?"

"Aylaen, I need for you to go back to the ship. Keeper will take you—"

"You are not getting rid of me," said Aylaen. "Treia is my sister. I'm coming with you."

Skylan heaved a sigh that seemed to come from the depths of his soul. He walked out the door and drew up, startled to find Acronis standing in front of him.

"You said to me, 'If we can find the spiritbone, we can save the city.' What did you mean by that?"

"I don't have time to explain," said Skylan, and he added shortly, as he hurried on, "Tell me how to find the arena. Then you and Keeper take Aylaen somewhere safe."

"What is going on?" Acronis demanded.

Skylan hesitated, then said, "Treia has the spiritbone of one of the Vektan dragons. I believe she is going to try to summon the dragon."

"I'm coming with you, of course. I wouldn't miss this for the world," said Acronis.

"You don't understand, sir," said Skylan, casting an anguished glance at Aylaen. "I can't allow Treia to summon the dragon! I must stop her—any way I can."

"You think you might have to kill her," said Acronis. "Kill the sister of the woman you love." Skylan stood, agonizing. Acronis rested his hand on Skylan's shoulder. "Trust in that god of yours. He's done well by you so far. I will take you to the arena. You will never find your way through the streets without me."

They left the fane. Aylaen was already on her horse, waiting with Keeper, who said he had handed the women safely over to one of the Temple guards.

Acronis lifted his head, breathed deeply of the night air. He did not know how many breaths he had left, but it didn't matter. All his life, he had been bound like a slave to something: to ambition, to politics, to wealth. Everything was gone. He had given it all away. He felt now as he felt sometimes upon his ship when he walked the deck in the moonlight and saw nothing around him but the vast dark sea and the vast dark sky and the stars that sparkled like the scales of a dragon.

He had seen the face of a goddess.

He could not wait to tell Chloe!

15

Treia stood in the center of the arena near the sacred fire pit, holding the Vektia spiritbone. Sliver moonlight spilled over the empty benches, pouring down onto the field in a cascade that seemed to grow brighter with every passing moment. Treia wished the hateful moon would fall from the heavens. She wanted darkness, needed darkness. She had to talk to Hevis. She had to convince him to give her the ritual, even though she had failed to give him the sacrifice.

In the palace, the Empress had been pleased to hear from the Priest-General that a dragon was going to come to fight for the Sinarians. The Empress didn't have to worry any longer about ham-fisted ogres lumbering about the Imperial Palace breaking the porcelain. She wanted to witness this spectacle and sent word that she was going to come to her box in the arena as soon as she changed her clothes, invited her friends, found her little dog, who had run off again, and ordered her slaves to pack the wine and food baskets.

The Priest-General was already in the arena, thinking of his future. The Empress blamed him for the ogre invasion, and by stopping the ogres and providing her with an evening's entertainment, he was certain to regain her favor. He had his eye on the Legate's estates and wealth.

The unfortunate fact that Acronis was not dead was only a minor impediment to the attainment of Xydis's goal. Semelon had reported that the Legate had ridden off in company with the barbarians. The Priest-General had men searching for him.

In the streets, the people, led by Zahakis, were taking upon themselves the defense of their city. Reports came to him that the first ships of the ogre fleet had begun landing their troops. Ogre soldiers were swarming onto the docks and beaches. As soon as sufficient numbers were assembled, their godlords would storm the watchtowers, deal with any defenders, and open the gates to Sinaria.

"I'm going to be sick," said Treia.

Clutching her stomach, she handed the spiritbone to Raegar and ran toward the latrines, which were located behind the grandstand.

Treia looked over her shoulder to make certain she had not been followed. Raegar would give her a few moments privacy in case she was truly sick, and then he would come to make certain she was all right. She did not have much time.

Covered by curtains, shielded from the moonlight, the latrines consisted of a long row of benches with holes cut in them situated directly over a trench filled with running water. The area was cleaned by slaves, but the stench lingered. Treia gagged and covered her mouth and gave way to nausea that had caused her stomach to roil ever since the Priest-General had put the spiritbone into her hands.

When she was finished vomiting, she gasped out the name of the god.

Hevis had been waiting for her impatiently, it seemed, for he appeared almost before she finished speaking his name. He was no longer a disembodied face of fire. He was a warrior, clad in armor, and he held a sword in his hand. He was grim and implacable and he said nothing, but waited for her to speak.

Trembling with terror, Treia kept her eyes lowered, fearing to face his wrath.

"Aylaen was meant to die," said Treia through quivering lips. "They were all meant to die! You were supposed to have your sacrifice—"

"But I didn't," said Hevis, and his voice was cold as black winter's night. "You should have killed her yourself. Knife in the back, poison . . ."

"I know, I know," Treia said, choked. "Forgive me. I will . . . next time. . . ."

"There may not be a next time," said the god.

Treia gave a strangled sob.

Hevis stirred, his hand flexing on the hilt of his sword. He shifted his gaze in the direction of the bay where the ogre fleet was gathering.

"But I find I cannot pass up this chance to strike a blow at our foes." Hevis raised his sword and shook it at the heavens. "Do you hear me, Aelon? Do you hear me, Gods of Raj? Do you hear me, Torval, as you sit sulking in your great Hall? Look at me and see true power!"

Treia drew in her breath and, greatly daring, raised her head. "Do you mean . . . you will help me summon the dragon?"

"The sacrifice will be mine to take when and where I decide to take it," said Hevis, turning his fiery gaze upon her. "Are we agreed?"

"Yes, yes!" Treia cried, sinking to her knees, faint with relief. She barely heard him and did not understand him, but it didn't matter. She was desperate and would have agreed to anything he asked of her. "What is the ritual?"

" 'The air blows on the fire that consumes the earth that boils the water that douses the fire. When the smoke rises, throw down the bone.' "

Hevis disappeared. Treia rose shakily to her feet, using a wall for support. She stood a moment in the darkness to collect her thoughts, imprinting his words on her mind. Then, feeling stronger, she walked back out onto the playing field. Raegar was already coming to look for her.

"Are you all right?" he asked, regarding her with concern. "You are white as milk."

She gave him a reassuring smile. "I prayed to the god. All is well."

"Thanks be to Aelon," said Raegar.

Skylan had impressed upon Acronis the need for haste, and at first they made good time. The road that led them through the Temple grounds was almost deserted. The sounds of chanting and prayers to Aelon could be heard rising from the Temple.

But when they reached the city streets, their progress slowed almost to a crawl. The streets were clogged with people and barricades, noise, light, and confusion. Seeing the Legate, resplendent in his armor, the people cheered him. He told them he needed to reach the harbor and ordered them to clear a path for him and his escort. They were eager to obey, but it took time to dismantle the barricades.

Skylan kept trying to reassure himself that Treia would not summon the dragon before dawn, but he was frantic with impatience to reach the arena. He sat on his horse, fretting and fuming at the delays. Everywhere they stopped, people begged the Legate for news. He would tell them that all would be well; the enemy would most certainly be driven back. They cheered him and his soldiers again when they left.

No one cheered Keeper. At one barricade, a rock struck the ogre on the back of the head and he swayed in the saddle, almost falling. Skylan rode to his side, but the ogre waved him away.

"I have a hard head," he said.

Skylan saw blood flowing down the back of the ogre's neck. Acronis looked very grim, and after that, they took the side streets, though the going was slower.

Just when Skylan thought they would never arrive, he saw the vast, open playing field through a break in the cluster of buildings. He noted with astonishment people in the grandstands and more people gathered about the fire pit in the moonlight. He recognized one of them, a man far taller than the others. Raegar was there, which meant Treia must be there as well.

Skylan was breathing a sigh, thinking they would be in time, when Acronis suddenly reined in his horse.

"What is it?" Skylan asked. "What is wrong?"

"Listen," said Acronis.

Skylan yanked off his helm and then he heard it—a dull, roaring sound that was like waves pounding on a distant shore. But they were far from the ocean and Skylan was trying to figure out what could make such an odd sound, when he saw an orange glow light the sky. Not dawn. He was facing west, not east. The orange glow grew brighter and then he knew.

The sound was from waves, but not of water. Waves of ogre warriors roaring their battle cries to the rhythmic beating of drums and blasting horns.

"They're burning the warehouses," said Acronis. "And the harbor fortifications. After that, they will set fire to the houses—"

Skylan didn't wait to hear more. He kicked his horse in the flanks and rode on. He needed no further guidance. The arena lay directly ahead of him. If he could see the flames, Treia would be able to see them as well, and she would know that the ogres were not going to wait for the dawn.

And neither would she.

Aylaen caught up with him, and rode beside him. "Thank you for coming to save Treia. I know you don't like her and that you're doing this for me."

Skylan saw fire burning in the fire pit. He could see Treia reflected in the light of the leaping flames and Raegar standing beside her along with other warrior-priests. They were pointing at the orange glow in the sky.

"I'm not trying to save Treia!" Skylan dragged his horse to a halt and turned to Aylaen. "You want to know the secret to the Vektan dragon? I'll tell you!"

He raised his hand, five fingers spread wide. "Five dragons. The only way to control one is to control five. All five at once. All five together. Five dragonbones at the start of every game."

Aylaen stared at him in bewilderment. "What are you saying?"

"Treia is going to summon *one* dragon. She won't be able to control it, not with the help of Hevis or Aelon or Vindrash or all the gods in the universe. Because it is only one dragon."

Aylaen went livid. "You're not going to save her! You're going to kill her!"

"If Treia summons the Vektan dragon, she will destroy us and everything around us. I have to stop her, Aylaen. Any way I can."

Skylan rode on. He topped a rise and galloped down it, only to find, to his dismay, another barricade blocking the highway. Men were stacking tables and barrels and chairs in a large heap. Skylan saw a gap and guided his horse's head toward it. Men yelled at him, waving their arms, trying to stop him. He kept going and they flung themselves out of the way of his horse's hooves. Lying low on the beast's neck, he urged the horse to jump.

He thought of the many times back in his homeland when he had ridden his horse, Blade, a wedding present from Draya. He had loved that horse. Together, they had jumped creeks, fallen logs, and hedgerows, running for the pure pleasure of feeling the wind in their faces.

The horse lifted its legs and made the jump, landing on the pavement beyond with a clatter of hooves. Gathering itself, the horse raced ahead. Skylan looked back to see that he had lost Aylaen. She was a good rider; he'd let her ride Blade sometimes, but she had never taken a jump.

He heard her calling his name, pleading with him to wait. He kept riding. It was better this way. She would hate him forever, but at least he wouldn't add to that the burden of forcing her to watch. Behind him, Acronis was yelling at the men, ordering them to dismantle the barricade to let them pass.

The row of buildings came to an end. The highway continued, leading to the Para Dix arena. On game day, the highway would be jammed with people hurrying to the arena, carrying their children in their arms.

This night, the highway was empty. Skylan urged his horse on. The bowl of the arena spread out before him. The fire burned in the fire pit in the center. He could see Treia reflected in its light.

He didn't know the ritual to summon a Vektan dragon. All he hoped was that it was long and complicated. He glanced again over his shoulder to see that Acronis, Keeper, and Aylaen had made their way through the barricade and were riding behind him.

He reached the outer row of seats, those that had been carved into the hillside. Skylan did not stop, but urged his horse down the stairs.

The war horse, trained to negotiate steep, rocky terrain, had no difficulty. As they reached the smooth grass of the arena, Skylan began to shout, calling Treia's name.

She was standing on the edge of the fire pit directly above the flames. She held a pitcher of water in one hand and an object that gleamed golden in the moonlight. Jewels flashed and sparkled.

Treia heard him shout and she turned her head. She probably couldn't see him, with her weak eyes, but she would know the sound of his voice.

Skylan yelled again with all the power of his lungs.

"Treia! Stop!"

She stared at him. Raegar, sword drawn, walked over to stand protectively beside her. Soldiers wearing the uniform of the Imperial Guard streamed out of the grandstand. The Priest-General pointed at Skylan and commanded someone to slay him.

Skylan saw the soldiers and dismissed them. They were on foot. They would never reach him in time. He kept his eyes on Treia and begged her, willed her, pleaded with her silently to stop.

She turned away from him, and, lifting the pitcher, poured water on the fire, partially dousing the flames. Smoke roiled up around her.

Skylan was weak with relief. Flinging himself off the horse, he hit the ground running. He was on one side of the fire pit. Treia stood on the other. She looked straight at him and gave a thin smile. Her lip curled slightly. She threw the spiritbone into the fire.

Skylan gasped in horror and jumped into the fire pit. Raegar started to leap in after him. Treia laid a restraining hand on his arm.

The spiritbone lay on top of a smoldering log. The fire burned hot. The water had doused part of the blaze, but tongues of flame licked the spiritbone.

"Too late," said Treia.

Skylan, looking up, could not see the stars. The gods, looking down, could not see the world.

The bright moonlight disappeared. The ogre warriors were plunged into darkness. They could see nothing beyond the fires of destruction, and they looked fearfully to their shamans, who stared uneasily at the black and starless sky.

The light that beamed from Aelon's temple went out. The people in the streets and on the barricades might as well have been struck blind. They, too, stared into the sky.

On board the *Venjekar,* the only light was the red fire in the eyes of the carved head of the Dragon Kahg. Sigurd hung the spirit-bone from the nail on the masthead where it belonged. Sheltered by the trees along the shore, the ship bobbed gently on the rippling surface of the river. The *Venjekar* had been hiding in the shadows, but now all the world was in shadow. The air was still, the heat oppressive. A pall of smoke from the burning buildings on the waterfront hung over the water.

"A storm must be brewing," said Sigurd.

In the arena, Treia was ecstatic. She had summoned the darkness. This was her doing. The fire in the fire pit still burned, and by its light, she could see that Xydis was impressed, Raegar awed.

A hot wind stirred her hair. She lifted her arms to the heavens and raised her voice.

"Dragon of the Vektia! You are mine to command!" She spoke the words, but no words came out.

Treia shivered. Where was her voice? She could feel the words in her throat, feel herself shouting them, but once they left her throat, they were swallowed by the darkness like the moon and the stars.

A sliver of terror pierced her. She tried again, concentrating all her being on the dragon.

"You are mine to command. . . ."

Empty nothings. Raegar was now staring at her in alarm. Xydis was starting to look worried. In the royal box, the Empress had applauded at first, charmed to see the moon and stars disappear, but as time passed and nothing else remarkable happened, she grew bored.

"We are leaving," she said, and picked up the little dog.

Wings, gray as smoke, trailed glowing sparks. Blue flame crackled and rippled over blue scales. Eyes, cold and pitiless and soulless, gazed down upon the world and saw a void that must be filled.

The Vektan dragon spread its blue fire wings. Rain fell in torrents. The dragon breathed and cyclones twisted out of its mouth. Lightning flared from its claws and thunder cracked from its mouth.

The wind began to rise and rise and kept on rising.

Panic welled up inside Treia. She could scarcely keep her eyes open for the rain blowing in her face. The wind smote her, trying to knock her down. She had to find the spiritbone. She had to hold it in her hands. Then, perhaps, she could gain control of the dragon.

"Hevis, help me!" she screamed.

But the god had fled, fearing Torval's wrath. It was Raegar who heard her. He turned to her, his face contorted with fear and rage. Beside him, Xydis was calling upon Aelon, demanding that the god seize the dragon and send it to fight ogres.

Aelon did not answer. He, too, was lost in the dark.

The rain deluged the fire, putting it out. The fire pit began to fill with water. Lightning flared and Treia saw the spiritbone and Skylan standing over it, reaching out his hand.

As Treia jumped into the fire pit, a bolt of lightning struck the touchstone boulder very near where she had been standing. The boulder shattered. Splinters of rock, sharp as spears, flew through the air. The shock wave rolled over the ground, knocking Treia down. She landed on her hands and knees in the water at the bottom of the fire pit.

The raindrops sliced flesh like lances, hailstones left bloody gashes. Then there was a shattering crash and the sounds of twisting lumber. The grandstands had collapsed. She heard screams and cries, but she couldn't look to see what had happened. Skylan had picked up the spiritbone. Treia leaped at him, smashing into him, fingernails tearing at his hand.

Strong hands closed over Treia's wrists and dragged her off Skylan.

"Treia, stop!" Aylaen begged. "There's nothing you can do. We have to reach the ship—"

Treia screamed and lashed out at her. "This is your fault. You should be dead! Why aren't you dead?"

Aylaen gasped and let go. Treia could not see Skylan for the rain and the darkness. He must have escaped. Treia tried to crawl out of the fire pit but the sides were made of brick that was wet and slippery. She caught sight of Raegar and cried out for him to help her.

Raegar stood staring at the body of Xydis. A splinter of the boulder had pierced the priest's chest. Blood and rain ran down his ceremonial robes. His eyes were wide open, glaring accusingly at the god who had failed him.

Hearing Treia's call, Raegar turned to her. She reached out her hands to him.

"Raegar, please!"

He looked at her and he looked down at Xydis and he looked back over his shoulder at what was left of the grandstands.

Raegar turned his back on her and ran, head down like a bull, through the rain and buffeting wind. He was leaving the arena, leaving her.

"Raegar!" Treia screamed, but her cry was torn to shreds by the wind.

A piece of debris picked up by the wind struck Treia in the head. She felt herself falling and she didn't care. She gave herself to the darkness, praying as the water closed over her it would be eternal.

Help me with Treia, Skylan!" Aylaen cried from the fire pit, where she was holding her sister's limp body, trying desperately to keep Treia's head above the rising water. "Something hit her! She's hurt!"

Aylaen had lost her helm in the wild ride from the city. Her red hair, plastered against her head, streamed like blood down her face.

"Skylan, she's my sister!" Aylaen said. "This is not her—"

"—fault?" Skylan asked grimly.

Aylaen opened her mouth and shut it again. She said nothing, but gazed at him with pleading eyes.

Skylan had hold of the spiritbone by its golden chain. Not knowing what else to do with it, he flung the chain over his head and thrust the dangling spiritbone beneath his armor. He took hold of Treia around the waist. She hung limply in his arms, dead weight.

"Give her to me!" yelled Keeper above the tumult of the storm.

The ogre's childlike face glistened in the flashes of lightning. Blood poured from a jagged cut on his cheek. The cut on the back of his head was still bleeding. Between him and Skylan, the two hauled Treia out of the pit. Keeper dumped her on the ground, then came back for Skylan and Aylaen.

Aylaen held up her arms and Keeper plucked her out. Skylan felt around his neck to make certain he had the spiritbone, then reached up a hand to Keeper. Placing one foot on the side of the fire pit, Skylan propelled himself upward. Keeper's heaving yank brought him the rest of the way.

The wind slammed into Skylan. The rain streamed down his face, blinding him. He grabbed hold of Aylaen and, clinging to each other, they fought their way through the driving rain and pounding hail, trying to reach Acronis, who was holding onto the horses. At times, they were blown to a standstill and could do nothing except try to keep their footing. Then the wind would lessen somewhat and they lurched on. Keeper came staggering after them, carrying Treia.

Skylan could not see the dragon, but he could hear its awful voice, howling and shrieking and rumbling. There was nowhere to hide from it. Death might come slamming into him at any moment. He had one thought in his mind and that was reaching his ship.

"The *Venjekar*!" he bawled at Acronis, moving close to be heard. "We have to reach the *Venjekar*!"

"And I must go home to Chloe!" Acronis yelled.

Fighting the wind, they managed to drag themselves onto the horses. Treia was starting to moan, regaining consciousness. She opened her eyes, staring around dazedly.

"Give her to me!" Aylaen had to shout to be heard.

Keeper glanced uncertainly at Skylan, who shrugged, knowing it would be useless to argue. The ogre hoisted Treia up into the saddle behind Aylaen. She grabbed her sister's hands and drew them around her waist, holding them fast.

Treia blinked her eyes and stared about in confusion. She had no idea where she was or what was going on. Aylaen kicked the beast into motion and Treia nearly tumbled off the back. She grabbed hold of Aylaen more out of terror than because she knew what was happening.

They rode out of the bowl of the arena. Once they reached the top of the hill, all they could see was rain and smoke, fire and death. They rode on.

Raegar ran through the city streets toward the shrine of Aelon, where the warrior-priests were gathered. He prayed as he ran. "Aelon, I can help you fight this battle, but you must help me! You must keep me alive!"

He said the prayer over and over, and either the god granted his prayer or Raegar was blessed by being far taller and stronger than most men. He waded through flood waters that carried others away.

He shoved aside heaps of rubble that impeded his path. Hit by flying debris, he shrugged off the pain and kept going.

The streets had turned into rivers. Bodies floated past him, bumped up against his legs. Here and there, some wretched survivor floundered in the water, searching for loved ones, crying out for help. Many of the buildings had collapsed or were collapsing.

Raegar ran on. Xydis was dead. Probably the Empress was dead, as well, as were many of the nobles who had been with her in the grandstand. Raegar was wounded, but he was alive. Sinaria was wounded, but she, too, would survive. Sinaria would need a leader, someone to take charge in this time of crisis, someone to stand defiant, someone to fight back.

When Raegar reached the Shrine, he saw, with fast-beating heart, that it was still standing. He found men and women gathered outside, pounding on the doors, which were bolted fast, keeping the unworthy from entering.

Raegar shoved people aside and beat on the doors, shouting, "I bring word from Xydis!"

They opened the door to him and he plunged through it. The wretched people outside tried to cram their way in. The warrior-priests pushed them out and slammed the door shut.

The Shrine was filled with Temple guards and warrior-priests. They had gone out to man the barricades and do battle, but when the dragon struck, they gave up the fight to seek refuge with the god.

Raegar was astonished at the relative quiet inside the Shrine. His ears rang with the din of the chaos outside, and for a moment the ringing drowned out the voices of those who gathered around him demanding news.

Raegar needed everyone to hear him, and he began to shoulder his way through the crowd. Mounting the podium, Raegar assessed the situation. He could not have asked for better. No one was in charge. No one had taken command. No one knew for certain what was going on. Rumors were flying; the latest being that the ogres were on their way to slaughter everyone.

He raised his hands and a hush fell. His imposing height and impressive appearance served him well. He was accustomed to the acoustics of the building, knew where to pitch his voice to gain the maximum effect.

"It is my sad duty to report that Priest-General Xydis is dead,"

Raegar announced. "He died in my arms of wounds suffered battling the dragon."

Gasps and cries rippled through the crowd.

"We commend his soul to Aelon," Raegar continued, his voice strengthening, "but now is not the time to grieve. Now is the time for action. The ogres set fire to our city. Their evil gods flooded our streets. The dragon summoned by Aelon did battle with them, and our god has been victorious! Our enemies are defeated. Even now, the ogre warriors are fleeing our city in panic."

Raegar was lying, of course. He looked down at the faces gazing up at him, faces that had been pale with fear but were now flushed with hope. They needed to believe Aelon was still in control, still watching over them.

His voice boomed and thundered around the hall. "It is true that countless numbers of our people have been killed. It is true that much of Sinaria lies in ruins. I have heard that our beloved Empress may be among the dead. My faith wavered. I doubted in Aelon. Yes, I admit it!"

His gaze swept those in the Temple. No one spoke. No one dared to breathe.

"I was given to know the truth. My faith is being tested. Aelon is asking me if I am strong enough to go forward in faith, carrying his banner, to complete the destruction of our foes!"

The crowd cheered. No more sneers, no more insults. These fine people were ready to follow him, the slave, the barbarian.

"Our enemies are now escaping Sinaria with a great treasure in their possession! A treasure they stole from us when their gods murdered the Priest-General. I say we go after them and take it back! Who is with me?"

The cheering was thunderous. Raegar had a difficult time forcing people to quiet down long enough to listen to his plan.

"Our path will not be easy," he told them. "We will have to leave this place of safety and endure the flood and the fire. But be assured, as I am, that Aelon is with us, that his hand will guide us."

He issued commands and men hastened to obey him. As for Raegar, his faith was restored. He had no doubts. Somewhere in heaven, Aelon vowed revenge.

The dragon, trailing fire from its wings and hurling bolts of lightning, swept over the city, the flames burning so hot that the deluge of rainwater could not put out the fires. The wind-whipped inferno leaped from building to building. Those trapped inside rushed out, only to drown in the flash floods that had turned streets into rivers. The barricades caught fire and were swept away. Burning wreckage swirling on top of blazing water surged down the streets setting fire to everything it touched.

Skylan saw at once that riding into the city was to ride into certain death. Acronis realized the same and turned his horse's head. Without a word, they followed the Legate. They galloped across grasslands, rode through olive groves, trampled vineyards. They saw farmhouses in flames, cattle and sheep and pigs running wild or lying dead in the fields. They found bridges washed out and had to ford raging streams.

Skylan immediately lost all sense of direction and he wondered how Acronis knew where he was. His way lit by the flaring lightning and the lurid glow of blazing pine trees, Acronis rode on unerringly, pausing at the tops of hills and rises to get his bearings, then leading them on. When the fire-streaming wings and hideous roar came close, Skylan and his comrades sought shelter in ravines, hunkering down, enduring the terror until the dragon had flown on to wreak havoc somewhere else.

They rode and rode until they came upon one of the man-made sluices that carried waste from the city. Skylan saw objects bobbing in the water. At first he thought they were logs and then a sheet of lightning swept across the sky. He saw faces and he realized that the logs were corpses, hundreds of corpses. He sat on his horse gazing into the murky water, into the staring eyes and gaping mouths, the straggling hair and cold flesh, and he knew he would see this terrible sight until his own eyes closed in death.

The bridge across the sluice was gone. They would have to ride through the dreadful river of carnage. Acronis led the way, urging his horse to keep going even when the bodies bumped into the beast, causing it to shudder.

"Don't look, Treia," Aylaen said, urging her horse forward.

"Look, Treia!" Skylan wanted to shout. He wanted to seize her and force her to look at what she'd done. Treia rode slumped over, her head pressed against Aylaen's back. Her eyes were tightly shut.

Aylaen made it as far as the bank of the sluice and then her horse stopped, shaking its head and shivering. Keeper took the reins from her hand and pulled the terrified horse through the water.

Skylan waited until the rest were safely across before he entered the horror-filled stream. A glint of metal caught his eye. He looked down to see a body wearing armor. The dead man's eyes stared straight into his and Skylan recognized Zahakis.

Skylan checked his horse. He didn't know what to do. He could call Acronis, perhaps carry the body out of the water. But even as the thought crossed his mind, he had to let it go. The dead were with the gods. This was a night when the living had to look after themselves. "We will meet in Torval's Hall," Skylan told Zahakis.

The body collided with another body and slowly turned in the water and drifted on down the stream.

Skylan urged his horse on.

They rode so long that he was afraid they were lost, and then he recognized, in a lightning flash, the practice field at the villa. Skylan took heart; they were not far now from the river where, hopefully, Sigurd was still waiting for them.

Acronis, eager to reach home, pushed his tired horse and galloped ahead of them. Then he jerked on the reins so sharply that his horse twisted and nearly foundered. Acronis sat in the saddle staring straight ahead, his face gray and set as a granite cliff in the rain.

His villa was on fire. Flames were eating through the roof and flaming from the windows. The outbuildings constructed of timber were all ablaze. The trees, the roses, the atrium that Chloe loved, were piles of ashes. As they watched, part of the roof collapsed, sending up an immense cloud of cinders and sparks.

"I remember you told me once that you send your warriors to meet their god in ships of fire," said Acronis. His voice was toneless, held no emotion. Skylan could see the flames reflected in the man's dark eyes.

Around them, the wind had lessened, the rain plummeted straight down, the lightning spread across the sky in sheets of blue-white.

"My daughter's funeral pyre," said Acronis, and a bleak smile touched his lips. He sighed and his voice quivered. "She would like this much better than being entombed in the catacombs. She wouldn't have liked the dark."

A bolt of lightning sizzled through the air, striking a nearby tree. They were so used to the noise that none of them flinched.

Acronis stirred. "Where is your ship?"

"My men carried it to the river."

"You plan to sail downriver to the sea?"

Skylan nodded. He was keeping a wary eye out for the dragon.

"Navigating the river is tricky, especially now that the waters are rising. I have sailed it since I was a child," said Acronis. "You will need my help." He glanced at Skylan. "If you will have me."

Skylan was astonished. He didn't know what to say. He could imagine Sigurd's reaction, that of the others. They might well kill Acronis the moment he set foot on the ship, and Skylan didn't know that he would much blame them.

"Poor Zahakis," said Acronis. "This is not much of an inheritance. Still, he will have the land. He can build his own villa."

"What are you doing?" Keeper roared, riding up to them. The rain was increasing. Hailstones began to fall again, rattling on Skylan's helm and his armor. "Waiting for the world to end?"

They kicked their weary horses to a trot and rode down the steeply sloping hills toward the slave compound. Skylan had been worried that something might have happened to prevent his men from hauling the *Venjekar* to the river, but the ship was gone and Skylan breathed easier.

He rode around the back of the compound and bent down over his horse's neck, searching for signs of his ship's passage. He found the trench the keel had cut into the ground, the flattened grass on either side. The trail was easy to follow and gave all of them renewed hope.

The dragon was still marauding, still raining down destruction from the heavens. One lightning bolt would turn the *Venjekar* into a fire ship. He would sail down a flooding river out to sea where the ogre fleet was between him and home.

Still, Skylan clung to the belief that if he could reach the *Venjekar*, all would be well. The Torgun had their freedom and they had their ship and they had their dragon. The Torgun stood together. Nothing could stop them. In his mind, he was already setting his foot upon the soil of his homeland.

Which made it all the more shocking to reach the bank of the river and find the *Venjekar* gone.

Skylan roamed the riverbank, cursing Sigurd for a fool and a coward for sailing off and abandoning his friends. But Skylan did Sigurd an injustice. Sigurd might be many things, but he was neither a fool nor a coward. The Dragon Kahg had made the decision to run.

The Torgun were elated with their freedom. They lifted up the *Venjekar,* and though their numbers were far fewer than would have normally been needed, they were able to haul the ship over the wall and drag the ship, singing, down to the river.

They were about halfway there when Wulfe appeared. Sigurd scowled to see the boy and told him to get lost. Instead of obeying, Wulfe handed him the spiritbone.

"Skylan said you would like me now," said Wulfe.

Sigurd stopped dead in his tracks.

"Where did you get that?" He snatched the spiritbone from Wulfe.

"The dragon gave it to me," said Wulfe. "I gave it to Aylaen and she gave it to Skylan and he said I was to bring it to you."

"Where is Skylan?" Sigurd asked.

Wulfe shrugged. He had no idea.

Mystified, Sigurd looked at the dragon. Kahg's eyes gleamed red in the darkness. Sigurd shrugged and ordered the men to keep going.

They launched the ship in the river at about the time Treia was pouring water on the fire in the fire pit. The Torgun boarded and were breaking out the oars, Wulfe was scampering down into the hold, and Sigurd was hanging the spiritbone on the nail on the prow when the Vektan dragon spread its wings and blotted out the stars.

The Dragon Kahg looked into the heavens, and although he had never before seen one of the Five, he recognized it immediately.

The Five Vektan dragons. All dragons honored and revered these wondrous creatures that were godlike, wise and powerful, all-seeing and all-knowing.

Ilyrion, the great dragon who had created the world and fought Torval for a thousand years, had not been defeated by Torval, as the Vindrasi believed. Dragons believed that Ilyrion, seeing that their battle was having devastating effects on the world she loved, had sacrificed herself. The Five Vektan dragons sprang from her bony crest as her blood rained down from the heavens.

The world belonged to the Vektan Five. Torval and the other gods were viewed by the dragons as the world's caretakers. Vindrash, born of the blood of Ilyrion, served the Five, giving each of five gods one of the Five spiritbones to keep safe.

Eons passed and other strange gods found the world and sought to dislodge the old gods. These interlopers could not find the power of creation; they had no idea it had been embodied in the Five Vektan dragons. Thus Kahg had been furious to discover that Horg had given one of the spiritbones of the Vektia to the ogres and the Gods of Raj. The dragons had been appalled to discover Sund's betrayal, that he had given yet another spiritbone to Aelon.

The dragons did not blame Vindrash for the losses. Their dragon goddess had been driven to the extreme of taking on human form in order to hide from her foes, who were growing in strength. The dragons were starting to fear that the old gods might be too weak to survive.

Now would come the time of the Vektia. Now the Five would return in triumph. Dragons, true dragons, would save the world.

"I will fly with him, the greatest of our kind," Kahg vowed, and his being began to coalesce around his spiritbone.

To fly with the Vektia! What dragon did not dream of that? Kahg would be nothing, of course. A grain of sand amidst glittering diamonds. The Vektan dragon would not even deign to notice him. But to see with his own eyes such magnificence, such awful beauty. To be able to live the rest of his life knowing he had flown in the shadow of the wings of gods.

But the shadow was dark and bloated. It blotted out the stars and swallowed the moon. It looked like death given wings, a tail, a head, and a crest. Death made to look like a dragon. Death made in mockery of dragons.

The Dragon Kahg was baffled. What was this hideous monster? Where was the Vektia?

Lightning crackled from the dragon's claws. The beast opened its hideous maw and a roaring wind swept down from the heavens, flattening the willow trees on the distant side of the bank, tearing the roots from the ground with rending, snapping sounds, and hurling them into the river. The wind struck the *Venjekar* a blow that seemed to Kahg to be personal, malevolent, aimed at him. The ship heeled and nearly went under.

It was then Kahg knew the truth as the gods had always known. Creation is destruction. Destruct to create. Create to destroy.

The Dragon Kahg struggled to right the ship in the lashing rain, to keep it afloat. The *Venjekar* left the shore and began to sail away.

"Sigurd! Stop!" Bjorn cried. "What are you doing? We have to wait for Skylan and Aylaen!"

"I'm not the one sailing the goddam ship!" Sigurd roared. He pointed at the dragon.

Shaken to the soul, Kahg wanted only to flee the hideous thing in the sky. He roared out the name of Vindrash. The goddess either could not or would not answer.

Hailstones thudded on the deck and the heads of the Torgun, driving them to seek shelter in the hold. Lightning smeared the sky. The smoke of the burning city lay on the banks like a hideous fog. The *Venjekar* crept along, hugging the shore, hiding among the rushes and the trailing branches of the ruined willows.

Kahg could hear the Vektia rampaging through the heavens, hear its howling. Its fury was mindless. The Vektia, wise and all-knowing. Kahg could have wept if he hadn't been so enraged. He hid the ship beneath the trees, not because he feared the Vektia might see him, but because he did not want to see it. He loathed the sight of it, made to look like a dragon.

Something hard and sharp struck him on his carved wooden snout. At first Kahg thought he'd been hit by a bit of windblown debris, but then the object struck him again, this time harder, chipping off a chunk of wood. He looked to see a hammer fall back to the deck, narrowly missing the boy who had thrown it.

Kahg glared. The faery child. The boy was a sodden mess; he

seemed oblivious to the rain. He picked up the hammer by its wooden handle, careful not to touch the iron head, and brandished it threateningly.

"You have to go back for Skylan!" Wulfe cried.

Skylan, Kahg thought. Which one was Skylan? The dragon could not keep all these humans straight. The ship kept moving.

The boy peered through his sopping wet hair in the direction of the sky. "That's not a dragon, you know. It's old. Really, really old. It used to run wild, but then the gods of the Uglies captured it and chained it up."

Kahg's red eyes flared. His gaze cast a garish aura on the boy.

"If you throw that at me again, whelp, I will smash you flat!" Kahg snarled.

Wulfe lowered the hammer and backed away. "You have to go back for Skylan."

Kahg changed course suddenly, bringing the ship around, a difficult maneuver in the wind-whipped river, but he managed.

"Thank you!" Wulfe yelled, waving at the dragon.

Kahg's eyes glittered. He had not reversed his course for the sake of the faery child or for this Skylan, whom the dragon finally vaguely remembered.

The Dragon Kahg had abruptly reversed course because he had been about to sail into the midst of the ogre fleet.

BOOK THREE

Skylan scoured the riverbank searching for some sign of his ship and praying to Torval that the *Venjekar* was not lying at the bottom of the swollen river. He could find no trace and he wondered bleakly what to do.

They could not remain here. The river was rising, and this part of the bank would soon be underwater. All were exhausted, including the horses. He was about to tell Aylaen and the others to move to higher ground, when he saw two red lights flaring from a gray wall of rain.

Skylan cried out and plunged excitedly into the water and was nearly swept away by the current. Keeper caught hold of him and dragged him back to land. Skylan shouted and the Dragon Kahg steered the *Venjekar* close into a small inlet partially sheltered from the wind by a gigantic willow tree.

Aylaen stood on the bank holding her sister in her arms. Treia was shivering violently. Blood oozed from the wound on her head. She paid no heed to all attempts to speak to her. If Aylaen had not been supporting her, she would have fallen to the ground.

Keeper and Skylan and Acronis stripped off their heavy armor and then waded into the water to seize hold of the hull and drag the ship close to the shore. Sigurd and Grimuir jumped over the side, assisting Skylan and Acronis as they tried to hang on to the ship long enough for the others to board.

"Where did you go?" Skylan yelled at Sigurd as they stood side by side, trying desperately to hold on to the ship that the river was threatening to tear from their grasp.

"Ask him!" Sigurd jerked his head toward the prow.

The dragon's eyes burned an angry red and Skylan decided to let the matter drop.

"Nice haul, by the way," Sigurd said, his gaze going to Skylan's neck. "The gold in that must be worth a fortune."

Skylan clasped his hand around the spiritbone and tucked it under his sodden tunic.

Keeper boosted Aylaen up and over the hull. Treia made no resistance, but she did nothing to help herself either. They could have let her sink beneath the water and she would have gone down without a murmur. Keeper gave a great heave and flung her onto the ship. Bjorn caught hold of her and eased her down onto the deck.

Sigurd had looked astonished to see Acronis, then he'd grinned. "Slave master now the slave. Good thinking."

Skylan said nothing, not wasting his breath in explanations that Sigurd would not understand. Acronis knew how to navigate the river, and he had knowledge of much more besides. Knowledge that might be useful to Skylan, such as how to sail the ship across the open sea at night without losing his way, how to read the squiggly lines on a map, how to use some of the mystifying instruments that Zahakis had brought on board.

"Keeper, help the Legate!" Skylan shouted.

The ogre didn't waste time. He lifted Acronis and tumbled him over the side. Acronis landed on the deck, where Erdmun and Farinn hauled him to his feet.

The river was rising steadily, eating away at the bank beneath them.

"You next, my friend!" Skylan ordered Keeper. "We'll take you to your people."

Keeper was about to clamor on board the ship when a gust of wind caused a large willow branch to whip around and strike the ogre in the head. Keeper's grip slipped off the hull and he started to go under.

Skylan shouted and grabbed hold of the ogre by his leather harness. Sigurd and Grimuir and others seized hold of him by any part they could latch on to—his harness, his belt. They managed to haul the ogre over the side, though they nearly swamped the ship in the process.

Skylan was the last to board. He was so tired he did not think he had strength enough. Sigurd and Grimuir reached down their hands. Skylan caught hold of them and he was once more standing with his feet on the deck of his ship.

"Now what?" Sigurd asked.

"We follow our plan," Skylan yelled. "Sail down the river to the sea and home!"

Sigurd scowled. "You mean we sail down the river and into the arms of the ogres!"

"They will be happy to see us," said Skylan. "We are bringing them one of their godlords." He pointed at Keeper.

Sigurd grinned.

"I could get to like you," he said, slapping Skylan on the shoulder.

Skylan leaned wearily against the rail. The horses were running off, heading for higher ground. He hoped they reached safety. He asked Torval's blessing on them, then.

He made his way across the heaving deck to see how Keeper was doing. He found, to his relief, that the ogre was conscious.

"Another bump on the head," Keeper said, and then he puked.

"You've got a cracked skull," said Skylan. "Come on, I'll take you down to the hold. We can't have anything happening to you, my friend. You are going to buy us safe passage through the ogre fleet."

Keeper grunted in understanding. He started to insist that he was fine, but when he stood up, he keeled over backward. Erdmun and Skylan caught him and between them they managed to help the ogre down the ladder.

Aylaen had brought her sister into the hold as well. Treia sat huddled on a sea chest, wrapped in blankets, staring at nothing. Water sloshed about the deck. Aylaen sat beside her, chafing her cold hands and talking to her reassuringly.

"It wasn't your fault, Treia," Aylaen was saying. "You couldn't know what would happen when you summoned the dragon. You must have all five of the Vektan dragons in order to control them. That is the secret of the Vektia. You couldn't know."

Skylan felt a chill of foreboding. He wished Aylaen hadn't told Treia the secret. She didn't seem to have heard, however. Her eyes were dull and lifeless. Aylaen wrapped another blanket around her sister and began to rock her like a child.

Keeper sat down with a groan on a sea chest and lowered his throbbing head into his hands. Skylan was about to leave when Wulfe appeared from nowhere and flung himself on Skylan with a glad cry.

"The dragon is upset," said Wulfe. "That's why he left. I know why—"

Sigurd began bellowing from the deck, shouting for Skylan. He extricated himself from Wulfe's grasp.

"Stay down here out of the way. Aylaen, see to Keeper. He's the one who needs your help."

Returning to the deck, Skylan saw a fearful sight. The Vektan dragon was right behind them, flying down the river, rushing at them. The water beneath its fire-lit belly foamed and churned and boiled.

"Why is it chasing us?" Bjorn cried.

Skylan put his hand to the golden necklace.

"Because I have its spiritbone."

He yelled for Aylaen. She hastened onto the deck. Seeing the dragon and the thundering wall of water bearing down on them, she stopped to stare in horror. Skylan fought his way forward, buffeted by the wind. He thrust the spiritbone of the Vektia into Aylaen's hands.

"Talk to the Dragon Kahg! He's the only one who can save us!" Skylan yelled over the howling shrieking of the wind and the near-constant thunder.

Aylaen looked up at the dragon, then she shook her head.

"He cannot stop the Vektia." Aylaen had to grab on to Skylan to keep from being blown over. "It's not a true dragon."

Aylaen looked into the dragon's eyes. The fire of his gaze seemed to ignite her red hair, surround her with flame.

"Aylaen!" Skylan cried, shaking her.

But she was far away from him and could not hear.

Aylaen walked the battlements of Torval's Hall. Her boots crunched on snow that was churned and dirty and stained with blood. The wind blew cold and fierce, stinging her cheeks and freezing her breath. She was dressed warmly in a fur cloak with a hood and thick wool gloves. She wrapped the cloak more closely about her.

She looked out over the battlements onto a vast, frozen landscape of ice and snow. The sky was a brilliant, aching blue. The sun was so bright it hurt her eyes, but it gave no warmth.

Torval, leaning against the battlements, stared out over the silent land. His spear rested against the wall. His shield stood beside him. His sword was in its fur-lined sheath. Some distance from him, Hevis and Joabis squatted in the snow, playing with dice made of walrus tusks.

Vindrash stood near Torval. She was clad in armor and fur and she looked at Aylaen and then looked away, back out over the frozen fields and plains to the distant mountains beyond.

"Is the fighting over?" Aylaen asked.

"For the moment," said Torval. "Our enemies have been forced to retreat."

"Thanks to me," said Hevis, tossing the dice. "I win."

Joabis swore and threw down a handful of jewels. Hevis gathered them up and stuffed them in a pouch.

"You won by revealing our secret to our enemies!" Torval said angrily.

"I was trying to help," said Hevis, shrugging. "Besides, it's not my fault. You should have told us the truth about the Vektia. You and your bloody secrets!"

He handed the dice to Joabis, then shifted his gaze to Aylaen. Hevis winked at her.

"You can stop the Vektia and save your friends. I can tell you how, but you must sacrifice—"

"You are wasting your time, Hevis," said Vindrash. "Aylaen knows how to stop the Vektia. She doesn't need you to tell her."

"You taught me a song," said Aylaen. "But it is only a song. I hear the words in my head. I don't feel them in my heart."

"To understand the song, you must become a Bone Priestess. No pretending. No playacting. You must dedicate yourself to me and to Torval, to Joabis and Aylis, and even Hevis." Vindrash added gently, "You have been faithful all your life. Even when you raged against us, you could not deny us."

"I would not be a good priestess," said Aylaen, shaking her hooded head. "I am selfish and willful, obstinate and stubborn, as you know, Vindrash. I have a quick temper. I don't like to follow rules."

Vindrash smiled. "Those are the faults of a child. You must leave childhood behind, Aylaen."

The bitter wind froze her tears on her cheeks. Aylaen knelt in the snow.

"If you can forgive me, Vindrash, I will serve you."

"Give me your sword," said Vindrash.

Aylaen handed the goddess her sword by the hilt. But the goddess gripped the sword by the blade. Blood ran from Vindrash's hand, dripped down the blade, and spattered red on the snow.

She gave the sword back to Aylaen.

"I win," said Joabis, triumphantly snatching up the jewels.

"For the moment," said Hevis, shrugging.

"Aylaen!" Skylan was shaking her, shouting her name.

The battlements vanished in shards of sparkling ice and Aylaen was once more on the deck of the *Venjekar*.

The Dragon Kahg had infused his spirit into the *Venjekar*. He had, in essence, become the ship. The dragonhead prow was no longer made of wood. It was flesh and bone and covered with scales. The dragon roared defiance and outrage as he carried the *Venjekar* downstream in a terrifying race with the Vektan dragon. The warriors were hanging on to whatever they could find to keep from being washed overboard.

Aylaen looked down at the spiritbone in her hand. The gold gleamed in the fire of Kahg's eyes, the emeralds were blood-red.

"Why didn't the spiritbone disappear?" Skylan cried.

The wind whipped his hair across his face. He was bare-chested, having discarded his armor, wearing nothing but the leather skirt and his boots and sword. He had cuts and scratches all over his body and his face and arms.

"The Vektia is tied to it," said Aylaen, "as the newborn babe is tied to its mother. As a man is tied to his wyrd."

She slowly placed the golden chain over her head.

"What are you doing?" He had to yell over the shrieking wind.

"What I have to," said Aylaen. "I am a Bone Priestess of the Kai. Vindrash has given me her blessing."

She looked back at the dragon. Kahg's mouth was wide open, gasping for breath. Spittle flew from his jaws. He had entered the world and he was now as vulnerable as the fragile humans he was try-ing desperately to protect. The Dragon Kahg rode the flood, keeping the ship afloat, keeping ahead of the raging Vektia. But his strength was waning. He was slowing. He could not go much longer.

Aylaen drew her sword and started to walk toward the prow. The Torgun warriors were hanging on for dear life to anything they could find to hold on to—the rail, the ropes where they would have mounted their shields, the mast. They urged her to go down into the hold or she would be swept overboard.

She couldn't hear them. All she could hear was the voice of the goddess.

The wind shifted, blowing against her, trying to stop her. She could not move against it, and she feared, for one terrifying mo-ment, that it would knock her off the deck. And then Skylan was there beside her. He caught hold of her and added his strength to hers. The two of them fought their way forward.

Aylaen placed her hand on the curved neck of the dragon.

"Turn, Kahg!" she cried. "Come about, face the Vektia!"

She lifted the spiritbone in her hand. "Take me to the Vektia, Kahg. It's the only way we can stop it."

The dragon spit a gout of flame and began to turn the ship.

The men had no idea what was going on. The dragon appeared to be taking them into the teeth of their enemy, but they could do nothing except hang on and pray.

Aylaen clasped the spiritbone of the Vektia in one hand, then wrapped her arm around the dragon's neck. Skylan stood braced with his feet planted firmly on the deck, holding on to her.

As she was turning, the *Venjekar* was hit amidships by a wave and rolled over. For a perilous moment, the ship floundered in the rushing water. The Dragon Kahg struggled to keep the ship righted and swung around to face the Vektia.

The Vektan dragon had no eyes. It could not see. It killed without seeing what it killed, without even knowing. And yet the blind head was searching for them. The Vektan dragon dove at Aylaen.

She let go of the dragon's neck. The Dragon Kahg rode the waves, swooping up and down, his eyes red slits of fire against the blinding spray. He was sailing right into the wall of water. They had only moments left before the Vektia crashed down on top of them.

"Hold on to me, Skylan!" Aylaen cried.

Skylan braced himself against the hull. He had no idea what she meant to do. The wind tried to tear her out of his arms.

Aylaen began to sing the song Vindrash had taught her. Holding the spiritbone high in the air, she drew her sword. "The thread is twisted and spun . . . then I seize it. . . ."

The dragon's sightless head focused on the spiritbone. The dragon opened its maw and darted down. The *Venjekar* lifted up.

"And he dies!" Aylaen raised the sword and swung the blade, shining with the light of thunderbolts, and sliced off the dragon's head.

The dragon's blind head glared at her and then burst into flame and vanished. The dragon's headless body whirled and wrapped around and around, wings drawn inward, tail whipping, the feet swirling. The dragon spun like a massive waterspout and then the Vektan dragon lifted up into the heavens. Thunder rolled, lightning spiked, black clouds boiled, and it was gone.

The warriors stared about dazedly, not sure what had happened, knowing only that they were still alive. The wind died. The water calmed. The current was still flowing swiftly, sweeping the *Venjekar* downstream, but the ship was no longer in peril of being crushed. Aylaen realized Skylan was still holding her in his arms. She could see the blue of his eyes. With the passing of the storm, the sky was alight with the coming of dawn.

Aylean sheathed the sword blessed by Vindrash.

"We're safe now," she said. "You can let go."

As he released her, she clasped his hand. "I'm sorry, Skylan. I hope you can forgive me."

He drew her close and she drew him close, and for a moment they were the only two people on the ship.

And then Aylaen saw Treia.

Her sister had come up on deck. She stared at the brightening sky, the ragged-edged clouds that were like tattered wings, the lightning that flashed in the distance and then was gone. She listened to the last, low rumble of thunder.

"You are the darling of the gods now, Sister," said Treia. "But they will turn on you as they turned on me. I was tricked into destroying everything I held dear. The same fate will happen to you."

Aylaen let go of Skylan's hand.

B O O K   T H R E E

The rising sun crawled out from under the storm clouds. Lurid light spread over the water. Skylan could see the bay and the sea beyond and the ogre ships, with their odd, triangular sails, thick as seabirds flocking to feed on a school of fish.

Ogres are terrified of dragons and, at the sight of this one, their godlords had decided to retreat. The ogre warriors who had survived the flood and fire in the city fled back to their ships, only to find the seas rising in the whipping wind, tearing off masts and shredding sails. Some of the ships sank, but most managed to survive the storm and they were now milling about the bay, searching for survivors.

The swift-moving current boiled beneath the *Venjekar*'s keel, hurrying the ship along with it. The Torgun dared not try to use the oars, for the boiling water would rip them out of their hands. Skylan and the Torgun warriors crowded in the prow of the *Venjekar*, watching the ogre ships in the bay ahead and speculating on what the ogres would do once they saw them. Acronis stood by himself, watching the death of his city.

"Look!" Wulfe cried. "Another dragon!"

Skylan whipped around, the terrifying thought in his mind that the Vektia had come back. A ship sailed through the debris-strewn waves of the harbor. There was something odd about the ship, but it was certainly no dragon.

Skylan's heart was still thudding in his chest.

He gave Wulfe a shake. "No more of your lies! Go below before I toss you overboard!"

"But there *is* a dragon," Wulfe insisted.

SECRET OF THE DRAGON

Acronis stared at the ship and said in puzzled tones, "It is a small war galley, with a single bank of oars. Or, rather, it should have oars." His brow furrowed. "There's no wind to speak of. And yet she's moving fast."

Skylan stared at the ship until his eyes ached. No banks of oars extended out from the ship's hull, sweeping over the water in beautiful synchronicity. No rowers strained at their task.

"How do you know the ship has a dragon?" Skylan asked Wulfe.

"I can see it," said Wulfe. He glanced up at the Dragon Kahg. "And so can he."

Skylan looked up at the Dragon Kahg and saw him watching the war galley.

"We can tell for certain," said Acronis. "The spyglass that Zahakis used when he was on board your ship. Is it still here?"

"The magic seeing glass?" said Wulfe eagerly. "I know where it is!"

He ran off and returned in a few moments, spyglass in hand, wrapped in cloth. Acronis put it to his eye, then handed the glass to Skylan.

"You better look at this," he said.

Skylan, somewhat hesitantly, held the glass to his eye. At first he could see nothing but water, and then the ship came into view, so close that it seemed it must ram them. He jumped and nearly dropped the glass. He lowered the glass to see the galley was still some distance away.

He looked again, focusing on the ship's prow—the long graceful neck and fierce head of a dragon. And there was a familiar figure standing at the prow, one hand on the neck of the dragon.

"It's Raegar," Skylan said, lowering the spyglass. "The galley has a dragonhead prow."

"The galley now has a dragon," said Aylaen. "Kahg told me. Her name is Fala. And the Dragon Kahg says he will not fight one of his own kind."

Raegar's ship was closing on them rapidly from the east. Warrior-priests crowded the decks.

"Maybe he's going after the ogres," said Sigurd.

Skylan turned to look at Treia, who leaned on the rail staring out at the galley, her face aglow, her cheeks flushed, her lips parted.

"No," said Skylan. "He's coming for us."

"I say we stand and fight the whoreson," said Sigurd grimly.

"He must have fifty warriors with him," said Skylan. "We are seven. And a dragon who won't help us."

He looked to the open sea. The tops of the waves spattered with gold as the sun goddess, Aylis, cast her light across the water. To the west was the open sea and home. But to reach the sea, they would have to sail past a hundred ships filled with ogres who were undoubtedly angry at being robbed of glory and loot. Some of the ogre ships must have spotted the galley for several ships were starting to turn to meet it.

The ogres could not yet see the *Venjekar,* which was concealed by a spit of land thrusting out onto the bay. The current would soon carry them into their view. Skylan tried to put himself in the boots of the ogres. What would they see? Two human ships sailing out after them, two ships bearing dragons.

What would the ogres think except that the humans and their dragons were coming out to finish them off? And perhaps that was Raegar's plan. After he seized the *Venjekar,* he would have two dragons to send after the ogres. And he would once more be in possession of the Vektia spiritbone.

And in possession of the secret!

Skylan looked over to where Treia had been standing. She was no longer there. She must have gone back down to the hold. Probably to change her clothes, make herself pretty for her lover when he captured them.

And as if he had any doubts about Raegar's intent, the tattoo on his arm began to burn. Skylan clutched his arm, as did the rest of the men.

"We can at least stop Aelon," said Acronis grimly. He turned to Aylaen. "Use the blessed sword. Quickly!"

Aylean drew the sword of Vindrash from the sheath. She seized hold of Skylan's arm and sliced into the tattoo, cutting it open. The sword flared with an angry light. The only pain Skylan felt was the pain of the wound. And that pain he could bear. Cheerfully!

"The blood will wash out the crystals imbedded in the wound, but you should soak it well in water," said Aylean, watching in satisfaction as the blood flowed down Skylan's arm.

"Congratulations. You are a free man." Acronis glanced back at the galley, which was gaining them, and added somberly, "At least for the moment."

The *Venjekar* had cleared the point. The muddy water of the river boiled into the sea, carrying the ship with it. An ogre ship sighted them. The *Venjekar* was closer to the ogres than to the galley, so close that Skylan didn't need a spyglass to see the ogres come rushing to the side to stare. The triangular sails shivered as the ogre ship changed course.

The other men were slicing open their tattoos; blood spilled on the deck. Aylaen thrust a roll of cloth at Skylan, and he hurriedly wrapped the bandage around his arm. As he worked, Skylan explained his plan.

"Keeper will hail the ogre ship and tell the godlord that we helped him escape. He'll warn them Raegar is coming with another dragon to destroy their fleet. He'll urge the ogres to attack Raegar and, while our enemies are fighting each other, we will escape."

"Will the ogres believe him?" Sigurd asked.

It was Acronis who answered. "I think you stand a good chance. Ogres revere their godlords. If he tells his people that you saved his life, they will let you go."

As Skylan ran to the hold to alert Keeper that he was about to be reunited with his people, he reflected that he was glad he had Acronis with him.

The older man and his knowledge would be useful when the Vindrasi, once more free men, sailed to their nation to recover the Torque and the Vektan spiritbone that had been stolen from them.

For the first time in his life, Skylan realized the immense importance of the Vektan dragons and the true value of the spiritbone that Horg had given to the ogres. He had known the spiritbone was sacred, but he had never fully appreciated its worth until now. If the gods of the Vindrasi possessed all five of the Vektia, they would control the power of creation. Aelon and the Gods of Raj would be forced to go find other worlds.

"Keeper!" Skylan called, sliding down the ladder in his haste. "Keeper, we're coming up on an ogre ship. I need you on deck!"

Keeper was where Skylan had left him, sitting on the sea chest, his eyes closed, his head and shoulders slumped.

"Only a lazy-ass ogre could sleep through all this commotion," Skylan said, laughing. "Come on! Wake up!"

He gave Keeper a punch on the arm.

The ogre toppled over sideways, sliding off the sea chest and landing with a thud. He lay still and unmoving in the water that sloshed around the deck.

Skylan put his hand on the ogre's neck, feeling for a pulse, though he knew he was wasting his time. The ogre's flesh was already starting to grow cold.

"Is he dead?" asked Treia.

She had been looking out through a chink in the boards, watching Raegar's ship gaining on them, watching her lover coming for her. She couldn't let Keeper talk to the ogres. She couldn't let the *Venjekar* escape.

"Yes, he's dead," said Skylan, his voice grating. He could never prove she had murdered him. She was too clever for that.

Treia shrugged.

"You can never tell with head wounds," she said, and she turned back to watch the galley.

Skylan looked down at Keeper.

"Now you are home, my friend," Skylan said softly.

He gave a bleak sigh and climbed the ladder and emerged out onto the deck. Sigurd peered down into the hold.

"Where's Keeper?"

"Dead," said Skylan.

There was silence. No one asked how or why. It didn't matter. The ogre ship was bearing down on them from the west. To the east, Raegar was urging the Dragon Fala for more speed.

"So what do we do now?" Sigurd asked.

"We are Torgun. We stand together," said Skylan.